AGATHA H *and the* VOICE OF THE CASTLE

A GIRL GENIUS NOVEL

AGATHA H AND THE VOICE OF THE CASTLE

A GIRL GENIUS NOVEL

PHIL & KAJA FOGLIO

NIGHT SHADE BOOKS
NEW YORK

Night Shade books may be purchased in bulk at special discounts for sales promotion, corporate gifts, fund-raising, or educational purposes. Special editions can also be created to specifications. For details, contact the Special Sales Department, Night Shade Books, 307 West 36th Street, 11th Floor, New York, NY 10018 or info@skyhorsepublishing.com.

Night Shade Books™ is a trademark of Skyhorse Publishing, Inc.®, a Delaware corporation.

Visit our website at www.nightshadebooks.com.

10 9 8 7 6 5 4 3 2 1

Library of Congress Cataloging-in-Publication Data is available on file.

Cover art by Tom Kidd
Cover design by Jason Snair

Print ISBN: 978-1-59780-295-6
Printed in the United States of America

To Our Dear Mothers, Ottillie & Rose, whom we often
drove to despair, and no doubt, still do.

PRELUDE

⚬⊙⊙⚬

"As we passed through the last of the great Iron Gates and approached Mechanicsburg for the first time, the Bishop was struck anew by the grandeur of the surrounding cliffs, the majesty of the encircling mountains, and the awe-inspiring fury of the River Dyne as it roared far beneath the Bridge of Thorns.

As we crossed toward the town, he rhapsodized at such length that I feared it would take a double dose of poppy-juice tea to settle him in for the night.

The more strategically inclined Captain Van der Vheer pointed to the same features and glumly explained why, for the last thousand years, the Valley of the Heterodynes deserved its reputation as unconquerable.

I am already resigned to never leaving this place, but I take some small comfort that, at the very least, my last memories of Earth will be filled with some of God's finest landscapes."

—*Excerpt from the journal "The Building of the Red Cathedral, or Why God Now Hates Us" by Brother Martanus, "The Unkillable." Located in the Papal Library of Banned and Forbidden Books, Avignon, France.*

CHAPTER 1

Mechanicsburg, Mechanicsburg,
Welcome to Mechanicsburg!
There's no finer city from
Saint Petersburg to Rome.

Mechanicsburg, Mechanicsburg,
The loveliest we've ever heard of,
Jewel of Europa and
The place where we call home.

How mighty are her mighty walls,
How shiny are her clanks,
How beautiful her mountains tall,
And for her snails we all give thanks.

How glorious her Hospital
Which helps folk far and near,
Bill and Barry Heterodyne
Built it for us here.

Mechanicsburg, Mechanicsburg,
Welcome to Mechanicsburg,
We thank you so for visiting,
With every erg and ohm.

Mechanicsburg, Mechanicsburg,
The greatest burg we've ever heard of,
Jewel of Europa and
The place where we call home.

—"The Mechanicsburg Tourism Song," Tom Smith

＊＊＊

rella Heliotrope climbed the stairs to her family apartment, her mind buzzing with news. She opened the hidden locks on the front door and peered inside. "Poppa?" she called.

The sitting room had been tidied in a rather haphazard manner. Couch cushions were lined up wrong side out, the great salvaged clank head that had been repurposed as a fire-front had been left with jaws agape, books had been stuffed onto bookshelves with no regard to order. Arella sighed. The old man did try to stay useful. She wished he would go out but more and more, he just stayed in the apartment. He was not taking retirement well.

She walked past walls lined with family mementos: portraits of old Heterodynes, monsters, ancestors, and nervous-looking dignitaries.

The apartment itself was more spacious than its exterior would suggest. It actually occupied the top floor of what, observed from the street, would appear to be three conjoined yet separate buildings. Even from the beginning, the family had sought to keep a low profile.

"Poppa?" she called again. He wasn't in the library, a room lined with meticulously oiled leather-bound volumes containing everything one could wish to know about Mechanicsburg and its former rulers.

He wasn't napping in his room. With a small pang of guilt, Arella saw that the votive candle before the portraits of her husband and his mother had melted down. She replaced it with a new votive, setting it securely into the cut-glass safety lantern.

"Poppa?" Arella continued on to the kitchen where she set her purchases down on the counter, trying to avoid a scattering of dirty bowls and small drifts of flour. She scowled. "Poppa?"

"I'm on the balcony," the old man's voice called out.

And indeed he was. Carson Heliotrope rested, ensconced in a large comfortable chair. The cat, Electrode, so named for its ability to store up static electricity, lay sprawled in his lap. The old man put down the book he was reading and smiled at her as she stepped out the back door.

"I got us a pork pie for supper, and some fresh onions."

Carson looked pleased. "Wonderful! I have some bread rising."

Arella had noticed the covered loaf pans arranged upon the balcony railing. "You shouldn't have!" She remembered the disarray she'd seen in the kitchen. "Really."

The old man waved a hand in dismissal. "Ha! Did it anyway." He cast an eye over the side of the balcony. Below, on the normally sedate Avenue of Schemers, there was an excessive amount of traffic and a suspicious number of people clustered together, conferring. His voice was deliberately casual. "Any news?"

Of course, Arella realized, *he knows something is up.*

"Yes, indeed," she reported. "They say a new Heterodyne heir has—"

But Carson had lost interest, waving at her to stop. "Ah. Enough." He sighed as he picked up his book.

Arella hesitated and then spoke slowly. "I don't know, Poppa… this one sounds different." The old man noisily turned a page. "It's a girl, for starters."

Carson grunted in surprise. "That *is* different."

Arella nodded and leaned back against the doorframe. "And she beat Baron Wulfenbach."

Carson frowned. "What, with a stick?"

"With an army." *Now* she had his full attention. "She appeared in Balan's Gap. Blew up half of Sturmhalten Castle." Involuntarily, both of them glanced up at the ruined castle that loomed over their own town. "After that, it gets…confusing. But the town was destroyed, or at least overrun with assorted monsters, and during the fighting, the Baron was hurt." She pointed a finger towards the large white structure crowning a hill in the distance. "He's here—in the Great Hospital. And…she had Jägers with her."

Carson had been staring at the distant hospital, but this information jerked his attention back to her. "Jägers?" His brain, which had spent too many sleepy days in the sun, was laboriously spinning back up to speed. "A nice touch, that. The generals will come down hard on them when they catch them." He snorted. "She should've just had the Masters along as well."

Arella nodded in satisfaction as she delivered her *coup de grâce.* "She did. Along with the Lady Lucrezia, Punch *and* Judy and even the High Priestess—you know, from the street plays."

The old man absorbed this—his mouth twitching and the corners of his eyes crinkling with remembered humor. "Master Barry would be furious."

"He didn't *look* furious," Arella replied tartly. "Of course, they were all three meters tall, glowed, and had wings—"

Carson just stared at her now. "Wings."

Arella shrugged. "Well, there is some argument about that, but otherwise, everyone who saw them was convinced that it was them." Arella fluttered her fingers upwards. "And then they all flew away into the sky. Presumably, to come here."

Carson nodded slowly. "And where is my grandson?"

"He was out all night," Arella informed him. "Probably because of the excitement."

To her slight surprise, the old man nodded in approval. "Yes. He'll be busy, I expect. Very good. Still…"

With a small grunt, he levered himself out of his chair, dumping the cat to the floor. "Arella, my dear, I am going out."

Arella handed the old man his jacket and cap. "You're going to the gate?"

Carson nodded as he carefully adjusted his cap to hide the terrible scars upon his bald head. Arella dutifully brushed the back of his coat. "I'll send down some lunch." She paused. "Do you really think she'll come, Poppa?"

Carson heard the faint whisper of longing within Arella's voice and sighed. *Even after all this time, even after we all know better, we still hope. Best take care of this one quickly.*

He patted her arm as he turned to go. "I'm sure she will. All the others have."

He descended the stairs to the street, drew in a deep lungful of the morning air, and took a look around. What he saw brought him up short. For a moment, he panicked, but then he remembered that the Masters were gone. With the familiar pang of loss mixed with reassurance swirling through his head, he took another look, taking mental notes.

It was worse. Worse than he remembered. He tried to think back. How long had it been since he had last inspected the town? Not just walked like a tourist, but looked, *really* looked, like a man who was responsible for things and would have to explain them to the Masters?

Obviously far too long.

There was litter in the streets. Not great drifts of it, to be sure, but that there was any at all would have caused his father to have a stroke. The façades of the shops were weathered. He saw a cracked window, and with a genuine shot of fear, he noticed that one of the small public fountains was no longer running, the bowl dry, filled with old leaves and a few cracked snail shells. What was his grandson *thinking*?

He meandered down through the closely packed streets, eyes half-closed…listening.

There was a rising tide of excitement bubbling through the citizenry. They always reacted to rumors of a Heterodyne, but this time it was sharper, fuller. Fanned, no doubt, by the large number of Wulfenbach troops and obvious out-of-towners who were holding forth on various street corners.

He paused outside a busy pastry shop. A few seconds later, a shop girl hurried out with a wicker basket of warm cinnamon butter snail buns, which she handed over with a small curtsy before darting back inside.

The proprietor of a Turkish teashop spied Carson as he turned onto the lane. He filled a blue ceramic mug with the thick campaign tea that he knew the old man favored, closed the decorative copper lid, and placed it into his hand as he passed. Carson, preoccupied, took it with a slight nod and continued on.

As he approached, Carson ran a practiced eye over the wall surrounding the main gate of the town. Constructed of a wide variety of materials, the thirty-meter-tall walls were a mosaic of stone, brick, and chunks of metal arranged into a solid line of defense, broken only by the great gate before him. Even there, he saw signs of neglect. A crack had appeared below one of the deactivated catapults. It was probably only cosmetic, since the hodgepodge façade hid an inner wall that had broken the armies of empires, but to allow even the appearance of weakness! If the old Masters had seen such a thing, it would've been mortared with his blood.

The great doors themselves were constructed of riveted iron and festooned with carvings of skulls and demons, with ranks of gargoyles leering down to glare at approaching travelers. Many were clutching the gilded trilobite that was the sigil of the Heterodyne family, rulers of Mechanicsburg.

Carson strode through the vast central gate, keeping to a raised walkway on one side of the passage. The usual cart traffic rumbled by. When he cleared the portcullis the gloom of the gate tunnel gave way to bright sun, and he paused a moment, blinking.

A young man who had been industriously sweeping the walkway removed his hat as soon as Carson appeared. "Master Heliotrope!" the boy called. "It has been a while since you've been by." He indicated a small stone bench that had been set into the stone railing that lined the roadway up to the gate. "But I had a feeling you might be here, and I have just finished tidying your bench."

Carson smiled as he settled onto the sun-warmed stone. "You are a good boy, Kars." He took a sip of his tea. "And how is your mama?"

Kars looked pleased. "Very well, sir. Thank you."

Carson nodded. "Do remember me to her." He ran an eye over the traffic. "Anything unusual today?"

Kars paused and leaned upon his broom. The two of them looked out across the landscape. A well-constructed road led from the gate, crossed the river, and disappeared off between two of the cliffs that encircled the valley. The road was lined with advertisements, touting various taverns and inns, as well as the numerous attractions that helped draw in the waves of tourists who came to see the home of the legendary Heterodyne Boys.

These days most of the town's visitors arrived by way of the airstrip across the river, but today the old road was noticeably busier than usual. Carson could see, even from here, that most of them were troops. This was even more unusual, as the Wulfenbachs habitually used airships for military transport.

"Forces from Balan's Gap?"

Kars nodded. "Mostly walking wounded. And they say they're establishing overland supply lines."

Carson frowned. Mechanicsburg *was* the closest town of consequence, but the Empire had the largest air transport fleet—

The old man bit his lip. *Of course. This must be a very troublesome Heterodyne claimant indeed for the Empire to send troops, even if they were trying to be circumspect about it. At least the merchants will be happy.* Prices were no doubt being raised even as he idled here.

Carson leaned back and closed his eyes. Kars waited a moment, but when nothing else was said, he nodded, and taking his broom, moved to the other side of the roadway.

Carson tipped his head back and regarded several of the gargoyles ranked along the outer wall.

"Another Heterodyne heir," he grumbled to the air. "And this time it's a woman, who seems to have gotten her ideas from too many Heterodyne shows." He shrugged. "I expect she'll be easy to discourage..."

He considered this statement. "But she apparently had enough power to take on Klaus Wulfenbach. Which makes me think she might be trouble."

Across the way, Kars continued with his work. He picked up a windblown twig and tossed it over the low wall that followed the road out of town, and Carson watched a leaf detach and briefly spin in an updraft.

Carson laced his fingers together. "And if she is, I expect you'll help me deal with her. I know you'll enjoy that."

A dray wagon loaded with empty barrels rumbled out from the gateway A large dog loped along behind it, tongue flapping.

After a moment of protracted silence, the old man chuckled and settled back on his bench. "Well, at any rate…until we're needed, I believe I'll take a nap."

As the sun slowly rose, the defenders of Mechanicsburg waited.

The Great Chronometer in the Red Cathedral had just boomed out the hour. Nine o'clock. From outside the gate, Carson couldn't hear the shrieks of the clockwork nuns fleeing the clockwork Jägers, but he was familiar enough with the routine that he could visualize each of the hourly shows as clearly as if he were there. His lips twitched in a faint smile.

So caught up was he in memories that, when the trio of horses stopped in front of him, he continued to drift. The young man on the lead horse had to repeat himself several times, in a slightly louder voice each time, before he was startled back to full awareness.

A tall, friendly-looking fellow looked down at him and nodded his head respectfully. Behind him was a young woman, most likely his wife: young, alert, and wide-eyed. Currently she was staring up at the gate. Fair enough, it took some getting used to. At the gateway, the walls blossomed outwards, and a person entering the town experienced the disquieting sensation of entering a lair of grinning, cavorting gargoyles and other assorted monstrosities. The old Heterodynes were accused of many things, but no one ever said they were unfair. They always enjoyed letting visitors know exactly what they were walking into.

Behind her was—Carson perked up a bit. The woman looked like one of those warrior nuns he'd heard of, from…the old man frowned. That convent fortress up near Lake Geneva…he cursed this further evidence of his aging memory. Twenty, no, even ten years ago, he could have reeled off the name of the place as well as what they usually ate for breakfast.

He shook his head. In the nun's lap was a—Carson's breath hissed inwards in shock. It was a child. A terrible, misshapen child, tightly wrapped in bandages. The only thing he could see was a pair of mad, glaring eyes. He shuddered.

Even before the rider spoke, the old man knew what he wanted.

"If you would be so kind as to tell us the way to the Great Hospital?"[1]

"Certainly. Straight down this avenue until you get to a square with a statue of the Heterodyne Boys. Turn left at the statue, and you'll start to see the signs."

The young woman broke off her staring at the gate and turned to him. Her eyes held him transfixed and the old man felt his heart skip a beat.

"Thank you, kind sir." She broke the connection as she turned to her husband. "Let's go, darling."

The old man let out a breath as the horses clopped off. *Well. Apparently one is never too old to feel foolish over a pretty girl.* He impatiently shook his head.

"It's unfortunate, that's what that is," he muttered. "Now's a particularly bad time to show up with a sick child. The hospital will be in chaos what with the Baron there and everyone all stirred up."

He glanced upwards. "Perhaps I could—" He froze, then twisted around and stared up at the gargoyles that lined gate into town. All of them—every blessed one of them—had shifted on their pedestals, gazing after the trio of newcomers as they entered the city.

Agatha glanced at her companions and couldn't help the small smile that crossed her face as they left the old man. The idea of

---

[1] The Great Hospital of Mechanicsburg was the first of the Great Projects that Bill and Barry Heterodyne undertook when Bill officially became the Heterodyne. Before that, an entire section of the town had been zoned for, among other things, biological experiments. The Boys tore it all down and cleansed it with fire. In its place, they built a hospital. The staff had to undergo a rigorous, and prolonged, retraining using assorted incentives, hypnotism, threats, and cattle prods, which was—on the whole—surprisingly successful. Today, The Great Hospital is one of the leading institutions of medical research. It is also known for its pioneering research regarding the humane treatment of the insane, which is greatly appreciated by the staff.

the boisterous and unrestrained Zeetha as a nun was almost as amusing as the thought of her being married to the normally prim and decorous ex-valet Ardsley Wooster, who had joined them in Sturmhalten. She caught a glimpse of Krosp's furious eyes and turned away. Intelligent he might be, but Krosp was still a cat, and his dignity was suffering greatly under those bandages.

As they finally cleared the tunnel through the great wall, Agatha had a strange feeling in the pit of her stomach. Mechanicsburg! She'd heard so much about it. It was the home of the Heterodyne Boys, after all, and for the last two months, she'd been slowly wending her way here—because she'd been told that *she* was a Heterodyne as well.

As far as the rest of the world knew, the Heterodyne Boys had vanished years ago, putting a stop to the devastations of the Other: the secretive power that had nearly broken Europa nearly two decades ago. Agatha sighed. She had learned much in her travels, and almost all of it bizarre and unsettling. She, Agatha, was the daughter of the hero Bill Heterodyne, and the Other had been her own, equally brilliant mother, Lucrezia Mongfish. Agatha figured that she was now the only person in Europa who found the Other not just mysterious and terrifying, but horribly embarrassing.

It would have been nice to be able to discount this as hearsay, but as Agatha currently had a copy of her mother's mind lodged inside her own head, determined to break free and wreak havoc, she had to accept that hers was a family with…special problems.

As the horses ambled down the street, they were approached by swarms of touts for many of the local establishments.

"Try the Rusty Trilobite, sir! Soft beds! Hot running water! And you can't even see the tannery!"

"Nothing like a hot mug of golden rum to clear the dust of the road, ma'am! Come on over to the Laughing Construct! And don't you pay attention to what anyone says—he's laughing 'cause he's *happy!*"

"Hoy! You look like a man of the world, squire. Stow the ball and chain and get yourself over to Mamma Gkika's. They'll treat you right."

"Would the poor little fellow like a fried trilobite? Just—*Sweet lightning*! Those *eyes*! Hospital's that way! Clear the road, you lot!"

Like magic, the crowd thinned, and they proceeded relatively unhindered. This allowed Agatha a chance to look around a bit. According to the books she had read, the city of Mechanicsburg was almost a thousand years old and had been the home base of the Heterodynes from the beginning. The architecture varied wildly. Over there was a row of shops, equipped with fully modern plate-glass windows, yet hanging above the doorways were old-fashioned pictograph signboards. Over here was a row of mullion-windowed apartments, easily several hundred years old, but a set of peculiar-looking wind turbines thrummed away on the roof.

And trilobites were everywhere. Mechanicsburg was built on a fossil deposit and the peculiar little creatures had been so common that there was even a trilobite incorporated into the city's famous coat-of-arms. So, Agatha had expected to see them, but in actuality, their presence was overwhelming. They were chiseled upon buildings as assorted architectural features, and emblazoned upon the numerous posters, signs, and broadsheets plastered upon almost every vertical surface. These advertised everything from local attractions to a wide range of products, all of which were (apparently) personally associated with, or endorsed by, the Heterodyne Boys themselves.

As for Bill and Barry, their likeness shone forth from pictures, statuettes, key-chains, mugs, belt buckles, and a thousand other bizarre and inappropriate items.

Zeetha saw Agatha's expression and leaned over. "It is a tourist town. Aside from the Great Hospital and the memory of the Heterodyne Boys, Mechanicsburg has nothing else worth selling…or so I've heard."

Ardsley Wooster snorted. "That is a perception promoted quite heavily by the Mechanicsburg Chamber of Commerce. They neglect to mention that they are the leading exporter of snails to most of Eastern Europa."

Agatha blinked. Over the last ten years, snails had become a dietary staple on more and more tables.

"But that's something to be proud of, I'd think. Why downplay it?"

Wooster glanced about and lowered his voice. "Because, according to the Baron's agents, Mechanicsburg is also the center of at least three major smuggling and black market operations. Thus they take pains to dismiss the importance of shipments to and from the city." He shook his head in admiration. "They are aided by the simple fact that it is a rare customs agent that is willing to burrow through a shipment of live snails—"

Agatha nodded. "I can see that."

"Especially since some of the fancier varieties bite," he finished.

Suddenly Agatha reined in her horse and pulled it about. The others realized that she had stopped and looked at her questioningly. She frowned and scrutinized the street they had ridden up. It looked normal enough—bustling with crowds of people, merchants calling out their wares, hawkers, and street performers…

It's all for show, she realized. The merchants might be ebullient and boisterous while enticing passersby, but the moment their audience passed, their grins faded and their posture changed. Agatha thought they looked like poorly maintained automata. The town itself was similar. While the shop areas seen by visitors were reasonably clean and maintained, from here she could see that the upper stories were in serious need of paint and repair. It was like the people of the town no longer cared.

Agatha pondered this as she swung her horse about and continued forward.

Wooster claimed to know his way around the town. He led them up several ramps and before too long, Agatha saw that they were on a raised highway that circled Mechanicsburg's inner core.

Before them lay the bulk of the town, dominated by a massive black stone crag that loomed in the center of it all. Apparently growing from the top of the natural promontory was a ruined castle, partially hewn from the crag itself.

It was a huge structure. The main tower, a square pagoda-like affair, was easily ten stories tall, emblazoned with an enormous gilded trilobite. To Agatha's eye, it was apparent that the structure had been built over the course of centuries. Assorted architectural styles and fashions were jumbled together in a most disturbing way. The rest of the castle—Agatha's breath caught as she took in the scope of the devastation. Many of the barbicans and towers were leaning away from the center. Atop the various roofs, the remains of assorted aerials, towers, and lightning rods could be seen drooping in disrepair. Vast sections of the curtain wall were blown out or were in danger of crumbling. The slopes of the crag were littered with chunks of the castle that looked small, but once you identified features such as windows, you realized that they must be several stories tall. From the base of the structure, where the masonry met the cliffs, an enormous gargoyle head spat a frothing torrent of water toward the rocks far below where it disappeared into a cloud of perpetual mist. This was the source of the Dyne, the river that meandered through the town before flowing through an elaborate set of gates to the valley beyond.

Wooster saw the look on Agatha's face and nodded in satisfaction. "Yes, that's it. Happy?"

Agatha still gazed up at the castle. "It's a mess. But, to be honest? From everything I'd heard, I'd thought it would be much worse."

Next, she turned her attention to the rest of the town. It was built on uneven ground, with stairways and bridges connecting neighborhoods as often as streets. The buildings were mostly three- and four-story houses, many with a business tucked underneath. To the west, an immense factory complex dominated the skyline. Striking black and white clouds of smoke and steam poured from tall, slender smokestacks. To the north, an ornate, red stone Gothic cathedral rose, defiant beside the dark bulk of the ruined castle. To the east, a miniature lake and several acres of greensward gave way to orchards—which abutted a large white building that could only be the Great Hospital. Before them was a vast open area lined with what looked like rather dilapidated barracks.

As a whole, once you got past the gates, the town was obviously run down. It was easy to spot the tourists—they were the ones strolling down the streets with a bit of a bounce to their step. The natives, though dressed more colorfully, simply trudged along, at least until approached by a customer, at which point they radiated colorful folksiness.

Wooster allowed Agatha to take it in for another minute and then delicately cleared his throat. "So, my lady. You have arrived in Mechanicsburg. Now what?"

Agatha looked at him blankly. Then she stared at the ruined castle. "I'm not sure," she confessed. "I was told to go to Castle Heterodyne, but…" she gestured at it vaguely.

"First things first," Krosp declared. "Let's get somewhere quiet and then get these bandages off of me!"

"Are you sure—?"

Krosp waved a paw. "This is a town. There will be cats. I'm a cat. I'll blend in better."

Agatha had some doubts about this. Krosp had once confessed to her that while his creator had designed him to be a tool of espionage, he had engineered Krosp so that it was more comfortable for him to walk erect. The cat had to be frequently reminded to walk on all fours and any attempt he made at subterfuge seemed likely to be subverted by his constant complaining.

As they clopped along, Zeetha covered Krosp with her cloak and with a few deft slices, cut him free of his bandages.

"Better." Krosp stretched luxuriously and continued. "So. The castle. I'd heard it was damaged by the Other." He eyed the ruin and turned to Agatha. "I don't suppose you can shed any light on that from…" He tapped his head.

Agatha shook her head. She knew that the entity trapped inside her was indeed her mother—Lucrezia—and that Lucrezia had confessed to being the Other, but this only made things more confusing. "I can't access her mind or memories." She thought about this for a moment. "—Thank goodness."

Zeetha acknowledged her predicament. "Lucrezia Mongfish was supposedly kidnapped by the Other. But if they are one and the same…"

"The part that confuses me," said Agatha, "is that everyone says that Lucrezia and the Heterodyne's infant *son* were kidnapped."

They pondered this. "Maybe," Krosp suggested, "they didn't know you were a girl. Heck, if you were young enough, your eyes might not even have been open yet." Agatha ignored this suggestion.

Wooster pulled his horse to a halt. When they all turned to look at him, he indicated the ruined castle. "Seriously. You've seen this castle. It's useless. Worse than useless. Coming here was foolish, as it was the obvious thing you would do. Everyone is looking for you—"

Agatha cut him off. "Mr. Wooster, we are here because when my foster mother was about to throw me to safety—just before she was cut to ribbons by the Baron's Von Pinn creature—she told me 'Get to Castle Heterodyne. It will help you.' She *knew* it was a ruin. She *knew* people would be after me. But this is where she told me to go." She looked the man firmly in the eye. "And since she was one of the few people I trust, that is where I am going. You did *not* have to come along."

Wooster reflected that he was still under strict—and secret—orders from Gilgamesh Wulfenbach to get Agatha to safety in England—with the threat that if he did not, Wulfenbach would boil the spy's beloved island off the map. He rubbed his brow. "I rather think I did, actually."

Agatha patted him on the arm. "Don't worry, Mr. Wooster, I'll visit England eventually, if only to make sure that my friends there are being well treated."[2]

Wooster straightened up. "In that, at least, you may rest assured, my lady." He took a deep breath. "Very well. Let us reconnoiter this family treasure of yours. If you find out enough about it, perhaps you'll change your mind about going inside."

Mechanicsburg sits in a small, rough-hewn valley, ringed by sharp mountains. It is a point of pride to the inhabitants that despite being

---

[2]   Before leaving Master Payne's Circus, Agatha had arranged for them to receive sanctuary in England. Since she had secretly reengineered their circus into a mechanical fighting force which had wound up wounding the Baron and damaging a significant part of one of his armies, it had seemed like the right thing to do.

the home of the most hated family for a thousand kilometers in any direction, the town has never been taken by an invading army. Much of the surrounding area is devoted to high-density farms and orchards, which contribute to Mechanicsburg's vaunted self-sufficiency. Salted around the valley are a number of stone towers, which throughout history have served as watchtowers, storage bins, or places of assignation.

In one of these, three Jägermonsters were leaning against some upper crenellations, longingly gazing at Mechanicsburg's front gate.

Maxim peered through a trim little wood and brass telescope. When Agatha and her party had ridden on through the great iron gates, he had stared for another few seconds and then collapsed the scope down and stowed it in a pocket. "Dey's in," he announced.

Ognian was slouched atop the wall, apparently just enjoying the sun. "Any trobble?"

Maxim glanced back. He could see that old Carson Heliotrope was getting up from his bench. "Hy dun tink so."

Ognian put his hands behind his head. "Dot's goot."

Dimo was drumming his fingers on the stonework. "Ve should haff gone in vit her," he muttered.

"No Jäger," a new voice reminded him, "is to enter Mechanicsburg until a Heterodyne iz vunce again in residence. Dot vas de deal."

Maxim turned with a grin. "Jenka! Nice schneekink dere, sveetie!"

Jenka tried not to look pleased. Even Dimo looked a bit more relaxed. "Hy vundered vere hyu vas."

Jenka leaned against the parapet and shrugged. "Keepink busy. Deliverink newz. Cawzink trouble."

The three sighed. Some Jägers got to have all the fun.

Outside the Great Hospital was a manicured park. Broad green lawns and beds of colorful flowers were laced with crushed white stone paths. On a typical day, depending on their condition, patients were either tending the flowerbeds or being wheeled around the walks by uniformed attendants.

Today, though, a squad of Wulfenbach troopers was herding everyone off to the edges of the lawn, while one of the Empire's sleek courier dirigibles began its final descent. To the dismay of the gardening staff, several clampoons were fired into the ground, trailing thick cables up behind them. With a groan, the great steam-powered capstans began to turn and the ship was smoothly winched down to the ground. Soon a small group of hospital staffers were waiting anxiously while a metal stairway unfolded itself and the main hatches opened.

The first person out was Gilgamesh Wulfenbach—in a long, military-style greatcoat with the elaborate collar and cuffs that were *de rigueur* amongst the Empire's intelligentsia. In his hand, he carried a slim iron cane, topped with what looked like a rather fragile blue glass tube. When they saw him, the troops and low-rank hospital staff at the base of the stairway snapped to attention. Everyone in the small crowd watched nervously, glancing at the elderly Chinese man who walked calmly to meet the new arrival. This was Doctor Sun,[3] the head of the Great Hospital, and he was clearly in charge. He was dressed in a long, immaculate white lab coat intricately embroidered with white silk in a pattern of cavorting dragons. Atop his head was a tall double-peaked hat emblazoned with a red trilobite, the symbol of the Great Hospital.

When Gilgamesh saw him, he paused and made a slight bow with his hands at his side. "Dr. Sun. I am honored by your presence."

The old man glared at him with a sour expression on his face. "I was expecting you last night. He is your father, after all."

Gil swallowed nervously. "Yes, sir, I was stabilizing a medical experiment. Leaving it would have been unforgivable. Actually there are aspects that you might find interesting."

---

[3]   Dr. Sun Jen-Djieh was the administrator and chief doctor at the first Great Hospital. He was a Spark whom the Heterodyne Boys and Baron Wulfenbach had met in China during their adventures there. (See *The Heterodyne Boys and the Even Greater Wall of China* for a reasonably accurate record of their meeting.) Shortly thereafter, the Emperor decided that Dr. Sun had been contaminated by exposure to foreigners and should be put to the Death of Five Hundred Tightenings. Dr. Sun decided that it was time to listen to his doctor and take an extended vacation in the West.

As a medical researcher, Sun could feel his buttons being pressed and did not appreciate it. "At the moment, I am interested in keeping your father alive. A subject I can assume is of some small interest to you as well."

They strode into the hospital, which was even more bustling than usual. "We are clearing out the entire North wing," Sun explained. "Luckily, we're not particularly full at the moment. Some patients are being released a few days early and we have requisitioned one of the closer hotels."

Gil paused in the doorway to the hospital room and gasped. Over the last few years, Gil had seen his father occupy numerous hospital beds, but Klaus had always been awake and garrulous—even entertaining—in his own way. This was certainly not the case now.

The ruler of the Empire was surrounded by an impressive array of quietly humming machines and gurgling tubes. He lay still and silent at the center, swaddled in bandages and plaster. The few patches of flesh not covered revealed extensive bruising.

Gil was shaken by his father's face. For once it was not set in its permanent expression of vaguely irritated disappointment—instead it looked shockingly weary. With a touch of hesitation, Gil gently brushed a lock of white hair away from Klaus's closed eyes.

Then he took a deep breath and turned back to the patiently waiting physician, who almost took a step back from the expression that now burned in Gil's eyes.

"What happened?" Gil asked quietly. "The reports I was given are…" he hesitated.

"—Unbelievable?" Sun suggested.

Gil nodded reluctantly. When one dealt with the inner workings of the Empire for any length of time, one became a bit gun-shy about using phrases like "unbelievable."[4]

Sun nodded. "If you want unbelievable, you should hear how your father got here. Allow me to tell you of one Airman Higgs.

"When the field medics found your father, he was severely injured."

---

[4]   A perusal of archived Empire records reveal that other red flags were: "Impossible," "Illogical," "He wouldn't dare," and the all-time favorite: "…couldn't possibly be that stupid."

Sun handed over a medical chart that had required additional pages.

"He was taken aboard the medical corvette W.A.F. Linnaeus, as was Captain DuPree."

Gil looked up at this. Bangladesh DuPree usually dealt damage rather than taking it.

Sun noticed his surprise. "According to her, she was injured while destroying a very dangerous merry-go-round."

Gil's eyes narrowed. "Head trauma?"

Sun nodded. "Oh, yes. Once the extent of your father's injuries were understood, the Linnaeus took off immediately for the hospital. Unfortunately, the fighting was still quite fierce, and the ship was hit by antiaircraft fire.

"The alarms woke Airman Third Class Axel Higgs. He reported for emergency duty only to discover the main cabin in flames and the rest of the crew dead."

Gil frowned. "What did they get hit *with*?"

Sun shrugged. "Who knows? Mister Higgs reported that the ship was overrun with monsters."

Sun paused and looked at Gil expectantly.

Gil nodded. "Yes, long range systems to deliver biological weapons. If this isn't something the Other cooked up, then at least someone's been studying his methods."

Sun resumed his narrative. "On his way to the evacuation gig, Higgs discovered your father injured and unconscious. While dragging him to safety, he encountered Captain DuPree, who was apparently delirious. She broke his arm."

Gil sighed and rubbed his eyes.

"Mister Higgs knocked her out. He then managed to get both her and your father into the gig and shoved off just as the ship began to go down. Now, Mister Higgs is not rated as a pilot or a navigator, but he was able to set the controls for Mechanicsburg and engage the automatic pilot.

"He then began to apply first aid to your father, which was when he was again attacked by Captain DuPree. This time she broke his leg.

"He managed to subdue her by breaking a chair over her head and began to tie her up. That was when she bit him." Sun passed over another chart. "That's infected, by the way."

"During the fight, she also got in a few good kicks to the gig's controls. Mister Higgs put out the fire and tried to set his own arm, apparently blacking out from the pain. He awakened as the gig was crashing into a farmer's pond.

"He dragged your father and Captain DuPree ashore, where he encountered a nesting goose. This broke his other arm.

"He headed towards the farmhouse, but as luck would have it, there were Wulfenbach troops there. They had been hearing strange reports coming out of Balan's Gap. Thus, when they saw Mister Higgs, and the way he was moving, they thought he was a revenant. So they shot him in the leg.

"They were *very* sorry afterwards, of course. They heard him out, saw to your father and DuPree, called for transportation, and gave him some rum."

Sun paused. "Actually they gave him a *lot* of rum. Even if they exaggerated how much they gave him, he probably had a touch of alcohol poisoning. But before he passed out, he told them everything."

He paused, and Gil realized the significance of what the old man had said. Sun nodded wearily at the growing horror in Gil's eyes. "The battle at Sturmhalten. The loss of the fleet, the monsters—everything. Of course the troops were already reeling from the news about this supposed Lady Heterodyne.

"Needless to say, by the time Mr. Higgs was here and we heard what he had to say, it was far too late for us to suppress the stories."

Gil closed his eyes. "You mean, the Heterodyne heir, my father nearly being killed, our retreat from Balan's Gap..." He waved a hand. "You're saying everyone in Mechanicsburg knows about this?"

Sun arched a shaggy eyebrow. "You're concerned about Mechanicsburg? My dear boy, news of this import is probably being discussed in the Forbidden City even as we speak."

Gil stared at him. When the implications of this news really dawned on the people of the Empire ...

Sun interrupted his thoughts. "Gilgamesh." The use of his first name by the old man was so surprising that Gil actually started. Sun placed a hand on his shoulder. "The situation is grave. You must take control of the Empire immediately."

Gil's mind went blank. This was the day he had feared above all others. He pointed at his father. "You said he'd recover!"

Sun rolled his eyes. "*Eventually.*" He waved a hand at the bank of medical equipment. "But even for me, this will be a challenge, even if your father allows me the time to fully repair him."

Gil had to acknowledge the truth of this. Klaus was, like many people trained in the medical arts, a "bad patient." He refused to get enough bed rest, second-guessed his physician, and frequently hooked himself up to accelerated healing engines of dubious design or brewed up chemical concoctions from items filched from the hospital gift shop that admittedly promoted healing, as long as one didn't mind some small side effects.[5]

"But more importantly," Sun continued, "there are many who will try to exploit the current chaos. It must be seen that there is continuity. That the Empire is stable."

Gil felt the weight settling upon his shoulders. "Yes, Sifu." He straightened up and his eyes looked older. "I will be staying here."

Sun looked surprised. "I had thought Balan's Gap—"

Gil waved a hand. "Balan's Gap is contained for now. But my father is here. Those people you spoke of—for many of them, the first step will be to ensure his death." He stepped up to the window and Sun could see him assessing the terrain.

---

[5]　According to the private journals of Klaus's personal physician, Dr. Merrliwee, the Baron never actually believed that he had the time to allow himself to heal up naturally from anything. After a series of escalating events that were, in retrospect, actually rather humorous, unless you were one of the poor souls involved, she took to shooting him with a tranquilizer dart whenever he got a papercut. After the third time this happened, Klaus reluctantly established "sickness protocols" that allowed him to at least remain conscious while "taking it easy." He also felt spurred to invent "cutless paper," which has saved the lives of thousands of office workers across the Empire.

"I'm guessing that everyone I'll need to prove myself to, at least in the short term, will be coming here."

Sun began to look alarmed. "You aren't expecting an outright attack… are you?"

Gil snorted. "I expect several. I'm convinced that the Royal Family of Sturmhalten wasn't working alone. I've sent Questers to all of the surrounding castles. I have to look strong? Fine. Someone is going to wind up with their head on a stick." He paused. "Metaphorically, of course."

Sun nodded. "And the uproar caused by this supposed 'Heterodyne' girl?"

Gil took a deep breath. "She's the real thing." Sun's jaw dropped. Gil continued, "Even my father admits it."

Sun actually looked flummoxed. Gil carefully tried not to notice. The old man would come down hard on him if he thought his aura of imperturbability had been cracked. Sun pulled himself together. "Then…then she must be handled very carefully. If she were to actually enter Castle Heterodyne now… the effect upon the town alone—!"

Gil actually smiled. "Ah. Now *that* is already taken care of, and is the one thing I do not have to worry about. There'll be no Heterodyne heirs showing up in Mechanicsburg today."

Ardsley Wooster grimaced, stuck a pinky in his ear, and wiggled it around.

His cloaked and hooded companion noticed and in a muffled but clearly female voice asked: "What's the matter…darling?" The endearment was obviously taking some getting used to.

"Itchy ear," the Englishman grumbled.

The hood rippled. "You know what that means."

Wooster nodded. "It means I need a good hot bath."

"After walking around in this outfit, so will I."

They strolled a while along the promenade that ran beside the River Dyne before turning aside to cross a stone bridge. Beneath them, the river roared through the arches of the bridge. Before them rose Castle Heterodyne upon its pedestal of stone cliffs.

High above, they could just see the massive main gate of the Castle—gargantuan ironbound doors shut against the world. From there, a wide road wound down the hill, each switchback guarded by its own gate tower, complete with portcullis. The dark cliffs between were dotted with patches of scrubby thorn that waved gently, even though Wooster could feel no wind. An equally formidable gate at the base of the whole business completed the scene.

The lower gate itself was set into a colossal stone wall which surrounded the entire castle mount. Small guard posts were regularly spaced along its length. A decoratively scalloped pavement of white stone provided a contrast, a bright, open space that dramatically separated the river and town beyond from the wall.

The hooded lady looked along the pavement and paused. She swung around and looked back the way they had come. Across the bridge, the town bustled with life and movement. Tourists swarmed the streets and pushcart vendors and street performers called out to customers with songs, bells, drums, and simple shouts. Shop owners stood in their doorways and nodded invitingly to passersby.

The lady turned again and examined the area before her. There were no guards or barricades, yet the white stone parkway was empty.

"It's a lovely place...though I'm surprised there aren't at least a few souvenir stands ..." she said uncertainly.

Wooster nodded and tucked her arm through his. "Curious, isn't it? As far as I can tell, there's no rule against setting up here. The locals just...don't."

"I don't even see any guards."

Wooster frowned and slowed to a halt. "Yes...that is a bit—"

Suddenly, a heavy wave of air pressure swept them. They blinked, and found themselves surrounded by a troop of guards. Uniformed men and women trained their weapons upon them, faces grim. As far as either of their captives could tell, they had not run or leapt into position, they had simply appeared.

The guards wore Wulfenbach uniforms—the badges and buttons adorned with the familiar winged castle proclaimed that—but their uniforms were unfamiliar, cut from black cloth in a slightly archaic style. The leader, a captain by his insignia, raised a strangely fashioned bayonet. "Do not move," he said. "My people will not hesitate to shoot." The captives froze.

The captain nodded and stepped forward. His hand darted out and grasped the hood of the cloak. "Let's have a look under this hood, Lady Heterody—"

He stopped in surprise at the face before him, framed with a full head of vivid, emerald green hair.

Zeetha blinked and frowned at the perplexed officer. "Lady *who*?"

The soldier couldn't take his eyes off of Zeetha's hair. "What is this?"

Wooster stepped forward and yanked the fabric of the hood from the soldier's unresisting hand. He pulled it quickly back over Zeetha's head as he snapped: "It's a fungus!" He made a show of tenderly adjusting the hood before wheeling about, the very picture of an outraged husband. "The doctors *said* not to expose it to light!"

The soldiers didn't lower their rifles, but they began to look uncomfortable.

"That ain't her!"

Zeetha and Wooster turned to see a soldier stepping out of one of the castle's guardhouses, where he had evidently been waiting surreptitiously. He was an older man, thick and squat, yet he moved with an ease that said he was as fit as any of them. He was decked out in a green and blue uniform topped with a jaunty top hat. The wings on his Wulfenbach insignia were neither the usual bird wings nor the bat's wings adopted by some of the Baron's troops—these were styled like the wings of a dragonfly. His right arm was in a sling, but his left hand waved the other troops off. The hash marks on his sleeve identified him as a master-sergeant. "I *said* that ain't her." He tipped his hat to Wooster and Zeetha. "Sergeant Scorp. Sorry for the inconvenience, folks, we'll have you on your way in just a minute."

Another of the dark-clad soldiers swung her rifle up slightly. "Hair color is easy to change, sergeant."

Scorp nodded. "True enough, ma'am." He turned and eyed the pair before him. "But I saw her. Was this close to her. Different face. Different build." He shook his head. "This ain't her."

The captain nodded and with a showy spin, sheathed his sword. "Right." He turned to Wooster and Zeetha and apologetically touched his hat. "Sorry about that, ma'am, sir. We got word that there's an escaped lunatic heading for the castle here. For her own protection..." he vaguely waved a hand at the rest of his squad.

"A lunatic?" Wooster frowned. "You don't mean that new Heterodyne girl everyone is talking about?"

The captain rolled his eyes and sighed. "Yeah, that's the one. I guess she missed the birth announcements about it being a boy."

Zeetha glanced at Wooster. "Maybe there was—"

"A mistake?" the captain snorted. "Get serious. I was born and raised here. My aunt was one of the Lady Lucrezia's midwives. I remember the day he was born. They rang the Doom Bell." The captain shivered.

"There weren't any daughters and Master Barry never had any kids. So...*no*. Now move along. Go visit the Heterodyne Museum on Vox Street. You can see his portrait." He turned away. "Squad—Disperse!"

And with a huff of wind, they vanished. Sergeant Scorp again tipped his hat and strolled back to the guardhouse.

Zeetha and Wooster held their silence until they were halfway back across the little bridge that took them back to the bustling town.

"Those soldiers," Zeetha said carefully. "They came out of nowhere."

Wooster grimaced. "That's...more true than you know. That was the Black Squad. If the Baron is using them—" He shook his head in annoyance. "I need a drink."

They toiled up a sloping street until they came to a small café. On a sun-drenched patio with an excellent view of the Castle gates, Agatha was finishing up a buttery bacon quiche. A small set of binoculars rested on the table beside her.

Zeetha and Wooster joined her at the table. A smiling waiter appeared with more quiche and a tray of chilled flutes filled with a crisp, sweet spring wine.

When he had gone, Agatha tapped the table thoughtfully. "Well, I guess I won't be getting in through the front gate."

Zeetha thoughtfully took a sip of wine. "They said 'for her own protection.' What was that about?"

Wooster glanced at the nearest table—occupied by a single old man apparently engrossed in his newspaper. An odd feeling of déjà vu flickered across his mind. Agatha cleared her throat and Wooster leaned forward and lowered his voice. "The castle is haunted."

The ladies stared at him blankly. Wooster looked embarrassed. "Well, I guess that's the easiest way to explain it."

Agatha looked skeptical. "Easy is rarely accurate."

Wooster sighed and looked about to signal the waiter for a refill. Agatha handed him hers. "Right. Some of this is common knowledge, some is from the Baron's files." A troubled look flitted across his face. "I doubt it's important enough that they would have bothered to make false files…"[6]

Wooster collected his thoughts. "Castle Heterodyne is purported to be a single, gigantic mechanism. In its heyday, it was apparently one of the Seven Mad Wonders of the World.[7] Details are a little sketchy, as the Heterodyne Boys never talked about it much and

---

[6]   Until Recently, Ardsley Wooster had served aboard Castle Wulfenbach as Gilgamesh Wulfenbach's valet. In actuality, he was working for British Intelligence. It would have been an extraordinarily useful position from which to winnow out the secrets of the Empire, if it wasn't for the fact that both Gilgamesh and his father had been aware of Wooster's true allegiances from the get-go and had been cheerfully feeding him false information. Spies find this sort of thing terribly embarrassing and are loath to mention it on their résumés.

[7]   The Seven Mad Wonders of the World is an informal list kept by the British Museum. Castle Heterodyne was indeed on it for at least two centuries (One must remember that neither the penchant for odd creations nor the British Museum are new institutions).

In addition to Castle Heterodyne, there are listed the Storm King's Muses, the Awful Tower in Paris, the London Dome, Mr. Tock of Beetleburg, the Secret Library, and a semi-open spot which was whimsically referred to as the "Impossibility of the Day." Since its fall into ruin, Castle Heterodyne's spot on the list had been usurped by Castle Wulfenbach.

their predecessors didn't encourage tourism. But from anecdotal evidence, it was quite amazing.

"Overnight guests spoke of awakening to discover their rooms in a completely different part of the castle. There were reports of mysterious voices and invisible servants. Intruders found themselves lost inside it for weeks, if they didn't disappear entirely.

"After the attack, it lay broken and abandoned for years. The locals refused to go near it.

"Eventually a young professor from Transylvania Polygnostic University led a team of researchers inside.[8] Their objectives were the Great Library and any other research notes they could salvage.

"Once they were deep inside, the Castle spoke to them. It demanded to be repaired. One of the team members spoke up against the idea, and the Castle made it clear that this was not a request.

"Six months later, one of the assistants finally emerged, much the worse for wear. In that time, the town had been taken by the Baron. The assistant explained that the Castle was directing its own repairs, but in an extremely haphazard manner. The job would take years.

"The food stores had run out and the assistant had been sent out to procure more food, tools, materials, and, if possible, more labor.

"The Baron had an idea. He managed to negotiate with the Castle, who actually remembered him as an associate of the Heterodyne Boys, and he got the professor and his remaining people out.

"To replace them, he offered to send in actual Sparks, which the Castle could direct as it saw fit. Ever since then, the Baron has used it as the ultimate punishment detail. I have to assume that once it's been made safe, he plans on looting it himself."

Wooster sat back and took another drink. Agatha slowly shook her head. "I've never heard about any of this." She paused. "One of

---

[8]   Professor Mordechai Donowitz, PhD. Tampering Within God's Domain and Chair of the Department of the Non-Humanities. The father of Hezekiah Donowitz, whom Agatha met while aboard Castle Wulfenbach. See our earlier textbook; *Agatha H. and the Airship City.*

the Heterodyne Boys novels,[9] *The Heterodyne Boys and the 20,000 League Boots*, mentions that they had an invisible servant in their castle, but that was one of the parts I never took seriously."

Wooster nodded. "It is easy enough for the Baron to keep it a secret, of sorts. Those people who don't believe that the place is haunted just think that the place is full of booby traps."

Agatha frowned. "But the Baron has had people working inside it for how long?"

Wooster did a quick calculation in his head. "Almost fourteen years, I believe."

"And people believe the place is still booby trapped after fourteen years?"

Wooster nodded. "Who is going to tell them otherwise? The locals? This is Castle Heterodyne. It's a point of *pride* for them."

Agatha sat back. "Well, if it remembered the Baron, perhaps—"

At that moment, Krosp dashed around a corner, scrambled under the chair of the old man reading his paper, and leapt straight onto the table. "Agatha!"

Agatha dropped her fork. "Quiet," she hissed. "Someone will hear!" Indeed, the old man was regarding the agitated cat with astonishment.

Krosp glanced at him and waved a paw dismissively. "In a minute he isn't going to care about a *talking cat*!" He grabbed Agatha's sleeve and tried to drag her along behind. "Come on!"

Wooster quickly dropped a few coins on the table while Zeetha cheerfully stuffed the rest of her quiche in her mouth and they all rose to follow.

"What's happening?" Wooster asked.

---

[9] The Heterodyne Boys traveled the world righting wrongs and fighting evil. Once they disappeared, publishers realized that people still wanted to hear about their adventures, and *The Heterodyne Library of Spark Snapping Adventure* was born. These books purported to chronicle the actual adventures of the boys, but as your humble professors are well aware, and do our best to avoid, it is the rare recitation of facts that suffers from the injection of blood and thunder, egregious villainy, and spicy romance. Thus, after a few volumes, the facts of the Heterodynes' lives became more and more unimportant, while the books themselves became more and more exciting.

Krosp continued to pull Agatha along. "You know how everyone in town is buzzing about how the Heterodyne heir is coming?"

"Of course," Agatha muttered. "We—"

Krosp jerked her around a final corner. "She's *here!*"

And indeed she was.

It was one of the larger squares in the town. In the center was the famous cast iron statue of the Heterodyne Boys—jaunty grins on their faces, giving their famous "thumbs up" salute.

The square was packed with people—townspeople and tourists alike—with more pouring in every second. Floating directly overhead was a small airship, newly minted, if the gleam still on its engines was any indication. It was astonishing both for the large gold trilobites emblazoned upon the sides of its gasbag, and the fact that said gasbag was a shockingly vivid pink.

The girl standing proudly upon the statue's pedestal—with the Boys towering behind her beaming down approvingly—was almost as pink herself.

Her outfit was a splendid confection straight from the overly-fussy fashion houses of Vienna, with a full skirt, puff sleeves, and a high collar, all framing a round, rosy face. Golden trilobites were scattered about her outfit, even nestled in her shimmering blonde hair.

Her voice, which was obviously being boosted by some unseen mechanism, was high, clear, and rang with noble sincerity.

"Greetings, people of Mechanicsburg! I am the Lady Zola Heterodyne—" There was a murmur of surprise from the crowd at this, which quickly died down. "—daughter of William Heterodyne! At long last, I have returned to my home!"

This got a burst of applause—discreetly led by the ring of men that Agatha now noticed surrounding the statue's base. They were all of a single mold: tall, weirdly slim, dressed in dark frock coats and striped shirts, with matching stovepipe hats nearly as tall and narrow as themselves. Their eyes were covered with black smoked goggles. Each man held a different, uniquely odd machine—each machine clearly the work of a Spark.

"I have long been in hiding, for there are many who have vowed to destroy me!" This provoked another burst of noise from the crowd. "But now, the Baron lies injured! Powerless! He can no longer defend the Empire, let alone my beloved Mechanicsburg!"

Silence washed over the square now. This was dangerous talk. "I fear that his incapacity will lead to war that will threaten this place— this beloved town of my ancestors! I have a duty to you, my people! There will be danger, but I *will* face it, for I *must protect my city*!"

She squared her shoulders and looked adorably resolute. "Thus, despite the risk to my person, I return to claim my own—and I begin with Castle Heterodyne! Come along and bear witness, for a new era begins!" And with that she unhesitatingly leapt from the base of the statue, provoking a gasp from the crowd which turned into cheers as she was effortlessly caught by two of the tall men awaiting her below.

The girl took her place at the head of a procession, surrounded by a phalanx of her tall dark men—the still-growing crowd falling in behind her. With a roar, they swept out of the square and followed her towards the castle gates.

Zeetha turned and saw Agatha staring, her mouth agape. She reached over and pushed Agatha's mouth closed with a delicately outstretched finger. "Do try to face the new era with some dignity," she advised.

Soon, enough of the crowd had passed that Agatha and her friends could join the tail end, and they turned the corner in time to see the girl in pink gracefully lifted onto the rail of the little stone bridge by two of her retainers.

She pointed dramatically at the castle and the crowd cheered.

"Will you look at her?" Agatha was slowly shifting from shock to outrage. "I cannot believe this! She's pretending to be me!"

Krosp nodded and glanced up at the pink dirigible, which was slowly drifting along in the direction of the castle. "Yes, this is going to be trouble."

The girl and her coterie had reached the castle side of the bridge.

Even though Agatha was looking for it, it was still startling when, with a puff of displaced air and a small cloud of dust, the members of the Black Squad materialized around the girl and her party.

Wooster nodded in satisfaction. "And that should take care of that."

The captain looked a lot more alert this time. His squad held their weapons at the "ready" position. "Halt."

The girl did so with a smile. Without taking her eyes off of the captain, she inquired, "Herr Vikel?"

One of the dark retainers nodded and activated the device in his hands. Instantly the members of the Black Squad shrieked and began to unnaturally twist and bend before they disappeared. Their weapons clattered to the ground.

The pink girl took a deep breath and then casually waved a hand. "Onward!"

Wooster let out a low whistle. "Interesting."

After a shocked moment, the crowd hurried to catch up and hundreds of people were now toiling up the winding road to the front gate of the castle. Agatha's group joined them.

Krosp looked over the rail at the steep slope and nodded in approval. "Nice. Very defensible."

Agatha frowned. "But why didn't Miss Perfect just fly up to the top in her perfect pink airship?"

Wooster considered this. "I think it's fairly obvious that this whole grand procession is for show."

Zeetha nodded. "She wants as many people as possible to see her enter the castle."

Agatha frowned. "But...can't they tell that she's spouting nonsense?"

Wooster gave her a smirk. "The only thing that makes it nonsense is that *she's* saying it instead of you." He waved a hand at the excited townspeople. "They've all heard about you, so they were expecting something like this." He paused. "Well, probably not like this, exactly. This is all a bit high-handed, although her showmanship is impeccable."

Agatha stumbled slightly and leaned against a railing panting, "Well her 'impeccable showmanship' is killing me."

Krosp sniffed. "I think you're still feeling some of the after effects of those chemicals they filled you full of in Sturmhalten."

Zeetha narrowed her eyes. "*I* think somebody's been neglecting her training."

"Training?" Agatha snorted. "Please. Right now, who cares?"

Seconds later, the crowd toiling its way up the incline hastily parted for Agatha, hotly pursued by Zeetha—brandishing a large stick.

Soon enough, Agatha reached the gateway and stumbled to her knees. "Sorry, Zeetha! Sorry! I do care! I really do!" she gasped under her breath. Her heart was pounding and she was afraid she might pass out. She swayed slightly, thinking maybe the rest would at least be good for her, when a well-manicured hand appeared before her.

"My, my…" The voice was light and melodic, with a faint Parisian accent, "such an encouraging reception! But there's no need to kneel, dear girl. I'll not rule by fear! Arise!" So saying, Zola's hand lightly curled around Agatha's upper arm and hauled her up straight, with surprising strength.

Up close, the face of the woman in pink was broad, but delicate. Her eyes were large and expressive and her wide mouth was set in a genuine smile of delight. Behind her, two of the tall retainers watched Agatha closely, the innocent-looking devices in their hands not *quite* pointing at her.

"Here, my dear, a little token of our meeting." She pressed a coin into Agatha's hand as she moved on.

Agatha stared at the coin and felt a surge of fury wash through her. It was a gold coin. Solid, by the weight of it. One face was an elegant portrait of the girl herself. The other was a trilobite. The heraldic symbol of the Heterodyne family. If nothing else, Agatha felt severely outclassed.

Wooster saw her face and pried the coin from her fingers. He could see that several nearby onlookers were interested. He slipped a familiar hand around her shoulders. It was like hugging an iron statue. "Mighty generous, eh, dear?" he said gamely. He pretended to notice her face. "It's not charity, dear. No need to be embarrassed."

The onlookers nodded in sympathy and then the sound of squealing metal drew everyone's attention. Several of the tall men were pulling back a set of gates that had been installed before the actual great door of the castle, which hung ajar, slightly off its hinges.

When she was sure that everyone was looking, Zola drew herself up and raised her hands for silence. "And now," she said solemnly, "I go to reclaim what is mine by right!" She then turned and, followed by her attendants, stepped through the door, disappearing from sight.

Everyone waited a minute but nothing else seemed to be happening. Agatha turned to Ardsley Wooster. "She just walked right in?"

Wooster nodded. "Well…yes. The trick is in walking out again."

Agatha drew herself up, her eyes hard. "Well, fine. That's just great. I'm going to go in there and show her—"

A quiet voice interrupted her. "Pardon me, my lady…"

Surprised, Agatha and the rest of her party turned to see the old man who had been sitting near them in the café. He had looked sleepy before but now he was alert and focused as he studied her intently. He made a small gesture towards the great doorway. "But shouldn't that have been you?"

CHAPTER 2

Like most towns, Mechanicsburg has located its airship terminals and freight yards outside of the old city walls. There are many fine things one can say about modern airship travel, but on the ground, it does require an inordinate amount of real estate. Luckily, the airship terminal that serves Mechanicsburg is located near a Corbettite rail terminal. If one is of a patient disposition, one may hop a slow freight shuttle directly into the town for free. For the traveler with more money than time, carriages, carts, rickshaws, and horses are available for rent. If one feels like a spot of exercise, it is less than a kilometer by foot to the North Gate. The intervening area is primarily farmland, which does allow one to appreciate the size and grandeur of the surrounding mountains. Some do like that sort of thing.

Due to one of the more fanciful of Airshipman traditions, no ship will ever fly directly over the town itself. This is a shame, as theoretically, the aerial views of Castle Heterodyne alone would be spectacular.

—*Out and About the Empire on Ten Guilders a Day* —Dame Mòrag MacTavish/Waterzoon Press/ Amsterdam he air was tense aboard the shocking pink airship that hung over Mechanicsburg. The captain stood quietly, apparently enjoying the glorious view of the mountains on the horizon, but his hands, clasped behind his back, were white knuckled. On the surface, everything appeared ship shape, polished, and crisp, but in his heart he knew that everything about this berth stank like bad balloon wax.

When the Aerofleet Merchant Board had first outlined the job it had seemed like a dream come true. Captain of a brand new ship—from the Stockholm Yards, no less! Conveying a lost heir to her new kingdom, along with her royal sponsors, who would win over the town with a display of loose wealth and largesse. If all went well, there was even the possibility of a permanent commission.

Then the rip panel had been pulled. The town? Mechanicsburg. The girl was a supposed Heterodyne heir, and her noble sponsors were a pair of privileged, overbearing ne'er-do-wells that he would as soon have had jettisoned before the ship warped away from the dock.

In addition, the preparations had been rushed, less than twenty-four hours from oath to float. He hadn't had the time to properly vet or shake down either the crew or the airship before they'd left, and he'd run them blue doing inspections and drills while on the fly. The old-timers, at least, had appreciated that. The fledglings had been too busy running to grumble.

The supposed heir had boarded ship in Vienna and no one had seen her since. She kept to her cabin—her needs seen to by her sponsors and the flock of silent minions she had brought with her.

The captain smiled humorlessly. Well, he'd done his part. The girl had been delivered safely. They'd touched down right in the main square of the town and she'd been escorted off in style. He'd been ordered to take the ship back up, to hover at an unnervingly low two hundred meters and await further orders.

The gentlemen who paid the bills stood in the main Observation Bay. The tall, equine one—Duke Strinbeck[10]—had been watching the girl's progress through an elegant brass telescope. Finally, he let out a huge gust of breath and lowered the scope.

"She's in the castle," he announced.

His companion, a portly, white-haired man who called himself Baron Krassimir Oublenmach, had been striding back and forth, seemingly deep in thought. Now, he positively beamed. "Excellent!"

Strinbeck regarded him with a slight frown, swung the tube up again and idly scanned the town. "I certainly hope so," he muttered.

Oublenmach grinned. He knew he made his fellow nobles feel uncomfortable. He clapped Strinbeck on the back. Oh yes, as stiff as a board. He could feel that even through his metal gloves.

"Come, come, young fellow, you're still worried?"

Strinbeck, who had never been much into the whole "fellowship" thing to begin with, pointedly detached himself from his overly familiar companion. "Of course I am," he snapped. "It's too soon. I don't like being rushed."

To his surprise, the older man took him seriously. In a rare flash of insight, Strinbeck realized that Oublenmach was as worried as he was—but better at hiding his misgivings. "You think Zola isn't ready?"

Strinbeck waved a hand irritably. "No, no. She's perfect." The hand flicked towards the window. "I'm worried about the castle."

Oublenmach regarded Castle Heterodyne with a frown. "Ah yes, the castle is the unpredictable element, is it not?" He faced Strinbeck and grinned that disquietingly evil grin of his. "But it always will

---

[10] His Grace, Josef Carmelita Strinbeck, was from a minor kingdom in Lithuania that had been overrun by unsettlingly large wind-up toys. You might think these circumstances would cause him to be mocked by his fellow royals, but variants of this absurd story were all-too-common amongst displaced nobility. Too many of the wrong sort of person found these events hilarious to begin with. Among the Fifty Families, to be anything other than properly sympathetic and solicitous when hearing the story of a fellow royal's overthrow by Sparks, no matter how ludicrous it sounded, was considered extremely gauche. As for the Duke himself, he was—by all accounts—snide, supercilious, and a born martinet. It had often been said that it was only his family connections that had stood in the way of his becoming an incredibly feared headwaiter.

be, sir. No matter how much we prepare. No, we had to move! All that lovely build-up in Balan's Gap? Old Klaus wounded? Either one of them would have been temptation enough, but both together? *Carpe diem!*"

Strinbeck irritably snapped his telescope shut and wondered what fish had to do with anything. "But what about that giant Heterodyne girl over Sturmhalten? Even your people haven't found her yet! Which is inexcusable! I mean, she was bloody enormous!"

Oublenmach began to laugh at the joke, and then his eyes glazed slightly as he realized that Strinbeck was quite serious. "One thing at a time, sir. One thing at a time. Once everything is in place, our girl will effectively be the new Heterodyne. *Vox machinae, vox populi,* eh?

"Then, when do we capture the other...aheh...no doubt enormous...girl, *she'll* just be another pathetic Heterodyne impersonator, and if she *does* give us the slip as it were and get in, why then, Zola will simply see to it that she's 'killed by the castle.' That is what it does best, is it not?"

"Let's just hope the castle doesn't squash our Zola first, eh?"

Oublenmach rolled his eyes. "Oh enough, sir! The dice are thrown and we've loaded them as best we could! Think positively, your Grace! The castle *will* fall to us! The Doom Bell *will* ring, and Europa will—"

Oublenmach's voice was rising with excitement, but Strinbeck cut him off with a sigh. Oublenmach was so enthusiastic that Strinbeck cringed whenever he had to endure a prolonged conversation with him. Right now, Oublenmach was positively exhausting. "Yes, yes! A new era for everyone. Do spare me the glorious blueprint. I'm going to have a bit of a lie-down."

Oublenmach dismissed him with a wave. This was the sort of casual impertinence that caused Strinbeck's jaw to tighten in fury. *Soon enough, you jumped up peasant,* the duke promised himself for the thousandth time.

Once the duke had left, Oublenmach turned to the captain, who'd been standing woodenly behind them. "Captain Abelard, I assume your drop-reels are properly engaged."

Abelard was used to getting questions from nervous passengers about the state of assorted equipment, but this was a surprise. The drop-reels were a rather unnerving method of exiting a low-flying ship. Not the sort of thing you'd expect a ground-hugger to even know about.

"Of course, sir."

"Excellent. Show me."

There was no polite way to refuse. Oublenmach was paying the bills and it was patently obvious that there was nothing otherwise occupying the captain's time. Thus a short while later, he was treated to the sight of the small man examining one of the cunning little devices with a practiced eye.

"You look like you know a bit about drop-reels, sir."

"Oh, indeed, indeed," Oublenmach called out cheerfully. "Saved my life any number of times."

As the captain digested this intriguing bit of information, he was caught by surprise as the little man slapped the cable release, causing the drum to begin unspooling.

"What the devil are you doing?"

Oublenmach had donned a pair of canvas airman's gloves and swung the drop-reel around, slapping the gripping jaws closed with a snap. "I am giving in to foolish fancy, sir," he said gaily. "Too much back-room plotting ruins a man's digestion, it truly does, sir! When I pick a man's pocket, I like to do it to his face, and I'll not steal an Empire any differently!"

Before the captain could stop him, he swung out and hung from the control rods. "If poor Josef asks, I've gone for a drink! *Au revoir!*" And with a laugh, he twisted the grips and dropped out of sight.

The captain swore and peered downwards. He then grunted in surprise. Annoying fellow he might be, but Oublenmach handled the drop-reel like an expert. As the captain watched, he disengaged at exactly the right moment and touched down lightly even as the reel spool began yo-yoing back up the line. He then waved a perfect signal-corps "safe aground" sign before turning and sauntering off.

It was a reflective captain who stowed and locked down the reel before making his way back to the bridge. He had thought that their assigned height had been a symptom of this whole poorly thought-out affair. *Too low to hide but still high enough to fall hard.* But he was reassessing that now. He was convinced that Oublenmach's departure, as spontaneous as he had tried to make it appear, had been part of the man's plan from the start and that the duke was in for an unpleasant surprise. What else was he misjudging?

He glanced out the window in time to see one of the freakishly odd birds of Mechanicsburg squawk at the sight of the ship and veer off. "We're still pink," he grumbled. "Let's not forget that."

He ran an eye over the bridge trying to see it with fresh eyes, and what he saw was not good. On a milk run like this, the bridge crew should be relaxed. Making idle chatter. Checking out a new town was always a source of entertainment, with crews observing the ebb and flow of the street traffic and making bets as to the locations of the best taverns and sporting houses.

But there was none of that here. The entire watch was on edge. With a practiced eye, the captain scanned the crew and found the center of the storm. It was Kraddock—and that was worrying all by itself.

Mr. Kraddock had started as a "rigger rat" when he was nine and claimed that he could still count the number of times since then that he'd actually touched ground. He'd fought skywurms in the realms of the Polar Ice Lords and seen the Great Western Wall of Fire. He'd survived air pirates, storms, hypothermia, blowouts, and the skybends, yet here he was at his wheel, fretting like a dirt-foot.

With a sigh, the captain stepped up behind the man. It was a sign of Kraddock's level of distraction that it wasn't until the captain leaned in and quietly asked, "A problem with your wheel, Mr. Kraddock?" that the old fellow snapped into a textbook picture of attention.

"No, sir!" he barked. "Wheel is secure, sir!"

The captain came around so that he was looking the man in the face. Oh, he was worried about something, all right. "Well what is it, then? Come on, out with it, old-timer."

The wheelman grimaced and tried to avoid his captain's eyes. "Well, Captain, I don't like to second-guess orders. 'Specially with an officer that's been around like yourself, sir. Not my place, you know? But… we're in Mechanicsburg airspace."

And that said it all right there. A lot of the newer crewmen were listening in, without trying to look like they were. No doubt they'd already got an earful of stories about the place. Outside the windows, in the light of day, the town looked positively picturesque. But Kraddock—and the captain—knew that that was just a new coat of paint on a sleeping dragon.

The wheelman saw the look in the captain's eyes, and felt emboldened. "A lot of the old hands…we…we don't like it. Sir."

But this was a bit too close to participatory democracy for the captain's taste. He stiffened. "The Baron has proved that Mechanicsburg airspace has been safe for close to twenty years, Mr. Kraddock," he said loudly.

Kraddock nodded vigorously. "Oh, yessir …but…"

Abelard knew he'd regret asking. "—But?"

"But, beggin' your pardon, Captain, but everyone knows it… We're kind of…conquerin' it, ain't we?"

And with a start, the captain realized that, like Kraddock, he was terrified at the thought of what they were involved in. He'd just tamped it down so far that he hadn't even known it.

But it *had* been twenty years… "Yes," he admitted. "Just like the Baron did. So?"

Kraddock hesitated. The captain rolled his eyes. It was too late to tell him to hold his tongue now. The best way to deal with this would be to lance it and let it all spill out. "You may speak."

The old wheelman nodded. "The Baron, yes. But… he was…an old friend of the family, as it were. And if he's ruling the place, he's doing it with a mighty light touch on the wheel, if I may say so, sir. Whereas, our…young lady…" He took a deep breath and his voice dropped to a whisper. "She ain't *really* a Heterodyne." He paused. "Is she?"

Captain Abelard made it a practice to never lie to the crew. On the other hand, he knew when to stop talking. He pulled down the General Address speaking tube.

"All hands—" he said crisply, "are to keep a weather eye out. Immediately report anything odd to two officers!"

A sigh of relief blew through the bridge. Strategically, nothing had changed, but they knew that their captain was taking things seriously. Kraddock saluted sharply and stood a bit taller. "Very good, Captain."

Abelard returned the salute and, with a measured calm, sat in the command chair. He felt a little better, but not much. For the thousandth time, he wondered why they had made the damn balloon—

"Pink," Gilgamesh marveled. He leaned full against the stone of the windowsill and stared. "It's *pink*."

Dr. Sun entered the room, a tray-laden nurse following several steps behind. "Have you seen—"

"I see it, Sifu."

The old man came to his side and gazed up at the hovering dirigible. "It is very—*pink*."

"Yes, I see that too." Gil swung away from the window. "I want the city sealed. I want a full squad of clanks sent up to the castle, and I want a full report on what's happening."

Sun nodded agreeably. "You will not go yourself?"

Gil shook his head. "No. I need to stay here with my father." He glanced toward the hospital bed where Baron Wulfenbach lay. "NURSE—!" He pointed his walking stick at the woman who had entered with Dr. Sun. She paused beside the Baron, a full hypodermic in her hand.

"What is that?" Gil's eyes narrowed. "Nothing was ordered for this patient."

The nurse gave him a matronly smile. "Don't worry, young man, this is just a vitamin that we give all—"

"*Do not move.* Sun?"

The old man's voice conveyed his fury. "She is not one of my people."

"Too late!" The woman screamed in triumph as she brought the syringe down towards Klaus. "Die, tyrant!"

Before Doctor Sun could move, a bolt of electricity spat forth from the tip of Gil's stick, catching the woman full in the chest. She was knocked back hard, bursting into explosive flames before she hit the far wall.

Gil strode to his father's side, brushing off bits of flaming debris. "My father appears to be unharmed," he told Sun. "That was lucky." He began a deep breath of relief but was surprised to find himself jerked about and staring into the face of Dr. Sun. The old man was furious.

"What the devil did you just let off in my hospital?" Sun roared at him, giving him a solid shake.

Gil held up his cane. It was a light, ornate swagger stick such as any fashionable young man might carry, but the blue glass bauble at the top was lit with a fading glow-heat pouring off it.

"Just a little something I've been working on, Sifu. A lot of it is Agatha's, but she was working from my designs. I've managed to solve most of the remaining problems. I was a bit worried about effect spread, but…"

His vision blurred as he was given another shake. He realized that Sun was staring at him with a stone-cracking gaze. He wound down.

"Pretty neat, don't you think?" he finished weakly.

Sun pinned him with his gaze for another second and then spun to the charred corpse on the floor. "An assassination attempt! In *my hospital*! Who would *dare*?"

Gil checked some of the dials on the medical machinery. "Now that they know my father is helpless? Many would dare." He shoved the dead woman aside with his foot. "She'll be but the first." He glanced at the now-coated walls. "I think we'll need a mop."

Sun rang for an orderly. "She certainly wasn't a professional," he sniffed.

Gil snorted. "No, she wasn't. She was too slow." Sun bit his lip as he considered this. Gil continued, "The professionals will wait. They'll let a few overly enthusiastic amateurs go first to see what happens." He kicked one of the larger charred lumps under the bed. "We should leave my father here. Let the assassins enter and then…disappear. Keep it a mystery. Keep them guessing."

"What? Keep your father here? In the same room as a corpse?" The doctor was appalled. "…Although… she *is* cauterized…" Sun frowned and slowly combed his hand through his beard. A knock at the door made them jump, but it was only an orderly. Sun met the man at the door, purposely blocking his view. He requested a broom, a dozen blankets, and several cartloads of ice. "At the very least we can sweep her up and put her in the closet," he said cheerfully as he shut and locked the door again. "There is still a fair amount of her I can use."[11]

He stood over the remains of the dead woman and looked at Gil with a raised eyebrow. With a sigh, the acting ruler of the Wulfenbach Empire rolled up his sleeves and began to clean up his own mess.

Sun shook his head. "I wonder why—"

"Why?" Gilgamesh interrupted as he shoved the closet door closed, "Because Wulfenbach troops turned the people in her village into owls—"

Sun blinked. "You what?"

Gil waved a hand. "—Or we might have deposed her favorite mad prince or hung her lover for piracy or banished the Heterodyne Boys or poisoned the well or raised the price of herring…" Gil wound down and took a deep breath. "The *reason* isn't important, Sifu. Neither is the truth. What is important is this: she was just the first."

The old man nodded. "Then you had better clear your mind and be prepared." He headed out the door. "As should we all. We must transfer as many patients as we can—"

Doctor Sun was about to close the door behind him when Gil stepped forward and put a hand on his arm. "Sifu—when you come

---

[11]   Make no mistake, Dr. Sun was a Spark, specializing in the more outré branches of medicine. This was by no means the first inconvenient corpse he'd had to step around while he worked. Usually on another corpse.

back? Don't forget to knock."

Sun nodded, and the door shut between them. Gil took a quick turn around the room, examining the vents and tapping at certain points upon the floor and ceiling. Satisfied, he again checked his father's machinery and finally allowed himself to once more stare out the window at the airship that floated above the town.

"That can't be Agatha," he muttered. "Unless they tried to fake us out by switching ships..." He dismissed this with a wave. "No, they'd want to hide, and I *told* Wooster to get her to England..." He gnawed on his lower lip.

"Wooster is *good*. If he's somehow failed and she's here...if that's her up there...then something terrible must have happened to him." Gil thought about this for a moment and his face darkened. "And if it hasn't—it will."

Agatha, Wooster, Zeetha, and Krosp followed the old man down the causeway. Wooster was furious with himself. "This old fellow is the one who gave us directions outside the city gates."

Agatha nodded. "He was also sitting next to me at the café."

Zeetha bit her lip. "Why didn't we notice—"

The old man's amused voice floated back towards them. "Because I did not *want* to be noticed." He smiled. "It's a knack."

He led Agatha and her friends away from the Castle and through the streets of Mechanicsburg. They followed him warily—he refused to say anything more until they were "somewhere more private," which they all agreed was wise, but unsatisfying.

Everywhere people were clustered on the streets and in doorways, talking with a great amount of gesticulating and hand waving. Voices were raised in argument and wonder. As far as Agatha could determine, the out-of-towners seemed inclined to believe the newcomer was the real thing, a genuine Heterodyne, returned at last! The natives were perfectly willing to concede that this might be true, in which case, any item purchased on this momentous occasion would obviously become a treasured memento. Thus, all of the merchants seemed to be doing a roaring business, with trays of souvenirs—or indeed anything that bore a "Made in Mechanicsburg" label—evaporating as fast as the delighted merchants could haul them out from their back rooms.

After a while, Agatha noticed that even though most people in the streets couldn't take three steps without being solicited for their opinion, the locals checked themselves when they caught sight of the old man by her side and smoothly intercepted anyone who headed his way.

Thus, it was within a bubble of calm that the group turned onto a small drawbridge decorated with legions of grotesque little monsters in red-painted wrought iron and crossed to a barren islet in the center of the river that wove through the town. Something struck Agatha as odd, and she paused to look about. Though the rest of the town was a textbook example of high-density urban design, there were no structures on the island itself except for the bridge platform that crossed it. Agatha peered over the chest-high walls but could see nothing except patches of scrubby lichen. A small metal sign bolted to the stones warned them not to leave the path.[12]

There was no other traffic here. Agatha stopped and faced the old man. "I think this a good place for us to talk. Who are you, sir?"

The old man regarded her for a moment, then leaned back upon a railing. "That is what I intend to ask you, Miss."

Ardsley shook his head. "I do not think we should reveal—"

Agatha overrode him. "But I do. I think he knows a lot. We know nothing."

She took a deep breath and stood tall. She looked the old man in the eye. "I am Agatha Heterodyne. My parents were Bill Heterodyne and Lucrezia Mongfish."

The old man smiled and nodded agreeably. It was disappointingly anticlimactic. "Interesting." He paused. "Where are they?"

Agatha blinked. There were a number of possible answers to that question, most of them awkward: ("My mother? Well, her

---

[12]   Tiny Monster Island is one of the more boring Mechanicsburg landmarks. Unless, of course, one is foolish—or unfortunate—enough to leave the path. Then it becomes very exciting indeed.

consciousness appears to be lodged in my head…") but she decided to keep things simple for the moment.[13]

"I don't know. I last saw Uncle Barry eleven years ago. I was raised in Beetleburg by…well…you'd know them as Punch and Judy."

This caused the old man to raise an eyebrow. "Not a hidden monastery in the Americas? *That's* different," he allowed. "Did Punch ever mention a Master Heliotrope?"

Agatha frowned. "No, because he couldn't talk."

Now both eyebrows went up. "Not many people know that."

Agatha leaned in. "They probably also don't know that he got the hiccups after getting an electric shock." The old man was silent. "I *know* you're testing me. I *can* keep this up."

An odd expression swept across the old man's face. "But—it's impossible," he whispered.

"Yeah, I think it's pretty weird myself." Krosp's voice was loud in his ear.

That snapped the old man out of his reverie and he turned on the cat that stared up at him with a smug gaze. "Don't you try to boggle *me*, Mister Talking Cat. This is Mechanicsburg and you are by no means the oddest thing in *this* town!" Krosp looked slightly disappointed but the old man didn't notice.

He had already turned his attention back to Agatha. There was a new gleam in his eye. "But you, my lady—*you* are something quite special."

Agatha blinked. "You…you believe me?"

The old man tapped a fingernail against his teeth. "Not yet," he admitted, "but I will listen."

With that he swept off his flat cap, revealing a pattern of odd scars upon his head as he bowed. "I am Carson von Mekkhan. Former seneschal and keeper of the keys to Castle Heterodyne. Welcome

---

[13]   Ironically, we now know from Carson von Mekkhan's journals, that if Agatha had taken the time to explain every improbable, bizarre event that had led her to Mechanicsburg, he might very well have believed her on the spot. The family history of the Heterodynes has never made for dull reading.

home, my lady." He straightened up and his gaze sharpened. "If my lady you be."

Wooster had started at the old man's name. "Von Mekkhan…von Mekkhan *was* the name of the seneschal. But—he died in the attack upon the castle. The family is extinct."

"You're remarkably well informed, young man." Carson's face grew older. "Yes, I died a bit that day…" He straightened up. "But the Masters always considered that a poor excuse. For the last several years I have been going under the name of Carson Heliotrope."

Wooster waved a hand. "The records clearly show—Lady Heterodyne, this can't be the seneschal!"

Carson pointed with his bony forefinger. "And I know, personally, that this young lady cannot be who *she* says she is!"

He then regarded Agatha with uncertain eyes. "But…" he continued slowly, "I'm an old man and I've lived in Mechanicsburg my entire life. One thing I've learned is that just because something is 'impossible,' doesn't mean that it cannot happen."

Agatha frowned. "Yet you say you don't believe me."

Carson grinned an evil grin. "This is a town built by science, my lady. Mad science, I'll concede, but science still. I'll *entertain* the idea that you are an impossible thing, but belief requires proof." His grin faltered. "You… you don't have any proof *on* you, do you?"

Agatha thought about the locket at her throat. It contained pictures of Bill and Lucrezia, but no doubt so did a thousand others for sale less than a hundred meters from where she was standing.

"Nothing concrete, sorry."

The old man clearly didn't seem to know if he should be disappointed or relieved. "Well, you could still be useful," he mused.

Agatha raised her eyebrows questioningly.

"You don't act like the usual bogus Heterodyne heir," Carson explained. "You're too low-key."

He offered Agatha his arm and the little group continued onward. They crossed another bridge and entered a neighborhood that displayed no tourist paraphernalia. The shops and cafés displayed markedly cheaper prices, and while everything still had a feeling of slow decay, the people here were more personable.

Krosp glanced upwards at the hovering dirigible. "Ah, so the one who entered the castle—"

Carson interrupted him. "No, she doesn't fit either. We get fake Heterodynes through here every year or so, sometimes more. Fewer these days than we used to, but they still come. They're either con artists or deluded, messianic crazies." He sighed. "The tourists love it, of course, and that's good for business. The townspeople..." He checked himself and continued on a different tack.

"But the one now in the castle—she's different. She has an armed staff. She has an airship. She has funding." He prodded Agatha in the arm. "She is being *managed*." And at this, Carson's face grew dark. "And that means someone is trying to take over my town."

At this point, they stopped walking, and with a sigh, Carson indicated they should enter a small shop. Agatha glanced at the name over the door: The Sausage Factory. However, when they entered, she was surprised to find not a butcher's shop, but a café. It was large and well lit with high, arched ceilings and the walls and furnishings were covered in decorative woodwork carved in the Art Nouveau style.

The gold and red tiled floor was crowded with small round tables covered with crisp white tablecloths. Cozy booths with tall wooden backs and scandalously carved privacy screens lined the walls. Along the back ran an elaborate glass-fronted counter, behind which were a number of intriguing machines as well as shelves crammed with bottles and row upon row of porcelain mugs in a variety of sizes. Within the counter were long glass shelves displaying assorted pastries and cakes, pies and quiches, sweet cheeses and blocks of halvah, and marzipan molded into trilobites and other festive shapes.

An amazing smell hit them as they walked through the door, combining the odors of fresh baking, warm butter, chocolate, nutmeg, cinnamon, and fresh coffee.

Zeetha stepped through the door and stopped dead. She took a deep, appreciative sniff, and declared, "I am living here now."

One of the waitresses, a plump girl with a dazzling smile, laughed. "Sorry, Mademoiselle, but there's a waiting list."

Krosp's face settled into a frown. "I don't smell any meat. Or even plants. What kind of restaurant *is* this?"

Carson snorted as he shepherded them between the tables towards the back. "It is a *coffee shop*. They started in Amsterdam quite a while back, but this is the first one in Mechanicsburg. This is where the business of running the town is done these days." His tone was disapproving—it was evident that the old man was unimpressed at this turn of events.

Wooster casually scanned the room and frowned. "I don't see Burgermeister Zuken here." At Agatha's look of curiosity, he explained, "He's the head of the City Council."

Carson snorted. "That fool? I should hope not!" He stopped next to a large booth that was tucked into a corner. Sitting alone at the table, an oversized china mug in his hand, was a tall, elegantly dressed young man. His hair was meticulously cut in the latest style favored by the dandies of Prague and he was dressed like a minor city functionary, a set of silver city seals adorning his lapels. It was obvious by looking at their faces that he and Carson were related.

"*This* is the fool you want," Carson declared sourly. "My grandson, Vanamonde."

The young man's mouth quirked upwards in a semi-smile as he gently deposited his cup in its saucer with a quiet "clink." "Am I now part of the tour, grandfather?"

"You could be," the old man said in a low tone. "You never leave this table!"

Vanamonde looked surprised. "But why should I? The seats are comfortable. Everyone knows where to find me, and lovely young women bring me coffee all day long."

At this he looked up and gave Agatha and her friends a warm smile. "Which you simply must try!" He waved to the other seats in the booth. "Please do sit down. Don't wait for my grandfather to do the polite thing, he rode with the Jägermonsters in his youth and never quite got over it."

Carson scowled but slid into the booth beside his grandson. The others filled the opposite bench. Instantly two of the waitresses swooped down and placemats, cutlery, and an astonishing selection of little pastries appeared before them; everything from warm, buttery croissants, to elaborate concoctions of custard, cream cheese, glazed fruits, and chocolate. Zeetha immediately began eating as many of these as she could and showed no signs of stopping. The second time the tray had to be replaced, she assured the obviously delighted pastry chef that she was "just getting started."

The waitress returned with tall silver pots that contained a rich black coffee. Only after this had been poured out and various condiments had been circulated along with a bowl of cream for Krosp, did Vanamonde lean back and place his fingertips together.

"I assume you're here about the heiress," he said to Agatha, conversationally. Agatha opened her mouth, but then merely nodded. The young man nodded back and began laboriously adding yellow crystals of sugar to his coffee with a tiny silver spoon. "She is a mystery, but her main backers appear to be a pair of gentlemen of fortune. One is a Baron Oublenmach, a disreputable character who purchased his barony with money accumulated through a long career that has included everything from confidence work to light piracy. The other is His Grace, Josef Strinbeck, a deposed Duke of Lithuania and an idiot.

"Their craft is a Flash-class ship fresh out of the Stockholm yards and paid for in cash by the way. Dutch gold, obviously laundered.

"It employs that new chameleon skin technology that wowed everyone at the St. Petersburg airshow last fall. They can make it any color they want. So—that ostentatious pink? That's quite deliberate.

"They clearly have an agenda, but they're rushed. Personally, I believe that they are part of some larger organization—and that they have set things in motion before everyone was ready.

"As for their cat's-paw—the young lady, who was dressed in Vienna but educated in Paris—she has entered the castle, but is, at the moment, still held up in the Courtyard of Regret. She has been handing out gold coins, which—" he consulted a small scrap of paper before him, "—assay out as 95 percent pure."

He stirred his coffee, tapped the spoon against the rim twice, and took a sip. "And that," he said, carefully *not* looking at his grandfather, "is what I have discovered within the last hour, while never leaving this table."

The old man rolled his eyes and grunted. Vanamonde turned a charming smile upon Agatha. "And may I have the pleasure of your acquaintance?"

Carson leaned in. "This is the Lady Agatha Heterodyne. Daughter of Master William and the Lady Lucrezia."

Vanamonde stared and only came to his senses when he realized that his hand had slipped and was now dribbling coffee into his lap. He slammed his cup down with a clunk and a splash, which only added to his distress. "There are *two* of them?" he blurted out.

The old man smiled toothily and passed him a napkin.

"No," Agatha said calmly but firmly. "There's her, and then there is me. *I* am the real thing."

Vanamonde stared at her. "But…a girl…"

Agatha looked at him steadily, but her eyes narrowed. "I promise not to get any cooties on you."

Vanamonde reddened. "That's not the point," he sputtered.

At that moment one of the servers appeared, pot in hand. "Need anything, Van?"

The young man waved at the rest of the table. "More coffee! Please!"

The waitress efficiently refilled everyone's cup and then paused when she saw that Agatha's was untouched. "Is everything all right, Mademoiselle?"

"Oh, yes," Agatha smiled. "It's fine, thanks."

After the waitress moved off, Zeetha leaned in close from within a small cloud of powdered sugar. "A problem?"

Agatha reddened slightly. "I've never *had* coffee," she whispered. "Lilith said a young lady shouldn't drink stimulants."

"We're trying not be conspicuous," Zeetha pointed out. "Drink your coffee like a warrior."

Agatha sighed. "Yes, Zeetha."

She gingerly sipped the hot liquid and almost spit it out. "Ew," she whispered. "Is it *supposed* to taste like this?"

Wooster looked upon her with the sympathy of a devoted tea-drinker stranded in the land of the heathen. "Cream and sugar help," he suggested. Agatha added copious quantities of both.

Meanwhile Van and his grandfather had their heads together. "No, really," the younger man was asking, "why are they here?"

The old man deliberately tipped some of his coffee into his saucer and added cream and sugar before sipping it delicately. Van tried to ignore this. He knew he was being baited.

The old man smacked his lips loudly. Van closed his eyes. "The girl has made a claim," Carson stated. "If she is legitimate, she is our liege."

Van's eyes flicked over to Agatha as she was gamely draining her cup. "Oh, please."

Carson shrugged. "If she isn't, she will still be useful. Strinbeck is a buffoon but Oublenmach is more of a schemer. If he's out in front here, it means he's making a big play. Strinbeck means the Fifty Families are involved somehow. I wouldn't be surprised if there were troops on the way."

Van sat up. "Troops?"

Carson nodded. "Oh, I'm sure that they'll be from someone or another who is ostensibly determined to be the first to recognize the new Heterodyne and will only be here to help support her during what will no doubt be a 'rocky period of transition for the town.'" He cocked an eye at his grandson, who nodded slowly.

"Rocky for us, I imagine, if we don't support her."

"That's my guess. With the Baron down, the Empire will hesitate. Thus, having our own heir will confuse things. Muddy the waters a bit. Slow things down."

"Cold."

Both men jumped back as Krosp's voice emerged from under the table. "And afterwards," the cat continued, worming his way onto the seat between them, "once the Baron's back in control, it'd be easy enough for you to get rid of Agatha." He rubbed his paws together. "I think I like you people."

Van blinked. "But, your friend—"

Krosp twitched his whiskers. "No, no, it's okay. You still think she's a fake." He smiled. "I know better."

Van realized he was clutching his coffee cup defensively and set it down with a thump. "Yes, I do think she's a fake."

Krosp leaned in and gave Van's cup a quick sniff. "You'll learn." Another sniff. "Pretty soon, too."

Both men glanced at each other. "Oh?"

Krosp batted at the mug with his paw. "This coffee you gave her. I'm familiar with some of the alkaloids in there…strong stuff?"

The younger man looked offended. "It's my own personal blend. Naturally, I emphasized its rejuvenating and brain-invigorating properties—"

Carson interrupted, "Once it sits for twenty-four hours, we use it to strip paint. Why?"

Krosp sat back, satisfied. Both men became aware of a faint, high-pitched vibration. They glanced around and saw Agatha, empty cup in hand, quivering. The sound came from the vibrations of the cup hitting the saucer with a sound reminiscent of a dentist's drill.

"I think," Krosp drawled, "that you're about to find out that Lilith was one smart lady."

A feeling of uneasiness spider-walked down Vanamonde's spine. He leaned towards Agatha. "Mademoiselle? Are you—"

Suddenly Agatha was *looking* at him. Looking at him so intensely that he felt pinned to his seat. He didn't see her move but suddenly her mug was on the table before him. *"This stuff is kind of interesting but I don't see what the big deal is."*

Van blinked. Agatha was talking quickly, almost too quickly to be understood.

"Well, my usual coffee engine is broken so we're using the backup machine—" He realized he was talking to an empty seat.

"*A-HA!*"

Van spun about to see Agatha standing on top of the counter, gleefully examining the interior of the café's coffee engine, parts of which were also littering the area. The mechanic Van had called in (out of desperation, since the device was almost spark-like in its complexity) looked up in annoyance at the interruption. Agatha picked up a condenser. "*Yes! I see! A simple double boiler with a rather clever condenser and percolation system that recycles the steam! Ha!*"

One of the waitresses, a stout woman with a no-nonsense air to her, who had been striding towards her, an iron ladle gripped in her hand, suddenly found herself nose-to-nose with Agatha, who demanded: "*Do you carry any information on the coffee extraction process?*"

The woman blinked. "Uh—We have a book for sale by the cashier. It's only—"

Agatha stood by the cashier now. There was a buzz of turning pages. "Ha!" She snapped the book closed. "*This is but a simple exercise in chemistry!*" The terrified cashier now found herself in Agatha's spotlight glare. "*Where is some raw coffee?*"

The girl froze. But Agatha had been standing still for as long as she could. "*Never mind I shall find it myself!*"

A tearing sound came from behind the counter. There was Agatha, her hands buried in an open sack of coffee beans. She pulled a fistful up to her nose, breathed deeply, and then frowned. "*Interesting! The end product doesn't taste anywhere near as good as the smell would lead one to expect.*" She swung about and gave the stout woman a grin. "*I can fix that!*"

The older woman shook herself. "Now, that's enough of that! You get out of there!"

Agatha stepped closer to her and fixed her with a stare. *"I need parts!"* She deftly plucked an order pad from the countertop along with a pencil and pressed it into the woman's hands. *"Write this down!"*

The woman's eyes narrowed. "Who—" Agatha's smile vanished and her voice harmonics changed. *"Write. This. Down!"*

The woman swallowed and put pencil to paper. Agatha began to speak.

On the other side of the room, Vanamonde's jaw dropped. "Did... did she just give a direct order to Rinja and...and not get smacked? But she couldn't—"

Van's babbling was cut off by his grandfather, who administered a sharp dope-slap to the back of his head. "She certainly could!" The old man sounded worried now. *"Listen* to her! Can't you *feel* it? This girl is a Spark!"

Vanamonde went pale. He swung around to Agatha's companions, who regarded him with a smug innocence. "You didn't tell us she was a Spark!"

Wooster looked at him over his cup. "We *told* you she was a Heterodyne."

Zeetha delicately nibbled a cream-filled éclair. "Naturally, one should assume that a Heterodyne would also be a Spark."

Krosp licked the last drop of cream from his bowl and snagged another container. "It's not our fault you didn't believe us."

Suddenly Agatha was there. *"Here's your book back."* The book appeared in Van's hand. It was warm. *"I can tell you wrote it even though you used a false name."*

"I—you can?"

"Oh yes, word choice, sentence structure—anyway, all the spelling corrections are marked in red."

Carson snorted. A slip of paper was thrust into Van's other hand. *"And here is a list of things I require, please."*

Van looked at it blankly. "Of course, my lady." Agatha vanished. Van shook himself. "Wait—What did I say?"

Carson's smile soured. "What our family has been saying to Sparks for generations. We wouldn't have survived, if we hadn't."

Van glanced at Agatha's friends and dropped his voice. "But…you could say that about anyone in Mechanicsburg."

"I am leaving!" Herr Mitrant—the mechanic who had been attempting to repair the café's coffee engine—now stood before Van. The stout little man was furious. "I am a Master Artificer!" He pointed at Agatha, who was rooting about in the man's toolbox. "And this girl is…she's…she's touching my tools!"[14]

"*And they are superb!*" You could actually hear spaces between Agatha's words now. Herr Mitrant made a grab for the wrench she was examining. Agatha let him grab the wrench, but he suddenly felt his wrist clasped in a grip like iron. "*You can tell a craftsman's abilities by his tools, and yours speak well of you. Show me your skill!*" She pointed to the defunct coffee engine. "*Disassemble those boilers!*"

Herr Mitrant opened his mouth, a look of offended rage on his face—

"*When we rebuild them, they'll go from cold to boil in eight seconds!*" The man paused. "Eight seconds? You can do that?"

Agatha grinned. "*It'll be fun!*"

An odd look crossed the man's face, and finally, with a jaunty "At once, Mistress!" he was off.

Carson nodded grimly. "That's right, boy, anyone."

Krosp opened one of the small packs that Zeetha had been carrying and began pulling out his coat. Obviously, he felt the time for subterfuge had passed. "I get it. A whole town of minions waiting for a Master."

The old man slumped into his seat and took a pull from his mug of coffee. The look he gave it made it clear that he had hoped for

---

[14] At this time, many trades still learned their skills starting at a very basic level. Most mechanics, carpenters, artificers, and other skilled tradesmen were expected to actually build, craft, and forge their own tools. A tradesman's tools were precious things indeed. They were never lent out, their loss was a crippling blow, and their owners were usually buried with them. Now Klaus liked to move with the times, and the Empire was responsible for great strides in converting the Empire's industrial base from hand made items to mass production, but he felt that there was a great lesson to be learned by the old traditions and thus he insisted that potential factory owners had to physically help construct their factories.

something stronger. "Pretty much," he acknowledged. "And one of *our* jobs is to keep outsiders from realizing that."

Vanamonde leaned in. "Grandfather," he said seriously, "this is getting out of hand."

The group at the table looked up. Everyone in the café was busy now. Patrons were clearing an area—shoving aside tables and chairs. Several of the shop staff were running back and forth from the storeroom in the back, presenting Agatha with a bizarre array of items for consideration. More worrying was the procession dashing in and out of the front door, bringing back tools, equipment and… more people.

A glassblower was dragged in, protesting vehemently—until Agatha showed him some hastily scrawled plans. Minutes later, assistants were hauling in armloads of glass tubes and rods and an oxyacetylene torch sputtered to life.

With a clang, a coppersmith dropped a load of brewing kettles on the floor. Carson and Vanamonde recognized shop assistants from nearby grocers and chemists. With a smell of ozone, old Staikov, the electrician, showed up with a double bandolier-load of battery jars.

The waitresses were moving constantly, serving coffee and snacks to the various workers, and the roar of conversation was taking on the same sort of coordinated hum one occasionally hears from well-organized beehives.

At the center of it, seemingly everywhere at once, was Agatha: exhorting, explaining, diagramming, praising, and then moving on to the next group. She paused and caught the eye of one of the waitresses. "Say, could I get another cup of that coffee?"

Carson and Vanamonde screamed in unison. *"NO!"*

Agatha considered them briefly and then, with a nod, moved on.

Suddenly, magically, there was an empty space in the center of the shop, materials neatly radiating outwards—every section overseen by a cluster of eager helpers. Agatha stood in the center, then spun about slowly, examining where everything was. She nodded once, selected a wrench, and began to build.

Watching Sparks as they work—apparently warping the laws of physics as they go—can be difficult for most sane, sober people to watch. With a wince, Zeetha turned away with a troubled look on her face. She buttonholed the elder von Mekkhan.

"This—" She waved a hand, to take in the entranced crowd of townspeople assisting Agatha. "Tell me this isn't some kind of…of mind control? You know, like slaver wasps?"

Carson snorted grimly. "You do the Masters a disservice. They didn't need slapped-together filth like the wasps to inspire the townspeople. Control like this is crafted over time. You are seeing the end result of *generations* of effort.

"For close to a thousand years, the people of Mechanicsburg have served the House of Heterodyne, the most depraved, unstable, crazed maniacs in the world, and in return, they shaped us.

"As long as we pleased the Masters, life was good. Mechanicsburg was the Heterodyne's home from which they would sweep out and periodically despoil half of Europa."

The old man waved his hands as if to encompass the entire town. "I don't know how good an eye for geography you have, my dear, but we are uniquely protected here by our mountains and our chasms. No one has ever managed to take Mechanicsburg by force, although certainly many, many powers have tried. The Masters wouldn't allow it."

He sighed and sat back. "And so we fed them and equipped them and made sure they had a hat on when it rained and waved them off to terrorize someplace else and grew fat and secure on the spoils they brought back. Some of us even went along for the trip." He saw Zeetha's face and shrugged. "You disapprove? Oh, I understand, you yourself—" he gestured towards her swords, "are obviously from some proud, warrior culture somewhere that hones its fighters and insists on things like honor and self-reliance. It's hardly unique. But I'm curious—who carts away your night soil? Your rulers? No, I thought not.

"As for the townspeople here, we are not Sparks. No, we are the sons and daughters of those who served Sparks. The ones who were loyal. The ones who were useful. The ones who were lucky. The ones who *survived*. As a result, it is...easy for us to get caught up in the Masters'... enthusiasms."

He looked at Zeetha with a touch of defiance. "I don't expect someone who isn't from Mechanicsburg to understand, but there is a lot of pride here. We served the Heterodynes, and we were *good* at it." He looked out across the bustling room. "It's what we did. What part of us *needs* to do. A lot of folks desperately want a new Heterodyne. Any new Heterodyne. Without one..." He thought about the signs of decay he had seen in the town and sighed.

Krosp looked skeptical. "But it's been how long? Surely the younger generation won't—"

A dead rat slapped onto the table in front of him. Startled, the cat looked up but saw no one. A small sound dragged his eyes downward. Hidden under a sinister-looking wide-brimmed hat, a cunning pair of eyes barely cleared the lip of the table. "My family," the boy muttered out of the side of his mouth, "has been serving as grave robbers to the Masters for over a hunnert years. I heard there was a new master, so I dug up a dead rat cuz that was all I could find."

Krosp stared the rat and tentatively batted at it with a paw.

"T'ain't poisoned," the boy assured him. "Trapped last night and interred this morning, so it's fresh, and—" the boy leaned in while glancing about furtively, "there'll be no questions asked about this one, he's from out of town."

Krosp picked the rat up, sniffed it, and bit off the head. "You're hired."

The boy squealed and dashed off, clutching what appeared to be a sandbox shovel.

"Don't *encourage* them," Carson hissed.

Krosp raised his brows. "Why not? Seems to make them happy enough."

"For the moment, yes. Usually when some joker comes through town claiming to be the long-lost Heterodyne heir, I try to keep him quiet, get him into the Castle as soon as possible, and he gets killed. Nice and simple.

"But it's not so tidy if the townspeople get their hands on him."

He waved a hand at the crowd surrounding Agatha. "They look like a nice bunch of folks, don't they? But they're descended from a long line of brigands and cutthroats and they don't like to be the ones played for fools.

"Trying to con these people is a very bad idea. When they break out the torches and pitchforks they know how to do it up right and, let me tell you, it's hell to clean up afterwards." He sighed, and rubbed his eyes. "Not to mention that it attracts the wrong sort of tourist."

Krosp swallowed the last bit of rat and licked his chops thoughtfully. "It also attracts the attention of the Baron, it's more work for you, and it's bad for business."

Carson gave a sardonic smile. "Smart cat."

Krosp's ears twitched and he frowned. "The mood in the room... it's different."

Carson sagged. "She's a Spark. The people enjoy working with Sparks. They've been having fun. But by now, a lot of them will have heard that, supposedly, she's a Heterodyne. That changes everything. Now they're watching her. Judging her. Now she had better be the real thing."

Agatha stepped back and examined her creation with a critical eye. It was a ramshackle construction. She saw one of the people nearby looking at it dubiously.

"Oh, this is just the support," she explained as she rolled up her sleeves. "Now we hook everything up together." With that she picked up a coil of copper tubing and began threading it through a small opening. As she did so, Agatha started to hum. The sound grew, filling the room and causing the townspeople around her to freeze in wonder. It was a bizarre, eerie melody that bored into the listener's head and made it impossible to look anywhere else.

Carson looked as if he'd seen a ghost. "She...she's *heterodyning*,"[15] he breathed.

Krosp looked interested. "What? The music thing? She does that all the time. Is that what it's called?"

Vanamonde stood entranced. "I...I remember this. Before the Masters disappeared..." He swung around and clutched at Carson's sleeve. "Grandfather, maybe she really is—"

Agatha straightened up and wiped her brow. In the sudden silence she held a hand up behind her head. "Hepler wrench!"

"*Yes, Mistress,*" the crowd roared and easily two dozen wrenches appeared for Agatha to choose from.

Krosp grinned at Carson who had collapsed into his seat. "Convinced yet?"

"NO!" The old man shook himself and sat up. "Not until the Castle accepts her control." He watched the room, which was full of a renewed sense of purpose. "But she's bought herself the time to get there," he admitted.

Krosp shrugged. "Then the sooner she gets there, the better."

"The cat is right," Wooster stated. "If the people on that pink airship are as organized as you believe, then they'll have spies in town." He gazed out at the chaos that filled the room and continued to spill out onto the street. "They'll hear about this soon enough and then Miss Agatha will be in danger. We must move quickly." That said, he sat down and deliberately poured himself another cup of coffee. "However, I doubt we'll be able to get her out of here before she is done 'fixing' your coffee engine."

Vanamonde looked relieved. "Thank goodness, do you know what that thing cost?"

---

[15]   In a world filled with mad science, heterodyning occupies a special place. It is a peculiar vocal tick that appears to be unique to the Heterodyne family. According to its practitioners, it cancels out ambient noise, making it easier to concentrate on the task at hand. If this is true, it means that the person heterodyning is able to instantaneously analyze all incoming noise and organically generate its harmonic opposite *subconsciously*, without engaging the brain's higher mental functions. As academics who have devoted their careers to trying to understand the Lady Heterodyne, we can assure you that the more you think about it, the creepier it gets.

Carson ignored him. He studied Wooster. "You've been around Sparks then?"

Ardsley nodded as he sipped his coffee. "Oh, yes." He examined Agatha with an educated eye. "As long as she's in the middle of something, I really wouldn't recommend trying to move her."

The old man sat down and nodded. "I agree."

There was a sudden odd sound and one of the large copper pots shuddered and imploded down into a small chunk of metal. The crowd cheered.

"How long?" Van asked.

Carson considered this. "Something like this? I'd say a strong Heterodyne would take about two hours to truly warp the laws of nature."

Krosp flicked an ear. "I thought you weren't convinced."

Agatha picked up the chunk of metal and saw Zeetha snickering. "I meant to do that," she said, and tucked the chunk into a space that accommodated it perfectly. A row of lights lit up.

Carson shivered. "I'm getting there."

A coded series of taps sounded on the hospital room door.
"Come in."

Dr. Sun gingerly swung the door inwards and then stopped in surprise. Gil was busy fighting with two men who were flailing away with, as it happened, flails.

"Huh," the old man looked interested. "You don't really see proper flails much these days, much less trained flail-fighters."

"I have news for you," Gil said sardonically. "You're not really seeing them now." With that he elegantly disarmed both fighters while running his sword through the one on the left.

The man on the right screamed and pulled a knife.

"I can come back if you're busy," Sun remarked frostily, tapping his foot.

"Not particularly," Gil said. He skewered the man's hand. The knife flew upwards and Gil snagged it at the top of its arc. He frowned in disappointment. "Hmf. I was hoping it was one of those Sturmhalten Sewer knives." He tossed it aside and looked at Sun. "You have news?"

Sun tipped his head back towards the hallway. "I have a soldier here with an interesting report."

"Send him in," Gil said, "I'll be done in a moment."

"Wrong," his opponent roared. He held up a small device in his uninjured hand. "Kill me and this dead-man switch will release and blow you and your bloody Baron to bits!"

A large sea-green hand closed over the upraised fist. "Vell, ve kent haff dot." A tall Jäger in a crisp white uniform then casually ripped the assassin's arm off. As the man screamed and collapsed to the ground, the Jäger swiveled about and gave the startled Gilgamesh a perfect salute. "I haff not yet giffen my report," he explained.

He looked down at the shrieking assassin and with a booted heel, gave a savage stomp, crushing his throat.

Gil swallowed. Thanks to the Baron's efforts, much of the Jägermonsters' casual cruelty and disregard for human life had been knocked out of them (or at least been better hidden). This fellow seemed untouched by the Baron's behavioral modification efforts. A sudden realization hit him.

"A Jäger? Here in Mechanicsburg?"[16]

The creature looked down at him and sneered. "Captain Vole. Mechanicsburg Security Division. I iz not a Jäger, sir."

Gil was used to having to humor a great many self-delusional people amongst the Empire's command staff, but there were some things that could not remain unchallenged. "How do you figure that?"

---

[16] When the Jägermonsters were absorbed into the Baron's forces, one of the conditions was that they stay out of their former home, Mechanicsburg. It was thought that they retained too many memories, loyalties, and associations with the place, and if they were ever to be rehabilitated, it would be best to remove them from a place where their assorted cruelties and atrocities were enshrined on various public monuments and featured in children's books.

The creature spat. "Der Jägers iz veak. Dey cannot let go of der oldt dead masters. I heff renounced der Jägertroth."[17]

Gil blinked. "You can *do* that?"

Sun stepped in. "It wasn't his idea." The tall Jäger looked away as Sun continued, "They threw him out. It was an unprecedented move."

Gil nodded slowly. "And your loyalty to the House of Heterodyne?"

Vole snapped his head back. "Pah. Non-existent, sir."

"Fascinating. Your news?"

"Yes, sir. Dere iz now, in der town, a second gurl claiming to be a Heterodyne."

Gil felt a tightening in his chest. "A second girl…is she also attempting to enter the castle?"

"No, sir." Vole shrugged. "She iz in a coffee shop."

"A coffee—what is she doing in a coffee shop?"

"Hy'm told she iz makink coffee, sir."

A touch of annoyance crept into Gil's voice. "Making coffee."

Vole grinned. "Dere haff been three explosions so far, sir."

The surety struck Gil like a bolt of his own lightning. "Agatha!" He turned to Dr. Sun. "It's her! It's *got* to be her!"

The old man frowned. "Wait. This is the genuine Heterodyne girl you said was 'already taken care of'? But now you look pleased that she's here."

Gil realized that he was, in fact, grinning like an idiot, and his pulse was racing. He took a deep breath. "You're right. I shouldn't be pleased."

Sun looked wary. "Oh?"

Gil continued, "Father is convinced she's dangerous."

Sun glanced over at Klaus's array of medical devices and the bandaged man they served. "Well, all the evidence does suggest—"

[17] The Jägers are remarkably close mouthed about the process that made them into Jägers, a secret of the Heterodynes that they appear ready to carry to their graves. However they talk quite freely and at great length about what it means to *be* a Jäger. The Jägertroth is the blood vow that one made before the Jägerification process was begun. It involves serving the Heterodyne family above all else, being willing to die for them (any number of times), and an acknowledgement that this vow is binding beyond the limits of time, space, death, and the perceived three dimensions. It is, according to all accounts, a pretty big deal.

"That is why I sent her to England."

Dr. Sun had worked very hard over the years, perfecting a reputation for heroic unflappability. He was usually very good at it. Thus, it was a shame for Gil that he had his back to him at that moment.

"You did what?[18] You sent a genuine Heterodyne heir to *England*?" It seemed something of a counter intuitive move.

Gil shrugged. "You remember my man, Ardsley Wooster? He was a British agent. I had to use him to get Agatha out of Sturmhalten. Allowing him to take her to England seemed like the best motivation."

Sun stared at him. Gil began to feel somewhat anxious under that unflinching stare. He tried to explain: "I wasn't going to let them keep her, of course. I told him that if they didn't keep her safe for me, I'd destroy them, okay?"

Dr. Sun was one of those Sparks who liked to believe that he trod rather firmly upon the path of sanity. He did this by maintaining a rock-steady focus upon the administration of the Great Hospital and only unleashed his own considerable talents when he was devising new medicines or treatments. He tried to avoid the politics of the Empire, but even he was familiar with the tensions between the two great powers. He knew well enough how much even a casual threat by the young Wulfenbach could affect the entire continent. He took a deep breath.

Gilgamesh made a soothing motion. "But if she's here, why then, it's a moot point." He smiled at his old teacher disingenuously.

---

[18]   At this point in history, the Empire of the Pax Transylvania controlled much of the continent of Europa. Thus, one would hardly be expected to believe that one little island nation to the west could cause any serious problems. You would be quite wrong. Due to England's extensive trading fleet, loyal colonies, cosmopolitan citizenry, and, of course, Her Undying Majesty, Queen Albia, powerbrokers around the globe refused to call a winner in the event of a straight-up war. Diplomatic relations between the Baron and England had started out cordial enough. Indeed, the British had been instrumental in helping the nascent Empire clear out some of the more entrenched nests of Revenants, Slaver Wasps, and Pirates in Western Europa. However, as the Empire had continued to expand in power, territory, influence, and market share, relations had cooled considerably. Luckily, both Empires were governed by genuine geniuses, who knew enough to stay out of each other's hair.

Sun raised an eyebrow—then began elaborately folding back his sleeves, a sight which caused Gil to go pale. "It's been a while since I gave you a thrashing," the old man remarked conversationally, "but under the circumstances, I'm sure your father would approve."

Gil desperately waved at the bodies of the assassins on the floor. "Is this the right time, Sifu?"

Sun smiled. "Do give me some credit, young Wulfenbach. Rest assured that the pain will stop the instant I am finished making sure you understand."

"Understand what?"

Sun pursed his lips. "Ooh, this might take some time."

Gil took a step back, wide-eyed. Fortunately for him, he was spared this particular lesson. It was interrupted before it could begin by a giant mechanical ant which came smashing through the wall. It waved its antennae and declared mechanically: "Death to the despoiler of East Kruminey!"

Sun looked startled. "East what?"

Gil flicked a finger and the tip of his cane began to glow with a bright blue light. "It's not really important."

"I suppose not," Sun conceded.

The tall Jäger, who had been following the conversation with great interest, stepped forward. "Allow me—"

Gil waved him back and shot a bolt of electricity at the ant's head. Surprisingly, it absorbed the charge and discharged it back at him from its antennae.

"Interesting," Gil grunted. He spoke to Vole. "No, I'll handle this. I want you to bring the Heterodyne girl here. The one in the town."

Sun looked alarmed. "No! Wait!"

Anything else he was about to say was cut off as another bolt of lightning shot from the mechanical ant and narrowly missed him but came perilously close to the insensate Baron.

"Go!" Gil yelled as he leapt onto the device's thorax.

Vole saluted and slipped out the door before Sun could interfere. If this girl truly was a Heterodyne, the ex-Jäger most definitely wanted to meet her.

Back in the Sausage Factory, the now finished coffee engine gave a final "blurk" and released a great gout of savory steam. Several electrical discharge points gave a last crackle as the whine of a dynamo dopplered down the scale. An orange light began to flash. Everyone in the café realized that they were holding their breath and they all released it at the same time.

Agatha picked up an ornate china cup, held it under a silver spout, and threw a switch. A stream of black liquid sensuously poured out. The aroma that spread had everyone breathing deeply. It was the aroma of fine coffee, redolent with undertones of cinnamon, chocolate, and possibly, a soupçon of diesel oil. But there was more to it than just the aroma itself. Every person who smelled it found themselves remembering a frosty morning or an inn alongside a rain-soaked road or a quiet café in that indeterminate time between night and dawn when the city was just beginning to awaken and one could imagine that you were one of the few people left on Earth. Their mouths filled with the memory of the coffee that they had sipped then and how it was the perfect thing in the perfect place at that perfect time and how it restored one's faith in one's own humanity and reaffirmed your place in the world and gave you the strength to go on and do something amazing. Everyone who smelled the aroma that spread from the coffee in Agatha's hand knew—they *knew*—that this coffee would be even better.

"It's ready," Agatha said brightly.

Carson ran a connoisseur's eye over the device that loomed over the tables. "Not bad," he conceded.

Vanamonde raised his head from beneath the table where he'd hidden when Agatha had turned the machine on. He looked like he'd been pole-axed. "But how did she…" He fished a watch from an inner pocket and checked the time. He then held it up to his ear to be sure it was still running. "But it's impossible!"

Krosp shrugged nonchalantly, though Van noted that the cat had been sequestered under the table right beside him. "Never seen a real Spark in action before, eh, kid?"

Agatha sniffed the cup and then faced the crowd and gave them a small salute. "Well, here's to Science!"

Instantly Vanamonde was before her, his hand covering the top of the cup. Agatha's lips stopped millimeters away.

"Wait," he said, as he deftly slid the cup from her hand. "As your seneschal, I should try this first, my lady."

He glanced over to his grandfather and muttered quietly, "If *regular* coffee set her off, who *knows* what this stuff would do?" He was astonished to see a tear appear in his grandfather's eye.

"Whatever happens to you, m'boy, try..." the old man said in a shaky voice, "*try* to remember that I'm so proud of you right now."

Van blinked and examined the no-longer-quite-so-tempting cup in his hand. For form's sake, he gave it a delicate sniff. "Excellent aroma..." He looked up and saw that everyone was watching him closely. With a feeling of trepidation, he took a delicate sip—

Light. Pure golden light burst upon his consciousness. The light one gets from a glorious clear sunrise at ten thousand meters in the sky with the fresh wind in your face. There was music—enlightening music—that filled his frame and made him want to dance and synchronize himself to its rhythms like a glorious symphony set to the tick of a metronome in tune with all of existence that gathered you in and showed you your place in the universe and how astonishing that it existed at all and how much more wondrous it was that you were there to appreciate its existence and realize that you were a part of it and that there was work to be done to make everything better and that you had an important part to play and that this was how it should be and you knew that nothing would ever be the same again because you now knew that the world and everything in it, all its glories and foibles, its madmen and saints, its agonies and its ecstasies, were necessary and that what we called "life" was how one surfed the edge of creation and that it was a glorious game and you were as good a player as anyone else and thus this moment and everything in it was—

"Perfect," Van whispered, tears rolling down his face. A red-gold vision resolved itself in front of him. The Heterodyne. Of course it was she. Everything he was and that his family had been for generations recognized her as the thing that had been missing from his life and in that moment of realization he became forever and irrevocably hers.

The vision looked worried and languidly waved a hand before his face. "Does it taste okay?" She bit her lip. "Are *you* okay?"

Vanamonde's mind tried to pull itself together. There was so much that needed doing, of course. Lists and schedules bloomed in the organized corridors of his mind. Everything would have to be reorganized. He began assembling a list of the various lists he would have to prioritize... But wait, the Heterodyne was still looking at him. How embarrassing. She'd been waiting for over an hour for him to answer.

"It's perfect," he assured her.

She nodded encouragingly.

Oh, how could he explain? He had to explain. He had to do whatever he could to make her life easier and more interesting. He took another hour or so to correctly formulate his response.

"The taste is a perfect blend of all the tastes and essences that make coffee what it is. A perfect blend—And yet I can discern each and every one, perfectly."

He realized that he was still clutching the cup and saucer. *And the coffee in it was still hot! After so many hours! Astonishing!*

"Even the way the liquid adheres to the inside of the cup—indicative of the way it flows along the taste buds—is aesthetically perfect. It reveals the mathematical perfection of the cup itself!"

He realized that he was declaiming now. His voice ringing out with the force of the pure truth he spoke. "The delicate smoothness of the china, with its own inherent temperature, which mitigates the otherwise extreme heat of the coffee itself—It is a thing of tactile and functioning beauty! Perfect!"

Now he was on top of a table and everyone was staring up at him. Yes! They must listen! This was cosmic truth itself! "And this! This perfect saucer!"

Carson sidled up to Agatha. "Lady?" He looked worried.

Agatha glanced back at Van as he began licking the saucer, his eyes rolling back into his head at the sensation upon his tongue. She gave a weak smile. "I can fix that," she assured him. She looked down at the still-full cup that she had eased from Van's hand. "Probably."

There was a crash, and one of the light fixtures exploded. The crowd shrieked and dropped to the floor.

Vanamonde allowed himself to drift downwards, like a perfect snowflake.

In the doorway, smoking pistol in hand, stood Captain Vole, along with a squad of what even Agatha could identify as bullyboys. "Hy seek de vun who claims to be der Heterodyne," he roared.

Agatha smiled at the sight. A Jäger! She began to step forward only to feel Carson holding her back with an iron grip. "Don't move," he whispered urgently. "Keep quiet!"

The tall monster soldier strode into the room. His gaze swept the huddled townsfolk on the floor, then took in the assorted mounds of tools and equipment and lingered on the tall, hissing coffee machine in the center of the room. He nodded in satisfaction.

"Hy know dot she iz here," he stated conversationally. "Step forvard now, gurl—" Smoothly he spun the gun in his hand and placed the barrel against a waitresses' forehead. She froze. "Or," Vole continued, "Hy vill begin shootink dese fools." He waved to include the rest of the crowd. "Hy giff hyu to three." He paused, and cocked the gun, "…Two…"

"Stop!" Agatha stepped free of Carson's hand. "I am the Heterodyne!" She marched up to the startled Jäger and poked him in the chest. "How dare you burst in like this and threaten these people! Stop this at once!"

The effect of this dressing-down upon the tall Jäger was dramatic. His face paled and his eyes widened. He took a step back and studied the girl before him while he rubbed his jaw. "Hyu… Dot voice," he breathed. "Dot schmell… Hy ken feel it…" he patted his chest in wonder. "Here. Ken hit be true? Hyu really iz—?"

Agatha smiled up at him. "Yes," she assured him, "I am."

The Jäger's eyes went cold and his gun came up. "Vell den. Dot changes efferyting!"

Without really understanding why, Agatha instinctively hurled the cup of coffee into the Jäger's face and dodged as the gun went off centimeters from her ear.

The monster soldier shrieked in rage as he shook the coffee out of his eyes. "Dem hyu!" Again the gun came up. "Now hy vill not just keel hyu—" he screamed, "Now hy vill keel *efferyvun*! Hy—" Vole paused, and a thick pink tongue ran across his upper lip. He looked surprised. "Dot iz verra gud coffee."

The large drop-steel monkey wrench Agatha swung at him caught him squarely across the back of his head. Vole blinked. "Vit a nize kick!"

A second blow drove him to the floor, unconscious. "Glad you like it," Agatha said, panting. She looked up at the frozen seneschal. "Herr von Mekkhan," she glanced at the rest of the crowd. "I'm putting these people in danger just by being here. It would be best if I got into the castle. Quickly."

The unmistakable sound of weapons being cocked caused every eye to swing back towards the front door. There stood Vole's companions. It was obvious that they had been chosen for their willingness to cause damage, as opposed to the Wulfenbach Empire's usual high standards, but while slow, they had finally registered their leader's trouble.

"I think you'll come with us, Miss, you are under arrest." He indicated the prone Jäger with the tip of his rifle. "Captain Vole seemed to have a grudge against you, but I don't. Not yet. Our orders are just to bring you in. Whether it's alive or dead is at our discretion. So let's all be discreet, hey?"

This unexpected display of civility and tact was spoiled by a paving stone hitting him between the eyes. Within an instant, bricks, bottles, and other debris showered down upon the remaining two soldiers, followed by a swarm of townspeople.

"Stop!" The mob froze and stared at Agatha. "They didn't shoot. Don't kill them." For a long couple of seconds nothing happened and then a tall man in a leather apron swatted a younger man on the back of his head. "Back to the shop! Get thirty meters of Number Three rope!" He glanced at Vole. "And four of Number Six chain." The young man left at a run and the crowd laid the unconscious men out. A team began dragging the still-comatose Jäger out onto the street. Others began sweeping through the café, collecting up tools and materials.

Agatha turned to Carson. "This will only get worse. Get me to the castle. Now."

The old man nodded. "It looks like I'd better." He turned to one of the café's waitresses, who was gently leading out a serene Vanamonde. "I'll have to ask you and the rest of the girls to keep an eye on my grandson."

The girl smiled. "Of course, sir. We'll get him home."

Van clapped his hands together and squealed. "Of course they will! They're perfect!"

The old man sighed. "With any luck this will wear off soon," he muttered.

The girl nodded. "I certainly hope so. He's creeping me out."

Agatha and Carson strode off. Krosp trotted alongside, while Zeetha and Wooster brought up the rear, scanning the area for trouble.

What they saw was not trouble, but evidence that trouble was on its way. Everywhere, spreading out from the now closed café behind them, shops were suddenly pulling their wares in from the street and pulling down their shutters, to the growing consternation of the tourists.

Seeing a growing crowd ahead, the old man steered them to a narrow flight of stone steps and they found themselves striding atop an ancient wall. This was obviously once part of some fortifications, but as Mechanicsburg had grown, it had been incorporated into the inner structures of the town. There were a lot fewer people here, and von Mekkhan took a deep sigh.

"Normally, I would just take you straight to the front gate," he said thoughtfully.

Agatha peered over the wall and saw a squad of Wulfenbach troops jogging along one of the streets below. "But that's not a good idea now."

Carson nodded. "It's not just Wulfenbach. The false Heterodyne's people will be looking for you as well."

Krosp leapt to the top of the wall and looked around with interest. "As seneschal, you must know all the doors. Even the secret ones."

"Of course, but it won't do to underestimate these people. If they think you're here, I wouldn't put it past them to have even the secret doors watched."

Wooster frowned. "They don't sound like they're terribly secret," he remarked.

Carson looked slightly embarrassed. "You can buy tourist maps that list most of them." Under Agatha's incredulous stare, he shrugged. "Sane people don't try to get into the Castle."

They turned a corner and before them loomed a gigantic tower. It stood almost ten stories tall, a squat, circular structure built of native rock, encrusted with the occasional decorative panel, rusty spike, and the ubiquitous trilobites. After the castle, it was probably the tallest structure in Mechanicsburg.

Atop this was a vivid red, pagoda-like structure from which hung an immense bronze bell, easily six meters tall. The surface of the bell, along with the huge chains that held it aloft, were covered in a thick green patina of age, except for a large bas-relief skull, which sported a large gilded trilobite set into its forehead.

"The Doom Bell," Carson declared proudly. "Only to be rung when a new Heterodyne is born, an old Heterodyne dies, or the Heterodyne returns from abroad."

"So I guess you'll have to ring it for Agatha when you're convinced she's the real deal," Krosp remarked.

Carson looked startled and then a growing expression of worry crossed his face. "We…we might…" he conceded. "Oh, dear."

That sounded like a subject that should be explored at a later date. "So what do we do now?" Agatha asked.

Carson snapped out of his musing. "What we do is send you in through the front door."

"What? But you said—"

The old man waved a hand dismissively. "The trick is to make it seem like you don't want to go in."

In the Great Hospital, Gilgamesh was slumped in a chair. He had a slightly sick look upon his face and he was breathing heavily. A small sound jerked his head up and an instant later he was by his father's side.

He scanned the array of monitoring instruments and nodded in satisfaction even as the Baron's eyes fluttered slightly and then snapped open. Gil took a deep breath, adjusted his clothing, ran a hand through his perpetually disheveled hair, and stepped into his father's line of sight. He was surprised at how gratified he was when, at the sight of him, the Baron noticeably relaxed.

"I see you're awake, Father."

"…" The Baron opened his mouth but nothing came out. Gil reached over and held a cup of water to the old man's lips. The Baron sipped and in short order emptied the cup. He slowly ran a tongue over his lips and tried again. "I must be," he whispered. "Dreams don't hurt this much." He closed his eyes. "How long?"

"Two days."

Klaus absorbed this. "Damage?" he asked.

Gil didn't need to consult the chart for this. "Seven broken ribs. Severe fracture, right leg. Fractured clavicle. Some crush injury, but the kidneys appear unharmed. First and second degree burns on upper back and lower arms. Third degree on lower back. Four broken fingers, three broken toes. Sprained and bruised muscles throughout, major and minor lacerations, and a concussion."

Klaus's mouth twitched. "Hmph. I've had worse." His eyes examined the room before him. "We're in Mechanicsburg." Gil nodded. Suddenly Klaus's eyes sharpened and he twisted his head slightly towards his son. This caused him to grimace. "Balan's Gap?"

Gil took a deep breath. "Contained." Klaus opened his mouth but Gil continued. "In addition to the forces already in place, I reinforced them with the 13th Chemical Division, the 2nd Armored Infantry Battalion, and the 117th Interceptors. I placed the Seismic Rangers and Chained-Fire Horsemen on picket, and the Heliolux Airfleet is maintaining communications." He finished—and waited.

Klaus paused…and closed his mouth. Gil felt the same elation he had experienced when he had passed his first doctorate exam. With great effort, he kept his face blank.

"Lucrez—", his father rolled his eyes towards him and again licked his lips. "The Heterodyne girl. Is she here?"

Gil nodded. "I believe so, although there is also an imposter."

Klaus wearily closed his eyes. "Nothing is ever simple where that family is concerned," he whispered. "Where is she?"

"She has entered the castle. I believe she is part of a larger plot taking advantage of your injuries. She has minions, equipment, up to and including her own airship. This tells me she has powerful backers."

Klaus frowned. "And she managed to coordinate all this while traveling in a circus across the Wastelands? She's more dangerous than I'd thought!"

Gil blinked. "Oh, no. Sorry, Father, that's the imposter. Agatha is still in town. She's making coffee at a café."

Klaus stared incredulously at his son and then his great head sank back onto his pillow. "Oh dear," he muttered. "I am still dreaming. *And* it hurts." He sighed. "How unfair."

Gil rolled his eyes. "Father, about Agatha—"

A hint of the old steel entered the Baron's voice. "She is the Other."

Gil spread his hands. "Coffee?"

Klaus rolled his eyes. "The flesh she wears is different, but she is Lucrezia Mongfish! I talked to her! She didn't even try to deny it! There is no mistake!" Klaus saw the emotions flickering across his son's face and tried to reason with him. "You must understand. This girl you care for is not what she seems. She was aboard Castle

Wulfenbach for what? Less than two weeks? I knew her for years. She's a consummate actress. Ruthless, manipulative, and convinced that she is destined for greatness." He closed his eyes, exhausted. "You must believe me," he whispered.

Gil refilled his father's cup and helped him to drink. As he did so, he spoke. "Father, I agree that there is a lot to consider. The preliminary reports from the teams inside Sturmhalten Castle are extremely worrying. Rest assured that I am aware that there are serious questions about her and everything that has happened since we found her."

Klaus and cocked a shaggy eyebrow. "—But?" he whispered.

Gil cleared his throat. "The very trait that allows Sparks to apparently warp the laws of physics seems to affect probability and statistics within their vicinity as well. Every visible action will be open to misinterpretation and their motives can easily be misconstrued."

Klaus looked startled. Gil leaned in. "Your words, Father, used to explain a rather catastrophic incident in your father's laboratory when you were eleven, if I remember correctly."

Klaus glared at his son. "I was lying. I knew the cat was there."

Gil tried to look shocked.

Klaus's eyes narrowed. "You are trying to change the subject. Even if she wasn't the Other, this girl is a Spark and that makes her dangerous enough. You do know that every single woman I have ever known who has possessed the Spark has tried to kill me?"

Gil crossed his arms. "I think that's just you, Father. How many women that you've been involved with *without* the Spark have tried to kill you?"

An odd look crossed Klaus's face. "I... I don't see what that has to do with anything," he muttered. "This girl—"

Gil made a chopping motion with his hand. "Father, I'm not going to argue about this now. I sent the Jäger to bring her here and then I—we—will examine her. Until then, you should rest."

Klaus's eyes widened in surprise. "The Jäger... Vole? Captain Vole? You sent *him* to fetch your Heterodyne girl?" Gil nodded, and a great weariness filled Klaus's face as he closed his eyes. "Well, that should solve everything. It's what I would have done myself." He took in a deep breath. "I seems I have misjudged you. Well done, son."

A chill skittered across Gil's heart. There was something he wasn't getting here... He leaned in. "Is this another test?"

The Baron twitched and a small pained sound escaped from his mouth. "Please," he whispered. "Don't make me laugh." He took another deep breath. "No," he announced. "There will be no more tests, my son. The time for such things is over. Now give me your report. What has been done?"

Gil stared at his father for a second—his mind racing—then he straightened up and organized his thoughts. "Castle Wulfenbach is not yet here. I have closed the city gates and established a perimeter. I am reinforcing the garrison. I was trying to do it subtly, with troops rotated out of Balan's Gap, which has also allowed us to secure the main road. Tourists and non-residents are being urged to leave. No one can enter except for vetted residents. The garrison here was never very large, and the false Heterodyne neutralized the Black Squad when she entered the castle. We're...still trying to locate them.

"With the remainder, I've reinforced the gates and entrances we know about, but I doubt we've found them all. I've put out a call, but we have no air power here, and thus I haven't been able to bring down the imposter's airship. Since it has no weapons to speak of, I haven't made it a priority. I have the remainder of the troops patrolling the streets and guarding the armory. I thought about activating the Mechanicsburg militia, but since we're dealing with an actual Heterodyne, I thought that could be a bad idea."

Klaus nodded at this. "Why are you still in here? Surely there are better command posts?"

"Word of your state has spread," Gil said frankly. "I feared assassination."

Klaus snorted. "Any attempts?"

Gil glanced to the side. "A few. Nothing worth mentioning."

Klaus absorbed this. "The work of your imposter's people?"

Gil shook his head. "I... don't think so. They've all been very disorganized, just random enemies taking advantage of the situation. To a degree, I believe the imposter's people are also taking advantage of circumstances but they're much more organized. They are following a plan." He leaned against the window and stared out at the town below. "Killing you would seem to be a necessary step, but it's been long enough that I have to conclude that our imposter's people haven't tried to do it."

Klaus frowned. "That does seem sloppy."

Gil nodded. "And I haven't seen sloppiness anywhere in this. No, if they want the Empire..." Suddenly Gil felt his eye drawn to the brooding pile that was Castle Heterodyne. An errant thought trickled through his mind. "If they...*want* the Empire..."

Klaus had long been able to recognize when the people around him were being clever. He knew when to be silent and when to prod. He waited a second and then cleared his throat.

Gil spun about. "But what if they don't?" He stared at his father. "What if all they want—at least for now—is *Mechanicsburg*?"

With a bound he was at the door to the room. He pulled it open with a jerk, startling the two troopers stationed outside. "Get Captain DuPree in here," he ordered. "Now!"

He then spun about and went to his father's side. As he spoke, he made a last check of the medical machinery and then began to perform a similar check upon his walking stick. "I'm afraid I must go after all, Father. When the main attack comes, it will not be here."

"Explain."

Gil waved towards the airship that could be seen floating above the town. "These people had a false Heterodyne all prepared. She was trained. Rehearsed. They could conceivably have known about Agatha, but you being injured? They couldn't have planned for that." He gave his father's hand a gentle squeeze. "We're not even a part of this yet. This isn't a direct attack upon the Empire, it's an outflanking maneuver. They're after legitimacy."

Klaus interrupted. "Claiming to be a Heterodyne won't get them that."

Gil nodded. "Not directly, no, but…" He paused to organize his thoughts. "You've imposed order, Father, but before you did that, ours was always a minor house. Before the Empire—"

Klaus snorted. "It was all chaos. Everyone was fighting everyone else. Fools."

"Yes, but before that? Before the Long War?"

Klaus looked startled. "Before? Why—you'd have to go back to the Storm King, but even—" A thought struck him. "Oh! The girl!"

Gil pounced. "The *Heterodyne* girl!"

Klaus stared at him. "Ridiculous! That's practically a fairy tale! Who would—"

"Everyone," Gil declared flatly. "They have a pet Heterodyne heir, and fairy tales have a great deal of power because everyone has heard them! If they do this correctly, Europa will submit to them and cheer while they do it. But in order to do it right, they need to take Mechanicsburg!"

Klaus nodded. It was obvious that this news invigorated the wounded man. The fact was that Klaus enjoyed a well thought-out bit of insurrection. It gave the troops something to do, allowed him to do a bit of fighting, and occasionally spotlighted some genuine grievances within the Empire. This one seemed to be particularly well thought out and Klaus was already eager to begin cracking it.

"The first thing I should do—"

But Gil had been ready for this and he pitilessly smacked his father sharply upon the chest, causing the Baron to gasp in shocked surprise and pain.

"*You* must *rest*! At least for now. *I* will deal with this."

Klaus angrily opened his mouth. Gil raised his hand and Klaus flinched and then grudgingly nodded. "Very well."

Gil took a relieved breath.

"But there is one last thing," Klaus said, and seeing the look in his son's eye, he raised his voice. "And it's important. The Heterodyne girl. Your Agatha, not the other one. She has a companion. She is a girl with a pair of unusual swords and long green hair."

"Green?" Gil looked intrigued.

Klaus nodded. "Bright green. Be careful. She is a formidable fighter." Klaus hesitated, which was uncharacteristic of him. His eyes shifted sideways. "There is a very good chance that she has been sent to Europa to kill you."

Gil blinked in surprise. "Kill *me*? What did I do?"

"Absolutely *nothing*," Klaus roared. The force of his anger shocked Gil and even seemed to surprise the Baron himself.

Gil's eyes narrowed. "Father, what did *you* do?"

For the first time, Klaus gazed directly at his son. Pride filled his face. "I kept you alive."

Gil was nonplussed and the Baron closed his eyes and settled back into his bed. "And now, as you yourself have said, I need to rest."

Gil stared at the supine man and then, as it would look bad if he strangled him, settled for waving his arms in the air. "Confound it, Father!" he howled.

Klaus cracked an eye open. "And you have work to do." He closed the eye again. "I will explain anything and everything when you return."

Possibly nothing else could have silenced Gil as effectively. "Everything? Even my..." his breath caught. "Even my mother?"

Klaus nodded wearily. "Anything you want." He sighed, "But especially your mother."

This was a bombshell. Gil had often asked about his mother but Klaus had always refused to answer. As he became better at reading people, Gil realized that the subject affected his father deeply and the mere mention of it would disturb the great man for days at a time. To finally have an explanation...

Gil took a deep breath. "Then rest up, father, I have many questions."

The corner of Klaus's mouth quirked upwards slightly. "Don't I know it," he whispered. Again his eye opened but this time the look he gave his son was soulful. "But for pity's sake—DuPree?"

Bangladesh DuPree was also one of the few people who had little or no fear of the Baron. When he was healthy, Klaus found this refreshing, in a guilty pleasure sort of way. But the idea of being trapped in the same room with her, where he would be subjected to her endless, cheerful running commentary on life, the functioning of government, and how everything would look better if it was on fire, had him seriously considering ways to knock himself out.

Gil smiled. "Oh, you have my sympathy, but she'll keep you alive."

This was certainly true, if only because Bangladesh was a highly functional homicidal maniac who never worried about what she called "the small stuff." It worried Gil that he had yet to fully figure out what DuPree considered to be "the Big Stuff," This was because whenever he thought he had an idea about what it might be, DuPree set it on fire.

"But my will to live…"

"For what it's worth, her jaw has been wired shut."

Klaus brightened immediately. "Good heavens. I wouldn't miss this for the world." He then felt a touch of paternalistic concern. "Is her jaw really that damaged?"

Gil suddenly focused on the machines near his father's head.

Klaus frowned. "Gilgamesh?"

The young man shrugged. "Well, I never actually said that her jaw was damaged at all."

An odd sound brought his eyes back to his father, who was grimacing. "It really does hurt when I do that," Klaus confessed.

Gil refrained from supplying the obvious medical response.

There was a light, rhythmic tapping on the door. After a moment, it swung open and Dr. Sun peered around the doorjamb. When no one shot at him, he stepped through, followed by a dark-skinned woman with long glossy black hair, wearing a crisp white captain's uniform. Her eyes glared furiously at Gil over a complicated bandage and wire apparatus that covered the lower part of her face.

Gil clapped his hands and gave every indication that he was pleased to see her. "Ah, DuPree! How are you feeling?"

Beneath the bandage, it could be seen that her jaw tightened. DuPree settled for raising a finger at him.

Gil tsked. "I keep *telling* you, Captain, it's 'thumbs up.'"

Her eye twitched.

"Perfect! Now I'm leaving you here to guard my father." Instantly her face grew serious. Gil continued, "Your orders are simple. Kill anyone who enters this room except for Dr. Sun or me."

DuPree went still. Her pupils expanded. Gil nodded at her unasked question. "I mean anyone. Men, women, children, service animals—anyone."

She began breathing faster and her hands darted about her person, checking the numerous weapons she had hidden about her person. "You can use any weapon you like," Gil continued coldly. "Just keep my father from harm."

DuPree stared at him and then suddenly wrapped her arms around him in a fierce hug. Gil endured this for several seconds and then gently pried himself free. "But," he dropped his voice and whispered to her, "put your trash in the corner and don't let my father see it. I don't want him upset."

With that he strode out.

DuPree looked after him quizzically and then shrugged. She stepped up to Klaus, who seemed to be sleeping. Turning about, she glanced into the corner of the room that was hidden from Klaus's view. She gasped. There was a small pile of corpses spilling out of the closet.

She stared after Gil with renewed respect. Setting him on fire just might be a challenge after all.

CHAPTER 3

Your Majesty, it is with great chagrin that I must again report our failure to assassinate the Heterodyne.

Considering the importance of the assignment, I followed your Majesty's advice and sent in not one team, but two. The second was led by none other than Don Giorello of Venice, whom you may recall, having served your Majesty so admirably in the affair of the burning windmill.

According to him, the infiltration of Mechanicsburg and even of Castle Heterodyne was easy enough. It was once they were inside that things fell apart.

I have provided, for your edification, a verbatim transcription of Don Giorello's debriefing:

The castle itself is alive. I say this now, to try to explain that which happened to myself and to my team, may God have mercy upon their souls. I understand that this might be considered a blasphemous statement, but I find that after the experiences of the last few days, I no longer care overly much for the opinions of a God who would allow such a thing to exist upon this sphere.

So. The castle, it is a constructed thing of stone and iron. A building where people live and eat and sleep. But it is also alive, and more than alive. It has intelligence. It is sentient. Furthermore, do not try to conceive of it as some ordinary beast, but rather like some enormous protean creature that is not relegated to one set configuration!

…Forgive me. I did not mean to roar so. No, I am calm now, sir. My state of mind will perhaps be best explained by my tale.

We gained access to the castle with an ease that should have warned us that there was something not right. I believe now that it was aware of us as soon as we entered, but allowed us to penetrate deeply within. I suspect—no, I firmly believe that this was so we would not be able to easily escape its influence.

The shape of our predicament unfolded slowly. No matter where we went, we encountered no other person, although we had, as planned, entered on the night that Bludtharst Heterodyne was throwing a Grand Fête for his field commanders. We heard music. The sound of many people. We were able to see brightly lit rooms filled with revelers through the windows, but no matter where we went, we were alone. No guards. No servants. No prisoners. No monsters. We began to think that if there were ghosts, than we were they.

More worrying was when we tried to leave. We could not. Never could we find a room with a window facing outwards. Never could we find a door that led anywhere but deeper into the castle. Doors behind us sealed themselves shut, melted into nothingness, or opened not onto the rooms whence we had come, but onto solid walls.

After two days of this, our nerve broke. We yelled. We begged for the Heterodynes' guards to find us. We tried crawling out of the windows, only to find ourselves crawling back into the very rooms we had left. While we slept, the rooms themselves would change shape, or abut different rooms than when we had last looked. Eventually they began to do this, not while we slept, but before our very eyes as we watched.

Six of my people were crushed or impaled by hidden mechanisms and traps. Some instantly, some hung screaming for almost an hour.

In the end, the last three of my people simultaneously killed each other, and of this sin I absolved them. In the end, only I remained. We had been inside for close to five days without food or sufficient water, and I was lying near insensate upon the ground, too weak to move and resigned to death.

Suddenly, a door opened, and in strode the devil, Bludtharst Heterodyne himself. He saw me and gave a great shout of surprise. Then a terrible voice—a voice I know never came from the throat of man nor beast—arose from everywhere. "Forgive me, Master. He is but an interloper with whom I was having some sport."

"Well he gave me a turn, you wretched thing," Bludtharst declared. "Toss him out."

The monstrous voice spoke again: "But, Master," it said, "he still lives. I am not yet done with him."

"Then let this be a lesson to you," the Heterodyne said dismissively, "to not leave your trash lying about where I might trip over it. Send him on his way. At once!"

The next thing I knew, I awoke to discover that I had been tossed upon a night soil cart that was passing out through the town gates.

When he had finished, Giorello broke down into tears and had to be sedated.

I have placed him under observation for his own safety, as I greatly fear that he will attempt suicide. In my judgment, he is a broken man and is no longer fit for field service.

As to the veracity of his account, I cannot say. While preposterous on the surface, it does corroborate stories and anecdotes I have heard from disparate sources over the years. Thus, I would strongly recommend against further attempts to infiltrate Castle Heterodyne.

—*Report from Baron Andrzej Petr Orczy, head of the Department of Assassination and Assorted Unpleasantness for Andronicus Valois, the Storm King. From the Storm King Collection of the British Museum.*

ᨔᧅᨔᷫ

Zola waited impatiently as one of her Tall Men twisted the dial a final degree and gingerly tapped a red button. There was a long, tense pause; then he gave a small shriek as the door before him slid aside. When he realized that he was not dead, a grin of relief spread across his face. "I did it!"

Zola scowled. "And about time," she declared. "I want to get inside. We're being watched."

One of her other Tall Men cleared his throat. "Forgive me, my lady, but it is only due to Tiktoffen's notes that we got through at all. We weren't expecting difficulty so soon." His eyes flicked upwards despite himself, "And I suspect even this could have been avoided."

Zola glanced upwards. There was yet another of her Tall Men, hanging head down—impaled upon a grim metal arm that had unfolded from the ceiling. This device, which terminated in a wicked spike, would be horrific enough, but the machine had then used the screaming man to scrub out a message in blood that still oozed its way down the wall:

THE HETERODYNE MUST ENTER ALONE.

The girl rolled her eyes at these theatrics but had to concede that it might have a dampening effect upon the enthusiasm of her assistants. This was a situation where a firm whip hand was called for.

"Be that as it may, I shall play this by my rules." She then hardened her voice. "We shall all enter together." The remaining men had been trained well enough—they knew that there was no option other than outright rebellion, and they had not been selected for their independence of spirit. Glumly, they formed up in ranks behind her and stepped through the doorway, which instantly slammed shut behind them.

While her Tall Men cringed, Zola coolly examined the area in which they found themselves. This had once been a main entrance to Castle Heterodyne and it had been decorated to impress. Inlaid constellations picked out in semi-precious stones were just visible behind the grime that coated the barrel-vaults high overhead. Cobweb-festooned chandeliers dangled, unlit.

The paneled walls were decorated with enormous paintings depicting the great capital cities of Europa—apparently in the aftermath of a visit from the Heterodynes. Here was Vienna in flames. There was Berlin, still and silent, carpeted in an array of exotic fungi. Strange, shadowy shapes crept through the recognizable ruins of Paris.

This last was the only one that seemed to affect the girl—she gave a slight shudder and quickly turned away.

The hallway suddenly flared into brilliance as half a hundred lamps came alive. The candelabra were wrought in an astonishing variety of disquieting shapes—figures of men, women, and bizarre creatures writhing in what would *appear* to be agony.

Beneath the grime and rubble, the terrazzo floor—with its fabled madness-inducing non-Euclidian geometric patterns—could still be glimpsed beneath the now tattered carpet.

Zola took a deep breath. To finally be here… She squared her shoulders. This is where it got dangerous. A second look around the area and this time she noted a plethora of paint and chalk marks. Hastily scrawled signs and sigils warned of the thousand and one traps that lined the hallway.

She turned to her Tall Men and almost screamed in frustration. They had actually spread out and were examining the nearest walls with interest.

"Freeze, you fools!" Sensibly, they did. Even behind their goggles, she could see their eyes desperately swiveling in her direction.

"Now listen to me," she said, foot tapping. "This is probably the best-mapped area of the Castle, but it is also one of the most dangerous. You must follow my lead."

She pointed downwards. "Avoid any area of the floor marked in white. It is a trap that will kill you."

She pointed upwards. "Do not stand beneath any area on the ceiling marked in red. It is a trap that will kill you."

She caught one of her men gazing in fascination at a wall sconce depicting a golden lady entwined with some sort of cephalopod. "Do not touch any metal surface. It is a trap that will kill you."

The man guiltily lowered his hand. "Are you trying to frighten us?"

Zola ground her teeth. "Of course I am! This place is dangerous! It is twisted, and diabolical and worst of all—"

Too late she saw another of her men reaching for a gold coin glittering innocently upon the floor. "NO!" she screamed, but it was too late. A trapdoor split open beneath him, sending him screaming into the darkness. There was a pause, and then the trapdoor rose back into place with a hiss. The coin glittered enticingly in the darkness.

Involuntarily, they all took a step back. Zola swallowed. "A—And worst of all, this place likes to think that it has…a sense of humor."

They all kept close to her after that, as she headed deeper into the castle.

Professor Hristo Tiktoffen trudged down the Hall of Nasty Iron Springs.[19]

He moved with a distracted look on his face as he sorted through an enormous notebook, generously interleaved with additional notes and maps. Most of the prisoners that inhabited Castle Heterodyne had learned to walk very carefully indeed, and it was not uncommon for them to take several minutes to decide where to next place their foot. Tiktoffen trod confidently, to the awe of those around him. It was whispered that he and the Castle had reached…an accommodation.

He came to a large metal door and, with a small grunt, shoved it open, revealing a large cavernous space. Within, cyclopean gears were frozen mid-turn, teeth and gear shafts dull beneath years of accumulated dust and grime.

He heard a faint, rhythmic tapping coming from behind a wall of interlocked gears larger than millstones. Tiktoffen cleared his throat. "Fraulein Wilhelm?"

The tapping stopped and a shock of delicately shaded pink hair appeared between two enormous gear teeth. Its owner peered cautiously at the professor, then grinned and dodged around the machinery to stand before him.

Tiktoffen gave her an avuncular smile and checked his notes. "Anything for my books today?"

---

[19] This was probably not what the Heterodynes and their servants-in-residence had called it, but in the fourteen or so years that the Empire had been disposing of its more dangerous prisoners, a rich body of lore, myth, and nomenclature had grown up around the castle's inner workings. When new areas of the castle were mapped, the amateur cartographers were encouraged to name things as vividly and memorably as possible.

Sanaa Wilhelm absent-mindedly scrubbed at a spot of grime on her orange coverall as she pondered. "I think so, Professor." She closed her eyes in concentration. "I was summoned to the north wall of the Room of Lead. I reconnected fifteen copper cables behind the third panel. That was at four thirty-six exactly.[20] There was a sort of a hum...and then nothing."

Tiktoffen's eyebrows rose. "Four thirty-six?" He shuffled through his stack of papers, muttering to himself. Suddenly he gave a small cry of satisfaction.

"Yes! Tark was in the Gallery of Razors—" He double-checked his notes. "—And yes! They flexed at four thirty-six!" He made a small notation on one of the sheets and tucked his pencil away with a glow of satisfaction. "Ten points for you!"

Sanaa's eyes lit up in pleasure. "Ten? Thank you!"

Tiktoffen was already flipping through his notes and waved a hand. "De nada. We've been looking for the Razor's power for over three years."

Sanaa got a faraway look in her eyes. "Ten points," she said to herself, just to hear it. "Wow! That's worth at least two months off my sentence! So to get out of here, I only have to get—*Ow!*"

As fast as a striking snake, Tiktoffen had lashed out and clipped the side of the girl's head. "Fool!" His jovial face had hardened instantly. "*Never* total your points out loud!"

Involuntarily, both prisoners glanced upwards towards an invisible presence that they knew loomed silently around them. Tiktoffen leaned in and addressed Sanaa in an urgent whisper. "When you've got enough to get out, *I* will know." He tousled her hair affectionately.

At that moment, Tiktoffen heard a familiar metallic panting. Through the doorway came a man in his thirties, unprepossessing in every way—except for the sharp-toothed mechanical mask permanently fastened to his lower face that had earned him the

---

[20]   All of the prisoners in Castle Wulfenbach wore chronometers strapped to their wrists, and were trained to record and remember the time whenever they performed a particular repair or observed something happen. As a result of this, almost all of them knew to the second when they died.

name "Snapper." When he saw Tiktoffen and Sanaa, he slowed a bit, but made up for it by waving his hands in agitation.

"Professor!" he called. His voice sounded hollow through the mask.

Tiktoffen gave a perfunctory smile. The man before him was one of the more unpredictable of the Castle's current residents. He was also uncannily smart, which was why he was still alive. This also explained why it had taken the Baron's people over two years to track him down, despite his striking appearance. "Snapper," he said. "What is it?"

The man's mechanical teeth ground together in excitement. "There's a Heterodyne in the Castle!"

Immediately, Tiktoffen was all interest. A new "Heterodyne" crashing through the Castle always revealed so much information. He snapped open his notebook in anticipation. "Did he come in through the Red Gate?" He turned another few pages, searching. "They promised to send the next one in through the Red Gate," he muttered. "I'm sure there's a deadfall we missed…"

Snapper waved his hands again. "No, sir! She made it into the Octagon! She's alive!"

The Professor looked at him blankly. "She?"

Snapper nodded vigorously. "And she's brought in minions!"

With that the older man took off at a dead run down the hallway. *No*, he thought to himself. *It can't be!* He skidded to a halt in a doorway. It was.

The Octagon was a large common room where the prisoners could congregate after they finished their shifts. It was directly off the kitchen and dormitories, and it was one of the few places where they had managed to replace the maddening red emergency lights with bulbs of a normal color. It was also in one of the permanent 'dead zones' in the Castle, and so was a popular place for the prisoners to relax. Some even chose to sleep there, just in case.

Many of the prisoners were there now, with more arriving every minute. The tables had been shoved against the walls, and in the center, a girl was getting undressed.

She was of middling height, and—once the ridiculously elaborate ball gown she wore over everything was stripped off—wearing a sensible pair of trousers and a simple leather singlet. Disconcertingly, they were still pink, but they were obviously working clothes. When she saw the professor, she gave him a cheerful smile that only highlighted the coldness of her eyes.

"Good morning, Professor Tiktoffen."

Tiktoffen stared at her in dismay. "Mademoiselle Zola! It is you! I can't believe it! What the hell are you doing here? Don't tell me you fools got *sentenced* here!"

Zola laughed airily. "Of course not! We came in on our own." The watching crowd gasped. She looked around the Octagon and was obviously unimpressed. "Well? Are you ready to leave this place?"

Tiktoffen restrained himself. He so very much wanted to slap her. "I didn't send for you," he roared. "It's too soon!"

The girl shrugged. "We've had to move things up."

The professor opened his mouth to object—

"Another Heterodyne girl has appeared." Despite her flippant attitude, Zola knew that Tiktoffen was smart. He instantly closed his mouth and waited.

Zola smiled. "The Baron tried to capture her. She defeated him, and in the process, announced her existence to the entire world. They were buzzing about her in Vienna when I left. We had to strike now before she gets here."

"Is…" Tiktoffen hesitated. "Is she the real thing?" Suddenly he felt it. A vast *attention* was focused on them now. Tiktoffen shivered. *Apparently The Octagon wasn't as dead as they had been led to believe.*

Zola shrugged. "Her pedigree is unknown. As always, the only test of import is if she can hold this castle. That's what people will understand. It's why you're here, remember?"

Tiktoffen collapsed into a chair and glared at her. "Of course I do! I've been in here for three years. There is nothing I want more than to get out and I am telling you that it is *too soon!*" He slammed his book onto a nearby table. "The Council needs to know how the Castle works?[21] That is what I have been *doing*! But unraveling the work of generations of lunatics takes time! I cannot tell you how to control the Castle yet! You've put the entire plan into jeopardy—for nothing!"

The girl picked up Tiktoffen's treasured book and leafed through a few pages. "No, not for nothing," she said comfortingly. "We understand that you can't control the Castle." She tossed the precious book into a trash barrel. "Instead, you will just have to help me kill it."

Tiktoffen gasped as if he'd been punched in the stomach. "*Kill* it?" In an instant he was up on his feet and fishing the book from the barrel. "The whole *point* of all this was to be able to *use* it! Its recognition will legitimize you!"

Zola ruefully shook her head. "The consensus is that the Castle may be too shattered to aid anyone. The legends all say that when Faustus Heterodyne brought the Castle to life, it was keenly intelligent. Able to observe and express itself everywhere within its structure, able to move and reshape almost every part of itself. In times of war, there are accounts of it actually aiding in the defense of the town. Now, even if we prune away the obvious hyperbole and inevitable exaggerations, does that sound like this place?"

Tiktoffen looked troubled. "I've admitted as much in my reports. The stories you mention could be easily explained as exaggerations of some of the phenomena we can still see today. But the incisive guiding intelligence? That seems to be gone. There's something, certainly. There are the voices that direct our repair efforts, but they often seem confused…"

"Confused?" Sanaa spoke up from the ring of fascinated prisoners that had gathered while the two had been talking, "Half the time it says it's guiding us to repair sites and then leads us into traps!"

---

[21] It is always frustrating to your professors when an organization chooses to use such mundane nomenclature instead of something a little more helpful to future historians. We are especially appreciative of the late, lamented *Most Secret Cabal of Unscrupulous Moldavian Chemists and Poisoners United Against the Tyranny of the Department of Safety & Ethics*, who were quickly betrayed to the authorities by the printer who had been hired to design their letterhead.

There was a heartfelt murmur of confirmation on this point from the rest of the inmates.

Tiktoffen acknowledged this. "That is certainly the case now, but I regard these problems as evidence that the guiding mechanism is damaged, not that it never existed. While I could accept that some of these old stories are exaggerations from enemies or prisoners, there are too many private accounts from the writings of the Heterodynes themselves."

The girl patted his arm solicitously. "Your work here hasn't been wasted, Professor, nor has that of your predecessors."

Tiktoffen looked surprised. The girl noticed and gave a small laugh. "Oh please, you can't seriously believe that you were our first inside man?"

The look on his face illustrated that this was exactly what he had believed. Zola smiled.

"If it makes you feel any better, you've certainly lasted longer than any of the others…but their information has also proved valuable. A recent analysis of all the collected reports suggests that we are not dealing with one single Castle entity. The current thought is that there may be as many as *twelve*."

Tiktoffen stared at her. He slowly sat down as this idea bubbled up through his brain. He spoke slowly, "But every source I've been able to unearth has referred to it as a single entity."

The girl nodded. "And it is quite possible that this was originally the case." She shrugged. "Maybe it even could do some of the things that the old stories claim. But I will say that relying upon the writings of the old Heterodynes to give you an accurate portrayal of *anything* seems a bit far-fetched, don't you think?"

Tiktoffen had to concede the point. Only the previous night, he had finished plowing through a journal by the Black Heterodyne,[22] which had gone on at great length about "how things would be so much simpler if everyone didn't have those purple insects crawling in and out of their faces all the time."

---

[22]   (1596-1655) His favorite color was "charred."

The girl continued. "But whatever cohesion existed must have been destroyed in the Great Attack.[23] We now believe that all that is left is a disorganized collection of sub-systems. That's what you've been dealing with. That's why none of it makes sense."

A wave of confusion washed over the ring of observers. The girl thought for a second. "Think of it this way; you've got repair systems that direct you to damaged areas. You've got anti-intruder systems that activate to keep you out of sensitive areas. Normally they're all part of the same system. But because of the damage, while they are still functioning, they're not talking to each other. The left claw doesn't know what the right one is doing."

She let them absorb this for a moment. "We're still going to use the Castle, but first we have to stop it from killing everyone. We have more than enough firepower on the way to allow us to hold Mechanicsburg through conventional means, especially if we seem legitimate. I will rule as the new Heterodyne, and I do *not* need the permission of a broken machine to do it."

Carson von Mekkhan swung the ancient ironwork gate closed behind him and locked it fastidiously. Agatha, Zeetha, Krosp, and Wooster peered into the gloom. The enclosure was evidently used to store road maintenance tools. Humming to himself, the old man selected a particular brick, gave it a twist, and a hidden door slid open with a deep groan. Carson frowned. "That needs oiling," he muttered. He stepped through, and indicated that Agatha and her three friends should follow. Once all were through, the door swung shut behind them and they were left in total darkness. Before they could react, there was a "clunk" as Carson threw an ancient knife-

[23] The Great Attack took place nineteen years before our current narrative begins. A massive explosion blew apart Castle Heterodyne from within, signaling the beginning of the War with the Other. Considered one of the most significant events of the last one hundred years, it began the sequence of events that destroyed almost forty of the Great Houses of Europa, laid the foundations for Baron Wulfenbach's Pax Transylvania, and culminated in the disappearance of the Heterodyne Boys. It directly set the stage for the story contained within these pages.

switch and a series of dim green lights began to glow. They now saw that they stood at the top of a wide stone staircase that wound sharply down.

"This isn't another sewer, is it?" Krosp asked as they started down. He'd had quite enough of those in Sturmhalten.

The old man shook his head. They came to the bottom of the steps and looked up at an elaborate series of groined vaults, the tops of which were lost in the cool darkness.

"This," Carson announced, his voice echoing, "is the true family crypt of the Heterodynes." As their eyes adjusted, they could see bizarre and elaborate sepulchers and coffins of marble and granite, decorated with tarnished metal and dusty gems. Unearthly statues lined the walls and carved skeletons were everywhere. It took Agatha a moment to realize that unlike other cemeteries she had visited, all of the statues and carved faces were grinning in a most disquieting manner. Even in death, the Heterodynes took a perverse pride in the fact that people were happy to see them go.

As they moved down the central corridor, names came and went in the darkness. Names that Agatha recognized as the monsters of stories she had heard as a child. Stories that everyone had heard. She realized that she was torn between dread and a sort of twisted admiration. These were the monsters that had shaped the face and the history of Europa. Sometimes for the worse, and sometimes, though it had certainly not been their intent, for the better—if only because of the heroism that had arisen in order to confront them.

It was all summed up by the inscription over the tomb of Bludtharst Heterodyne, who had been responsible for the creation of the Storm King's coalition: *HE COULDN'T HAVE DONE IT WITHOUT ME.* *True enough*, Agatha thought, although she suspected the Storm King might have appreciated having an option.

Wooster fished a watch from his waistcoat pocket, gave the back a half-twist that revealed a softly glowing compass, and frowned at it. "I seem to have gotten a bit turned around in all those tunnels," he admitted. "We started at the Cathedral,[24] but now we're closer to the castle, yes?"

Carson nodded in approval. "Very good, Mister Wooster."

Zeetha looked around and took a deep breath of the limestone-scented air. "Are all the Heterodynes here?"

Carson pulled an ivory pipe from his pocket and leaned against an ornate coffin. He plucked a clump of crumbly black moss from the stone surface, and tamped it into his pipe. "Well." He thought about this as he pulled an elaborate silver lighter from another pocket and lit the pipe. "There are a few of them that are represented by only a few ashes or scraps of armor," he conceded, "but aside from Master William and Master Barry, one way or another, the Heterodynes have always come home in the end." He took a deep puff and released a savory cloud of faintly glowing green smoke. "A place has been reserved for them, for when they arrive."

Agatha studied the man. "You're convinced they will return," she declared.

Carson hunched his shoulders and gave a faint smile. "In one form or another." His teeth gleamed in the shadows.

Agatha stood tall. "And yet you say it's impossible that *I* could be a Heterodyne. Even though…every…everything tells me that I am."

The old man nodded amiably. "Oh, yes, I can see why. Punch and Judy, your effect upon the people of the town, not to mention Captain Vole's reaction…" Another ruminative puff. "Still, whatever you are, you are not the heir everyone expects."

"And why can't I be?"

Carson looked at her and took the pipe from his mouth. He gestured towards her feet with the stem. "Because you're standing on him."

---

[24]   The Red Cathedral of Mechanicsburg was the result of a bet between Prince Vadim Sturmvarous of Balan's Gap and Dante Heterodyne, known to history as 'The Good Heterodyne' (Not because of any intrinsic nobility of spirit, but because he was very good at being a Heterodyne, which meant rather the opposite). The Prince had hoped that the cathedral would serve as a nucleus of goodness in Mechanicsburg, which, over time, would spread to the rest of the inhabitants, and, he dared to dream, the Heterodyne family itself. The cathedral's dedication ceremony involved the sacrifice of the Cardinal sent from Rome to oversee it, and things went downhill from there.

Agatha jumped and stared down. A tiny marble slab was set into the stone floor. The inscription was succinct:

KLAUS BARRY HETERODYNE
Beloved son of Lucrezia and William
With us but 407 days—
Forever in our hearts

Agatha had to move her foot to see the dates of birth and death.

Peering over her shoulder, Wooster's breath caught. He looked up. "He died in the attack on Castle Heterodyne?"

Carson nodded.

Krosp's tail twitched. "The name—"

He was cut short by Carson. "He was named Klaus at Master William's insistence. It was done to honor his old friend who had vanished over two years previously." The old man paused, "Two years and three months, to be technical about it."

"Yes…" Ardsley said slowly, "I can see why you'd want to be clear about that."

"I don't," said Agatha, "What am I missing?"

Carson looked at her and then looked away. Agatha blinked in puzzlement. The old man was embarrassed.

Zeetha merely chuckled infuriatingly.

Ardsley cleared his throat. "There were…rumors that before she married Bill Heterodyne, the Lady Lucrezia had…trouble deciding between him and Klaus Wulfenbach."

"It was a well known fact around here," Carson said tartly. "And the Lady Lucrezia was not one to be bound by…propriety or cultural mores, let us say. But luckily, for dynastic reasons, everyone was satisfied with the math." He looked at Agatha expectantly.

The light dawned and Agatha flushed. "How did he die?"

"When the Other attacked Castle Heterodyne—"

"But why would she?" Agatha stopped short at a overly loud cough from Zeetha. There were very few people who knew that Agatha's mother, Lucrezia, had been the Other. To most of the world, the Other was still a figure of mystery. Perhaps, Agatha thought, she should leave it that way for now. She took a deep breath. "I'm sorry," she said to the old man. "Please. Tell me what you know of the attack."

The old man took a long drag on his pipe and settled back on the slab. He closed his eyes and thought for a moment. Absent-mindedly he steepled his fingertips before his chest. When he spoke, his voice was firm and his wording concise. "I was not in the Castle on the night of the attack. Indeed, I was no longer seneschal. I had retired three days before and turned the duty over to my son.

"The Masters were away. The town of Huffnagle was being overrun by…hm…giant vegetables, as it turned out. I was enjoying the luxury of playing with my grandchildren.

"At eight-seventeen p.m., there was an earth tremor and a massive explosion rocked the town. It came from the Castle—so I left the children with their mother and went out to see what I could do…"

The town was in chaos. The Castle had been hit. Entire towers leaned drunkenly outwards. Flame roared from windows and as Carson watched, a section of the battlements collapsed, tumbling down the crags to the slopes below.

Flaming bits of the Castle had been blown throughout the entire town, and fires were breaking out all over. To make matters even worse, the automatic fire suppression systems were either malfunctioning or were slow to activate and the fires were growing everywhere he looked.

He saw a crowd gawping at a fountain of flame slowly spreading over the Rusty Trilobite, his favorite tavern.

"Grab some buckets," he roared. People jumped at his voice and then ran to obey, as they had done for the last thirty years.

Carson continued: "Castle Heterodyne had a staff of two hundred and seven. Sixty-three died that night, including the new seneschal—my son." He paused again, catching his breath as the old pain washed through him.

The Jägers were weeping. He'd never seen that before, even at the death of a Heterodyne. They lined the corridor, blood oozing from wounds they'd incurred clearing debris. He saw that a section of the ceiling had come down. The skeletal Herr Doktor Torsti arose from a crouch, his joints snapping in that unfortunate manner he had been so proud of, the eternal rictus of his mouth stretched into an unfamiliar expression of sadness.

As he drew near, Carson saw a crumpled figure that appeared to be trying to crawl from beneath the rubble. With a chill, he recognized the Coat of Office. He found he had dropped to his knees, and just when he thought it could not get any worse, he identified the pathetic bundle clutched in his son's arms…

The old man raised his head proudly. "He died trying to protect the young master. Serving the House of Heterodyne to the end."

Agatha realized that she was crying, silent tears running down her face. "I'm so sorry," she whispered. "He must have been very brave. All of your family must have been so brave for so very long…" She took a deep breath and looked the old man in the eye. "Thank you."

The old man blew out an embarrassed breath and stood up. "A 'thank you', is it?" He jammed his hands into his pockets. A moment later, he realized that the pipe he held was still lit and he pulled it back out of his pocket and waved it at Agatha impatiently. "Now I *know* you're not a member of the family!" He looked away and after a moment continued:

"The Lady Lucrezia was missing…"

It took four Jägers and two of the bone puppet golems to smash down the doors to Lucrezia's laboratory. Inside, clouds of acrid smoke rose from the large fireplace. Wearing a breathing filter, Carson pushed through and saw the remnants of charred file boxes. The Lady Lucrezia's precious notes. In the ashes below he saw the smashed remains of vessels that, from their markings, had contained volatile chemical accelerants. He felt his skin begin to tingle and checked the seal on his filter. Crumpled before this pyre was the pale form of the Lady's mysterious, nameless warrior-assistant. Her pupil-less eyes stared upwards and an ugly gash had opened her throat. The rest of the room gave testament to a pitched battle, with glassware and equipment tossed about and thoroughly smashed.

The Heterodyne Boys returned within hours, and Carson was there— waiting for them in the front hall. Master Bill nearly went insane. It took two of the Jägergenerals to hold him down, roaring and swearing. The Three Prometheans finally managed to convince him that the young Master was beyond hope. Even they—the Heterodyne's ancient and final arbiters of death and non-death—had been crying, and when Master William damned them to the Caverns of the Red Slow, they had merely bowed in unison and gone their way without protest.

Master Barry surrounded himself with a deadly calm. He was the one who took charge and made sure that all who had been within the Castle were rescued or accounted for.

Carson paused. "Except for the Lady Lucrezia. There was no sign of her anywhere, and the Castle was…Well the only way to describe it is 'raving.' It's gotten more coherent over the years, but then—"

He seemed to realize that he was wandering, and with an impatient shake of his head continued. "After everyone who could be rescued was rescued, and all that could be done had been done, the Heterodyne Boys secreted themselves in Master William's laboratory." The old man took a deep draw from his pipe and stared down the corridor of memory. "I heard them arguing. Arguing like I had never heard them do before. About what, I couldn't tell you, but it went on for almost two days. From the sound of it, Master Barry was…more in control, but Master William was the Heterodyne and in the end Master Barry conceded. They left the next day."

Carson paused again and reemerged into the present. He looked Agatha in the face. "And we never saw them again." Even now there was a note of hurt betrayal in his voice. "We heard of them, of course. Everyone did. Someone was trying to wipe out the Sparks of Europa.

The following years saw the destruction of forty-three major houses. Slaver wasps and their revenants were everywhere. People thought they were seeing the End Days.

"And anywhere there was a mention of wasps, you would hear about the Heterodyne Boys. They were always in the thick of things. Always fighting the Other. Always searching for the Lady Lucrezia. For close to three years…"

Carson shrugged. "And then…nothing. One day people simply realized that the attacks upon the great houses had stopped. We assumed that the Masters had found the Other and had beaten him. But no one ever knew for sure. They never returned, or even sent us word. They had vanished.

"There were still packs of revenants, and outbreaks of wasps, but they were… undirected. Without purpose. Inevitably, of course, the remaining Sparks emerged from within their fortresses and began to accuse each other of being in league with the enemy. They resumed fighting amongst themselves. Things became worse than ever…" Carson sighed, "and that was when the Baron returned."

Carson eased himself onto a low sarcophagus and considered his next words. "There are many who grouse about the Baron now, but when he first appeared, the people flocked to him…and with good cause. Where the Baron strode, peace reigned, and the people were desperate for peace. All too soon he was at the gates of Mechanicsburg—polite as the devil when he wants a drink, but here nonetheless.

"It's not that I didn't trust him. Truth be told, I always rather liked him. More important, the Masters had liked and trusted him. But even so, I would not be the one to surrender the secrets of the Heterodynes to an outsider.

"And so, the records showed that the seneschal of Castle Heterodyne, Carson von Mekkhan, had died, as had his eldest son—who bore his name. The younger children were erased from the records, and thus the House of Wulfenbach believed us—and the knowledge we possessed—to be gone.

"Eventually, after he had learned what he could—little enough, but still more than I'd have liked—Klaus set up a new City Council, reached an accommodation with what remained of the Castle, took the Jägers and the Nurse, and left."

Agatha interrupted at this point. "Wait—the Nurse?"

The old man nodded. "A construct of the Lady Lucrezia's. She had been the young Master's nursemaid. When she was found trapped in the rubble of the Castle, she had gone quite off her head and was nearly incoherent. She had to be locked up or she'd have killed even more of us."

"Was this...Von Pinn?"

The old man almost choked on his pipe. "You *know* her?"

Agatha nodded slowly. "She was on Castle Wulfenbach. The Baron had her guarding the children who served as hostages."

"Ah." The old man thought about this and nodded. "Klaus always did know the right monster for the right job."

Krosp interrupted, "So there's a new City Council?"

Carson waved a hand dismissively. "It was always the job of the seneschal to see to it that Mechanicsburg ran smoothly. It still is. In fact, it works so well that old Klaus has never had any cause to complain. The Baron's new City Council was still made up of Mechanicsburg people. They answered quietly to me, and now, to my grandson, Vanamonde." Carson paused. "I assure you, he is more competent than I let on."

"A shadow government." Krosp twitched his whiskers. "I really do like you people."

Wooster looked skeptical. "But the Baron is famous for being able to infer things from the subtlest of hints. How could you have possibly kept all this a secret?"

The old man shrugged. "The Baron sails high above Europa in that floating castle of his. It's very easy to see things from on high. More than people comprehend. Patterns are apparent, if you know what to look for. But Mechanicsburg has always been an insular place. A lot of our business takes place out of sight. The town sits atop caverns and passages that have been explored and expanded for centuries. A lot more goes through them than what is seen by the light of day. Klaus might *suspect* that all is not as it seems," he conceded, "but the Baron is an outsider. Fooling him is a sport. More to the point, the Empire is big and we've never caused him any problems. We've even assisted him, once or twice. Klaus is focused on results."

"No one notices that you have an undue amount of influence around here," Krosp interjected.

The old man smiled. "Why, our family holds an important hereditary position. We are even honorary members of the City Council!" He fumbled about in an inner pocket of his vest and drew out a small, worn placard. "Here you go."

Agatha examined the ivory card. It had been carefully etched, in an impressive gothic script. She looked up. "Doom Bell Ringer?"

Wooster gave a snort. "It hasn't been rung in years."

"And a good thing too," Carson muttered as he replaced his card. He stared at Agatha and looked troubled. "But there are signs that business could be picking up."

Agatha looked around. "So I assume that you can get us into the Castle from here so we don't run into any of the Baron's people?"

"No, no," Carson said as he stood up. "I said the front door and I meant it. You'll go in chains, of course, like a normal person." He saw Agatha's expression. "Klaus uses convicts to work in the Castle. The troublesome Sparks and monsters that the Empire wants gone for one reason or another. It's a death sentence for most of them, and considering the people Klaus sends in, I don't think anyone weeps for them.

"But not everyone dies. Ostensibly they're there to repair the Castle, and a number of them get interested in the work. There's a system, with points awarded for dangerous work or good behavior and sometimes someone actually completes their sentence and gets out."

The old man caught up a lantern and lit it from the coal of his pipe. He waved them all to follow him. He activated another hidden door and they again descended a long winding staircase. Carson continued, his voice echoing back up the stairwell.

"It used to be that the prisoners were sent in every morning and taken out to a barracks every night. The idea was to let people see the Baron's justice at work or some such nonsense.

"Didn't work, of course. It just brought a lot of bad characters into town. There was a whole slew of bookies and other low-level trash who'd whoop it up right outside the castle gates—taking bets on who'd come out that day and so on. It made the whole town look bad. We started to lose the higher class of business.

"We were looking into a way to get rid of them that wouldn't have the Baron sending in the Questers when one day, without warning, the Baron himself suddenly had them all rounded up and marched into the Castle along with the prisoners."

Carson's grin could be seen in the darkness. "And none of them ever came out. Klaus never was very good at the subtle." He fished a large key from his belt and unlocked a small unobtrusive gate. He held it open while they all entered, then locked it carefully behind them. They turned the corner into a wide, relatively well-lit hall that sank into the darkness. Carson started down and continued: "After that, the prisoners were housed inside the Castle. No more coming and going. But they still have to eat, so supplies are sent in twice a week. And whereas the supply crew is thoroughly scrutinized when they leave, nobody really expects anyone to try to get in, or particularly cares if they do."

Zeetha nodded appreciatively. Agatha frowned. "But then, why are we down here? Surely the supply runs don't start here in the Crypts?"

The old man's snort of amusement wafted back. "No, we're here because you need to be told what to do once you get into the Castle, and believe me, I wouldn't do this for just anybody."

A softly glowing mimmoth skittered across Agatha's foot. She flinched but controlled herself. "You can't tell us this information anywhere?"

"I don't know it."

The implications of this sank into the group. Krosp voiced the obvious conclusion: "And the person who does know, lives down here? That's kind of creepy."

Carson reached the bottom of the stairwell and turned to face them. "Not a person," he said heavily. "Not alive."

Krosp raised his paw. "Creepy?"

"Hell, yes." The man grasped an iron escutcheon and gave it a twist. With a groan, a section of brickwork slid back and to the side, revealing another set of stairs, lined with upended crypts adorned with grinning skulls that, to no one's surprise, turned to watch as they passed by. Carson waved a hand. "Don't pay them any mind, you're with me." He paused. "I wouldn't dawdle, though." Everyone obligingly bunched up. Zeetha moved protectively to Agatha's side.

Wooster cleared his throat nervously. "Um…We're not going to meet some ancient undead Heterodyne vampyre or…or something. Are we?"

Carson spat. "Oh, and wouldn't *that* be the perfect capper to my day."

Wooster licked his lips. "That…actually that wasn't a 'ho ho, don't be *silly*, old chap, there's no such thing as vampyres down here.'"

"I ain't being paid to lie to you, Brit."

"You mean…"

"But that's not who we're looking for today."

The spy hunched himself down a bit. "You mean there are days when you do go looking for…them?"

"Didn't say they were *good* days."

"Oh."

Carson sighed. "Better than this, though."

Wooster glared at the old man. "I am done talking to you."

"I appreciate the effort, young fellow, but the day's already a loss."

"Aren't they great, ladies and gentlemen?" Zeetha said brightly, "They'll be here all week."

Agatha gave a snort of amusement.

"What *are* we looking for?" Krosp demanded.

They reached the bottom of the stairs and Carson spun a wheel, which brought the lights up. "This. The throne of Faustus Heterodyne."[25]

And indeed, what had at first appeared to be just a nest of dials and gears, was, if you looked at it correctly, a seat at the center of a tangle of cables and pipes that spread outwards every which way before burrowing into the walls, floors and ceiling.

Wooster let out a gust of breath. "There's no one in it."

The old man slowly removed his waistcoat. "Not yet," he confirmed in a hollow voice. "That's my job."

"I see I'm never going to learn."

Carson grinned and clapped him on the back. "Then you've learned something already." He turned to Agatha, who was examining a large bank of controls with great interest, "Your pardon, my lady, but… if you could assist me in the warm-up sequence? I'm supposed to do it myself, but…"

For the first time Agatha noticed that the old man was showing his age. The long climb and the task ahead had clearly taken a toll on him.

"You sit down. I'll take care of this." She told him. When he began to protest, she raised her voice. "*SIT!*" Involuntarily, the old man sat. "Now *you* rest, and tell *me* what to do."

A nearby chest contained oiled rags and tools, and soon enough, under the old man's direction, Agatha had the others wiping and tightening connections while she ran through an impressive diagnostic sequence that, while it told her that the machines were functional, failed to provide her with any clue as to their purpose. Occasionally she became so intrigued by the machines that she began to drift into a Spark fugue, but these were always short-circuited by Carson, who seemed to always know the right time to distract her.

---

[25]　Faustus Heterodyne has been rated as one of the stronger Sparks ever produced by the family. It was he who crafted the intelligence that inhabited and energized the Castle. Naturally, he used his own mind as a template, which pretty much explains all of the Castle's little murderous behavioral quirks, up to and including its unsavory love of weathervanes.

Carson saw Krosp looking at him after the third instance and shrugged. "It's a knack. You'll pick it up if you live long enough."

In a very short time, Agatha tightened a final screw and threw a large red lever. There was a faint crackling from within the depths of the device and with a groan, wheels began to turn and lights flickered on throughout the chamber. A faint whiff of ozone and burnt insulation began to fight with the smell of limestone. She turned to Carson. "I think that's everything. Did I do it correctly?"

The old man took a last pull on his pipe, knocked it against a girder, and climbed to his feet. "I certainly hope so. I haven't done this in a long time."

"Why not?"

"Because it *hurts*," the old man snapped. "A *lot*."

Agatha looked distressed. Seeing her face, the old man's expression softened slightly. "But mostly," he admitted, "because, up until now, I hadn't thought that any of the claimants that had wandered into Mechanicsburg had a chance of being a real Heterodyne."

Agatha absorbed this. "So what is it we're doing down here?"

"I'm going to let you talk to the Castle."

"And that hurts you?"

The old man nodded. "From down here? Yes. But no one else can do it."

"Why couldn't…say…Wooster do it?"

The British agent jerked in surprise. "Hold on—"

Agatha waved a hand. "Just as an example."

"Hold on—why me?"

"Because I'm curious."

The old man nodded and removed his cap, revealing the fearsome scars set in a perfect square upon his bald pate. His voice rang with pride. "Because *I* am the Seneschal of Castle Heterodyne. Because I'm the one with the special holes drilled into my skull and the sockets embedded there." He rolled his eyes: "Vanamonde should have had it done years ago. But…well, the Heterodynes were gone, and…" He shrugged.

Carson lowered himself onto a leather-padded seat, cracked with age and spotted with mildew. He gingerly drew a large, complicated-looking machine towards his head. Agatha could see that it was a helmet, supported by an array of counter-weighted arms that swung it easily into place. Four spring-loaded clamps were positioned roughly above the scars on the old man's head. His hands danced across the ancient control board, and with a final grimace, he snapped the last switch.

Instantly the four clamps flexed, driving the metal rods downward into his head with a sickening sound, and the old man screamed. The helmet crackled with electricity and the tubes began to glow. Carson sat stock-still, the only movement a faint trail of blood that slid out from under the helmet and slowly dripped off his chin. Agatha stared in horror and reached toward him, then stopped dead when Carson spoke.

His voice was odd. Dry and slow, as if it had bounced back and forth across great distances before finally finding its way out through the old man's pale lips.

"It has been four hundred and thirty-seven million, two hundred and fifteen thousand, three hundred and fifty-three seconds since this system was last activated," the old man whispered. Suddenly his head jerked to the side, causing everyone watching to jump back. A delighted grin spread across his features, and when he next spoke, his voice was stronger, but no less disturbing. "Why, it's still old Carson! And here he swore he'd never be back!" His head swiveled around and examined the group staring back at him. "He must be very certain indeed!"

He leaned forward. His hand jerked upward and unfolded, pointing directly at Ardsley Wooster. "So you think you're a *Heterodyne*, eh, boy?"

Wooster stumbled back a pace. "What? No! Not at all!"

The thing inside Carson's head paused, and then cocked his head to one side, as if it was listening to an unseen voice. "A *what*?" he asked querulously.

Agatha stepped forward. "I am Agatha Heterodyne. I am the daughter of Bill and Lucrezia Heterodyne."

Carson's body rocked back in its seat. Across the helmet, lights flickered between red and green. "A girl?" His head snapped back to Wooster. "This is a trick."

Wooster shook his head. "No."

"Really. *You're* the Heterodyne."

"No."

"You're just acting like a miserable, cringing lackey."

Wooster realized that he was, in fact, hunched back against a pillar—shying away from the malevolence he could feel radiating off of the old man. He straightened up. "No."

Carson's attention snapped back to Agatha and examined her minutely. Agatha felt a growing annoyance. The old man snapped his fingers. "You're really a man, but you like to wear women's clothing."

"*Enough*," Agatha roared, her voice spiraling into the harmonics of madness. "I am the Heterodyne! Now stop wasting time with this idiocy and tell me what I need to know!"

The entity inside Carson froze and then shuddered. "*The Voice*," he whispered. Lenses on the helmet spun as he leaned in and again the lights danced. "I believe you are the Lady Lucrezia's child. Heh heh—" A nasty grin twisted across his lower face. "But are you the Master's? We shall see…"

Agatha grit her teeth. "You certainly shall!"

The entity in the old man's body considered her again. "Hmm. The Heterodyne blood so rarely produces girls. The last one was—"

"Me," Agatha stated defiantly.

The old man's mouth twitched in amusement. "Perhaps. There are ways to tell, once you are inside." He raised a finger dramatically, "Fail—and you—"

"Yes." Agatha interrupted. "If I'm a fake, I die. I've been told."

The entity sat back. "Well," he said slowly, "maybe not. Or at least… not right away…"

Agatha blinked. "What?"

"You are a Spark, are you not?"

Agatha nodded slowly, "I am."

The entity sighed. "Then, girl or not, false or not, I am prepared to make a *bargain* with you."

Agatha stepped back. "A bargain? With you?"

She considered this.

Wooster cleared his throat. "It's not unprecedented. It made a bargain with the Baron."

The entity nodded. "See? And I did not even try to kill him."

Wooster rubbed his jaw. "Did he ever try to enter?"

"I grow tired of these foolish questions," the entity snapped. "There is an enemy inside the Castle. A false Heterodyne. She intends to destroy me. The very idea is preposterous, and yet—I fear that she may have actually have found a way."

"Wait—" Krosp furrowed his brow. "If she wants to prove to everyone that she's a Heterodyne, then shouldn't she be trying to *control* you? I thought that was the test."

"Indeed it is. But...heh...she has realized that control is not possible."

"Ah," Zeetha interrupted, "because she's not really a Heterodyne."

The entity paused. Agatha found herself suddenly convinced that there was something important that the...thing...wasn't saying. Finally, Carson's body shrugged.

"In part," it admitted. "But mostly because I am severely damaged. Wulfenbach's people have been trying to repair me for years. Overall they have failed, but still they have been useful. I have directed them where I could, and thus I am much more coherent than I once was.

"My central brain—the part of me that you are now speaking to—is isolated. My control circuits were severed in the explosion. It seems the power systems are largely untouched, so my secondary systems are running automatically—and they are *stupid*. Running at cross-purposes. *Fragmented*. You will get in and repair the break in the central control conduit."

Agatha nodded. "Ah! So there's a secret way into your inner keep?"

The entity paused, still grinning. "Hmmmm. I suppose that *would* have made things easier for you."

Agatha sighed. "Wonderful. So I will be going in through the front door."

"As all honest men should…"

Agatha ignored this. "Then tell me this: how do I evade these rogue defenses? I assume that there's a key or a code word or something that will let me progress safely."

The entity frowned. "Dear me, no. Foolishness like that is the sort of thing that can be exploited by enemies. I was constructed better than that."

"Well, I'd better have something more helpful than just your good wishes or it won't do either of us any good."

The entity nodded. "I…concede the point. Very well. I will give you the map."

Agatha brightened. "A map? A map that will show where I need to make repairs? Why, that's perfect!"

The entity waved its hands. "It is not here. You must get to it. This will be…difficult."

"Do you want me to help you or not?"

"This is the best I can do!" the entity roared. "Every instinct I possess is geared to keeping strangers out and away from the family secrets! If you are captured, I would rather be destroyed than allow them to fall into the hands of an imposter!"

"You're not making it easy for the real Heterodyne, either."

The entity leaned in. "A real Heterodyne will find a way. They always do. Get to the Masters' Library. There you will find the map you need."

Suddenly another voice was heard. "Sniveling sand-dragons! Is Carson actually hooked up to that brain-sucking abomination?"

There was a clatter of footsteps, and one of the young women from the coffee shop appeared, leading a tall old man. He was dressed in a rich outfit topped with a rather gaudy hat of office. It was obvious that he was an official of the town.

The girl spoke. "Lady Heterodyne, this is Herr Wilhelm Diamant. He's responsible for the transport and care of the prisoners in Castle Heterodyne."

The old man ignored them and stepped close to examine Carson. "Did you people force him into this?"

The entity grinned. "Carson von Mekkhan came to me freely, Herr Diamant. He truly believes this girl is the new Heterodyne," it chuckled. "Though he will never admit it."

"That old fool," Diamant snarled. "All the Heterodynes are dead!"

Suddenly Herr Diamant gave a shriek and Agatha saw him hoisted into the air by an assortment of clamp-like mechanical hands. Another set of manipulators, equipped with knives, many of them rusted but still quite sharp, swung into the light.

"You disloyal dog," the entity hissed.

Diamant shuddered and stared at the entity in terror. "No! I—"

"Obviously it has been far too long since you felt the Masters' displeasure!"

"Carson!" the old man moaned. "Call it off!"

The entity paused and then tittered. "I think you've annoyed him as well." A blade lazily began to spin as it edged closer to the trapped man.

"STOP!"

Everyone jerked in surprise. The blade pulled back. Agatha strode forward and confronted the entity face-to-face. "I am here now, and I'm telling—No, I am *ordering* you to let him go!"

The entity inside Carson snarled. "You are not the Heterodyne yet!" The blade spun faster and aimed itself towards Herr Diamant's eyes.

Agatha viciously slapped Carson across the face. "I say enough! I am the Heterodyne! You'll do what I say now—because if you ignore me and hurt him—then I will walk out of this room and find another way to stop these people!" She leaned in. "But that will take time. Time you don't have. They'll shut you down and you'll be dead, having utterly failed the Heterodyne family. Is that what you want?"

The effect of these last words was dramatic. The entity gasped as if punched and flinched at her final question.

"No," it whispered.

"Then release him," Agatha demanded.

The entity hesitated. "Can't I just…wound him? Just a little?"

"No!"

The entity slammed Carson's fist down in frustration. "Why not? He needs to be reminded who is his Master!"

Agatha wheeled about. "The only disloyal thing I see here is you! *Release him at once!*"

Carson huffed, "Fine! Have it your way!" With a snap, several manipulators opened and Diamant dropped to the floor. "Maybe I just won't kill anyone at all! How would you like *that*?"

Agatha ignored it and bent to help the old man to his feet. "Are you all right, Herr Diamant?"

The old man stared at her and clasping her hands in his, awkwardly dropped to one knee. "I am your loyal servant until the end of days, my lady," he declared fervently.

Behind them, the entity looked on with interest. *Ah, an unusual variant upon the Old Game.*[26]

Agatha addressed Herr Diamant. "So you can get me inside the castle without attracting attention?"

Herr Diamant nodded. "Yes, my lady. Give me your measurements, and I'll have a suitable set of clothes prepared for you. My cart is outside." He glanced at the others. "I shall see to it that your companions are safely settled until—"

"Wait," Zeetha interrupted, "We're going in, too."

"No!" the thing within Carson thundered. "*The Heterodyne must enter alone!*"

---

[26] Those unfortunate enough to be dragged before one of the old Heterodynes were usually subjected to a version of what we today would call "Good Cop, Bad Cop." However, considering the personalities involved, a more correct label would be "Bad Cop, Insanely Evil Cop." This was never a fun experience, especially when both sides were played by different personalities manifesting within the same body—and neither of them were actually playing.

Wooster cleared his throat. "Allow to me point out, sir, that the rules of your game have already been negated. The false Heterodyne entered accompanied by a full complement of retainers. In the interest of parity..."

"Several of the usurper's creatures are already dead," the entity said with evident pride. "The rest will soon follow. The Heterodyne must enter alone!"

Krosp folded his arms. "Nuts to you, you overclocked music box. You'll do what Agatha wants."

"That's right," Agatha said. "And I say I'm going in alone." This prompted an eruption of protest from everyone else, which was only silenced by the entity's voice raised in argument, apparently with itself.

"*No!* I want to tell her! No, I'll do it now. Now give it back! You never let me have any fun!" This ended with the seated figure gripping the metal helmet and wrenching it upwards. Carson gave a shriek of pain as the device slid free of his skull and several fresh rivulets of blood slid past his nose. The old man took a deep breath and then his eyes snapped open. A maniacal grin spread across his face.

"*AHAHAHAHA!!*" he cackled. "I win again, you wind-up pile of rubble!" The others looked at him suspiciously. Von Mekkhan's voice was shriller than before, with traces of the Castle still evident. Apparently the effects of the connection took a while to wear off.

Agatha looked concerned. "Are..." She glanced at the holes in the man's head. "Are you all right?"

"Of course!" the old man crowed. "The Castle can't hold *me*, by damn! That's why it's my job!" His hands snapped out and gripped Agatha's arms. "And you! You made it back down! Magnificent!" He gave another peal of laughter.

Agatha frowned. "You don't...*sound* all right."

The old man rolled his eyes alarmingly. "Oh yessss. So I've been told. Our contest is not pleasant, but it is *invigorating*! But don't worry, the effects will fade all too soon!" With that he dissolved into another bout of high-pitched giggles.

Agatha thought about patting him on the arm and then changed her mind. "Um... good. So, was there something you had to tell me?"

Carson stopped his laugher as if someone had flipped a switch. "Oh yes. I won, I get to tell you. Ahem. Lady Heterodyne!" The old man grabbed his hat and Agatha's arm and began dragging her back up the stairway. "We must get to the outer walls! An army is advancing upon the Black Gate!"

Gilgamesh stared out over the smooth, flat plain before Mechanicsburg. It was covered by a pleasant counterpane of neat fields planted with a wide variety of crops. Many of these were in their full summer growth, gently rippling in the breeze that skirled down from the surrounding mountains. It was a bit of an anomaly, really. Gil had studied a fair bit of civil engineering and had observed any number of towns as they underwent successive cycles of peace and strife. During peacetime, walled cities tended to expand. Secondary industries and agricultural stores would accumulate outside the city walls, along with the hovels of beggars and other squatters. Over time these temporary residents built more and more elaborate structures and engaged in practices that required the watch to be sent out often enough that it became a *de facto* part of the town. This was how towns grew.

But Mechanicsburg was different—as it was in so many other things. Inside the wall was a bustling, vibrant community, but once outside the walls, all was pastoral. Low hedgerows and farms stretched to the feet of the encircling mountains. The tallest structures were the evenly spaced picket towers standing quiet and deserted amongst the fields. The lower slopes of the mountains were covered in orchards, store houses, and obviously planned lumber groves.

Gil nodded in approval.

Behind him he could hear the shouts of the minions and mechanics setting up his newest creation. He had set them to installing it even before he had visited his father. A crackling hum and a burst of satisfied murmuring amongst the technicians let him know that the devices were beginning to be activated. Excellent.

He then turned to the spot from which there had been absolutely no sound at all.

"Captain Vole."

The huge Jäger stood painfully at attention. The parade-ground perfection of his stance only emphasized the disheveled state of his outfit.[27] "Sir," he began, "I—"

Gil cut him off. "—Did *not* bring me Agatha Heterodyne. Yes, I noticed."

"Sir. She attacked me, sir."

Gil ran an eye over the Jäger's outfit. "With a deadly coffeepot, apparently." He locked eyes with the Jäger. "Now, why would she do that?"

Vole opened his mouth. *"Because I tried to kill her, sir,"* was a poor excuse on any number of levels, so he closed his mouth.

"I told you to bring her to me," Gil reiterated, "and yet here you are, dirty, injured, and quite, quite alone. I've been told about you, Vole. I know what happened."

The Jäger let out a breath and waited for death.

"You went stomping in there and tried to arrest her, didn't you?"

Vole blinked. "I—vot?"

Gil nodded. "You underestimated her and she bested you! She's a Heterodyne! Doesn't that mean anything to you?"

Vole realized that whatever intelligence the young Wulfenbach had received about him, it hadn't been very good. "Yez," he ventured. "Hit does mean someting to me. Next time Hy vill be ready for her."

Gil turned away. "I doubt it. But it is no longer your concern."

---

[27]   As has been mentioned before, all Jägers develop little hobbies over the decades. Captain Vole had discovered the joy of meticulous dress. Thus the stain caused by Agatha's thrown coffee, along with the residue of the dung, offal, rotten vegetables, and other unsavory fluids that had been poured upon his unconscious form by the people of Mechanicsburg—who had long been itching to express their feelings about his betrayal— had found a perfect canvas.

"No!" Vole stepped forward. This chance couldn't be allowed to pass. "Hy vill get more troops and—"

"No." Gil was frequently grateful to his father for teaching him the art of cutting people off before their tirade could gather steam. "I had wanted you to bring Agatha here so I could help protect her. But considering how easily she beat you—" Vole's teeth ground together audibly—"I am forced to accept the idea that Agatha can take care of herself for a while. I'm not particularly happy leaving it at that, but apparently I have little choice." Vole twitched. "Right now the fake Heterodyne is the problem."

This idea was so surprising that Vole actually snorted. Gil cocked an eyebrow.

"Der kestle vill kill dot vun," Vole explained. "Probably already has."

Gil turned away and leaned his arms upon the battlements. "You think so? I don't. This is too well planned, so it makes no sense to go to all this trouble just to have this girl killed when she crosses the threshold.

"No, she has to have something up her sleeve if she is to get the Castle to legitimize her." Gil was quiet for a moment as he drummed his fingers upon the weathered stone. "Ideally she'd *control* the Castle, but our people have been trying to do that for years. It can be bargained with, but I think my father has done as much as possible in that direction…" He looked over at Vole. "I think it most likely that they'll try to kill it."

Vole frowned. "Kill der kestle?"

Gil waved a hand. "Well… shut it down. Make it safe."

Vole's lip curled with a perverted sense of hometown pride. "De pipple uf Mechaniksburg vould not ekcept dot as proof dot she iz a Heterodyne."

Gil nodded. "Neither would my father."

Vole paused and then admitted, "Not onless she danced nekkid through de ruins vile trying to shoot down the moon, turned all de tourists into feesh, and den built a very dangerous fountain out of sausages."

Gil's focus had derailed slightly at the image generated by "denced nekkid," so it took him a long moment before he was able to concede the Jäger's point and move the conversation forward.

"Let's assume that the dissenters aren't important. That the opinion of my father isn't important."

Vole looked skeptical. Gil soldiered on. "If the outside world believes that a new Heterodyne has taken control, then the schemers behind this fake Heterodyne girl might just pull this off."

Vole frowned. "This iz pointless. Yez, vhat der rabble uf Mechanicsburg tinks vould count for nottink outside der town. But dismissink hyu poppa—"

Gil nodded. A slight movement near the horizon caught his attention. "An excellent point. The only way it could work is if he was busy somewhere else when it all went down."

Vole considered this. "Right now he iz busy not dyink. Does dot count?"

Gil fished inside his coat and pulled out a complicated little monocular. He casually examined something in the distance. "I don't think that was part of the original plan," he admitted, "but now that it's happened, they'll be tempted by the opportunity. They'll want to capture him—have him under lock and key. Or, if they're smart, they'll want him dead. That would probably suit everyone much better, I'm sure."

Vole was ready to give up. "Hyu keep talkink like dese guys iz schmart. Dose clowns attacking hyu poppa iz as organized as a bag of fleas."

A smile lit up Gil's face. "Yes! 'Clowns.' That's the perfect word, Captain. Foolish creatures who exist to cause a distraction while the real players prepare off-stage."

Vole looked at him blankly. Gil sighed. Suddenly, the ground trembled with a sound like a distant explosion. "Never mind. Sound the alarm. The real players have arrived."

In the little outpost, Ognian screwed the telescope tighter into his eye. "Hoy!" he called to the others, who were lounging like cats in the sun, "Someting iz heppenink!"

Jenka opened one eye and looked at him suspiciously. "Dis had better not be anodder gurl takink a bath."

Maxim grinned and nudged Dimo in the ribs. "Hy dun tink ve gets dot lucky twice."

Dimo grinned back. Good times.

Jenka snagged the telescope and examined the distant town. "Hyu iz right," she said grudgingly. "Dere's pipple appearink all alonk der walls. Dey's pretty excited about someting."

Maxim's ears twitched. "Listen—iz dot der alarm gongs?"

Dimo shrugged. "Hyu gots der goot ears—but Hy ken see dot dey iz closink der gates!"

Ognian peered downwards. "Jenka? Vy iz Füst runnink avay?"

Jenka leaned over the rail in time to see her trained bear retreating over the hill. "He's vat?" A look of surprise flashed in her eyes. "*Get serious*," she screamed.[28]

Instantly all three of her companions snapped to attention but it was too late. A giant metal foot smashed the tower to bits around them, sending them flying through the air.

They crashed to the ground, bounced to their feet, and stared in amazement.

Five enormous spider-like clanks filled the plain. Each boasted five stout armored legs that rose and fell, sinking deep prints into the earth as they ponderously moved forward. Their hides were armor-plated. Each was topped by a colossal machine cannon. Arrays of exhaust pipes poured forth gouts of black smoke. A balcony of sorts girded each machine, and they could see squads of riflemen staring down at them in amazement.

Ognian was the first to react. "Hey!" he yelled. "Dey busted our tower!" He shook his fist at the machine as it majestically passed over them. "Who's gun pay for dot?"

---

[28] The Jägermonsters were created by the Heterodynes to serve as shock troops, reavers, and nightmare fodder. They are incredibly hard to kill and shrug off wounds that any other soldier would consider incapacitating. As a result, when not actually fighting, they tend to ignore what's going on around them. This occasionally leads to a nasty surprise when they realize that something is actually trying to eat them. However, at this point, all but the youngest of the Jägers was several centuries old, and at that age, any surprise is a welcome diversion.

Aboard the lead war clank, His Grace the Third Duke of some kingdom that technically no longer existed,[29] flashed his oversized teeth in a grin and adjusted his periscope. "Haw! We caught those fellows completely by surprise, General Selnikov."

Behind him, His Lordship, late of Balan's Gap, nodded. "Yes, *that* worked, at least."

The duke fiddled with the scope. "Why, those are Jägers!" He looked up hopefully. "Shall I let the men shoot them?"

Selnikov considered this and then shook his head. "No. We're still pretending that we want to do this without bloodshed."

The duke looked at him. "Oh," he said, pronouncing the "E." "But surely they don't count. They're Jägers."

"Anywhere else, perhaps. But this is Mechanicsburg. Never burn a bridge unless your foe is on it, Your Grace." Selnikov rubbed his fingers together. "Does the air feel odd to you?"

The duke sucked on his teeth. "Odd?"

"Yes…sort of…greasy…" Selnikov frowned. He'd felt nervous. He'd felt this sort of thing before—but where?

Atop the city wall, the side of an elaborate set of chimney pots shivered and then swung aside, revealing the head of a metal stairway. From the shuff of dislodged dust emerged Agatha, Zeetha, Herr Diamant, von Mekkhan, Krosp, and Wooster.

Zeetha looked around. "And where are we now?"

"Top of the outer wall," Herr Diamant informed them. "The old passages can take you almost anywhere if you take the time to learn them." He pointed to an ancient bank of steam-driven arbalests. "The old Heterodynes liked to operate the defenses personally." He started

---

[29]   You might think that—once their particular corner of the world went to the effort to reorganize itself so thoroughly that not only were they no longer expected to show up for work, but a large percentage of the people in the area would stop what they were doing to arrest and/or kill them—deposed royalty would do something sensible, like learn an honest trade or at least change their names. What they actually do is find some other court located somewhere with a healthy enough infrastructure to allow it to absorb a few dozen more of God's Chosen. That said, the host nation usually finds any number of exciting and extremely dangerous things for them to do.

walking and indicated a mass of rusted tubes topped by a corroded copper gargoyle, its mouth stretched impossibly wide. "The Baron disabled the controls to the screamer guns long ago, but if you'd like to take a look at them—"

Agatha interrupted, pointing to a group of men intent on a device that gleamed with polished glass and fresh grease. "Screamer guns? Is that what they're working on?"

Diamant shook his head. "Oh, no, that's something new."

Agatha was intrigued. From where she stood, the device looked like a sleek brass cylinder, mounted to the stone walkway by a set of heavy-duty ceramic insulators. Thick power cables looped off in both directions. As they watched, a worker in thick goggles threw a final switch and, with a crackle, a large glass dome filled with flickering tendrils of blue energy. The crew gave a small cheer as the man shut and bolted a final metal hatch. Only then, as they turned away and began gathering their tools, did they notice Agatha and her friends.

The man in the goggles stepped forward, stripping off thick rubber gloves. "Why, it's Herr Diamant, yes? We have all the supplies we need, thank you."

Another technician closed the cover on a steel box and carefully snapped shut the clasps before straightening up. "Indeed, we're done. We have just turned everything on." He waved his hand and Agatha now saw that another cylinder, with its own flickering dome, stood some distance away and another beyond that. Similar devices were spaced out atop the wall as far as she could see.

"What are they?" she asked.

Diamant looked embarrassed. "We're not sure. Some project of young Wulfenbach's."

The second technician leaned forwards and dropped his voice conspiratorially. "Don't ask us. But we've been unloading and installing them since he arrived this morning."

Further disclosure was cut off by the team leader lightly tapping the speaker on the head with a spanner. "Quiet, you."

Meanwhile Agatha's eyes had grown large. "Wait—you're saying that Gil is—"

"BATTLE CLANKS!" The shout came from Wooster, who had been looking outwards. "Huge ones!"

Everyone ran to the wall and stared out at the vast contraptions hauling themselves toward the gates.

Agatha clasped her hands together. "Magnificent," she breathed.

"They *are* here to attack us," Krosp reminded her.

"Yes!" she agreed. "I can't wait to see them in action!"

Herr Diamant smiled. "Well, that's encouraging."

Krosp stared at him.

The old man shrugged. "What? Her grandfather used to open the gates for things like this, just so he could get a better look."

In the Great Hospital, Klaus Wulfenbach stirred. Outside, a resonant, mechanical sound was building. Bangladesh DuPree gazed out the window. When Klaus spoke, she noticed that his voice was already stronger than it had been at breakfast. "Those are the Mechanicsburg Alarm Gongs. DuPree, what's happening?"

DuPree's shrug became a businesslike snap—knives appearing in her hands as the door opened. The knives vanished when she saw that it was only Dr. Sun.

"The city is under attack. An army of war-clanks. Coming up to the Western Gate."

Klaus glanced at the nearest window. "I should have a decent view from here. Get me—Ow!"

The exclamation came from Sun lightly tapping Klaus on the chest. "Oh, so that still hurts, does it?"

"Of course it hurts," Klaus snarled. "You know every pressure point and nerve cluster I have. I still have to get up."

He tried levering himself up from the bed. With a detached air, Sun tapped a muscle in Klaus's shoulder, and the Baron collapsed back, grimacing. "Sun—"

"You shouldn't move."

"I need to see what we're up against."

"You'll damage yourself."

Klaus snorted and waved a bandage-wrapped arm. "I doubt any damage I will incur will be worse than this, and if it is, I'm in no better place for it, now, am I?"

Sun looked at him and with a sigh, quickly detached the assorted drips, feeds, and catheters, taking care to do so in the most painful way possible. By the end of the procedure, Klaus was paler, but still determined. He thrashed about feebly and sank back onto his bed.

"There," Sun declared with a touch of satisfaction. "Are you convinced? You cannot—"

"DuPree," Klaus interrupted. "Get me to that window. No matter what."

DuPree nodded and gave Klaus a "thumbs up" signal. The Baron glanced at Sun. "I think you could construct a simple—" DuPree grasped the edge of the Baron's bed and tipped it over with a crash. The Baron blacked out briefly from the pain. This was no doubt a blessing, considering the agony he experienced when he awoke a few seconds later to find that DuPree was dragging him by his shattered leg towards the window.

Sun forced himself to remain still as DuPree jerked, pulled, and slammed the gasping man into position. This was not the first time that Sun had patched the Baron up, and Klaus was one of the worst patients he had ever had to put up with. While he himself would never do what DuPree was doing, he reasoned that there was a small chance that this might actually teach Klaus a lesson.

A final gurgle of pain signaled DuPree draping Klaus over the windowsill. She patted him on the back and his knuckles whitened.

"Th-th-thank you, DuPree," he gasped. "That should be the worst of it."

Sun stepped up. "Please stick around, Captain, you can haul him back."

Klaus's eyes rolled back up into his head.

Back on the lead war-clank, the Duke exclaimed in delight. "Oh, I say! Someone is coming out! To surrender, I imagine."

Indeed, at the base of the great ironbound gate, a small postern door had swung open and a single man stepped forth.

Atop the wall, Herr Diamant frowned. "That's not one of the City Council."

Ardsley Wooster took one look and felt as if the floor had dropped from beneath his feet. "It's Master Gilgamesh! He's here!"

Krosp's ears flicked forward with interest. He gazed at the five gigantic metal behemoths and then back to the single small figure striding out towards them. "Well. This could solve some problems," he opined.

Agatha felt her breath catch in her throat. "What is he doing? He's all alone! He'll be killed!"

Zeetha raised her eyebrow. "Oooh? And why do you care?"

Agatha's face went red. "Because... Because the Baron will blame me?"

Zeetha nodded with a small smile. "Oh. Of course." She patted Agatha's arm. "We'll just root for him then."

Agatha didn't know it, but she was on Gilgamesh's mind at the moment. He was growing uncomfortably aware that, for someone as smart as everyone insisted that he was, he could be just as idiotic as anyone else who wanted to impress a girl. Surprisingly, he took some comfort from this.

Occasionally Gil looked at the silly doings and squabbles of the people around him and wondered if he was actually a member of the same species. He knew that this thought probably hit most people at some time in their lives, but Gil had the added factor of having a father who could easily have made it a legitimate question.

Thus—on those occasions when Gil found himself doing anything that he had ever seen or read about that had made him roll his eyes at the foolishness of the human race—he made sure that he took a moment to cherish the experience.

He toiled to the top of a small hillock and craned his neck up at the lead machine that now towered over him. *I think this is worth about four seconds of cherishing,* he mused, *then I can go straight to terror.*

The faces of several dozen uniformed men peered down at him. A few of them uncertainly raised their rifles. At the sight, Gil felt a small wave of hope. Muzzle-loading muskets. Whoever had financed this expedition had spent all the treasure on the walkers and bought the soldiers whatever weapons they could find handy. No doubt they expected the town to roll over at the sight of the giant machines. This meant that if it came to shooting, as long as he could avoid the first volley, he had some chance of getting away before they reloaded.

Gil stood tall, checked his stick a final time, took a deep breath, and bellowed upwards, "What is your business here?"

Wooster felt a jostle, and turned. To his surprise, the tops of the walls were filling with people. Townspeople. They were pouring up the stairwells, grumbling and querulous.

"I say," he said. "What is this all about?"

Krosp leapt atop a chimney and looked around. Troopers were shepherding the townspeople along, steering them away from the machines dotted along the wall and keeping them facing the action below.

"Wulfenbach soldiers are forcing the townspeople up onto the wall," he reported.

"But most of the defenses aren't working," Diamant protested. "They can't do anything useful."

Suddenly Wooster had an epiphany. "They can observe." Wooster turned back to the scene outside the walls. "Someone wants everyone in town to see this." He swallowed. "And I believe I know who that 'someone' is."

"Gil?" Agatha looked horrified. "But…but what is he thinking?" As soon as the words were out of her mouth, her mind flashed to the devices Gil had positioned around the wall. Certain structural elements suddenly suggested intriguing possibilities. Agatha's eyes went wide. "Oh," she said quietly.

Zeetha's eyes narrowed. "Oh? What 'Oh'? You know what he's thinking?"

Agatha bit her lower lip. "He's thinking he's not the one in trouble."

Aboard the walker, the duke laughed. "B'god, they do grow them stupid here, what?"

"Be quiet, you idiot," Selnikov snarled. *Something isn't right.* Raising his voice, he answered the tiny figure below. "I am Rudolf Selnikov—a Commander of the Knights of Jove! I hereby take command of the Empire of the usurper Wulfenbach in the name of the House of Valois!"

The tiny figure below put his hands on his hips. Selnikov felt the floor drop out from beneath him. He knew—*knew*—that the foot of the person below was slowly tapping. *Why did he know that?* Gamely he soldiered on. "Surrender the town, the Heterodyne girl, and the Baron! Cooperate, and no one will be harmed!" *Well*, he silently amended, *no one anyone will care about.*

The person below nodded once. Selnikov felt sweat start upon his brow, then realized why he was so rattled. This young jackanapes was acting exactly like that devil Klaus would! The *impertinence*—!

"I am *Gilgamesh* Wulfenbach. Son of Klaus!" The voice calling up to him sounded annoyed. "I will say this only once! Leave now, or you will die!"

Selnikov had been exposed to the strange ways of Sparks on an almost daily basis for most of his life, and had nevertheless managed to live to a rather respectable age. He turned to order a retreat. But before he could do it, the duke beside him gave a snort. "Stupid and as mad as a fruitbat, apparently." He raised his voice. "A gold piece to the fellow who shoots this rascal!"

That was it. The muskets were popping and there would be no retreat. Only one possible way was left to get through this mess. "All guns!" Selnikov screamed. "All guns open fire! Quickly!"

"Use the artillery," Selnikov roared. "Fire the coil gun!" Around him soldiers were raggedly firing their unfamiliar weapons.

"Damnation," one swore as he tried to dig another ball out of the pouch at his belt, "I hit him! I *know* I did!"

Another cursed as he tried to aim. "The gyros are keeping us steady, but they're not keeping us *still*!"

Below them, Gil raised his stick. "Time's up."

There was an almost imperceptible *click*—and then the sky opened. A bolt of lightning struck the lead machine, briefly wreathing it in a veil of blue-white discharge before various things inside it exploded, adding to the earsplitting sound of thunder.

The machine stood still for a moment, then twisted and slowly fell to the side with a booming crash.

Several thousand mouths fell open and almost twice that many eyes bugged from their sockets. The first sound, aside from the slow pinging of the metal as it cooled, was Agatha's delighted scream of triumph as she stared entranced at the scene below.

Gil would have found this intensely gratifying, if he could have heard it, but at that moment he was wondering if he would ever hear anything ever again. With echoes of thunder ringing in his ears, he again raised his stick, its tip glowing brightly. He roared towards the remaining machines, "Anyone *else*?"

A moment of terrified silence ticked past and then shouts arose from the machine to the right of the smoking clank. "We surrender!"

A shower of weapons fell from the next machine over. "So do we!"

Still, there is one in every crowd. The third machine swung its mounted cannon about and let off a poorly aimed shot, which blew apart a patch of road several dozen meters to Gil's left. Again he raised the glowing stick. Again there was a click, and again a bolt of lightning crashed down and blew the machine to molten fragments.

As the legs crashed outwards, Gil strode forward. "This is not a *trick*", he shouted. "I did not get *lucky*! I am Gilgamesh *Wulfenbach*, and I am in *control*!"

High above the walls at the hospital window, Klaus watched the action outside the town, his face lit with an unholy glee that even DuPree found unnerving. "They're surrendering. Good!"

"Good?" Sun looked pale. "That was amazing."

Briefly Klaus appeared to relax. Muscles taut with tension released for the first time in years. "Yes. Yes it was." He gazed down at his son with undisguised pride, then snapped back to his usual tense self. "Get me back to bed," he ordered Bangladesh. "Quickly, before he comes back."

There followed a period of screaming that Sun tried very hard to ignore. When it was done, he turned back to find Klaus again stretched out in bed, white-faced and sweating but still with a ghastly grin on his face. Sun shook his head, and set about reconnecting the assorted drips, feeds, and hoses to his patient. He hissed at the messages that his reconnected meters began to display. "I hope it was worth it," he snarled.

Klaus grabbed his hand in a steely grip. "Anything," he whispered, "even being paralyzed for life, would be an acceptable price for seeing what I have seen my son do today." With that he released Sun's hand and collapsed backwards, eyes fluttering closed while he muttered, "He will *survive*."

And then, the Master of the Empire slept.

Atop the walls of Mechanicsburg, the presumptive mistress of the town was leaping and twirling in glee, while a growing crowd watched. Finally Zeetha reached out and grabbed Agatha by the sleeve, dragging her to a halt. "A little decorum?"

Agatha couldn't contain her excitement. "Did you see what he did? That was a logical extension of the electrified sword I built by modifying the electrical discharge system *he* showed me back on Castle Wulfenbach!" She took a deep breath. "It's an elegant demonstration of some of the underlying principles of our research!" she explained happily.

Zeetha eyed the two smoking ruins on the plain below. "Very elegant," she agreed amiably.

Krosp and Wooster were leaning over the battlements—peering into the chaos below. "Is Master Gilgamesh all right?" Wooster slapped the stonework in frustration. "I can't see!"

Krosp nodded. "Too much smoke from the burning machines. I can't tell."

Agatha looked stricken. "What? Of course he's all right!"

Wooster shrugged, uncomfortable in the face of Agatha's conviction. "Perhaps, but there *were* a great many shots—"

There was a crackling flare from behind them, and—with a muffled explosion—one of the mysterious brass cylinders erupted in a tower of flame. The technicians, who had left their tools to watch Gil's performance with the rest of the crowd, rushed back to the device as it deformed and then melted.

"But we *just* set it up!" one of the mechanics wailed. "No one was even *near* it!"

Agatha hissed in annoyance and turned around, searching. "Oh no," she muttered. "There goes another plume…three…" Pillars of smoke marked the locations of several of Wulfenbach's machines, with more of them erupting as they watched. Some of the mechanics responsible for them were in hysterics—others were carefully edging away, trying to blend into the crowd.

After a minute or so, it appeared that no more were going to combust, but Agatha still looked pensive. "I figure that at least half of them went up. Oh, dear."

Krosp looked at her. "You know what they are?"

Agatha shrugged. "I think it's fairly obvious that they're some sort of supercharged atmospheric ionization engines." She saw the cat's blank stare. "Well," she said unapologetically, "It's obvious to *me*."

Krosp still stared. "…So?"

Agatha sighed. "So if they are, then Gil used them to electrically saturate the air around Mechanicsburg. Thus he had access to a tremendous amount of potential power. But how…" She paused and gazed upwards thoughtfully. "Ah, of course! That walking stick! It must be some sort of focus—an aiming device!" Her voice began to take on the subtle harmonics Krosp now knew to listen for. "Very elegant," she murmured. "Oh, I have *got* to get a look at—" Krosp gave her hand a casual nip, effectively derailing her runaway train of thought. "*Ai!* Um—Well, he obviously didn't have time to test it. His concept is sound, but I suspect he didn't have enough engines to prevent the whole thing from overloading. There's an unbelievable amount of power in lightning, you know."

Krosp nodded. "So I see." He waved a paw towards the smoldering hulks. "But he can relax. These guys are surrendering."

Agatha bit her lip. "I sure hope so. Because without these engines supplying him power, his focus device is now useless."

The last of the walker crews lined up before Gil. He eyed them closely. There were close to two hundred of them. Almost evenly divided into engineers and marines, if he was any judge. A few of the ones with more braid on their shoulders looked at him with anger in their eyes. They were the ones he had to disarm.

He pointed to one of the more disgruntled-looking officers now. "You! You'll speak for these men. Do I have to do any more convincing?"

The officer looked at the young man standing above him, armed with only a glowing stick. He hesitated and his eyes narrowed. He opened his mouth, and from around him his men roared, "No! Spare us! We surrender."

With a snarl, the officer closed his mouth and nodded jerkily. "We surrender, sir," he said.

Gil nodded and twirled the stick in his hand. It gave a small 'beep' and the glowing tip faded out. Gil stared at it a second and then casually rested it on his shoulder. "That's good," he said honestly.

"You all know how the House of Wulfenbach treats captured soldiers," he continued. "You may join our forces and retain your present rank, or return home to your families with a month's pay, a full pardon, and an honorable discharge. Our troops will be here shortly to collect your arms. You have until then to make your decision."[30]

He gave them a minute to let the expected murmurs of relief swell and subside. "All I want is your Commanding officer!"

That stopped them. As a rule, even if they weren't festooned by several kilograms of gold braid, said officer was easy enough to spot. Either by all his men trying to shelter him—or by them all pointing at him. Klaus Wulfenbach had formulated set responses for both instances. This time, however, there seemed to be some genuine confusion. Several of the men tentatively raised their hands, but to Gil's educated eye, he guessed that they were the ranking officers aboard individual machines. Finally, he swung his head back to the disgruntled fellow he had noticed before, who—seeing Gil focusing his attention upon him—squared his shoulders and stepped forward. *Oh, yes*, Gil thought, *this man could be trouble.*

"Our commander was General Lord Rudolf Selnikov. You hit him with lightning, sir."

Gil nodded. That sort of thing happened. "Second in command?"

"His Grace the Third Duke D'Fisquay. You also hit him with lightning, sir."

Gil had met the Duke D'Fisquay while he was in Paris. Statistically speaking, the population of Europa was now slightly more intelligent. Still, it was inconvenient… "Third?"

"Engineer First Rank Niccolangelo Pollotta, sir. He was in the second machine."

This was taking too long. Gil sighed, "Fourth?"

"That would be me, madboy!" And then the officer was leaping forward with a dagger upraised. Gil saw it approaching—pointed at his throat—

---

[30]   This practice was one of Klaus's more radical innovations, and one of his most effective ones. It relied upon the simple truth that most of the soldiers in a rogue Spark's army were not there out of any great loyalty to said Spark but because they did not want to be turned into fish (or whatever). That said, there is camaraderie and comforting routine in military life that many young men enjoy, and the chance to be a part of the Winning Side has a strong allure. Thus the army of the Empire was one of the few in history that got larger with every battle it fought.

A stout throwing knife seemed to appear in the man's eye and he collapsed to the ground, twitching only once before lying still.

Gil became aware of people behind him, around him—wait—people?

"Hoy!" A green-skinned Jäger made another knife dance along the tips of his fingers as he addressed the shocked crowd of soldiers. "So who else vants to be promoted?"

Gil frowned. "I..." His thoughts were becoming disorganized. What was happening? "I could have handled that."

Another Jäger—a female—insinuated her arm under his. "Ov cuzz. Now lean on me all sobtle-like befaw hyu falls down."

Gil realized that this was good advice.

Atop the walls, the crowd was beginning to disperse. Agatha and her companions remained, searching for any sign of Gilgamesh. Wooster pointed at a double column of troops marching towards the city gate. Another squad, in the distinctive blue uniforms of the Wulfenbach infantry, was moving out to meet them.

"They're surrendering to the Empire's troops. I guess Master Gil managed to keep them calm." Wooster found that he was actually pleased about this. It was true that the Wulfenbachs were Britannia's most dangerous rivals but, privately, he put that down to the irreconcilable differences between the Baron and Her Undying Majesty, Queen Albia.[31] In his opinion, an Empire run by Gilgamesh would be easier for Her Majesty to deal with. Gil was more relaxed about certain things. Ardsley had been Gil's friend for two years, and his valet for six months. Aside from the job title, little had been different. He knew that things between them could never be the same as they were, but he did hope that they might, somehow, remain

---

[31] As has been mentioned before, Sparks tend to establish hierarchy. They are never comfortable until they know what the order of precedence in a particular situation is, as well as their place in it. Aside from the politics inherent in running two adjoining expanding empires, it would be safe to say that neither Klaus nor Albia were willing to relinquish primacy to anyone. The miracle was that they had never actually gone to war. Subsequent research has revealed that each Empire was waiting for the other (obviously weaker-willed) Empire to declare war first, in the mistaken impression that they would then have the choice of weapons. This was an idea promoted by a desperate diplomatic corps, who were constantly astonished that it actually worked.

friends. The necessary first two steps towards this brighter future would be both Agatha and Gilgamesh remaining alive.

Agatha scanned the smoking field. "But where is Gil?"

Krosp sighed in resignation. "He'll be back."

Agatha felt a tap upon her shoulder. Turning, she saw Carson, looking a bit more composed. It was obvious that the old man was a bit embarrassed about some of the things he had said while sharing his head with the spirit of the Castle, and he spoke with a stiff formality. "Now that we've all seen the show, we have to get you into the Castle as quickly as possible." With that he spun about and strode off.

They hurried to catch up. "Those fools in their machines were just the first. The Empire is weak at the moment and all the vultures will be on the move."

Agatha glanced back at the pillars of smoke coming from the shattered machines. "You think that'll be seen as weak?"

Carson grimaced. "No, that'll be seen as impressive. It'll make a lot of them think twice. But the Baron was defeated at Balan's Gap. A crack has appeared in the Empire's heretofore-impenetrable façade. A lot of powerful Sparks will see this as the best chance they've had in a decade!"

Krosp nodded, "A rebellion against the Empire, eh? Depending on who wins—"

Carson slammed his hand down on the stonework. "To hell with who wins! They'll come here to fight! Mechanicsburg will be caught in the middle. Our only chance to even have a town left at the end of this is to be a *player* instead of just the *terrain*. For that, we need the Castle up and running and a Heterodyne in charge of it." He looked Agatha in the eye. "Not just some fake who's playing her own game with the Empire. A genuine Heterodyne who cares about this town. If you *are* a Heterodyne, the best thing you can do is get the Castle repaired and running again—and as soon as possible."

Agatha absorbed this and nodded once. "All right." She turned to Herr Diamant. "Let's go."

Zeetha looked surprised. She pointed towards the battlefield. "What about your boyfriend?"

Agatha looked at her. *She's testing me,* she thought. "He's not my boyfriend." She held up a hand to forestall any argument. "Yes, I worked with him for a little while, and yes, we got along all right, and yes, I'll admit there's an attraction, all right?" The memory of a kiss warmed her face. "But that was before he knew I was a Heterodyne. Before *I* knew I was a Heterodyne. That changes everything.

"That…that Jäger back in the coffee shop? He may have been a Jäger, but he was wearing a Wulfenbach uniform and he tried to kill me. Was he sent by the Baron? Was he sent by Gil? Or by someone further down the chain of command? I just don't know.

"When it comes down to it, I don't really know him. I don't know if *anyone* does."

Agatha looked out at the devastated walkers and sighed. "But I do know that he can be dangerous. So I think it would be smarter to deal with the Empire—and him—from a position of strength." She looked back at Carson. "And being a Heterodyne and holding the Castle, well, that's the strongest position I can think of right now."

She sighed and waved a hand at the town below the wall. "If I am a Heterodyne, then this is my family's home. I have to fight for it, or at least do my best to keep it safe, because it's the only place where a Heterodyne can expect to be safe."

Zeetha punched Agatha lightly on the arm. "By Gwangi, I'll make a warrior princess out of you yet!"

Agatha slumped slightly. "Any time." Then she looked at Zeetha again. "Actually—" She looked slightly embarrassed and lowered her voice. "I mean, even if he does turn out to be a vicious madman out to pickle me, I… well, I'm still kind of worried about him. While I'm in the Castle, could you find him and make sure he's okay?"

Zeetha looked surprised. "Me?"

Agatha dipped her head. "The *Kolee* asks this of her *Zumil.*"[32]

---

[32] "Kolee dok Zumil." According to Zeetha: "Sort of like teacher and student…sort of like grindstone and knife." The contract and promise that bound the Lady Heterodyne and the Princess Zeetha together as teacher and student, among other things. At this time, Zeetha had just started the martial training of the Lady Heterodyne that would serve Agatha so well in later life.

Zeetha snorted. "Well, I *was* going to sit around in a café worrying about you, but—sure. I can take care of him."

Maxim and Oggie proved remarkably effective at herding the captured soldiers off the field and towards the gates—where the Wulfenbach troops waited to deal with them.

Dimo and Jenka kept Gil on his feet between them, without it appearing that they were propping him up. Gil acknowledged the Wulfenbach Captain's salute and waved him off to do his job.

"Hokay," Dimo said, a grin plastered across his face. "Now traditionally, hyu should stride triumphantly out uv de smoke and thru de city gates. But ve dun vant hyu spoilin' tings by passink out, hey?"

Gil looked at him with a frown that would have been more effective if the Jäger's face wasn't slowly receding. "I'm… I'm fine," he insisted.

"Hyu iz not, keedo," Jenka said quietly, "Hyu iz hit. Ve ken schmell der blood. But Hy dun tink hyu iz hit too bad."

Maxim strolled back. "Hyu poppa's troops vill finish op tings here. Hyu'd better come vit us."

Gil took a wobbly step. The Jägers looked at each other and gently raised him slightly off the ground and carried him towards the base of the city wall. "Wearing armor," he said with exaggerated clearness. "Not…totally insane."

Dimo kept his opinion to himself. "Hy dun see nottink on hyu head."

"She…they…needed to see that it was me."

Dimo considered this. "Vat hyu need is a big hat vit hyu name on it."

This statement caused Gil to focus on his rescuers fully. "Really? Wait… you…you're not Wulfenbach Jägers."

"Nope. Ve iz der goot lookink vuns."

Gil didn't even try to examine this. "Are you kidnapping me?"

Jenka laughed. "Nah! Ve iz on hyu side."

"That's good," Gil conceded. "Why?"

Dimo rolled his eyes. Alarmingly, he did it in different directions. "Hmf. An Hy vas tolt hyu vas schmot." He waved his free hand at Mechanicsburg. "Hyu iz defendink our town. Hyu fallink down in front of efferybody ain't goot for der town, or for Mizz Agatha."

That got through to Gil and he made an effort to straighten up. "Agatha? Is she here? Can't fall down in front of Agatha, no." It was only Jenka's grip that kept him from, in fact, falling.

"He's losin' it, Dimo."

The green Jäger scratched his nose. "Hokay, Hy tink hyu vant de 'mysterious disappearance after de battle' ending. A beeg hit vit de ladies, as lonk as hyu know ven to quit, if hyu know vat Hy meanz."

Gil had no idea what he meant. "Do you do this sort of thing a lot?"

"Ho! Yaz!" Ognian cried jovially. "Lotz of pipple have tried to take dis town! And somevun's gotta make shure de boss gets home aftervards."

Dimo saw Gil's head start to sag, and tried to keep him engaged. "Zo—iz verra nize of hyu to save miz Agatha's town for her."

"She's a very nice girl."

"Dot's right. Verra nize."

Gil stumbled again. When he regained his feet, his face was covered in sweat. "I feel…strange," he whispered. "I didn't think I'd been hit that badly."

Jenka reassured him. "Oh, hyu izn't hit too bad. But—" She looked at him shrewdly. "Iz dis de first time hyu faced down an entire army all by hyuself vit a weapon hyu vasn't sure vas gunna vork?"

"Well…yes."

Jenka gave a laugh. "Vell den! Dot's just hyu body bein' all sooprized hyu ain't all blowed op and dead!" She gave him a squeeze. "Next time, hyu von't eefen blink!"

"Next time…" Gil almost swooned at the concept. "I really think I have to lie down now," he whispered.

Dimo nodded. "Hyup! Vun 'mysterious dizappearance' comin' op!"

Ognian leaned in. "Hokay. Hy sez ve skulks in through de Sneaky Gate and takes him to Mamma Gkika's."

Maxim considered this. "I dunno if she gun like dot, brudder."

Gil waved a hand, almost sending both him and Jenka off balance. "Where? No, get me to the hospital."

Jenka yanked him back to true. "No vay, sveethot. Looks like ve iz kidnappink hyu a leedle after all. Ve dun vant no vun to see hyu until hyu iz stompin' around all scary-like again."

"No! My father must be guarded, and Agatha will be in danger! I can't stop now!"

Dimo snorted. "Hyu kent protect hyuself right now."

Ognian leaned in and gave Gil a light slap to the face. Gil's eyes focused on the Jäger. "Hyu vant to help Mizz Agatha? Den ve takes hyu to Mamma Gkika. She fix hyu op fast and goot."

Maxim leaned in as well. "Goot enuf, anyvay." So saying he bounded on ahead to the city wall that now loomed above them, and started rapping on blocks. Ognian hurried over and pointed at the sun overhead. The two got into an argument. Jenka gently deposited Gil against the wall, where he watched Ognian and Maxim with obvious confusion.

Dimo sidled up to Jenka and spoke in a low voice. "He likes Mizz Agatha. Hy ken tell. But Hy dun know if ve should trust him vit dis." He indicated the wall.

Above her scarf, Jenka's eyes looked resigned. "Ve gots a Heterodyne back. Voteffer happens, tings iz gunna change. I say ve takes de chance."

Meanwhile, Ognian had apparently won the argument. He strode over to a different set of blocks, gave one a rap, another a kick, and the section of wall behind Gil slid to the side, causing him to fall over backwards.

Ognian helped him up. "Sorry, keedo. De Sneaky Gate iz like dot."

Gil stared at the opening wide-eyed. "I know what a hidden door looks like. That was not there a minute ago."

Maxim shrugged. "Dun vorry about it. It von't be dere next time either." He stepped into the passage. "From here iz easy peasy!"

The wagon, perched upon one fat wheel, bumped and clunked down the Mechanicsburg street, its engine popping and chuttering. People saw it coming, recognized the chain-draped exterior, and stepped out of the street, dragging along the occasional clueless tourist. You didn't want to interfere with the Prisoner Van.

Herr Diamant sat at the controls, easily weaving past the remaining carts that trundled through the streets. He spoke into a brass tube that conveyed his voice back into the prisoner compartment, where Agatha was changing into a properly disreputable suit of clothes that Herr Diamant had given her.

"There are things you should be aware of," the tinny voice informed her. "The leather case by the door has your papers. They state that you're in for mass-poisoning."

Agatha interrupted. "Murder!"

Diamant chuckled. "People are not sent to Castle Heterodyne for stealing a loaf of bread, my lady. These are people that the Empire wants to go away.

"You must be wary. Most of the truly crazy ones die rather quickly. At the moment, there are two you should keep a particular eye out for, a fellow named Snapper, and another named Vasquez. They're the only really psychotic ones.

"Many of the others are Sparks. They might prove useful, if you can get them on your side. Especially the old-timers. Promise them amnesty, if you must."

Agatha was surprised. "I can do that?"

A bark of laughter came back through the tube. "Prove yourself the Heterodyne—hold the Castle—and there is *nothing* you can't do in Mechanicsburg."

Agatha considered this as she began fastening buttons. Diamant spoke again. "The red pouch? That contains a map that shows the current floor plan of the Castle. The areas marked in green are considered safe."

Agatha examined this. "There's not much marked in green."

"No," Diamant admitted. "The area in blue is the Main Library."

Agatha frowned. "I don't...I don't see any way to actually get there."

"It was never easy. The Castle itself will have to guide you there."

"Terrific." She sat down and pulled on the stout leather boots, and carefully did up the side buttons. "So, who's the Baron's agent in there? I'm sure he's got one. I would. I'd want to know as soon as possible if they found anything really dangerous or useful."

"Of course. That would be Professor Hristo Tiktoffen. He's a prisoner himself, but he's also the 'Man in Charge' once you get

inside. He maintains the records and helps keep the others in line."
The wagon juddered to a halt. "We're here," Diamant announced.

Agatha gathered up the rest of her supplies. "Have you found out
anything else about that false Heterodyne girl that's inside?"

Diamant sighed. "No. But remember, your very existence is a
threat to her, so assume that she'll try to kill you. I'd recommend
avoiding her at all costs." He lowered his voice. "Don't forget to put
your manacles on, my lady."

Agatha found the steel cuffs and, with only a touch of hesitation,
snapped them around her wrists. They were connected by about
ten centimeters of chain. Agatha took a deep breath. "All right, I'm
ready."

Diamant made a show of throwing open the door and calling
out loudly. "We're here. Move lively! Unload those supplies!" He
indicated a pile of boxes and sacks that contained foodstuffs.

As Agatha loaded them onto a small hand truck, a Wulfenbach
guard hurried up.

"Herr Diamant! You can't send someone in today! That damned
Heterodyne girl is in there—"

The old man sniffed. "Just another imposter. She won't last and the
others still have to eat." He hooked a thumb back at Agatha. "Besides,
we want this one off the streets." Agatha glared at the guard.

Diamant pulled a thick ledger off the wagon seat. "But if you don't
like it, do feel free to go over my head. The Baron himself is here in
the hospital, I'm told. I'm sure he wouldn't mind if you went and
asked him about it."

"Aw, go kiss a construct," the guard grumbled. "Fine. Send her in
then."

Diamant shrugged and offered the man a pen. "Very wise, I'm
sure. Sign here, please."

The guard laboriously made his mark and Diamant snapped the
book shut and retrieved his pen. Then he turned to Agatha and all
the warmth left his voice. "Here you are. Take this load to Professor
Tiktoffen. He'll unlock you when he's checked you in and explained
the routine."

Agatha just glared. Diamant sighed. "You're being given a chance. A final chance, and more than you deserve, no doubt, but the Baron sees something in you, so a chance you'll have. Watch your back, work with your fellow prisoners, and good luck to you."

"Try to escape," the guard said with relish, "and I'll shoot you like a dog."

Agatha picked up the handles of the hand truck and tried to look tough. "Fine. Can I get going now?"

The guard waved her towards the gates. Agatha was interested to note that the "Front Gate" was actually a row of gates of varying sizes, from a small postern gate all the way up to gates the old Heterodynes could have passed siege engines through. To Agatha's shock, the towering, intricately carved central doors were faced with solid gold. It spoke volumes that the gold was untouched.

The door that she was herded to was smaller than any of the main gates. It was constructed of ironbound wood reinforced with rows of iron studs.

"Hoy! Castle!" the Guard called out. "Open up! The Baron has sent a new prisoner for Repair Detail."

There was a pause, then—with a groan—the gates swung open. They were thicker than Agatha had first supposed them to be, and instead of mere wood, she saw that they were full of dense mechanisms. When they touched the wall to either side with a dull *boom*, a sibilant voice—similar to the one that Agatha had heard in the crypt—echoed forth. "Enter."

Unhesitatingly, Agatha steered her cart through the doors into the darkness beyond. As soon as she cleared the lintel, the doors slowly swung closed and locked behind her with a deliberate series of clunks.

Outside, the two men watching turned away. The guard wiped the cold sweat from his forehead and leaned on his rifle. "It still gives me the spooks when it does that," he confessed.

Herr Diamant glanced back at the door and sighed. "Young man, you have no idea."

CHAPTER 4

THE STORM KING

An opera in three acts by Portentius Reichenbach.
*A Brief Overview Provided as a Courtesy to Our
Patrons Who, For No Doubt Very Good Reasons,
Were Late Or Simply Not Paying Attention.*

⚜

The First Act begins in the pass of *Balan's Gap* as the *Army of Atrocities*, led by *Bludtharst Heterodyne*, is fought to a bloody standstill by the *Coalition of the West*, led by *Andronicus Valois*, who is hailed as *The Storm King* in the unforgettable *Hammerhead Chorus*.

After the famous comic interlude wherein the maid *Capezia* steals the shoes, and the Coalition receives the blessings of the *Five Good Emperors*, in the haunting *It Has All Happened Before, But It Gets Better Every Time* roundelay, Andronicus witnesses the beautiful Heterodyne Princess *Euphrosynia* being menaced by the mad sorcerer—prince *Ogglespoon*, a Heterodyne ally whom her father wishes her to marry.

The highlight here is the scandalous-for-the-time *How Dast You Duet*, which caused almost a quarter of the men attending to faint at its premiere performance in Munich.

Andronicus falls madly in love with the Princess but is tormented by second thoughts which are raised by his dour, two-headed construct servant, *the Brothers Polyphemus*, in the cunning and occasionally terrifying *What Could Possibly Go Wrong* dance number.

These trepidations are dispelled by the haunting *Prophecy Aria*, in which the *Spirit of Europa* herself foretells that peace will only be achieved when the Storm King and the Heterodyne Princess are wed.

The Second Act begins as Europa's prophecy is conveniently echoed, for those who were visiting the concession stand, by the *Nine Muses*, who say the same thing, but use different words, in the groundbreaking *You'll Only Hear What You Want To Hear Chorus*.

The scene then changes to Prince Ogglespoon's Castle, where the forced marriage is already in progress.

It begins with the infamously bawdy Jägerchorus and the tune *She Dun Gotta Be A Lady, She Iz Gunna Be Hyu Wife*, (which can be heard in taverns and public houses to this day), as they celebrate the upcoming wedding.

This is followed by the intricately choreographed *Rescue Dance*. In its most recent performance by the Vienna Mechanikopera, the company has hewed to the original chorography, and thus utilized all seventeen soup waiters, three ladder teams, and the original roller-skating giraffe, which had only been recently rediscovered in a barn in Essen. We are grateful to the Vienna Mechanikopera for lending us these props under the condition that "we never have to see them again."

The scene again changes, to the interior of the Storm King's legendary Steam Palanquin, where we are treated to the tender *Lover's Duet* between Euphrosynia and Andronicus.

In a letter to his sister, Reichenbach reveals that he got the idea for this song by listening to the mating call of the Irish Elk while on a trip to Dublin. It is a performance known to test the vocal range of any performer.

Finally, we have the heart-wrenching *Abduction Adagio*, where Euphrosynia is stolen away by a vengeful Prince Ogglespoon, who traps the Storm King in the infamous Bonsai Hedge Maze.

As the Second Act closes and the thunder rolls, the Storm King makes his famous vow, to search for Euphrosynia forever with the heart-wrenching aria, *Nothing's More Important To Me and I've Got the Empire to Prove It*.

In the Third and Final Act, we shall see how that vow brought about the tragic end of the Coalition of the West, the Knights of Jove, and the Storm King's reign itself.

—The Mechanicsburg Opera and Musical Debating Society gratefully acknowledges Professoressa Kaja Foglio, who has graciously allowed us permission to use excerpts from her book: *It Is Not Over Until The Fat Lady Explodes—A Helpful and Concise Synopsis of Ten Operas That Deal With The Spark*. (Transylvania Polygnostic University Press)

❦❧

As the great doors closed shut behind her, Agatha felt a shiver run down her spine. A smaller series of booming clunks caused her to turn—just in time to watch intricate mechanisms built into the doors snapping into place. She was in, and no mistake.

The wide hall was lined with brooding stone statues—giant armored knights with animal heads that leered down at any tiny mortals who dared enter.

Red lights were artistically placed as if to maximize the drama of the statues' looming shadows. To Agatha's eye, these looked remarkably like the danger lights that would come on in one of Doctor Beetle's labs when something had gone terribly wrong. This did not add to her peace of mind, but Agatha guessed that serenity would be in short supply until she got the Castle repaired.

She noticed a faint movement in the shadows, and stopped. "Hello?"

"You have got to be kidding me!" From around a pillar oozed a young man with mean-looking eyes and a terrible scar that carved his mouth into a permanent sneer. "They actually sent someone in today? Well. Lucky me." He strolled on over. "So let's see what you've got on the cart, there."

Agatha pulled the cart back slightly. "You have the key to unlock these shackles?"

The young man waved a hand dismissively. "Nah. But I gotta check it for—"

"Anything I'm stupid enough to let you steal? I don't think so. I'm not going to start out my time here by getting in trouble with the management."

The young man gave her a nasty little grin. "Heeyyy—don't be like that. You're gonna need friends in here."

"I'm glad you're friendly. Now where can I find someone in charge?"

This was evidently the wrong thing to say. "In charge?" The man snarled, and pulled a sharp-looking punch knife from somewhere in his clothes. "Right now that would be me, you cow! You see anybody else in this room?" He stepped forward. "Now, if you're lucky, I'll be the Guy Who Lets You Live."

Agatha frowned and rammed the heavy hand truck into the young man's shins. He screamed and fell to his knees. "You filthy harpy," he howled. "I'm going to—"

Agatha rammed him again, smashing him to the ground. "My leg!" he squealed. "You broke my damn leg!"

"I doubt it," Agatha said coldly. "I got decent grades in my anatomy classes. You'll probably just have a nasty bruise for awhile."

For a heartbeat, she was at a loss as to what to do next. Then she remembered her time onstage. *How would the villainous Lucrezia Mongfish handle this?*

She kicked the punch-knife away and placed her boot solidly on the side of his neck. "Now this…" She leaned forward a little, putting her weight into it. The man froze. "*This* could seriously mess you up. But it's the least of what I'll do to you if you screw with me again. Do you understand?"

"I—I—"

Impatiently, Agatha leaned in again, harder. "Yes!" he shrieked. "I understand!"

Agatha removed her boot and the man scrabbled away on his hands and knees, not even taking the time to climb to his feet before he was out of sight.

That was disturbingly satisfying, Agatha realized. This troubling train of thought was derailed by the sound of slow clapping from behind her. She was so caught up in the whole 'performance' mindset, that she almost took a bow before she caught herself.

"Nice!" The voice belonged to a diminutive girl clad in an orange coverall. She had a shaggy mop of pink-tinted hair, a set of mischievous eyes, and a huge grin, with a distinct gap between her front teeth.

She straightened up from the wall she had been leaning against and sauntered over. On her way, she stooped to pick up the punch-knife. She examined it and gave a dismissive snort. Agatha flinched as she tossed it onto the hand truck. "That's yours now, if you want it. Right of conquest." She stopped about two meters away from Agatha and examined her with open curiosity. "I'm Sanaa Wilhelm. Nice to meet you." She stuck out her hand. Agatha made a snap judgment and shook it. Sanaa nodded.

"Well, now that you've wiped your feet on the doormat," she hooked a thumb in the direction of the vanished man, "Welcome to Hell. You are—?"

Agatha realized that she hadn't even considered a false name. "I'm…Pix."

If Sanaa noticed the slight hesitation, she chose to ignore it. Agatha continued, "Do I have to fight *you* now?"

Sanaa laughed. "Nah, that's a boy game. In here, we girls stick together. 'Play fair, do your share, and we're there.'" Then her face got serious. "If you don't, you'll be dead soon enough. It's real easy to wind up dead in here. People do it all the time. You got any problem with that?"

Agatha shook her head. "It's a better deal than I got out there."

Again, Sanaa flashed a grin and patted Agatha on the shoulder. "Ha! Knew you was smart! Knew it when I saw you! Now, you're new, so you got kitchen duty." She sighed in resignation. "I don't suppose you can cook?"

Agatha nodded with confidence. Old Taki, the circus cook, had cheerfully shared several of his "secrets"—tips on feeding large groups of hungry people, many of whom had knives. "I can cook. It's just chemistry."

Wilhelm brightened. "Really? Oh gosh, we need a good cook! The guy doing it now's a mechanic, and he's a complete idiot. I'd rather eat his engines!"

"If you're really good, you might not have to do any repair work at all! I mean, you'd be stuck in the kitchen all day…but still, it's a pretty sweet deal."

Agatha frowned. The last thing she wanted was to be confined to the kitchens. She wanted to be out and moving as quickly as possible.

Wilhelm continued. "So—what did you do to wind up in here, anyway?"

Agatha gave her a sardonic grin. "Poisoned thirty-seven people who complained about my cooking."

Wilhelm just looked at her for a moment, then changed the subject—going into the details of the worker's routines and the location of various facilities. "And we girls all bunk together. That way we can watch out for each other."

Agatha nodded in approval as Sanaa continued. "So, we all eat twice a day, both at six—"

Agatha realized what was disturbing her. The complete blandness of what Sanaa was talking about. She interrupted. "This is all everyday stuff."

Sanaa looked surprised. "Well…yeah. In here, the routine stuff is what keeps you going."

Agatha waved a hand. "Okay, but didn't a Heterodyne girl—?"

Sanaa's face soured. "Oh. Her. Yeah, she's here. She's holed up with Professor Tiktoffen. You'll meet him." Her eyebrows went up. "Oh wait—I get it! You think she'll fix the Castle and turn off all the deathtraps and la, la, la! We'll all go home in time for supper!" She snorted. "Well, forget it. People've been working on this man-eating trash heap for years. And she thinks she's gonna waltz in here, snap her fingers, and be the new queen? Shyeah.

"I been in here too long. There's no easy way out. Just in." Suddenly she whirled upon Agatha and leaned in. "But…and you gotta know this…I did see someone get out. Just once, but I saw it. She was smart. Collected her points, played the game, and walked out free. She did it. You can do it. Just like I'm gonna do it." Her eyes darted up into the shadows and her shoulders hunched slightly. "Just as long as this place don't get mad at me first."

They walked quietly for a while, leaving the entry corridor and stepping into a larger passageway. Boxes and bales of supplies were stacked against the graffiti-covered walls. Agatha couldn't help but read some of it as she passed by. Most of it railed against the Baron, the Castle, various magistrates, or just fate in general. There also seemed to be a great deal of wanton destruction. Entire walls looked like they had been smashed with hammers. Sanaa saw the direction of Agatha's gaze.

"Most of the Castle is alive. You might've heard, but I'm telling you, you really don't know what that means, yet. This area is one of the few that…isn't. It's just a building. So sometimes, when you want to smash the whole place down, this is one of the few places where it's safe to just go nuts."

She must have seen a touch of disapproval upon Agatha's face. "You just wait until someone you like gets squished, or you've been grinding away on some pointless job for fourteen hours because if you stop, *you'll* get squished. You wait until you been in here a couple of years and you wake up and realize that you're probably going to die in here and that you'll do anything to not get assigned to the Room of Rust and Hooks, or maybe you're just shaken because the new kid you've been explaining things to trusted you and got killed doing what you told her to do. Something you've done yourself. Something you've done a hundred times before. And that's if you're lucky. You just wait and see. You'll be taking a hammer to that wall before the month is out."

Agatha said nothing, which was, apparently, the correct response, because when Sanaa next spoke, she seemed her previously cheerful self.

"We're almost at the kitchen. That's where they'll take those shackles off."

"So why don't the Old Timers want this 'cushy job'?"

Sanaa started with a touch of guilt. "I knew you was smart," she muttered. "Okay, there's a reason they make the newbies do it," she admitted. "No one wants it. The kitchen's a Live Room. Now, nobody's ever been killed in there, which is, frankly, kind of weird. We think it gets more pleasure just messing with us, and whatever deal it made with the Baron—well, it knows we gotta eat. Anyway, it's so annoying, it gets to the point where you'd rather face death somewhere quieter."

Agatha considered this. "You're putting me on."

Sanaa gave her an honest grin. "Ha! Oh, don't you worry, people will have you fetching devil dog chow and left-handed trilobite tighteners soon enough!" She paused. "Go along with the first one or two of those, by the way. You'll fit in better. But if you get suckered more than four times, you'll be everybody's little minion." She looked at Agatha. "You don't look like the kind of person who wants that."

Sanaa stopped outside a doorway. "Okay, here's the kitchen, and here's our lousy cook." She raised her voice. "Hey! Moloch! Supplies are here."

Agatha froze in horror at the name—and, indeed, it was her old acquaintance Moloch von Zinzer whose head popped around the corner.

It was Moloch who had first brought her to the attention of the Wulfenbachs. Indeed, it could be argued that he was the one person responsible for everything that had gone wrong for her lately.

When Agatha first stumbled across them, Moloch and his brother Omar had been a pair of itinerant soldiers—remnants of a small private army that had challenged Baron Wulfenbach and lost. It said a lot about Europa at this time that they were unremarkable for that.

They had wandered into the town of Beetleburg, where Agatha had been living for the past eleven years, and had robbed her. They stole the golden trilobite locket she had been told to never remove—the strange mechanical locket built by Barry Heterodyne to keep Agatha's mind suppressed and far from the brilliance and madness that would identify her as a Spark.

The device in the locket—with its mind-deadening effects—had quickly killed Omar. Moloch, believing Agatha to be responsible, had sought her out to extract revenge. But Agatha's Spark had already begun to manifest and—in the subsequent confusion that nearly always follows a Spark's breakthrough—both she and Moloch had been captured by Baron Wulfenbach. Eventually, she had managed to escape. Apparently, he had not.[33]

He had no love for Agatha, and, indeed, would probably relish exposing her, leaving her trapped in the castle, short-shackled to a hand truck. This would reduce her chances of success to almost nothing.

Desperately she tried to think of a way out. Moloch saw the two women and his eyes widened. His jaw dropped and the mug he held in his hand slipped, spilling hot liquid down his shirt. "Sanaa!" he breathed.

He suddenly gave a yip of pain as the liquid began to soak through his shirt. He looked down. "Oh, no! Let me get a towel!" He turned to go and smacked into the doorjamb. Dazed, he turned to them, a crazed smile upon his face. "I'm…I'm okay! I'll just use my apron! That's what it's for! Yeah!"

He raised the apron in his hands and brought it to his face. Unfortunately, he had neglected to put down the mug, so the rest of the scalding liquid was sloshed over his face. He screamed from behind the apron and flung the mug away.

It hit an obviously handmade shelf loaded with dishes and bounced back onto his head. Moloch snagged it out of the air. He turned to the two appalled women with a triumphant grin upon his face. "Ha! See? It didn't even break!" Then the shelf fell over onto him, burying him in a heap of shattered crockery.

---

[33]   A more exhaustive and entertaining relating of these events can be found in our first textbook; *Agatha H. and the Airship City*. Reading this is not mandatory, of course, unless you wish to pass our course.

Agatha and Sanaa stared at the still form for a moment, then Agatha leaned in. "Do you think he's—"

Sanaa rolled her eyes. "Smitten with me? Yes, I know. It's amazing we get anything to eat at all, really." She sighed. "He'll be fine when I'm gone, or so I'm told."

She stepped over to Moloch, grabbed a handful of his hair, and hauled his head up. "I don't have time for this. I have to get back to work." Moloch stared at her blankly. Sanaa spoke loudly. "Pay attention, fool." She pointed at Agatha. "New. Girl." She gave his head a shake. "Unlock her!"

Moloch blinked. "What?"

Sanaa rolled her eyes. "New girl! Shackles! Get key!" Moloch continued to stare at her wide-eyed.

Sanaa gave a small scream of frustration. "Don't keep me standing around here or I'll smack you—"

That did it. "Yes!" Moloch began thrashing about on the ground like a fish. His hand dived into various pockets. "Yes! Key! Right!" he babbled.

He produced a shiny key. "Ha! Here! See?"

Sanaa plucked it from his hand and turned her back on him to open Agatha's cuffs with a quick twist and snap. "Well, thank goodness for that," she muttered.

She wheeled back and caught Moloch rising onto one knee. She grabbed his face and squeezed his bearded cheeks until his eyes bulged. "Now pay attention. Here is key!" She waited until Moloch took it and repocketed it. "Good! Now I will tell the Professor she's here. She says she can actually cook, so show her where everything is, then let her get started. Got it?"

Moloch nodded as much as he could. Sanaa let him go and straightened with a sigh. "That should do it." She turned back to Agatha. "See you later, Pix, I got work to do."

"Thanks, Sanaa."

The girl waved as she turned to go. "No problem. Just fix us something edible for a change." She paused and than turned to Moloch. "And you taste everything she cooks, okay?"

She gave Agatha an apologetic shrug and trotted off.

The two stared after her for a moment until she turned a corner and was gone. Moloch sighed. "Isn't she wonderful?"

Agatha looked at him sideways. "Yes," she admitted. "I like her already." Tentatively, she put a hand on Moloch's arm. "I…I don't know your reasons, but I really appreciate your not telling her who I am."

Moloch blinked and looked at her in surprise. Then he actually registered who she was.

Then he screamed.

The so-called "Sneaky Gate" was a narrow tunnel through the city walls. It went on for several meters in solid blackness after the door they had come through slammed shut behind them. Finally, Oggie, with Gil over one shoulder, pushed a half-sized door open and led Dimo and Maxim into a tight alley. Maxim looked around and smiled. "Hokay! Ve iz close by dis time!" He began to lead the way out of the alley, and nearly plowed straight into Captain Vole. The Jägers stared at each other in surprise. Maxim reacted first, his face breaking into a huge grin. "Vole! Hyu olt veasle-eater! Hyu iz schtill here!" His eyes glanced upwards. "Und dot iz a mighty fine hat!"

For just a second, a smirk rippled across Vole's face—then he erased it with a snarl. He turned away and saw Gilgamesh.

"Master Wulfenbach! Hyu iz injured!"

Gil struggled to get to his feet. "Yes…a bit…"

Vole sniffed. "Hy ken schmell de blood and it iz hobvious dot hyu iz about to collapse." He snagged the young man's hand. "Hy vill get hyu to de hospital."

"No! Wait!" Gil tried to resist, but found himself pulled effortlessly along. "You're correct! I do need to rest, but if word gets out that I'm injured, everything I just did out there will be pointless. If there is another attack before I can make repairs to the lightning rod—"

This stopped Vole dead. He turned around. "Hyu lightning schtick is broke?" He considered this and a slow grin spread across his face. "Den anodder attack vould be a goot ting."

Gil shook his head. "No, you misunderstand, my machines are broken—"

"Hy onderschtand perfectly. De two Heterodyne gurls iz both beeg trouble for hyu poppa. Hiff dere iz anodder attack, den de castle ken be destroyed, both gurls killed. Hit vill be verra sad—" He chuckled. "Ve vill get hyu poppa beck into hiz big airship, and from dere ve ken deal vit de…repercussions. Yez, hit vill all vork owt just fine."

A hiss diverted his attention from his musings. Jenka was practically vibrating with rage and the other Jägers were glaring at him with an ice-cold fury.

"So it iz true." Dimo said. "Hyu are no longer a Jäger."

Jenka pointed at Gil. "Ve iz gunna tek dis guy someplace safe und help protect der town and der Kessle and der family, as ve swore to do. Stend aside."

Vole sneered, releasing Gil and standing tall. "Devoted slaves to de last. Hyu dun ondershtand. Efferyting has chenged! De family iz dead and hy intendz to keep it dot vay." He glared down at them. "Vich of hyu iz gunna shtop me?"

"Oh, that would be me." The voice from behind caused Vole to spin in such a way that Gil's flying kick met his jaw perfectly, sending him slamming into the wall. He crumpled to the ground and stared up at the younger Wulfenbach in surprise.

"What do I have to do?" Gil asked the air around him. "I just took down an entire army of war clanks and I'm still being treated like a halfwit child!" He pointed at Vole. "Now you listen very carefully. The Heterodyne girl is not to be harmed. I won't allow it!"

Vole cocked an eyebrow, and then launched himself, snarling. "Hyu jabberink veaklink!" He swiped at Gil with a clawed hand that, if it had connected, would have knocked him back several meters. He seemed surprised when the younger man merely pirouetted like a dancer and sighed.

Vole screamed, "Hy vill keel hyu! Vill be onfortunate accident! Hyu poppa vill stitch hyu back togedder vitout de schtupid bits!" Then he lunged.

Again Vole missed, but this time, as he sailed past, Gil grabbed the back of Vole's head and added his own strength, sending the Jäger face-first into the wall. "I keep trying to be reasonable." Gil muttered. "To be fair." He deflected another attack. "I try to *talk* to people."

Vole made another charge, which Gil stepped quickly into. He gripped Vole's tunic and tossed him over his shoulder. Vole crashed to the ground on his back—hard. "And no one ever takes it as anything other than weakness!" Gil finished.

Vole raised his head and shook it. Gil looked down at him. "You listen to me trying to be civilized, and you all think, 'Oh, he's nothing. Him, we can ignore. Him, we can push around. We can do whatever we want—he won't be able to stop us.'"

He turned away. Vole flexed his back, sprung to his feet with a single movement and, screaming, launched himself at Gil from behind.

With perfect timing, Gil bent and gently placed his stick on the ground. Vole sailed past overhead.

Gil stood up. "No one ever takes me seriously unless I shout and threaten like a cut-rate stage villain." He sighed again.

Vole tried again and suddenly found himself seized by Gil, who effortlessly held him up above his head. "Well, you know what?" the young man asked conversationally, "I can *do* crazy. I really can. And it looks like I'm going to have to."

With that, he slammed Vole to the ground. "Agatha is in danger." Another slam. "This whole town is in danger." Another. "If I'm going to be able to help her at all, I'll have to give up all this 'being reasonable' garbage—" Another slam, and this time he somersaulted up and came down hard on the Jäger's head with both feet. "And show you idiots what kind of madboy you're really dealing with!"

Vole thrashed slightly and Gil kicked him in the face. A sudden realization made him pause. His eyes got wide for a long moment. "Oh. No. Oh no!" He again addressed the air with the attitude of someone experiencing a terrible epiphany. "This...this must be how my father feels *all the time*!"

He thought about this for another moment and sighed. Then he glanced down. He pulled Vole's head up so that he could glare directly into the now-terrified eyes. "So. Are you going to follow orders? Or are you going to keep attacking me until I have to kill you—at which point I'll just have to use one of *these* Jägers instead?" So saying, he hooked a thumb towards the astonished group that had watched him dispatch Vole.

This attention shook Ognian out of his stupefaction and he raised a point of order. "Ectually, ve dun take orders from hyu."

Instantly three fists smashed into his jaw, sending him to the ground.

"What was that?" Gil asked.

"Notting!" Four voices answered as one. "Ve's goot!"

Gil turned back to Vole. "So?"

"No!" The cowed Jäger bleated. "I'z sorry, sir! Vot iz hyu orders, sir!"

Gil nodded. "I am going with these Jägers. Tell no one except my father that you have seen me. I have much to do, so I shall be busy. Right now, I want you to find the body of whoever was in charge of those war clanks. The sooner you get his head to my father or Dr. Sun, the easier it will be to get coherent memories. Do you understand?"

"SIR! YES, SIR!"

"Then go." And pausing only to grab his hat, Vole loped off towards the burning machines.

The group watched him go in silence. Finally Dimo nodded respectfully. "Not bad."

Gil shrugged. "My father once wrote a monograph on how to communicate in the workplace."[34]

"...Iz dot so?"

Gil nodded. "All seven popes ordered it burned."[35]

---

[34] *Don't Make Me Come Over There!* Empire Publishing Office/Dusseldorf

[35] After the disastrous sacking of the Vatican by the Anabaptist Alchemical Army in 1566, the Papal Court was scattered. At the time of our story, after several centuries of internecine fighting and intrigue, there were seven recognized Popes; the Pope of Avignon, the Ottoman Pope, the Pope of the Tsars, the Pope of Belfast, the Gypsy Pope (who, confusingly, is not affiliated with the Romany), the Pope of the Mountains, and the mysterious Sicilian *Papa de Tutti Papi*.

Dimo snorted. "Vell, Hy guess hyu iz feelin' better."

Gil stared off at the burning machines. "Is he gone?" His voice was a whisper.

Dimo blinked. "Vot?"

"Vole. Is he gone?"

"Yah. Uv cawrze. He run off…"

"Good." And with the gentlest of sighs, Gilgamesh Wulfenbach collapsed face forward, completely unconscious.

The Jägers stared down at him. Ognian rubbed his jaw and grinned. "Hy *likes* dis guy!" He leaned down and swung Gil up over his shoulder with one hand. "He's fonny! Let's get him fixed op qvick, yah?"

Jenka winked. "Hif only becawze hyu Mizz Agatha likes him!"

All the Jägers perked up at this. "Iz dot so?"

Jenka nodded. "Accordink to de Generals."

Dimo grinned. "And he likes her too! Dot's mighty goot to hear." He glanced at Gil, "He seems like a sturdy vun. And vit Mizz Agatha, hy tink dot's gunna be impawtent."

Maxim set his hat at a jaunty angle. "Hy vill teach heem how to impress de gorls!"

Ognian gave Gil a pat. "Hy vill teach heem about de birds and de veasles!"[36]

Dimo assured Jenka, "Und hy vill teach heem how to avoid dose two."

She nodded. "Den ve might ektually see more Heterodynes yet."

The current Heterodyne was kneeling on Moloch von Zinzer's chest, her gloved hand frantically clamped over his screaming mouth. "Quiet," she hissed. "Quiet! I don't want to hurt you, but I will if you act stupid!"

Moloch's scream dwindled to nothing. Agatha wasn't sure if this was because he was listening, or because she was blocking his air

---

[36] Like almost everything else, sex education in Mechanicsburg has its own…unique take. As a result, Mechanicsburg girls tend to be rather forward, know what they want, and have no qualms about asking for it, especially when they are wearing their weasel pajamas.

intake. "Now I'm going to take my hand away. I'm giving you one chance. Don't make me regret it!"

She gingerly removed her glove and Moloch took a deep breath. Then he spoke—very fast. "I really must apologize for threatening you back on the airship. I was really scared and under a lot of stress and—"

Agatha gently placed her hand back over his mouth, cutting off his stream of words. "Keep quiet," she said gently, "and we'll call it even."

Moloch looked surprised. "Really? You're not going to kill me?"

"Not unless I have to."

"I can work with that."

They rolled apart and climbed to their feet. Moloch examined her. Agatha had changed since their time on Castle Wulfenbach. When he had first met her, she had obviously been a soft townie. From what he could see, she was now in much better shape. But more importantly, mentally, Agatha had seemed to be in a vague, pleasant fog a lot of the time, occasionally snapping into a terrifying sharp focus. Now… she seemed even more focused. A lot more focused. Looking at her now…she was obviously watching him, but her eyes—her eyes were moving. Constantly. In quick little snaps. Every other snap brought them back to Moloch, but she was looking at everything.

Moloch had always had a good "survival sense." He knew when it was time to retreat. When to avoid the gaze of a sergeant looking for "volunteers." This sense had only been sharpened here in Castle Heterodyne, where a misstep could cause him to be killed in any number of unexpected ways.

That sense was screaming at him now. Screaming in the same way as when he had found himself hauled up before Baron Klaus Wulfenbach himself and discovered that the Ruler of all Europa had made a mistake. About him.

The Baron had thought Moloch a Spark because of a machine that Agatha had built. He had never really understood why they had all automatically assumed it was him and not Agatha but he was not going to be the one to tell the Baron that he'd made a stupid mistake. So he'd tried to fool the smartest man in Europa.

There was a certain perverse pride to be felt because he had managed to do it for longer than two minutes, but at the three-minute mark, the fear of discovery had begun to erode the satisfaction, and by the time the whole thing had come crashing down several days later, he had almost been relieved that it was all over.

There were some who had argued that his sentence to Castle Heterodyne had been a bit harsh, considering that it was usually reserved for deranged Spark criminals, excessively loyal minions, constructs, and such.

However, it was also the traditional punishment for those who had *impersonated* Sparks, and thus, here he had been sent.

Moloch had no illusions about some hypothetical degree of "fairness" about life in general and his in particular. He just did what he always did—the best he could with the crap he had, and, occasionally, life handed him little unexpected victories. He wondered if this was supposed to be one of them. Schadenfreude did not come naturally to Moloch. He had to admit that although she had been the root cause of his current set of problems, Agatha had never actually betrayed him, done him direct harm, or treated him as anything other than a comrade in misfortune.

Thus he discovered that he could actually work up a measure of sympathy for her under the current circumstances.

"So, the Baron finally caught you, eh? Took longer than I thought it would," he admitted.

Agatha shrugged. "He didn't catch me and he isn't going to. I came in here on my own."

Sympathy went out the window. "That's insane!" He considered what he had said. "Oh. Right. You're supposed to be a real Heterodyne, aren't you?"

She smiled. "That's what I'm told."

He thought about this some more. "Wait a minute. That means you're like… you're like the Queen here or something."

Agatha nodded. "Or something."

"So get us out of here!"

She sighed. "I'm working on it." She looked around. "This is the kitchen? It's smaller than I'd have expected."

It was small for a castle this size. Even so, one wall boasted an enormous fireplace in which three entire cattle could have been spit-roasted end-to-end. There were huge griddles and ovens along another wall, clearly designed by someone with the Spark. Pipes and ductwork wound up and into the walls, steam vents with oddly constructed valves clacked open and shut, and a large cast-iron cauldron slowly bubbled over what looked like an industrial grade Bunsen burner.

Makeshift shelves held stacks of cheap china and tin plates and cups. Others held heaps of supplies, bottles of spices and sauces, and sacks of beans, flour, lentils, raisins, noodles, and rice. Large cast-iron pots and pans hung from the beamed ceiling, along with ropes of sausages, at least twenty large smoked hams, and bunches of onions, garlic, peppers, and other dried herbs.

Another rack of shelves held easily four dozen slightly burned loaves of bread.

An enormous zinc tub in the corner, positioned under a dripping pump, was filled with oily-looking water and a towering stack of dirty dishes.

Overall, it was obvious that home economics was not Moloch's strong suit. He sighed.

"Oh, this isn't the Master Kitchen. I don't think we've even found that yet. This place was built for Venthraxus Heterodyne's favorite cook."[37]

Agatha looked at him askance. "How do you know that?"

Moloch sighed. "It told me."

Agatha looked around. "Ah! The kitchen itself? I was told that it talks."

"WELCOME FOOLISH CREATURE! I AM YOUR DOOM!" The shout seemed to come from everywhere at once. Agatha jumped and

---

[37] Luigi del Basteri awoke one morning convinced that he was the reincarnation of one of the Borgias (which one varied from day to day). Venthraxus thought this was very funny and built Luigi his own kitchen, locked him in, and had him cater select parties. This worked out fairly well, until, in a moment of absent-mindedness, he tasted some sauce.

stared around her, then up at the beams of the ceiling. The sausages, pots, and all other hanging goods rocked back and forth gently at the vibration.

"Oh yeah," Moloch confirmed wearily. "It talks."

The voice was similar to the one that Agatha had heard in the crypt. The difference—this voice was deeper, more unearthly—she attributed to the fact that it wasn't being channeled through human vocal cords. In fact, try as she might, she couldn't see any speaker grill or even a vibrating membrane. The voice just seemed to emanate from the corners of the room.

"That's pretty creepy," she observed.

Moloch groaned and stepped away from her. "No! Shut up! Now it's got to show you how creepy it can get."

Before she could ask for an explanation, a knife on one of the cutting boards suddenly quivered and stood up upon the point of its blade. It stood there for a moment and then with a spin, launched itself at Agatha. Hours of training with Zeetha paid off and she stepped to the side. But instead of burying itself in the wall, the knife spun about. Dozens more utensils took to the air and began swirling about her, like a glittering flock of birds. "How is it doing this?" Agatha cried. She snatched up a large cutting board. Instantly two knives buried themselves in it. Suddenly Agatha realized that none of the knives had actually touched her.

Though Moloch had stepped off to one side, he was being menaced by a dangerous-looking eggbeater which he batted at with a pot lid. "How the hell should *I* know," he snapped. "It's supposed to be *your* damn castle, isn't it?"

His words struck home. Agatha straightened up, flung the cutting board aside, and demanded, "Knock it off!"

The utensils froze in midair. "Your voice…" The castle sounded uneasy. "Who are you?"

Agatha addressed the air. "I am Agatha Heterodyne! Daughter of Bill Heterodyne and Lucrezia Mongfish, and I am your new master."

All of the utensils crashed to the floor. "Oh, really?" The castle began to chuckle evilly. "Another brave claimant! And a girl this time. How odd."

"Stop it!" Agatha snapped. "You know me. I talked to you in the crypt."

When the voice again spoke, it was more serious. "I do not know you, silly girl, I lost access to the crypt years ago."

Agatha felt a touch of apprehension. "You don't recognize me?"

"Oh, it's no matter. You have made your claim. Now you must prove it."

"Well, that's what I'm here to do."

A knife sped through the air and deftly sliced Agatha's arm. She screamed in shock and pain. "What are you doing?"

"Blood!" the castle declared. Another knife tore at her leg. "The truth is in your blood!"

"Stop!" Moloch shouted, "You'll collapse my soufflé!"

The knives fell to the ground. "Oh." The castle declared. "Sorry—wait…"

But Moloch had already grabbed Agatha by the arm and dragged her out of the room. They halted, gasping outside the doorway.

Agatha turned to him. "Collapse my soufflé?"

Moloch shrugged. "It's a kitchen."

"I AM NOT A KITCHEN!" The voice roared from inside the room. "I AM CASTLE HETERODYNE!" And a fusillade of sharp utensils burst from the room, smacking into the opposite wall before spinning and clattering harmlessly to the floor.

The two of them stared at the mound of cutlery. Moloch glared at Agatha. "I thought you said you were a real Heterodyne!"

"I am!"

"Then why isn't the Castle listening to you?"

Agatha cocked her head to one side and considered this. "I don't know. Interesting, isn't it?"

He stared at her. "*Interesting!* It tried to *kill* you! I've *never* seen it do that!"

Agatha winced as she rubbed the cut on her arm. "Kill me? No—I don't think so. It could have just put a knife in my eye." She checked the cut on her leg. "These are fairly superficial." Indeed, both of them had already stopped bleeding.

She turned to Moloch. "And I did speak to the Castle in the crypts." She paused. "The voice in the kitchen—that must be one of the secondary systems it mentioned. I should have realized that its memories would be fractured as well. I'm going to have to…introduce myself to each one. And convince them, too, I suppose."

Moloch glanced back at the kitchen doorway. A cleaver shot out and imbedded itself in the opposite wall. "Yeah, that'll work."

Agatha considered this. "So this is the only 'live room' in this area?"

Moloch nodded. "Yeah. That's why we stay here to eat and sleep."

"I've seen artificial intelligences before back at the University. Unless it's something very limited, like a clank, they tend to take up a lot of space. If this one is confined to one room, I'm betting it's not very…sophisticated. I think that once I find systems that operate over larger areas, it'll be a bit more reasonable."

Moloch eyed her. "Reasonable, it's not. It's broken."

Agatha smiled. "Well, that's why I'm here. Once it's repaired, I'm sure it'll be fine."

Moloch scratched at his beard. "Yeah, but how are we gonna do that? They've been trying for how many years? We don't even have—" He stopped short. "Wait—did I say 'we'?" He stared at Agatha in horror. "No way. What am I saying?"

He stepped back and ran a hand through his hair. "You listen to me. I am not your minion![38] Forget it! No, no, no, no, *no*!"

Agatha waved a hand. "I'm sure I don't know what you're talking about."

---

[38] Unless one is raised in the minion mindset, it is difficult to understand the allure of the lifestyle. Outside observers merely see put-upon underlings who live and work in insanely dangerous positions, whose lives are ruled by dictatorial psychopaths who have little regard for their lives or sanity. Acclimatized minions realize that everyone on Earth lives under these strictures, they just don't fool themselves. With clarity comes freedom.

"Most of the people in here are either Sparks, or the loyal minions of Sparks who were too stupid to stop fighting for the losing side when the Baron arrived. I've seen where that gets you. I am nobody's happy little helper, you got that?"

Agatha nodded solemnly. "I got it."

Moloch crossed his arms. "Good."

Agatha sighed. "So I should get started. Where can I find some tools?"

Moloch indicated a set of bins against a wall. Agatha discovered they contained a wide assortment of worn but serviceable tools as well as a rack of tool belts and cases. She spent several minutes selecting and loading a sturdy toolbox. Finally satisfied, she grasped the handles and discovered that it now weighed easily fifty kilograms.

Moloch snorted and pushed her aside. With a few deft moves, he weeded out two-thirds of the items, selected several different ones, and slung the box's strap over his shoulder. "Let's go."

Agatha nodded and off they went.

Several minutes later, they were striding down a long corridor lined with dials of widely varying sizes. Agatha was able to identify numerous pieces of meteorological equipment along with pressure gauges and counters that seemed to record various aspects of the castle, its inhabitants, things that were taking place in the town below, the flow and movement of the river, the clouds above, and things that moved unseen beneath the earth. There were clocks that kept different units of time, measured the rate at which the local crops grew, the speed of various planets, and disturbingly, one that clicked back a notch every time she breathed.

She gazed at it all in wonder and felt a growing excitement. Who knew what wonders were here, waiting in this castle? What things of mystery and magic had lain here, unseen for years, just waiting for her to arrive and claim them?

Her foot caught and she stumbled, but Moloch caught her and steadied her. "Snap out of it," he said. "You can gawk or you can walk, but don't gawk and walk at the same time. It'll get you killed."

Agatha nodded. "You're right. What else should I know?"

He scowled. "I don't know where to start. Usually you'd report to Professor Tiktoffen, and then you'd—well, I guess you'd work with me in the kitchen, and I'd bring you up to speed over time."

Agatha shook her head. "Forget that. It's better if I don't talk to anyone before I head deeper into the Castle."

"Yeah, I'm guessing that other Heterodyne girl isn't your sister or something?"

Agatha snorted. "Only if sisters try to kill each other."

Moloch barked out a laugh. It was the first time Agatha had heard him do *that*. "You're an only child, aren't you?" Agatha looked at him blankly. He continued, "Fine. So you running into her would be bad."

"Very bad. In fact it would be better for you to forget that you knew me."

Moloch rolled his eyes. "If only I could."

Agatha glanced at Moloch. For absolutely no reason she could understand, a wave of fondness washed over her. He certainly hadn't asked to get caught up in her affairs and her time with Master Payne's Circus had shown her how ordinary people felt about being forced into proximity with those who possessed the Spark. She lightly patted his shoulder.

"Relax. I am the Heterodyne. I'll get the Castle repaired and then you'll be free to go and I'll be out of your life."

The eyes that Moloch turned upon her almost caused her to miss a step. They were the eyes of a man who has seen many a proposed simple stroll down to the corner store devolve into a small war.

"Relax," Agatha said reassuringly. "I have a plan."

They turned a corner, and almost ran into Zola—the very faux-Heterodyne Agatha had hoped to avoid. She was resplendent in pink, striding confidently forward and followed by an interested crowd of prisoners. Walking attentively at her side was, unexpectedly, Agatha's least favorite teacher from Transylvania Polygnostic University, Professor Silas Merlot.[39]

The two groups ground to a halt and stared at each other for what was easily several seconds.

Merlot's jaw snapped shut first. "You!" he breathed.

"RUN!" Agatha screamed, and took off.

To his horror, Moloch found himself running along behind her, the bag of tools banging against his shin with every step. "This is a terrible plan!" he shrieked.

"Who was that?" Zola demanded.

Merlot seemed frozen. "That was Miss Clay! It's her fault that I'm in here! She ruined my life!"

Zola stared at him. "Miss Clay? You said that you were in here because of the Heterodyne girl."

Merlot whirled upon her. "She *is* the Heterodyne girl! She is! And I am going to kill her for what she did to me!" With that he was pelting off after her, murder in his heart.

Professor Tiktoffen swallowed. "Good heavens. I've never seen Merlot act like that." He turned to Zola. "You don't think he'd really kill her, do you?"

Zola grimaced. "Well somebody had better, and the quicker the better!" She raised her voice so that all the prisoners heard her. "All of you! Find that girl! Freedom and gold for whoever kills her!" That did it. With a roar, the crowd followed.

As she ran, Agatha tried to examine the map that Herr Diamant had provided for her. As one would expect, trying to read an unfamiliar map of an unfamiliar place—while running with a mob

---

[39]   Professor Silas Merlot, PhD University of Salzburg, had been the long time second-in-command to Professor Tarsus Beetle, the late Tyrant of Beetleburg. There are those who are not Sparks but seem destined to become Sparks. Merlot was one of these and was continually frustrated by his inability to Break Through. This resulted in a sour disposition and a growing hatred of Agatha, who he saw as receiving a disproportional amount of the Tyrant's attention. The fact that Tarsus was aware of Agatha's true identity while Merlot was not, did nothing to ameliorate his feelings when the truth came out. The simple fact is that some people are born nasty.

of dangerous people determined to kill you hot on your heels, no less—was extraordinarily difficult. Finally Moloch couldn't stand it any longer. "Where are we going?"

"Something called the Red Hall. Where is that?"

"Turn left here!"

They crashed through a doorway into a long, colonnaded hallway. Periodically there were doors and exits to stairwells. The walls here were still covered in graffiti but as Agatha flashed past, she realized that here most of it was actually instructions or warnings about what lay behind various doors. She also realized that Moloch was yelling at her. "This was a mistake! We'll be trapped!"

"Not yet!" Agatha jogged forward, one eye on the map, counting under her breath. "Three… Fourth door… There! The fifth hallway! Come on!"

Moloch lunged forward, grabbed her shoulder, and dragged her to a halt. "Wait! We can't go in there! That's Uncharted Territory! It's full of traps! The Castle will kill us for sure!"

"There they are!" They both turned to see a crowd of prisoners pour into the hall and head towards them.

With a scream, Moloch hoisted the toolbox up over his head in a semblance of protection and darted down the uncharted hall. Agatha followed. They had passed over ten meters in before Agatha realized they were no longer being followed. She stopped and turned back. Sure enough, the mob had stalled at the entrance, as surely as if by an invisible wall. "They've stopped," she observed.

"Of course they stopped!" Moloch said bitterly. "They're waiting to see us get turned inside out! Not even the Trapmasters ever got this far! We're now completely at the mercy of an insane mechanical monster that *has* no mercy!"

A soft sound was all the warning Agatha had, but she shoved Moloch back in time so that the stone block that had fallen from the ceiling missed him completely. She raised her voice. "But it's *my* insane mechanical monster and I'm here to make sure that it knows it!"

There was a pause and then a complete dearth of falling blocks. Agatha nodded. "Good. I think I've gotten it curious." She held out a hand to help Moloch up. "Besides," she said quietly, "At this point, we really don't have much choice. We just have to keep going and hope for the best."

The two of them took a final glance at the seething crowd at the hallway entrance and pushed onwards. In a moment, they had turned a corner and vanished.

The prisoners looked at each other and sullenly turned back, only to be met by Zola, striding towards them, growing visibly more furious with every step she took. "What are you fools doing?" She pointed down the hallway. "Go after them!"

A woman wreathed in veils made an obscene gesture. "Eat knives, cow. You go down that hallway, you die."

In a single fluid movement, Zola dipped her hand to a holster at her waist, drew forth a compact little pistol, and shot the woman through the forehead.

The others stared at her. Zola took a shooter's stance. "No. You die if you *don't* go in."

The group stared at her and then, like a terrified amoeba, slowly crept down the hallway.

Darkness.
Light.
Darkness again.
Light. Ah. Eyelids. A vague cloud of sentience slowly coalesced and realized that it was Gilgamesh Wulfenbach. *I'm still alive*, he realized. *Yay.*

There was a creak from beside him, and an unfamiliar woman's voice. "Ah! You're awake! Relax, you're safe."

Gil rolled his head towards the speaker and caught sight of her. He tensed. The woman was young, not yet twenty-five, he guessed. She was muscular, a fighter of some sort, if the scars she carried were any indication. She wore mostly leather and canvas, with two unusual-looking swords strapped to her back. The light in the room was dim, to spare his eyes, he guessed, but he could see that her hair was a rich green.

"Am I?" he asked.

The girl raised her eyebrows and grinned. "Yup. Couldn't be safer."

She stood up, went to a tray on a nearby dresser and poured something into a pewter mug. While she was busy, Gil looked around. He wasn't tied down or restrained. He was feeling somewhat unsteady—a glance at his lower legs revealed several bandages. The astonishing thing about the room was how it was decorated. The only word that applied was "excessively." Every centimeter looked like it had been painted or carved by someone with too much time, a rather limited imagination, and a dearth of artistic talent. The scenes portrayed tended to be battles, monsters, and monsters battling with other monsters. Another glance and he realized that the more gaudily dressed monsters were supposed to be Jägers. Impossible, deformed, grandiose Jägers sporting towering, elaborate, impractical headgear, but clearly Jägers.

The room had only one exit, which appeared to be unlocked. There was nothing within reach that could be used as a weapon, or indeed, really anything useful at all within reach. It appeared to be a repurposed storeroom of some sort. The open beamwork of the ceiling seemed excessive for a house and there were no windows, so they were in a commercial structure of some sort.

Either the walls were thick or there wasn't anything happening outside the door. The air was close and had an odd, gamey odor that tugged at his memory, overlaid with the smells of antiseptic, unwashed bodies and, oddly, old beer.

The bed he was on looked like a standard issue hospital cot, with linen sheets and wool blankets. The dresser was sturdy wood, elaborately carved, as was the chair the girl had been sitting in. The floor was dressed stone.

Gil made this examination while the girl was getting his drink and composed his face by the time she returned to his side.

"I'll bet you have questions," she said as she sat back down, "I know I have." She indicated the drink in her hand. "Sit up and have some of this."

Gil moved carefully and found it surprisingly easy. His legs stung a bit but it could have been far worse.

He settled himself back and reached for the mug, calculating furiously. If he threw the drink at the girl, that should give him enough time to—

"Don't try it," she said.

"What?"

"Just now. You were thinking that if you threw your drink at me, you might be able to overpower me."

Gil tried to keep his face noncommittal. The girl smiled. "Body language. Eye movement. You tensed the muscles of your arms... You couldn't do it, by the way."

Gil nodded and sipped the drink. This, to his surprise, turned out to be some sort of spicy concoction, redolent of lemon and malt. He sipped it again. "I suppose I couldn't," he ventured.

The girl regarded him. "So I'm curious. People you trust told you they were going to see to you, you woke up, so if I was going to hurt you, I could've done it a hundred times over, and yet, when you saw me, you got all tense. Now why is that?"

Damn my father and his love of secrets, Gil thought. He regarded the girl and spoke slowly. "I've been told that someone who looks like you might be out to kill me."

The girl's reaction was unexpected. She sat up straight and grinned so wide that she brightened the dim little room. "Reeeeally?"

That was when Gil threw his drink into her face—or—wait—where was the mug?

It was in the girl's hand, not a drop out of place. She grinned again and took a sip, and made a face at the taste. "Very nice," she said. She casually tossed him the full mug, which Gil caught in midair. "I might even have been in trouble if you weren't messed up." She paused. "And if I were drunk and had a broken arm and—"

"Yes! I get it, thank you."

"Good. Now drink that up, it's supposed to be good for you, and don't worry, I'm not going to kill you." She shrugged. "Not yet, anyway." She paused for effect and made a devilish face. "Agatha wouldn't like it."

Everything else left Gil's mind. He sat up. "Agatha! Where is she? Is she all right?"

The green-haired girl made a show of frowning sternly at him. "And why should I tell you? Weren't you the one who just sent a Jäger to kill her?"

Gil's face went pale. "WHAT?" he roared. "I did no such—" He suddenly remembered Vole. He studied the girl's face. "Maybe I did," he said slowly, "But I never told him to kill her. He's not like other Jägers, but I never thought he'd…"

He remembered his father's reaction to his sending Vole after Agatha and his hand tightened upon his mug. "But my father wasn't surprised…My father is convinced that she's…the Other." He looked for a reaction in the girl's face and saw nothing. A chill went through him.

He set his drink down. "If you know something, tell me. I mean…I don't really know Agatha that well, but I…I don't want to believe it."

He took a deep breath. "If it was just about me, I would take my chances. But the Other devastated Europa. I've read the accounts. I've seen the results. And now the reports coming out of Balan's Gap—whatever went on there was the work of the Other. There's no question. And there's also no question that Agatha was right there in the middle of it all."

He looked the green-haired girl in the eyes. "I've never known my father to be wrong about anything. Anything! Not until Agatha came along. He was wrong about her then, and I hope he's wrong about her now, but what if I'm missing something?"

He paused, his mind swirling with conflict. He was sure it could be seen on his face but he kept going anyway. "The last thing I want is to unleash all that death and destruction upon the world—again—just because I fell in love." As he slumped forward, the fine gold chain around his neck shifted and a small ring-shaped gas connector slid into view.[40]

The girl eyed it and nodded slowly. She took a deep breath and pinched the bridge of her nose, a gesture that, oddly, reminded Gil of his father.

"Okay," she muttered from behind her hand, "You've convinced me." She straightened up and looked at Gil seriously. "Agatha is fine, for now. She sent me to make sure that you were all right after that stunt you pulled outside the city."

Gil leaned forward. "Did she like that?"

The green-haired girl rolled her eyes. *Sparks.* "Yes, she did. But because she's a smart girl, she's not ready to trust you, but I can tell you that she likes you." She held up a preemptory finger. "And not just because you blew up invaders on her doorstep—though that never hurts."

The girl then reached down and grabbed hold of Gil's hair, dragging his face up to hers. "But I don't care who you are, Agatha is my *Zumil*, and if you hurt her—I will kill you."

Gil didn't try to pull back. "I don't know what a 'Zumil' is, but I get the idea. However, there is this whole Other thing…"

The girl rolled her eyes and released him. "Yeah, that. Okay, I've heard you're smart, and I really do believe that you care about her, so I'm going to explain things to you and hope you can actually help her, because she could probably use it."

The girl took a deep breath. "Agatha isn't the Other. But apparently, her mother was. Or is. I'm a little unclear about the details, but the Other took over Agatha's mind for a while. They had some kind

---

[40] As related in *Agatha H. and the Airship City*, this particular gas connector was used by Gilgamesh as an impromptu ring during his disastrous first proposal of marriage to Agatha. In our second textbook, *Agatha H. and the Clockwork Princess*, we saw how it had been planted upon a convenient corpse in order to convince the Wulfenbachs that Agatha was dead. The fact that Gil had kept it, and continued to wear it is, in your Professoressa's opinion, indicative of a morbid personality.

of machine back in Sturmhalten Castle that was able to shove the Other in there."

A cold fury filled Gil's face. "The Sturmvarous family. Another thing my father was correct about."

She held up a hand. "But Agatha is back in control now. She's got a locket. It's something her Uncle Barry built for her a long time ago. She says that it damped down her brain—kept her from Sparking out while she was growing up. It let her hide—gave her a chance to grow up like a normal person. She'd lost it before I met her. She said it had gotten stolen in Beetleburg—"

"Oh!" Gil's eyes widened. "Von Zinzer! Yes, I see…go on."

"Now for some reason, the Baron had it on him when he tried to capture Agatha back in Balan's Gap. Looking at it now, it's obvious that this Other was in control of Agatha at the time. She put this locket on and I saw the Other get shut down hard." She sat back and spread her hands. "And Agatha's been herself ever since."

Gil processed this for several moments. "So the only thing keeping the Other in check is this locket?"

The girl shrugged. "Maybe. Maybe not. We haven't taken it off her to find out."

Gil shook his head. "This is very bad. It means—"

"It means that when you get her alone, you make damn sure that she keeps that locket on."

Gil's train of thought derailed with a crash. He stared at her. "I'm reasonably sure that there are more important considerations than that."

The girl made a face. "Not if you want to avoid kissing the Other." She saw Gil's face and sighed. "Look, I said Agatha's interested in you and it's obvious that you're interested in her, even though the two of you don't really know much about each other. That means it's a physical attraction. So the best thing to do is get it all out of your system first so you can start talking to each other intelligently."

Gil's face was now beet red. "I never thought there was anyone out there with a poorer grasp of romance than myself."

"Romance?" The girl snorted. "Are you kidding? I thought you were the Baron's heir. You're the one saying this is serious. I agree. Surely you understand that you shouldn't let infatuation cloud your judgment. Agatha still has a head full of romantic notions, but she wasn't raised as royalty."

Gil's eyes narrowed. "And you were? Who are you, anyway?"

The girl stood tall. "I am Zeetha, Daughter of Chump. Heir to the throne of my mother, Queen Zantabraxis, ruler of Skifander and the Dark Countries."

Gil raised an eyebrow. "Chump?"

Zeetha's eyes flashed. "A great warrior. And yes, I know what it means in your language. An amusing coincidence, yes?"

"I really couldn't say. How smart was he?"

A frown darkened Zeetha's face and then vanished. She gave Gil a small nod. A point to him. "Honestly? That's still a topic of debate amongst my family."

"What's your opinion?"

Zeetha looked down. "I…I never met him. He ran off a month after…ah…I was born." The admission apparently called up many emotions for her, though she made a clear effort to hide them. She took a deep breath. "It is one of the reasons I came here with Professor Consolmagno—to try to find him.[41] One of the few things he told my mother about himself was that he came from a place called Europa." A wry look crossed her face. "He neglected to mention how large it was. Agatha helped me when I needed it. She is now my pupil, and I, her protector."

When nothing more was forthcoming, Gil asked, "And where is that? I've never heard of this Skifander."

Zeetha sighed in obvious disappointment. "Your father has heard of it."

---

[41] Professor Guylian Consolmagno, PhD, University of Rome. Leader of the first Europan expedition to Skifander, though he evidently was surprised to find it. He died, and his expedition notes were destroyed by air pirates upon their return. He might have taken some solace from the fact that Zeetha subsequently eradicated the pirates and destroyed their base, but this assumes a small-mindedness and lack of forgiveness that one rarely sees amongst the better class of academics.

Gil shrugged. "My father knows a lot that he hasn't bothered to tell me about," he said frankly. He looked at her. "Like why he thinks that someone from Skifander would want to kill me."

Zeetha paused and then leaned back. "I'm going to be honest with you. I have no idea *why* he'd think that, but I can't say that it surprises me that he *does* think that."

Gil rolled his eyes. More games. "I don't have time for this."

Zeetha grinned. "Sure you do. You're not going anywhere like that."

Gil waved a hand. "I feel fine."

"I'll bet you look fine too."

Gil stared at her blankly and then peeked under his blanket and froze. "Where are my clothes?"

Zeetha's grin grew even wider. "How should I know? I didn't undress you."

Gil paused, relieved. "You didn't?"

"What, do I look like a doctor?"

Gil coughed. "No, but..."

Zeetha smiled sweetly and indicated the doorway. "The girls did that."

Three girls were now crowding the doorway, staring blatantly, grinning, and nudging each other. All were dressed in colorful military uniforms and all were equipped with pointed ears and sharp, white teeth.

"Hey! He is alive!" said one.

"Mamma knows what she's doing," said the shortest, examining Gil with a predatory look in her eyes.

Gil stared back at them and pulled his covers up higher. "They... don't look like doctors either."

They all laughed at this and came farther into the room. Now that they were closer, Gil could see that the ears and teeth were merely costume pieces.

"So you're the new Lady Heterodyne's boyfriend, eh?" said the tall one. She leered at Gil in a most alarming manner. "I see that she's gonna be a pretty lucky girl."

"The Castle hasn't accepted her yet," the middle one said flatly. She turned a jaded eye on Gilgamesh. "And she hasn't picked him yet either."

The shortest girl gave a surprisingly athletic bounce and settled atop the dresser. "That's right! You gotta spur a horse around the yard a bit before you buy him!"

The others chortled. Gil took a calming breath and started with the obvious. "You're not really Jägers."

The tall girl cocked her head to one side. "Of course not. No Jägers allowed within the city limits of Mechanicsburg."

The middle one nodded. "That was the deal."

"You're in Mamma Gkika's, bright boy."

Gil paused as a memory surfaced. "That…That was a bar…where the Jägerkin used to hang out…" A few more things clicked into place. "Barmaids? You're barmaids dressed as Jägers?"

The tall one laughed. "Not just barmaids, m'lord, now it's dinner and a show!" At an unseen signal, all three of them assumed obvious poses. The first looked demure and serious. "'Four Gears!' according to *Professor Strout's Guide to Roadside Scientific Atrocities!*"

The second looked at him shyly. "'A magnificent perversion of science' according to *Steamy Steam Quarterly*," she said breathily.

The third crossed her arms and looked truculent. "'Never heard of it'—Mechanicsburg Chamber of Commerce."

Gil looked bewildered. "But…but the Jägers have a *terrible* reputation! People are afraid of them! They hate them! And here you're telling me that tourists come here and *drink* with fake ones?"

The three girls looked at each other and smiled.

"You'd be surprised."

"You'd be shocked."

"I don't drink."

Gil stared at them. He shook his head. "Oh, no. No! This is just too ridiculous! There's got to be something more to this. I'm just not buying it, otherwise."

A richly amused voice rolled out from the doorway, "Vell lucky for hyu, dollink, dis iz on de howze."

There was no question that the figure filling the doorway was a genuine Jäger. She was also, unmistakably, female. Well over two meters tall, the smiling Jäger had a head of brilliant aquamarine hair piled up in a complicated chignon held in place with a slim stiletto. Her face was broad, which accommodated the large, sharp-toothed grin spread across it. Her eyes had a touch of the Far East and her ears were long and pointed.

She was dressed with a voluptuous elegance that announced both her profession and her demeanor with exquisite clarity. When she moved, it was with a sensual grace that was completely unexpected because of her size, and thus even more effective. She came over to Gil's bedside and looked him over with a wicked smile that had him repeatedly checking to make sure that his blankets were still covering him.

"So hyu iz avake now. Goot." She graciously extended a hand. "Velcome to mine howze. Hy iz Mamma Gkika."

Gil automatically took her hand, and as he did so, he was engulfed in a delicate cloud of spicy perfume that caused him to shiver in anticipation. Of what, he wasn't sure. "Charmed, Madam."

Mamma smiled even wider and leaned down to examine his face, exposing an amazing décolletage. This was a test Gil had learned to pass in Paris, and he kept his eyes locked with Mamma's. The Jäger raised an eyebrow approvingly.

Gil then examined the hand he held, noting the demurely trimmed claws. "You're a genuine Jäger, but you're—are we still inside Mechanicsburg?"

Mamma nodded. "Hyu iz a schmott vun." She indicated the other girls. "Ven pipple see lots of false Jägers, dey dun look so hard at real vuns."

"I see."

"So—" Mamma turned to Zeetha. "How'z he been?"

"Noisy. Suspicious. Cranky."

Mamma waved her hand. "Dot means nottink, he iz Klaus's boy." She turned back to Gil. "Hyu vas vun chopped op kid ven my boyz bring hyu in. Lets see how hyu iz doink now, hey?" She reached for his sheet.

Gil edged backwards. "Madam! Please!"

Mamma rolled her eyes. "Don be han eediot, keedo, Hy needs to see dose vounds, and de gorls heve seen better, hy'm sure."

The three glanced at each other and the short one piped up. "Not many, I'll give him that."

Gil sighed. He'd gotten worse from Bangladesh. It was Mamma's expression that brought him back into the moment. Her look of surprise caused him to glance down, which was when he became aware of the device attached to his thigh.

"What the devil is that?" he exclaimed.

"Iz a leedle monitor patch vun of de Masters cobbled togedder avile ago," Mamma replied. "End accordink to dis, hyu iz hokay." She looked up at him and there was a look to her eyes that revealed the steel beneath the harlot. "If Hy had to guess, hy'd say dot hyu poppa has deduced a few more uf de Jägerkin's secrets den he lets on. Dis leedle ting is ready to come out."

"'Come out?'" Gil asked. "How deep is it? That's right atop the *Profunda femoris* artery. You can't just rip it—yaAAAAAH!"

"Sure hy ken." She frowned at Gil. "Ho, don't be soch a beeg baby. A leedle pain iz goot for hyu."

"I'm probably bleeding to death!" Gil pressed down on the wound. "You shouldn't just…" His breath caught. He moistened a thumb and wiped the blood away. When he looked up, there was a growing confusion on his face. "This is almost completely healed. But—the size of the wound…" A new thought struck him. "I must have been out for days! Agatha! My father! What's been happening?" He leapt to his feet in a panic.

Zeetha grabbed one of his arms while the tallest of the girls grabbed the other. Gil gave a shrug and they went spinning off to crash against the walls. He stood there breathing heavily. "I've had enough of this! I'm leaving now!"

Mamma stepped up to him. "Not like dis, hyu ain't. Hyu gots to—"

Gil lashed out—his hands striking Mamma's shoulders, sending the large woman reeling back, a look of astonishment on her face.

Gil gave an inarticulate roar of fury. Then Mamma's fist slammed into his jaw, lifting him off his feet and sending him flying back. He flattened against the wall and then dropped back onto his bed. Everyone waited. One of Gil's hands moved slightly and everyone tensed. "What just happened to me?" Gil asked.

Mamma gave a snort and with a ripple, was once again the relaxed chanteuse. "Goot boy. We giff hyu some Battle Draught. Iz strong schtuff. Close op hyu vounds fast!"

Gil sat up and gingerly peeled back a bandage on his arm. The skin underneath was slightly red but otherwise unmarked. He looked up. "But this is amazing! Why isn't this being used in the hospital?"

Mamma looked distressed. "Battle draught iz brewed for Jägers. Iz not always… so goot for normal pipples."

Gil looked at her. "But you gave it to me."

Mamma nodded. "Hy did." She looked at him for a moment and then nodded again as she made a decision. "When you poppa took in the Jägers, we swore to serve de House of Wulfenbach. Vun uf de vays ve did dis, vas by keepink a close eye on hiz son." Gil tried to interrupt but Mamma plowed on. "Ve knew—" she tapped her nose, "—dot hyu vas de Baron's son. Ve knew before hyu did, and hyu vas guarded."

She leaned back against the dresser and regarded Gil with a grin. "And ven somevun iz vatched as much as hyu vas, tings get noticed. Hyu poppa spent a lot of time vit hyu in his laboratories. More den hyu realize since hyu vas asleep half de time, but he improved hyu. Oh, hyu tried to hide dem, but hyu vas a keed, and hyu let tings slip. Hyu is faster den most pipple, jah? Stronger. Hyu dun sleep moch. Tings dot vould help hyu survive." Mamma poked him in the chest. "Hy figure if ennybody ken take a leedle battle draught, it vould be hyu."

"But why take the chance?"

Mamma stopped smiling. "Because hyu poppa vants to keel Miz Agatha and de Jägers tink dot she iz der Heterodyne, vich means dot she iz under our protection."

Mamma shrugged. "Now, maybe she izn't a Heterodyne. Personally, hy dun see how soch a ting could be pozzible. But der Castle vill decide, not hyu poppa." She leaned forward. "De trobble iz dot ven hyu poppa decides to kill somebody, dey usually die pretty dem fast, and hy tink dot de only ting dot could schtop Baron Wulfenbach—vould be anodder Wulfenbach."

"I will not fight my father."

Mamma nodded with approval. "Dot's goot, becawze he's got a whole bunch of army and hyu dun got nottink. My hope iz dot hyu can out-*think* him."

Gil stared at her, his jaw hanging open. "Out-think. My father."

"Hyu deed it vunce already, sveetie. Hyu knew Agatha vas de Spark in Beetleburg."

"How do you know—?" Gil hesitated. "I can't count on that happening again."

Mamma grinned. "Ov cawrze not. It vill be schomting else. Hit alvays iz. De impawtent ting iz dot hyu iz alive and on de field."

Gil took a deep breath. "So—that whole temper thing. What was that?"

Mamma shrugged. "De Jäger draught didn't make hyu brain melt, but hit looks like der might be side-effects. Hyu better vatch dot temper, kiddo."

"Or else I might start frothing and attacking people?"

"Could be. Or maybe hyu make a beeg snarly mouth and hyu face steek like dot."

Gil stared at her. "Can I get dressed now?"

The other women simultaneously groaned in disappointment.

Mamma clapped her hands. "Ov cawrze. Now hyu clothes vas a mess, so my boyz iz findink hyu some new vuns."

And indeed, a minute later, there was a knock on the door. It opened and Maxim poked his head in. "Hey, Mamma! Ve found some real snappy schtuff from de prop room and der lost and finders keepers!" So saying, he passed through a mound of clothing. Meanwhile Dimo and Ognian had seen the Jäger-girls and immediately begun flirting.

Gil examined the clothing. It seemed to consist of equal parts armor and miscellaneous clothing from around the known world. Gil, who had inherited his father's appreciation of smart dress, was appalled.

He held up a pair of leather pants equipped with spikes at the knees and groin. "I can't wear this!"

Maxim leaned in, as one man of the world to another, and waggled his eyebrows suggestively. "Hyu could go find Mizz Agatha mitout dem…"

The red blush started in Gil's face and traveled a long way down before he snarled and grabbed an armored pair of underpants. "Fine!"

Everyone in the room took a close interest in his dressing—to the point where they got into arguments about his choice of assorted garments. This did not improve his mood.

A knock at the door revealed yet another Jäger girl. She whispered a message to Mamma, confided to Gil that she appreciated trousers tight enough to let a girl know which way a man dressed, and then vanished. Gil started looking for a different pair of pants, but Mamma interrupted. "Hyu hurry op now, keedo. Dere's sum pipple vaitink to talk to hyu."

Gil found a comfortable waistcoat, which was only marred by what appeared to be a functional pair of bear-traps mounted on the shoulders. "I can imagine. Does this place have a back door?"

Mamma chuckled. "More den hyu vould belief. But no, dese pipple it vill be goot for hyu to talk to. Trust me on dot."

Finally Gil stood in something that at least felt comfortable. He exited the room and came face-to-face with a long mirror. He stopped dead. "I can't wear this," he declared.

"Ashtara above, why not?" Zeetha declared. "You look perfect!"

"I look like I've picked over every battlefield for the last fifty years. From the losing side, no less."

Maxim grinned proudly. "Yah! Dot's goot schtuff."

"Don't be ridiculous! I can't have people see me like this!"

"Oh, of cawrze not," Maxim agreed.

Gil paused. "What?"

Maxim pulled a large, colorful object from behind his back and displayed it proudly. "Not vitout hyu hat!"

A tableful of Jägermonsters was chatting away. A careful observer would have noted that easily three-quarters of them were severely injured. This did not stop them from laughing, shoving, and drinking copiously. One of the few undamaged soldiers was discussing the latest orders and troop movements.

"De Baron haz ordered us all op to de North Border."

A Jäger missing an arm, with a surprisingly clean bandage wrapped over his eyes, snorted. "Dun tell me dot de Reindeer Boyz iz giffing him trouble?"

The first waved a hand. "He dun tink we'z dot schtupid. He didn't say nottink, yet. Hit vas just as far as he could send uz."

They became aware of a ripple of excitement coming towards them. Other tables, also full of Jägers, were exclaiming in awe and astonishment. The crowd parted and Gilgamesh strode past, escorted by Dimo, who was happily basking in the reflected glory. The Jägers stared at the figure clad in ridiculous, ill-fitting, and mismatched armor and their eyes locked upon the space above his head. Their breaths caught—and they rose to their feet and, as one, repeated the cry that was now filling the room.

"HEY! NIZE HAT!!"

The hat was, indeed, very nice. It had spikes and gilded wings, meters of gold lace and frogging. It had a small cheerful flame spouting from a chemical burner mounted at the top, and it had large gold letters that proclaimed that the wearer was *"Gilgamesh Wulfenbach: Schmot guy!!"*

Gil had had enough. "Everything…is going to go boom," he growled.

"They're quite serious, you know."

The voice that broke Gil's murderous rage was calm and smooth. A tall young man sat at a nearby table—his elegant dark suit adorned with several discreet medallions of office. The fellow looked at Gil with the open, honest eyes of a born manipulator and continued, "You may think they are mocking you, but I see someone they respect. And that, my dear sir, is very rare. And very useful." He gestured to an empty chair.

From beside the man, another person leaned forward. It was a dwarf—no, a—a cat. A huge white cat in a uniform jacket that would have shamed a comic-opera Bavarian princeling. "Oh, yeah," the cat said. "And by the way, nice hat."

Gil had a feeling that the cat was not impressed. He stared at the two and slowly sat down. "You're the ones waiting for me?"

The young man fastidiously set down a coffee cup and placed his fingertips together. "Yes. We—"

At this point, the cat hopped up onto the tabletop and, walking on his hind legs, stalked up to Gil. He stuck a clawed finger in his face. "Hold on. First, I want to make this absolutely clear. I don't trust you. I don't like you. I think that you are just out to use Agatha as a pawn in some inferior plot to overthrow your father and take over the world. Well I'm on to you, pal, and you're cutting into my territory!"

The young man sighed and grabbed the back of the cat's coat— forcibly hauling him back to his seat. "Thank you, Krosp, for getting us started on such a diplomatic footing."

The cat spat. "I'm serious. Mess with me and your shoes are mine."

Gil looked at Krosp and nodded slowly. He glanced at the man holding the cat's coat, "And you are?"

"Vanamonde von Mekkhan. I am the seneschal of Castle Heterodyne." As he spoke, Van poured Gil a mug of steaming black liquid from a small ceramic pot. "Have some coffee."

Gil frowned as he picked up his cup. "The seneschal? But that family—" He took a sip, and stared into his cup. "That's…really good coffee," he said reverently.

Van hid his head in his arms and sobbed into the tabletop. "YOU SHOULD HAVE TRIED IT BEFORE!" he wept. "It was perfect! *Perfect!*" He trailed off into further sobs.

Krosp looked at Van with irritation and leaned towards Gil. "Anyway, we're here to help you." Then he hissed at him.

Gil looked at the two of them, deliberately set his cup down, and began to stand up. "I'm going now," he said firmly.

Zeetha, who had been standing behind him, pushed him firmly back into his chair. "Sit down," she said.

She pointed to Van. "Forget the City Council, he's the real power here in Mechanicsburg. He drank something Agatha brewed up. She says it'll probably wear off."

Van looked up. "But it was—"

"Yes," Zeetha said gently. "We know." She gestured to Krosp. "This is Krosp. He's Agatha's cat."

"KING!" Krosp declared.

Zeetha nodded. "And I think that explains that." She indicated the room at large. "And let's be honest, they're probably the sanest people here."

The room was immense—a great barrel-vaulted cellar, easily one hundred meters long and half that wide. Thick pillars rose among the tables. One end of the room was filled with an expansive bar, behind which several bartenders were constantly busy. The walls behind them were lined with giant casks, each of them capable of storing the yearly output of a small brewery. A squad of waitresses endlessly shuttled back and forth, each carrying an impossible number of festively decorated tankards.

Opposite the bar was a cabaret stage. Gaslamps hissed along the front, and it was hung with a thick red curtain emblazoned with the badge of the Jägerkin, a grinning demonic skull. At the moment, the three faux Jäger girls Gil had met earlier were strutting about onstage, doffing assorted items of clothing while melodically assuring the audience that come what may, they still had their hats.

The appreciative audience was composed entirely of Jägers— several hundred at least. Some were sitting at small private tables or in booths but most sat at the immensely long wooden tables that filled the center of the hall.

Almost every square centimeter of wall was covered by weapons, armor, and peculiar bits of madboy tech, some of it hundreds of years out of date. Gil realized that these were trophies: souvenirs of enemies that the Jägers had gone up against in the service of the Heterodynes— and later, of the Wulfenbachs. With a start, Gil recognized the vermilion uniforms of the Viscount Eisenstein's Lobstermen.

"Mamma Gkika's isn't just a bar," Zeetha said. "The Jägers won't let anyone but a Heterodyne work on them—so when one gets too injured to fight, he comes here. Mamma patches them up as best she can. In the really bad cases—she keeps them comfortable while they wait for the family to come back. So they can get properly repaired, you know?"

Gil nodded slowly. "This answers many questions. I had been afraid that they killed their wounded rather than let us get our hands on them." He saw a Jäger with no legs and one arm pour a tankard of ale into his mouth and then challenge another to an arm wrestling match. He turned back to Van and Krosp and smiled. "I'm glad that's not the case."

Zeetha nodded. "I can't wait to see Agatha's face when she finds out. She hates doing chores."

Gil looked at her. "Then what are you doing here? Shouldn't you be with her?"

Zeetha shrugged and waved her hands at the ceiling. "The Heterodyne must enter the Castle alone," she quoted in mock sepulchral tones.

Gil shot to his feet. "She's already in the castle? That thing is a death trap! We have to go in and help her!"

"We really are going to be be-e-est friends," she said as she locked an arm around his neck and dragged him back into his seat. "I approve of this plan and intend to help in any way possible."

Gil paused, "You do?"

Zeetha nodded. "Absolutely. As far as I know, she just had to *enter* alone. Nothing says we can't follow in after her." She turned to Vanamonde. "Right?"

Van cleared his throat. "I don't think it's ever come up."

Gil turned to him. "My father—"

Van interrupted, "Yes, your father. He's been busy. I would like to know what he's been doing."

Gil sat back and gave Van a wan smile. "While I'm sure that at a cellular level my father has been quite active, he won't be doing much of anything for a while."

Krosp snorted. "Anyone else I'd call disingenuous, but from you I'll accept stupid."

Van looked annoyed. "Krosp, please…"

Krosp slammed a pawful of paper flimsies down onto the table. "For starters, he's been giving a bunch of weird orders."

Gil looked alarmed. He scooped them up and examined them. His alarm grew. "These are…*How did you get these?*"

Van waved a hand. "Please. People give orders, other people write them down, people carry them from place to place, others must execute them… But that is all unimportant. What is it exactly that he's doing?"

Gil waved the papers. "He's probably administering the Empire. I assume that most of these orders were sent out by Boris, under my father's seal. He's severely injured! Bedridden! In my medical opinion, he won't be up for weeks."

Krosp snorted again. Van ignored the cat and kept his eyes on Gil. "So. Even his son underestimates him."

Gil looked alarmed. "What? What do you mean?"

Krosp smoothed his whiskers. "Oh, he's up, all right."

CHAPTER 5

THE CAVERNS OF MECHANICSBURG

The town of Mechanicsburg sits atop a land honeycombed with caverns and lava tubes. It is famous among Europa's spelunking community as it offers a wide range of expeditions ranging from the simple all the way up to the insanely dangerous Class Five, which requires breathing apparatus, submersible gear, a demonstrated proficiency in at least two weapon types, a signed and notarized indemnification release, and a registered copy of one's last will and testament. (If you are familiar with Europa's spelunking community, it will come as no surprise that Class Five expeditions are perennially booked up a year and a half in advance, so reserve your spot as soon as possible!)

Lest this put off the curious amateur, let us reassure you that the sights and sounds that can be experienced on the Beginner's Tour are unique and well worth the laughably small chance of being attacked by bloodbats.

In addition to their natural wonders, the subterranean levels of the area have long been home to assorted servitors and creations of the Heterodynes. These colorful denizens of "Under Town" are always good for an exciting story about "the old days," and are renowned for their handicrafts and the various species of exotic fungi they cultivate, which are available for sale or trade. (It is only a statistically insignificant number of unlucky visitors that are chosen for the quaint local ritual known as the *Surface Tithe*, and those who survive to witness it call it "an unforgettable treat that gave us a new appreciation of life"— *Professor Strout's Guide to Roadside Scientific Atrocities.*)

Highlights on the Beginner's Tour also include the Snail Plantations, the Cursed Springs, the Ruins of the Subterranean Empire, and the Cavern of Transmutating Elements.

Expeditions may be booked through any number of Deep Delving Shops. We recommend Lindenbrook's Subterranean Adventures, located on Heterodyne Square.

—*One Thousand and One Things To Do In Mechanicsburg*/ It Seemed Like A Good Idea At The Time Press.

❧✦❧

D r. Sun gave the coded knock and opened the door to the Baron's sickroom. He had been handed the usual stack of papers as he passed through the halls. He frowned as he examined them.

"Klaus? What is this nonsense I hear—" A muffled sound made him look up. Bangladesh DuPree glared at him. She was chained to the foot of Klaus's bed, which was otherwise empty. Sun's eyes darted around the room. Assorted bits of important medical equipment were missing, as was his patient. His eyes went back to the papers in his hand. Realization dawned. "He wouldn't," he whispered.

Less than two minutes later, he erupted from the doorway to one of the inner courtyards, scattering a crowd of nervous orderlies. "Of *course* he would!" he muttered.

Sun paused and straightened up. *Center. Focus. Breath like a fern unfolding. You are the lynchpin of your House. Show no stress.*

Striding across the lawn was a large clank—the kind normally used for transporting supplies or dealing with dangerous constructs. Now, ensconced behind the two trained nurse pilots, Sun could see that Klaus had installed a bank of medical equipment, as well as his actual hospital bed. An I.V. bag swayed above him as the colossus strode about the manicured walkways, on what was obviously a test run.

"*Klaus!*" Sun screamed.

From above, the ruler of Europa paused and peered down at him. "What?" He asked innocently.

Sun realized that he was actually jumping up and down in rage. This only served to make him madder. "Are you trying to kill yourself? Or me? You are on strict bed rest!"

"Well, of course," Klaus said reasonably. One of the walker's giant manipulators waved at Sun. "That's why I made sure to recalibrate the controls to respond to minimal hand movements."

Sun again shrieked with rage and began furiously kicking at one of the giant legs. A few of the orderlies noted with fascination that the industrial grade metal was denting under the onslaught. "That is not the point! After what happened *last* time, you *promised* you'd let me do my job!"

A giant hand gently scooped the old man up and brought him close to the operator's cupola. "*Unless* it was an emergency. This is an emergency."

Sun waved his hands in the air. "You *always* say that! It's *always* an emergency!"

Klaus ignored this. "The Other is alive and here in Mechanicsburg. The Empire is being attacked. Hostile forces are still within the walls of the town, and my son is nowhere to be found."

Sun took a deep breath and folded his arms together. "So you're going to handle it all personally? Being a successful emperor means being able to delegate authority! Occasionally, you must let other people do things for you!"

Klaus rolled his eyes. "I know that. But there are some things that only I can do."

"Like what?"

"Like fight a war."

Sun raised his fists to the heavens. "You are a terrible emperor!" When he looked back at Klaus, Sun's eyes were filled with an icy rage. "And a terrible patient!" Methodically, he began tying back his long flowing sleeves. "I should have had guards upon your guards. I see that now. Obviously I must take a page from your book and do everything myself." He took a deep breath and went still.

For the first time, Klaus began to look nervous. A giant metal finger gently poked Sun on the shoulder. The old man began to look positively serene. Sweat appeared on Klaus's brow.

Suddenly, a shouted voice caught their attention. "Grandfather! Stop making yourself the center of everything!"

Sun frowned and peered down. He saw a slim young woman in a green silk version of the hospital uniform striding towards him,[42] followed by Captain Vole. "You are needed in surgery," she declared.

Klaus wisely said nothing and smoothly deposited Sun onto the ground. "What has happened now?"

Daiyu pointed. "This miserable creature—"

Vole interrupted her. "On orders from Master Gilgamesh, Hy haff brought hyu de leader ov dose var schtompers. He iz in need uv medical attention."

Sun sniffed. "I will be the judge of that. Where is he?"

Soundlessly, Vole reached into a stained canvas sack and pulled forth the surprised-looking head of General Rudolf Selnikov.

Sun blinked and harrumphed. "Yes. Well...*tricky*, certainly, but I've seen worse. Let's get him prepped."

The Baron interrupted before they could leave. "Vole!"

The Jäger paused and then made to hand the head off to the older man.

Sun waved a hand at his granddaughter, who gave a heavy sigh

---

[42] Sun Ming Daiyu. MD, PhD. Granddaughter of Dr. Sun. Daughter of the Wulfenbach ambassador to the Court of China. She was raised with Gilgamesh aboard Castle Wulfenbach, where she met Agatha. While not a Spark herself at this time, she was one of those on the short list of people expected to break through at any time.

and snagged the head by its ear. They took off, with Sun bellowing for the orderlies to begin prepping one of his operating rooms. Those who knew him could see that he was looking forward to the challenge. At the entrance, he paused and whirled about—startling the Baron with a fiery glare. He pointed at Klaus and then at the hospital. The message was obvious. Then he spun back and strode into the building.

Klaus heaved a great sigh. *Of course he would protect the Great Hospital. What was Sun thinking?* He focused his attention on the Jäger waiting below. "Vole, where have you been?"

The Jäger looked indignant. "Dere vos a lot uv dead guys und busted machines to dig through! Dot's not as much fun az it sounds like!

"Plus, Hy took some time to tok to sum uf de guards. Az Hy suspected, both of de Heterodyne gurls iz now in de Kessle." He paused, and his next words were slower. "De second gurl, de vun Hy vas sent to get, she iz der real ting. Hy ken tell," he said defensively, although Klaus had said nothing. "De Kessle vill listen to her, if it vill listen to ennyboddy."

"That's not good, Captain." *The idea of Lucrezia in possession of an even marginally functional Castle Heterodyne?* Klaus grimaced. "No, I don't like that at all." He leaned forward, "Now enough of your evasions, where is my son?"

"He iz at Mamma Gkika's, Herr Baron."

Klaus rolled his eyes. "I have got to get that boy married," he muttered. "But it could be worse. He'll be distracted for the moment." He leaned back down. "I have orders for you to deliver and I think it would be best if he doesn't hear about them. However, I will want him safely removed from Mechanicsburg before things get under way."

Vole saluted crisply. "Hy vill drag him avay from here, after Hy beat him senseless, sir."

Klaus stared at Vole for several seconds. "That might work," he admitted.

Back in Mamma Gkika's, Gil shuffled through the papers before him, his mind sorting and calculating automatically. Vanamonde and Krosp watched him silently. Zeetha was happily gnawing away at what appeared to be a turkey leg almost the size of her arm.

The orders concerned a lot of the sort of thing one would expect in a town that was both hosting the Baron and expecting civic disturbances[43]: the movement of road crews, paymasters, fire fighters, extra troops, quartermasters, emergency communication systems—

Gil paused, and suddenly shuffled back several sheets. His gaze sharpened. He checked a few names—

When he looked at Van, his face was aghast. "He's going to destroy Castle Heterodyne," he whispered.

"How?" Krosp asked with professional interest. "The town is legendary for never being conquered."

Van looked worried, "Yes, the old Heterodynes chose this spot for a reason."

Gil slapped the papers down onto the table. "Sure, if the defenses were working, an army couldn't even get up the pass." He leaned in. "But the defenses *aren't* working. My father is *already* in control of the town. He can walk the necessary machines right up to the castle walls if he wants to."

He pulled a paper from the stack. "Road crews. It's true, these days we mostly use the Rumbletoys as earthmovers. But their subsonic wave throwers could liquefy the rock the castle sits on!"

Another paper. "Firefighters? The Ninth Ætheric Vapor Squad usually fights fires in cities and forests, but kick their gas condensers up a notch or two and you could spray the castle with liquid Nitrogen and then crack it open with a hammer."

Another. "Emergency Communications System. The Heliolux Airship Fleet. If we order it, their mirror and lens arrays could melt this entire town off the map." He thought about selecting another but instead just tossed the entire pile in front of Vanamonde.

---

[43]　Experience showed that the two were closely interconnected.

"I'm sure you get the idea. For almost twenty years my father has been collecting Sparks and their tools, repurposing them for peaceful uses within the Empire. But rest assured, he always remembers that they were initially built as war machines, and he knows how to use them."

Everyone stared at the pile of paper. Van took a deep swallow of coffee. "This is…not perfect," he muttered.

Zeetha swallowed. "He's bringing all that just to get at Agatha?"

Gil sat back and snorted. "No, he's bringing a hell of a lot *more* than that. According to the time signatures, *this* was the work of ten minutes. I assure you that for the Other, he'll bring in everything in a hundred kilometer radius, if not more."

Now everyone stared at him. Gil shrugged. "He believes he has cause." He leaned forward and stared back at them. "And let's be honest here, he *does* have cause."

Van's eyes narrowed. "So you think we should just let him—"

"You still don't understand," Gil interrupted. "It's not a case of you *letting* him do anything. If all you've seen are the *official* reports about what happened at Balan's Gap—" Van was flustered enough that he allowed himself to look guilty, confirming another of Gil's suspicions. "—you don't know a *tenth* of what's happening there. If Agatha doesn't surrender herself peacefully, the Empire is going to come in and *cauterize* this place." Gil sat back and took a sip of coffee. "Frankly? The best thing you can do is evacuate the town."

Vanamonde drew himself up. "We serve the House of Heterodyne. We will not desert her."

Gil frowned. "The Heterodynes have been gone for years. You can't tell me…" His eye was caught by Mamma striding out onto the stage. "What's this?"

Van fished out a large silver pocket watch and looked startled. "Is it that late already?" He stood up. "It's time for us to take this conversation somewhere more quiet." All around them, servers were efficiently scooping up mugs and plates, some still full, dumping them into narrow three-wheeled carts and heading for a bank of swinging doors as quickly as they could.

Mamma waved her hands. "Hokay lads, leesen op! Efferboddy knowz dot dere's beeg tings afoots, yah? Ve gunna hav to get beck to vork."

There was a guffaw of laughter from the room. Mamma smiled. "Bot not yet. So iz time for heveryboddy to blow off sum schteam, hey?"

Gil realized that he was sitting alone. He stood up and spotted Vanamonde, Zeetha, and Krosp quickly weaving through the crowded room towards the doors. He wasn't sure why, but something told him to take off after them. Around him, the Jägers at the tables were still and silent, leaning forward with a palpable air of anticipation.

On stage, Mamma made a show of fishing a glittering silver whistle out from her ample décolletage. She held up a clawed finger. "Vait for de vistle, now!"

If anything, Van increased his pace through the crowd. Gil noted that he was obviously worried about something.

Gil caught up to the three. "What's going on?" he asked.

Mamma raised the whistle to her lips and blew a single clear, pure note.

Van flinched. "It's the evening bar fight."

Pandemonium erupted around them. Jägers howled and leapt about, swinging, clawing, and smacking Jägers that they had been laughing with just seconds ago (although, to be fair, they *were* still laughing).

Gil had been caught in several bar fights around the Empire and had to admit that this had to be the jolliest he'd ever been in. A Jäger tumbled back screaming with laughter, with another Jäger latched onto his ear with his teeth. Jollity aside, it was definitely time to go.

Suddenly a furry bundle of claws enveloped his head. After a second, he realized that it was a panicked Krosp, who, as cats are wont to do in times of danger, had scaled the tallest thing in sight. "Evening bar fight!" the cat yowled. "They do this every day?"

Van ducked beneath a thrown chair. "They're Jägers! What did you expect?" He staggered as a tankard bounced off his head. Gil caught his arm and kept him from falling to the ground. Van nodded his thanks and pushed forward. "Just be glad it's not Thursday," he shouted back. "That's poetry slam night."

The inevitable finally happened and a Jäger was thrown towards them. Gil grabbed the creature in midair, swung him about, and let him slam into another churning pile of combatants.

Van went white and clutched at his arm. "Don't do that again! At the moment, we're still considered noncombatants!" Suddenly he paused and glanced around. "Where is Miss Zeetha?"

All it had taken was a single misstep and Zeetha had found herself separated from the others. Initially she had been all-too-willing to leap into the fracas but had quickly discovered that she was garnering undue attention as an exciting novelty.

"Woo!" yet another admiring monster yelled at the sight of her. "Fight mit *me*, varrior gurl!" A boot to the face knocked him into another melee, but Zeetha found herself getting pushed backwards towards a corner, which was bad news.

Suddenly, she felt no pressure on her back.

She turned and stared. She had been pushed into a small pocket of calm. At a corner table sat a slim, rawboned man. His hair was a golden brown, twisted in the back into an airshipman's queue and extending forward in a pair of lovingly maintained muttonchops. Incongruously, he was wearing a Wulfenbach airshipman uniform. Apparently while the fighting had raged all around him, he had, with a rather sleepy-eyed look on his face, been quietly nursing an enormous tankard of beer, smoking his pipe, and, Zeetha realized, with an uncharacteristic jolt of annoyance, gazing appreciatively at her as she fought.

"Hey!" she yelled. The man blinked, and shifted his focus up to her face. "Wake up, you fool! We're cut off! Aren't you paying attention?"

The fellow removed his pipe. "If you want to make any headway towards the door, you'll need more than just your fists," he advised her.

A large Jäger with flapping ears reached for her, and Zeetha gave him a right cross that caused him to spin twice. When he stopped, he was facing in a different direction, and with a laugh, he launched himself into another fight.

"Well I'm not going to use my swords in here," she declared, "Agatha wouldn't like it."

The man nodded and took a pull from his tankard. "Of course not. No weapons. You want to keep it friendly." He unfolded himself from his chair. "Hold on." He then snagged the chair he'd been sitting on and threw it into the face of a Jäger who had been about to tackle Zeetha from behind.

Zeetha looked puzzled. "You just said: No weapons!"

Although his eyes remained half closed, the man looked surprised. "That wasn't a weapon, that was a chair," he explained.

Zeetha grinned. "Then give me a chair!"

The man smiled slightly and handed her one. "Aye, aye."

Zeetha took the chair, and sweeping it back and forth, began clearing a path towards the kitchen doors. The man's eyes followed her and he smiled. Then a slight frown crossed his features and he glanced longingly towards his beer. As he pondered, another Jäger flew through the air and smashed into his table, reducing the tankard to dripping shards.

With a philosophical shrug, the man put his hands in his pockets and slouched off after Zeetha, who was slowly progressing through the room. If Zeetha had watched him she would have been struck by how the man never was where you thought he was. Fists, bottles, tables, and casks flew towards him but somehow he never was there when they arrived.

When he caught up to her, he cleared his throat. "So, uh, what brings you in here?"

Zeetha's chair disintegrated as she broke it over a stout Jäger wearing a fancy pickelhaube. "Oh, you know, I came with some guys."

"You need to find them?"

"Yeah, I'm supposed to make sure one of them doesn't get into trouble."

The airshipman glanced about at the seething chaos and seemed to accept this statement at face value. He picked up a new chair. A barrel sailed past his head. "Smart guy?" he asked as he handed it to Zeetha.

Zeetha considered this. "Yeah, I guess."

"Found 'em. Is he the one with the cat on his head?"

"Probably." She paused. "Wait—how did you know they're smart?"

"They're not fighting a bar full of Jägers."

"Ha!" Zeetha laughed. "Good one!" Then both of them realized what he had said. "Wait a minute, what are you implying?"

The airshipman turned, and the look in Zeetha's eyes caused him to break out in a cold sweat. A long dormant survival instinct awoke within him. He smiled disingenuously. "Miss, you look so extraordinarily dangerous that I wouldn't think of implying *anything* I couldn't directly observe."

To her astonishment, Zeetha found herself blushing. "Do I really look dangerous?"

"Absolutely. Now let's get you back to your friends."

Zeetha nodded and then analyzed the entire exchange. "*HEY!*"

But the airshipman was wasting no time. Zeetha frowned. He wasn't pushing or shoving, and, in fact, never seemed to actually hit anyone, but they were now moving at a respectable clip and Jägers melted away as he approached.

From near a doorway, Van detected a different pattern in the melee, and pointed. "Here she comes."

Gil recognized the hallway as the one he'd entered by. He looked back towards the room he'd awoke in. "Wait, I need—"

From that very room, Dimo, Ognian, and Maxim emerged. "Here iz hyu zappy stick," Dimo sang out.

Ognian carried a small sack. "Here iz de sctuff hyu had in hyu pockets!"

Maxim presented the *pièce de résistance*. "Und hyu hat!"

Gil stared at the hat with loathing. "I do *not* need—"

Krosp interrupted him in a low voice. "The hat. The *special* hat. The hat the Jägers made to show you how impressed they are with you. The Jägers who saved your life and are devoted to Agatha. The girl you want to impress. The girl who doesn't trust you, but *does* trust the Jägers. *That* hat?"

Gil instantly took all the loathing that he had reserved for the hat, doubled it, and now directed it at the cat, who, disappointingly, did not burst into flames but simpered at him. "Helping," he purred.

"…I'll take the hat," Gil said leadenly.

Disconcertingly, every Jäger within earshot paused in their fighting and cheered. "YAY!"

Van turned to Krosp. "An excellent call, Krosp. That was very diplomatic."

Krosp grinned maliciously. "It makes him look like an idiot."

Thanks to the lull in the action, Zeetha and her escort were able to push through the last few meters relatively easily.

It was obvious that the airshipman was uncomfortable. "Here are your friends. I'm off."

For some reason, this seemed to make Zeetha even more annoyed. "So go already."

"You! Wulfenbach airman!" Gil's stern bark caught them both by surprise. "You're with me." Before the airman could say anything, he found the improbable hat thrust into his hands. "Carry this."

The airman's eyes narrowed. "Who…"

Gil grinned. "Oh, I'm sorry, I'm Gilgamesh Wulfenbach."

For the first time, the airman's mask of imperturbability cracked. He turned to the others. "You're…he's just sending me out for a crate of balloon juice. Right?"

"I'm afraid not," Van said.

Maxim pointed proudly. "Iz on hiz hat!"

The airman dragged his eyes downward and examined the legend on the front of the hat. When he looked up, he appeared to have aged several years. However, he snapped to a loose approximation of "attention" and gave a salute. "Airman Third Class Axel Higgs reporting for duty, sir."

"Welcome aboard, Mr. Higgs." Gil paused. "Higgs…Oh! You're the one who rescued my father!"

Higgs looked surprised. "Um…could be," he admitted warily.

Gil took his hand and shook it. "I want to thank you. There's a promotion somewhere with your name on it." Higgs looked uncomfortable. "Oh, well…"

Suddenly, Gil's gaze sharpened and his hand tightened. "Wait a minute, I heard you were seriously injured." He stared at the man for a second—

Dimo gave a roar of a laugh. "He shoo vas!" He punched Gil in the arm, "Joost like *hyu* vas ven ve brought hyu in here!"

Gil considered this. "Oh, yes, I suppose so. But why—?"

At that moment Mamma Gkika stepped up. Behind her, the fight continued. She tucked an errant lock of hair back behind a long elegant ear. "Iz hyu folks leafink? Vell please come again!"

She turned to Airman Higgs. "I'm glad to see hyu iz feelink better, sveethot. A gurl likes to pay her debts, yah?"

Higgs shuffled his feet. "I told you that you don't owe me anything, Ma'am."

Mamma tilted her head to the side. "Vell, I suppose dot's a *leedle* more true now den it vas yesterday." She turned to Gil.

"Hyu account is schtill op in de air, young man. Hyu gots a lot uf credit for slappink dose guys down mit de lightning." She leaned in and gave him a hard look. "But if hyu cause Miz Agatha trouble, den der vill be a reckonink."

Gil looked her in the eye. "Of course I'll cause her trouble. But I'll do my best to protect her."

Mamma's cheeks dimpled as she laughed and patted his cheek. "Oh, dis vill be so *interestink*," she crooned. Then she straightened up. "Hokay, get out uv here!"

Gil turned back to Higgs. "Anyway, you're assigned to me, now. Come along."

Higgs sighed. "Yes, sir."

As they moved off, Zeetha sidled up to him. "So, what did you do for the Jäger lady?"

Higgs kept his eyes straight ahead. "Nothing much. She's makin' more of it than she should."

Zeetha would have continued but they came to a steep set of stairs, almost a ladder, that disappeared up into the darkness. They scrambled upwards for what Gil estimated was close to twenty meters before they came to a wooden hatch that Van opened by throwing a lever set into the wall. The hatch swung up and over on silent, well-oiled pneumatic hinges and they clambered up into—

"A wine cellar?" Gil looked around in astonishment. "How deep underground are we?"

"Deep." Van selected a lantern from a well-supplied shelf. "And we're still two levels down."

Gil nodded slowly as they passed rack upon rack of bottles. He noted that it wasn't only wine stored here. They passed alcoves neatly stuffed with what appeared to be assorted food stores. Mechanicsburg was still well prepared in case of siege.

"Is this sort of thing common around here?"

Van raised an eyebrow.

Gil waved a hand. "These extensive cellars. I mean, we're still finding underground passages in Balan's Gap, and I spent a lot of time in the Paris Undercity,[44] but does every city have stuff like this? I grew up on an airship. We didn't really have a basement, per se."

The Jägers laughed. "Vell, dey's not all as extensive as ours," Dimo said thoughtfully.

"Or else Europa vould have collapsed after a hard rain!" Maxim chimed in.

Gil raised his lantern and looked around. "Are there monsters?" He looked back at the Jägers. "Present company excluded, of course."

Dimo laughed again, "Ho, yaz! But dey all vork for de Heterodynes. Ain't dot right, Franz?"

This last was asked at a shout, and Gil realized, with a start, that the <u>giant statue they</u> were walking beside was not a statue, but instead,

---

[44]   The city of Paris is famous, amongst those who are interested in such things, for its elaborate sewer system. There are also an extensive series of catacombs, quite a number of hidden vaults, a few natural caverns, some subterranean rivers, a thriving ecosystem, and at least one hidden civilization, along with two known enclaves of thieves, one of which runs a famous black market and the other the smugglers' railroad, all of which is ruled by the Shadow Court. Frankly, it's a wonder that any people are left to wander the streets above ground.

a living creature. Zeetha and Krosp realized it at the same moment. Both jumped and then looked annoyed at having done so.

The monster's great head swung slowly towards them. Its skin was cracked and pebbled and covered in a grey coating of dust. Enormous nostrils blew out a gust of air redolent with flammable hydrocarbons, and a pair of sleepy green-gold eyes opened slightly. Gil noted a tarnished brass dial set into its nose. The needle flickered at the far left, and there was a trilobite symbol set into the space between its brows. The rest of the enormous body was hidden in the shadows.

"Yeh, yeh." The gravelly slow voice roiled over them. "Heterodynes forever. Now shottop. I'm trying to get some sleep here."

Gil stared at the creature with awe. "I didn't think there were any dragons left,"[45] he breathed.

The dragon slowly shifted his attention to him and again sighed. "Until de Heterodyne returns," he muttered as his eyes closed, "you iz correct."

The sound of deep breathing filled the cavern.

At the next stairway, Dimo stopped. "Dis iz as far az ve goes," he said to Gil. "Hyu iz on hyu own now."

Zeetha looked disappointed. "You're not coming? Why not? We could use you."

Dimo shrugged. "Ve iz not supposed to be in de town until de Heterodyne iz back officially. Den dey rings de Doom Bell. Until dot happens, ve gots to stay underground, vere ve's technically not in de town."

---

[45]   Back when they called it "Mad Alchemy," the creation of dragons was actually fairly popular. There were any number of towns and kingdoms that wanted them as protectors, or mascots, the most famous being the City of London. Inevitably, however, being long-lived, frugal creatures, they tended to amass hoards, which people tended to want to steal from them. Thus, most of the dragons were wiped out. The few remaining alchemists who could create them were annoyed at this and started creating dragons that were much, much harder to kill. But "harder" is not the same as "unkillable," and after a dragon *was* finally killed, the knights went after the smart-ass alchemist that made it. And even a philosopher stone that granted immortality did not grant protection from a meter or so of Toledo steel. And thus the secret of making dragons was presumed lost. This is technically untrue, as apparently the *real* secret to viable, successful dragons was never found, which was: make them philanthropists.

Zeetha looked skeptical. "But didn't you go through the town to get here with him?" She pointed at Gil.

Dimo winced but it was too late. Ognian and Maxim's eyes had widened and they looked at each other in obvious distress.

"She iz right!" Ognian said with a troubled voice. "Ve broke de solemn oath ven ve brought Meester Gil in through de Sneaky Gate!"

"But de regular tunnels vas too far," Maxim said, "and he vas too injured!"

"Ve had no choice! But ve gafe our vord!"

"Now our honor is foreffer shattered!"

"Ve kin only redeem ourselves mit honorable death!"

"Yez! Svift, painful, honorable death!"

Ognian drew a wicked looking knife from inside his coat. Its blade glittered in the lantern light. "Hyu knife, brodder," he intoned.

Maxim's own knife appeared. A tear ran down his face. "Right here, brodder!"

Simultaneously, they reached up and placed their knives at each other's throats. They closed their eyes—

Dimo cleared his throat. "Ve didn't actually get *caught*, hyu eediots."

The two Jägers stared at him owlishly for a moment and then with a relieved sigh, repocketed their blades.

"Scary," Oggie muttered.

"Yeh," Maxim agreed. "Dot vas a close vun."

Gil and Zeetha exchanged glances.

Dimo strode over and clapped Gil on the shoulder. "Goot luck, Meester Gilgamesh! Ven hyu sees Miz Agatha, hyu takes care uf her until ve gets dere, hokay?"

Gil snorted. "If she'll *let* me."

Van, meanwhile, had been collecting the lanterns, extinguishing them, and storing them on a rack similar to the one in the wine cellar. He turned to the others now. "All right, folks, one last gauntlet and we're out."

Gil looked apprehensive. "What, more monsters?"

Van shook his head. "Tourists." He opened the door and a pulsing wave of sound boomed outwards. It was a driving polka beat that vibrated the floorboards and rattled the tableware. Gil and his party found themselves in another bierstube, but this one was brightly lit and hung with garish Jäger trophies and pictures that inevitably portrayed the Jägers as buffoons and dimwitted clowns.

The place was packed with tourists, drinking and dancing, along with teams of saucy girls barely dressed as Jägers.

Van put his mouth next to Gil's ear. "*This* is the Mamma Gkika's you've heard about," he yelled.

Krosp had clapped his paws over his ears. "No wonder nobody can hear the Jägers fighting down there."

Gil nodded. "Let's get out of here. I have an idea, but we'll have to move quickly and quietly."

As he spoke, a meaty hand grasped his collar and hauled him up onto the stage. It was a large, drunken patron, who waved Gil around in the air and bellowed; "Hey look! It's Gilgamesh Wulfenbach! The guy who saved the town!"

Immediately the hall erupted into cheers. Vanamonde sagged against the wall. "So much for quietly."

Krosp shrugged. "So we're doomed. Cope."

"No, really, we're doomed," Moloch moaned. "No one's ever been in this part of the Castle."

"The map says to go this way," Agatha said confidently.

"But the traps aren't marked."

Agatha nodded. "Then that pink harridan won't follow us."

"WRONG." A ghastly voice echoed through the cavernous room they had been traversing. Moloch whimpered and hugged the tools tighter. The voice of the Castle continued, "This is very interesting. They want to kill you so much that they are killing each other." It sounded amused. Then its tone became aggrieved: "Why is that? Don't they know that killing all of you is *my* job?"

Agatha took a deep breath. Another personality fragment. This one, at least, sounded…different. More complex. "They want to kill me because I am the rightful Heterodyne, and the girl leading them is a usurper."

"Oh, really?" The Castle was obviously interested now.

"Yes, really. I spoke to you in the crypt. You told me to get to the library."

There was a pause. When it spoke again, the voice was thoughtful. "The Crypt? I don't remember any crypt, but the library *is* where you should go…"

"I know you have trouble with your memories. You don't control as much territory as you know you should. It's one of the reasons I'm here to repair you. The other girl is a false Heterodyne. She wants to shut you down and kill me. The people after me are her minions."

"Ah. *That* I understand." This was followed by a snap and a scream from behind Agatha. She whirled and found Moloch stuck in a trapdoor in the floor, saved only by having wedged himself with the pack he had been carrying.

"He's with me!" Agatha said, as she helped haul him up.

"Ah," the Castle admonished. "Then you *should* have said, 'the people after us.' If you are a Heterodyne, you must remember that words are important."

Moloch yanked his feet free just as the opening in the floor resealed itself. "I hate this place," he gasped.

The Castle chuckled. It then made several helpful suggestions regarding where they should go and thereafter kept up a stream of idle, if slightly disturbing, chatter as they navigated the hallways. Agatha took the time to look around a bit. The damage to this part of the castle seemed superficial, though parts of the floor were slightly off-kilter.

Windows were cracked, furniture was tipped to the side, and there was a thick coat of dust everywhere. Cobwebs hung thick, and rotted drapery and tapestries hung from the walls. The air was thick and silent.

"It's obvious no one's come this way since the explosions," Agatha muttered.

"*Technically*, that's not true," the Castle replied. "Master William visited the library before he left. He told me to guard it, that it was the most important room in the entire castle. But since then, you are correct."

They turned a corner and saw a gigantic wooden door, labeled with tarnished brass letters that spelled out "BIBLIOTHECA." To either side of the door stood a statue of a solid-looking young lady carrying an axe in one hand and a large lantern in the other. Evidently the artist had thought that these accoutrements were stylish enough that the ladies could skip any other semblance of clothing.

Agatha smiled. "Well, I appreciate you letting me get here so easily." With that, the lanterns the statues carried began to glow along with their eyes, and with a grinding sound, the two statues turned their heads to look at them.

The Castle chuckled. "It will only be easy if you are an actual Heterodyne."

The statue on the left hefted its axe. When it spoke, its voice was eerie and whispered. "One must die—"

The other statue continued smoothly, "—so another may pass." The axes were lifted and the blades began shifting back and forth between Agatha and Moloch. The statue on the right whispered, "You must decide who must die—"

The statue on the left continued, "—so that one of you may pass."

Moloch shrieked and dropped to his knees. Agatha thought furiously. "I choose..." Then she pointed to the statue on the right. "Her!"

Instantly, the blade of the left-hand statue flashed out and smashed the head of the other statue. Ceramic and clockwork exploded into fragments. The right-hand statue shuddered once and then slumped into stillness. The statue on the left then paused. "Wait a minute..."

Agatha nodded. "Excellent. That secures passage for my companion." She indicated Moloch, who was staring at the smoking stature with an open mouth. She then stepped forward. "Do we have to play the same little game to secure *my* passage?"

The eyes of the statue flicked from Agatha, to the other statue, to Moloch, to the other statue, to its axe, to Agatha... and then it stepped back and the shaft of its axe slammed into place on the floor.

"Test passed!" it declared, and then its eyes went dark.

"Well," Agatha said, "that was a lot easier than I thought it would be."

Moloch shuddered. "The horrible thing is that I know you're serious." He then walked up to the large double doors. "So this is the library. How is this going to help? It's just a bunch of stupid books."

The Castle was clearly offended. "*These* books contain the secrets of the Heterodyne family."

"What, like *A Thousand and One Ways to Kill People*?"

The Castle chuckled, "Oh, there's far more than that."

Agatha, meanwhile, had been tugging and pushing at the great brass and onyx handle with no success. "The door's locked."

The Castle paused. "The door is not locked."

Moloch put down the supplies and gave the handle a twist. It clicked but nothing happened. He looked for hinges, and seeing none, gave a shove with his shoulder. The door shifted slightly.

"*That's* your problem," he announced. "I'll bet the doorframe's warped. The door is just stuck."

"It always sticks a bit," the Castle agreed.

Something about the way the Castle said this set off an alarm bell in Agatha's mind. Nothing she could put her finger on, but...

"Stand back," Moloch said, hunching his shoulders, "One good smack oughta do it." He then launched himself at the door.

"Wait," Agatha yelled. It couldn't stop him, but Moloch did manage to check himself in mid-rush, which is why he grabbed hold of the great handle as the door burst open. This prevented him from sailing freely out into open space. It did not, however, prevent him from screaming.

"Impressive, isn't it?" the Castle chuckled.

"There's no library here!" Agatha looked down onto a rubble-strewn courtyard several stories down. "There's nothing here at all!"

"Yes!" Von Zinzer yelled. "*Lots* of nothing! Help me!"

Agatha leaned out and managed to get a tenuous grip upon some of the door's brasswork. She braced herself and slowly began to swing it closed with her fingertips. Finally Moloch got close enough that his feet could touch the stone sill and he lunged back inside, sprawling onto the floor and taking deep breaths. Agatha stared out at the open area.

"This is another test." She waved her hand outwards. "The library *is* here, isn't it?"

"Very good," the castle said approvingly. "The door you seek is right in front of you."

Agatha stared out again and squinted. Nothing. Suddenly, her depth of focus shifted slightly and she saw, tucked into the far wall approximately fifty meters away, a small, unassuming opening. She pointed. "That's it? Over there? What, am I supposed to fly to it?"

Again the Castle chuckled. Moloch pulled himself into as small a ball as possible. "Flying is not necessary. But I *do* insist on a leap of faith."

Suddenly, there was a rattling of stone upon stone, and before Agatha's astounded eyes, the rubble on the ground shifted, wobbled, and slowly floated upward. A vast cloud of bricks and paving stones drifted upwards, rotated in place for several seconds, and then condensed into a narrow, irregular path of stones that floated in mid-air between the two doorways.

There was a final "clink," and the Castle spoke. "There. Our own little 'Bridge of Trust.' Anytime you are ready, 'My Lady.'"

Moloch stared at the floating path in horror. "Ready to *die*, you mean. There is no way I'm going—"

"Correct." The Castle was serious now. "The Heterodyne must enter alone."

Agatha nodded. She pointed to Moloch. "Please don't kill him while I'm gone."

Moloch looked appalled. "Hold on—you're not actually going, are you?"

Agatha took a deep breath. "Of course I am." And she stepped out upon the pathway. She expected it to give slightly or to sway, but the stones beneath her feet were as solid as if they were resting upon rock. She had listened to enough of the stories that the circus' aerialists had told around the fires at night to know not to look down, though this was proving difficult to adhere to. She took a step. Then another...and another after that. She was about to release the breath she had been holding, when a clunking sound caused her to freeze. She turned as quickly as she dared and looked back in time to see the stones that were positioned against the doorway begin to wobble and then fall, one by one, to the courtyard below. Slowly the disintegrating edge moved towards her.

Agatha sighed, turned back, and continued onward.

"You're very trusting," the Castle remarked.

"And you're very annoying."

"Aren't you afraid I'll drop you?"

"No."

Now the Castle sounded peeved. "Why not? I could, you know."

Agatha continued moving. "You're like the people in Mechanicsburg, I think. You want a Heterodyne. You keep threatening to kill me, but you're not sure, so you're herding me towards the library where I might actually be able to repair you, if I am who I say I am."

She took a deep breath and continued. "Besides, from how much fun you're evidently having from these games, I imagine you'd be disappointed if I didn't survive long enough to take whatever test there is to prove my legitimacy."

"Games? I don't know what—"

Agatha gestured downwards. "This path, for one. You could have easily made it three meters wide and as straight as a ruler."

A note of embarrassment crept into the Castle's voice. "Yes... well..."

"So, thank you."

The Castle clearly hadn't been expecting this. "For what?"

Agatha stepped off of the bridge and into the doorway. As she had surmised, a dark passage twisted off to the right and vanished into the darkness. "For getting me so annoyed that I didn't have a chance to get scared or disoriented. You did that."

The Castle was silent.

"Now no more games," Agatha said.

Behind her the last of the stones pattered to the ground. "Agreed," the Castle said. Then the floor opened beneath Agatha's feet and she dropped out of sight.

A fall, a jolt, a disorienting slide in the darkness. With a cry of shocked surprise, Agatha crashed through a wooden lattice and landed upon the floor of a new room. She took a minute to catch her breath and rub at her painful hindquarters. "I thought I said—"

"*SILENCE!*" With the Castle's roar, iron shutters slammed back, revealing a magnificent stained glass window. Through this, the afternoon sun washed the room with bright shades of red, yellow, and purple. Agatha stared.

The room was large and high ceilinged. Directly beneath the window was an unadorned altar of black stone. The walls and the ceiling were lined with bones. Human bones, inset and tessellated in patterns that caught the eye and always brought it back to the altar.

Agatha had heard of churches decorated like this, walls and furnishings supplied by victims of plague or war, but reading alone had failed to prepare her for the actual experience. She took a small step and almost fell over. The floor was paved with skulls.

"This is no longer a game," the Castle said. "This is where you will prove your claim, or where you will die.

"Over the centuries, there have been other times when my masters have gone missing. You are not the first stranger who has come to me claiming the family name. Sometimes they strode in leading armies. Sometimes they skulked in on moonless nights. One flew in on wings made of bone and brass. All claimed to be lost Heterodynes, and all found their way here to this room to be tested.

"Sometimes they were delusional. Sometimes they were...false men. Puppet things of shadow and dead meat. Sometimes they were simply...honestly...wrong. They never left.

"Now it is your turn. Take comfort in knowing that if you fail, there will still be a place for you here, forever."

Agatha took a deep breath. "Then let's get started."

A rumble emanated from beneath her feet. The vibrations swelled until the room shook and Agatha lost her footing, landing atop the pavement of juddering skulls. Before her, the floor bulged upwards. Skulls rolled off, bouncing away as a vast mechanical claw thrust its way up into the light. Another appeared. They bent, and slammed into the ground, levering a vast serpent-like form up from the depths. Corroded brass covered by cracked dials writhed upwards. Agatha could see furnaces glowing within the thing's structure. A great head shot upwards, paused as it reached the ceiling, and then swung down towards Agatha.

As opposed to the utilitarian gears, springs, and dials of the rest of the mechanism, the face had actually been sculpted. It took the form of an enormous gargoyle—all fangs and spines. Nervous as she was, Agatha had to admire the workmanship that went into its creation—it actually seemed to change its expression as it hovered less than a meter from her.

"Yes," mocked the Castle's voice. "Do let us get started." The gargoyle's great jaws, easily two meters wide, split open in a great gap-toothed grin. "Place your hand in the mouth."

Agatha stared into the dark recess. There were...things moving in there.

"...And?"

The mouth drifted open even wider. "And if you are of the family, I will know."

Agatha squared her shoulders and slipped her left glove off before gingerly inserting her hand between the great teeth. "I am a Heterodyne," she declared. The mouth gently closed down, trapping her hand. "I...I know I am," Agatha said gamely. "How will you know?"

The eyes widened innocently. "Blood."

Agatha had steeled herself for pain, but she screamed nonetheless.

Gilgamesh Wulfenbach gritted his teeth as he felt Krosp climbing up his back. The cat had evidently decided that he liked the height that Gil's shoulder provided, and Gil (correctly) assumed that the pain and inconvenience this gave him was considered a bonus.

Krosp dipped his head so his whiskers were tickling Gil's ears. "So," he said—one eye on the road ahead, "just for laughs, you wanna share what this great plan of yours was?"

Gil brushed a whisker away. "To quietly find my father and explain the situation." Krosp gave a snort. "And if that didn't work, drug him into insensibility until I could sort things out."

Krosp raised an eyebrow. "His doctor would allow this?"

Gil snorted. "If your reports about what my father is doing are correct? Dr. Sun would hand me the syringe."

Krosp considered this. "That's…not a bad plan."

Gil shrugged. "Thank you."

Krosp looked around at the huge crowd of revelers that seethed around them, yelling, cheering, playing musical instruments, and chanting various slogans as they stumbled towards the Great Hospital. "Got another? Preferably one that instead of stealth, involves half the town?"

Gil nodded seriously. "I'm working on it."

The appearance of an apparently genuine Heterodyne had brought forth a tremendous wellspring of excitement and jubilation in the populace of Mechanicsburg. This was only slightly dampened by the fact that no one was sure *which* Heterodyne girl was the genuine article and both of them were still in the Castle, but it was the considered opinion of the populace that the real Heterodyne would shortly appear, preferably with the fake's head on a pike.

Once Gil had been identified by the denizens of the tavern, he had quickly become the focus of all the pent-up bonhomie and Spark-associated goodwill.

Thus wherever he went, he was accompanied by an ever-growing crowd of boisterous well-wishers.

He found this very odd as usually whenever people in general discovered a person was a Spark, the crowd tended to run in the other direction.

He shook his head. *This is Mechanicsburg,* he reminded himself.

Riding above the crowd, Krosp noticed a snail-seller pause. The man began looking around wildly. Krosp sniffed. Was that coal gas?

With a roar, a column of flame erupted from the nearest lamppost, sending the snail-seller stumbling back until he collided with his cart.

The crowd screamed. Some in fear, some in delight. This only intensified as, one by one, other lampposts also burst into flame. Soon every street was lined with brightly burning posts.

Gil stared. "This is no ordinary gas leak! What—" He turned back to his companions, and saw the look on Vanamonde's face. He grabbed the man's coat and dragged him closer. "Von Mekkhan! You know what this is?"

Van's eyes looked like they had seen something impossible. "The Lady Heterodyne," he said, gesturing at the lamps. "She must have woken something. The town is… is beginning to defend itself."

Gil looked at him blankly. "Defend itself from what?"

Aboard the pink airship serenely drifting above Bill and Barry Square, things were quiet. The lights had been dimmed to night-watch levels. The only oddity a seasoned flyer would have noticed would have been gleaned from the gauges and dials themselves, which revealed that the batteries and boilers were still operating at full strength. Usually at night they would have been switched off and set to standby mode.

Captain Abelard grimaced as he checked his instruments for the hundredth time that day. An airman learned that as far as airships were concerned, less was better. This naturally led to an abhorrence of waste and the thought of fuel being burned while the ship simply hovered gnawed at him. The only balm was the agonized grousing of Duke Strinbeck, who was apparently the man paying for it all.

The captain glanced over at the man responsible for this "wasteful extravagance" and sighed. Kraddock was a damn fine wheelman and no mistake, but right now he looked like a middie who'd been given the wheel for the first time and told, in strict confidence, that the only reason the ship stayed up was because the wheelmen kept telling themselves that they were really birds.

The thought brought a touch of a smile to the captain's mouth. He'd always loved that one. But not here. Not now.

The second mate came onto the bridge. Shift change already? Indeed it was. Lieutenant Waroon activated the shipboard intercom and deliberately rang the ship's bell twice, paused, and then once again. "Three Bells," he announced. "Stand down for the Night Crew!"

The Night Crew, who, as tradition demanded, had stood off the bridge until it was their time, entered and went through the official turnover procedure.

Captain Abelard ran a tight ship, but a happy one, and so the crew felt free to chat briefly, not that there was much to report. As Ensign Stross reported to his replacement, "Dead simple and boring all the way, Mate."

But, as the captain had expected, there was trouble with Kraddock. His replacement stood by and requested the wheel but the old man refused to relinquish control.

Abelard sighed. It happened sometimes. "Airman's Grip" they called it, when, for whatever reason, a crewman latched ahold of something and simply refused to let go, convinced that if they did something terrible would happen.

It usually was the signal that an airshipman was ready to settle down and leave the air. The captain shook his head. He'd have never in a million years have thought that would happen to an old cloud-nuzzler like Kraddock.

He stepped over, and spoke in a low, but firm voice. "Hey, old timer, shift's over."

Kraddock turned and saluted sharp enough, but his face was enough to cause the captain to draw in a quick breath. The wheelman was sweating like a ballast tank and his eyes looked like a pair of bloodshot boiled eggs. The captain wondered if he had blinked in the last several hours.

"Something is wrong, Captain," the old man said. "I can feel it."

Sturgeon, the other wheelman, rolled his eyes. "Patch the gas leak on him, will you, sir?" he appealed to the captain. "He's been like this all day."

"And don't I know it. Ensign Kraddock, you are relieved—"

He was interrupted by one of the spotters. "Captain! Fire on the ground!"

The captain paused. "Let me see."

The spotter pointed to a small park near the castle. Sure enough, it appeared that one of the lampposts was on fire. Odd.

The captain nodded. "Very good, Mr. Owlswick. Helio the co-ordinates to the town watch and—"

"No!"

The bridge crew turned as one man and stared at Duke Strinbeck as he stepped onto the bridge. Captain Abelard took a deep breath. *Now what?* "Your Grace?"

The Duke crossed his arms. "No communication with the town until Oublenmach gives the order. Were we unclear?"

The captain frowned. "But, your Grace, fire spotting is one of an airman's sacred duties."

The Duke waved a hand dismissively. "I am your employer, and I don't give a bent gear about your 'sacred duties.' You will—"

"Another fire!" This time it was the starboard spotter.

Both the captain and the Duke paused.

"And another!" This time it was the navigator, peering out the windows.

"Two more over here!"

Mr. Owlswick gasped. "I don't believe it! Sir! There's dozens of them! Everywhere!"

"*GET US OUT OF HERE!*" Kraddock's shriek caused everyone to leap into the air. "*NOW!*"

So frantic was the man that two of the bridge crew grabbed him as he tried to head towards the captain. "He's gone mad!" one of them shouted.

Kraddock ignored them and addressed the captain, desperation in his voice. "Captain! Get us up! Get us out of Mechanicsburg airspace!" Kraddock's hand, dragging one of the men holding him, pointed towards the ground, where hundreds of sparks could now be seen below. *"It's the Torchmen!"*

Captain Abelard drew in a sharp breath as the old stories roared through his mind, but before he could say anything there was the unmistakable sound of a gun being cocked. Silence fell instantly. The Duke pointed his weapon at Kraddock. "I will shoot any man who tries to move this ship," he said coldly.

Fury filled Captain Abelard. "Get that gun off of my bridge," he roared, shaking a fist.

Strinbeck stared back. "Don't touch me. We stay here!"

This galvanized Kraddock, who again began to thrash against the men holding him. "Take us up!" he screamed. "We'll all die!"

Strinbeck's eyes narrowed and he placed the barrel against Kraddock's temple. "*You* will die now unless you shut up."

"And don't threaten my crew," the captain snarled.

The two glared at each other. The pause was broken by Mr. Owlswick's shout. "Captain! The fires! They...Sir, they're *moving*!"

Captain Abelard froze. "It is the torchmen," he breathed.

Strinbeck rolled his eyes. "I don't like your tone, hireling."

Captain Abelard had seen military action, fought hand-to-hand against pirates, and was once the last man standing at the end of a glorious fight at Montgolfier's Rest—the notorious airshipman's bar in Paris—but the punch that he landed upon Strinbeck's jaw was the most satisfying one he had ever thrown. The aristocrat went down like a cut sandbag and crashed to the deck, motionless.

"That's *Captain* to you," Abelard snarled. Then he grabbed the intercom. "All hands," he roared. "Dump all ballast! Emergency climb! Engines ahead full! *We are birds! Fly for your lives!*"

Immediately the report came back. "Ballast dropped, sir!" They could feel it in their guts when the ship lurched beneath their feet.

The bridge crew took over.

"Engines to speed."

"All hands rig for pressure loss!"

"Full speed ahead, Mr. Ajayi. What's our bearing?"

"Due North, sir.

"Due North it is."

Below, over a thousand fires burned. At the heart of each fire, a decorative gargoyle—one atop each of the town's lampposts—shivered and swiveled its head upward, seeking until it found the rapidly climbing airship.

There was a great cracking sound across the town, and the burning figures stood atop their posts. There was another great snapping and hundreds of sets of flaming wings extended. They reached down in unison and, grasping the center light globe, drew it forth, revealing a long, steel lance. As one, they all pointed their lances at the little airship and launched themselves upwards.

Aboard the airship, the great flaming swarm of torchmen could be seen coalescing above the town and heading towards them in a tight spiral.

"They're coming right at us!" Mr. Owlswick shouted.

"Engine's in the yellow," the engineer reported.

The captain stared at the advancing wave. He didn't like what the trigonometry was telling him. He again grabbed the intercom.

"All hands! This is an *Emergency Dump!* Food! Fuel! Ammo! *Everything!*"

The bridge crew looked shocked. This was a desperate measure indeed. Reserved for those situations where every gram made a difference in weight and speed.

Behind him, Kraddock, now a model of professionalism, smacked the back of both wheelmen's heads. "Hold your wheels!"

Hands that had gone lax snapped back to true North. One of the newer wheelmen, called out: "Kraddock! You know about these things. How far will they follow us?"

The old man's eyes went distant. *"If you'd live to see the end of day, from Mechanicsburg you'll two leagues stay."*

Silverstein looked lost. "Two leagues? Um...whose leagues?"[46] He thought again. "And what's that in kilometers?"

Kraddock stared at him. "How the freefalling hell should *I* know," he roared. "We just stayed away from the damned place!"

Lieutenant Lorquis removed a set of earphones. "Sir! Chief says that he's dumped everything but the bag!"

Mr. Owlswick piped up. "They're still gaining, sir."

The captain thumped a fist down on a bulkhead. "Blast! There's got to be *something* we can toss!"

"You scum!" The voice caught everyone by surprise. It was Duke Strinbeck. He had pulled himself up to a sitting position. "You dare to strike my royal personage? I'll have every member of your crew flayed alive! I'll see to it that you never collect a pfennig of your pensions! *You'll never fly again!*"

Lieutenant Lorquis exchanged a glance with the captain. Occasionally, problems solved themselves.

Less than a minute later, the two men returned to the bridge. Lorquis ran his tongue over a split lip. The captain fussed at a lost button.

"That did it, sir," Mr. Owlswick sang out. "We're pulling ahead."

This announcement fell flat. The rest of the bridge crew was tense and silent. Lorquis took a deep breath. "So, uh, Captain...we pirates now?"

---

46   A legitimate question. Before the Baron enforced the adoption of the metric system, local units of measurement were based on systems designed by such diverse sources as the Romans, Charlemagne, Moorish Spain, the Bible, Greek mathematics, how many steps it took a man to find enlightenment divided by his love of a good woman, and the size of assorted potentates' feet. However everyone insisted on using the same names. Thus depending on where you were in Europa, a "foot" could be anything from fifteen centimeters to fifty, and it just got worse from there. Especially if you were a cobbler.

The captain froze, and then deliberately stood tall and brushed off his coat. "No. He didn't count. I'll log him in as 'Lost Due to Own Stupidity.'"[47]

The lieutenant and the rest of the crew relaxed. "Just checking, sir!"

The navigator called out, "Heading, Captain?"

Ah, now that was a question. Captain Abelard had had a belly-full of these conspirators, but they were powerful, there was no denying that. He had to think carefully about what came next. Or so he believed.

"Whoa!" That was Van Loon, one of the wheelmen. "Captain! Clouds moving in fast out of the West! I've never seen—"

"Wait." Kraddock gasped. "*Hard to starboard!*"

The wheels spun and the bridge crew was suddenly blinded as they were caught in a web of searchlight beams. Castle Wulfenbach's spotters had seen them and now the enormous grey expanse of dirigible loomed before them. Apparently Castle Wulfenbach had been running dark, but now decided that this was pointless. Thousands of lights burst forth from the structures covering her hull, making it appear as if a flying city were bearing down upon them.

"Captain! We can't let them delay us! The torchmen are still following us." It was the new kid who suggested it. "If we slide *around* 'em, then the torchmen will go after *them*, and we can—"

Kraddock's fist slammed into the kid's jaw, and the other airmen nodded grim approval. Sometimes airmen fought other airmen, it was true, but that was under orders or for similarly good reasons. Until then, you were all part of the Brotherhood of the Skies.

"Heliographs," Captain Abelard roared. "Signal flares! Sound the sirens! Warn them what's coming and tell them we offer all aid and assistance!" He then grinned at his crew. "And I'll bet that's the first time anyone's said that to the flyin' whale."

---

[47]   A notation that appeared all too often regarding new airmen. It also tended to close the ledgers on suicides, thieves, crooked gamblers, and practical jokers. It says something that when this verdict was eventually delivered to Duke Strinbeck's next of kin, none thought to question it.

The crew chuckled as Captain Abelard gazed back at the onrushing wave of flaming death. *And I'll also bet they'll take it*, he thought.

On the ground below the crowd *ooohd* and *ahhd* as the torchmen rose after the rapidly departing dirigible. A few tasteless people were noisily taking bets as to whether or not the craft would escape.

Gil heard Vanamonde sigh with pleasure. The young man was staring upwards, possessive pride radiating from him like a beacon. He saw Gil looking at him and he pointed upwards. "Look at them! Still operative after all these years!"

Yes, Gil thought to himself. *Father will be annoyed that he missed that.*

Van continued, "Back then, 'Made in Mechanicsburg' really *meant* something!"

Gil pondered this as he stared upwards. Something about the patterns of the flying looked…off to him. "If I remember correctly, it usually meant 'death and destruction.'"

Van shrugged. "That's still something."

The meaning of what he was seeing became clear, and Gil gasped as a dozen flaming machines smashed to earth. Instantly, Van was all business. "Fire fighters," he shouted. "To your stations!" His voice seemed to break the spell and dozens of locals threw down their drinks and raced off into the night.

Van frowned as a few more of the torchmen hit the ground.

"I don't understand," Krosp muttered. "That airship isn't shooting at them."

Van looked embarrassed. "They haven't been properly maintained. Not since the Castle was damaged. Since the Baron took over, we haven't even dared test them."

"And yet she still got them running." The admiration and excitement was obvious in Gil's voice. "She's amazing. Together we will—"

Krosp batted at his ear. "Focus! We've got a problem!"

Everyone gasped. The Castle Wulfenbach airship had now appeared from out of the clouds. It was clear even from the ground that it was the torchmen's new focus, and—unlike the tiny pink dirigible—the capital of the Empire was equipped to fight back.

Almost as one, a hundred anti-aircraft guns flashed. Several seconds later, the sound of the fusillade reached the people on the ground, rolling over them like a continuous roar of thunder. Dozens of torchmen exploded into burning fragments. Now the hundreds of smaller support ships that traveled with the behemoth airship could be seen, and they also began firing. Unfortunately, their presence complicated the battle. The compact group of torchmen broke apart and spread out. Weaving and ducking amidst the flock of ships attacking them, grazing envelopes, igniting gondolas, leaving trails of burning devastation behind them, they made it almost impossible for the Wulfenbach ships to fire on them without hitting their own allies.

Before long, several of the smaller ships could be seen bursting into flame and spiraling down to the ground. Luckily, it appeared that all of them would fall to earth outside the city limits.

Gil stared upwards, aghast. "This will complicate things. My father is already convinced that she's a threat, but I don't think he'd considered her effect upon Mechanicsburg itself. There's no way he'll listen to me now."

Krosp sounded worried. "So what can we do?"

Gil nodded. "I do have an idea," he admitted, "but it's a bit desperate." He signaled to the others and then took off in a slightly different direction. "The only uncertainty," he muttered, "revolves around just how much my father actually cares about my physical well-being."

They rounded a corner and Gil gasped as Krosp's claws sank into his head. Behind him, the remnant of the crowd that had kept up shuddered into silence and began skidding to a halt at the sight before them.

A full squad of Wulfenbach troops filled the street: two dozen troopers armed with rifles, their bayonets glittering in the light from the surrounding fires. Three of the tall brass trooper clanks, armed with machine-cannons, loomed behind them. Bringing up the rear was a gigantic green-furred monstrosity wearing a set of goggles and a tall plumed hat.

At the head of this assemblage was Captain Vole. When he caught sight of Gil, his mouth split open in a fang-filled grin. He pointed dramatically at Gil's chest with a clawed finger. "Hokay, brat! Hy haff been charged by hyu poppa mit collectink hyu, end escortink hyu beck to Castle Wulfenbach, vere hyu vill be safe!

"Hy haff been also told dot Hy ken beats der schtuffinks out uv hyu if hyu giffs me teeny veeniest problem. Hyu gots dot?"

Gil turned to Krosp, Zeetha, and the others. A small tear trickled from his eye. "He really *does* care. This is perfect!"

Krosp flattened his ears. "How is this perfect?"

Gil spoke rapidly. He could feel the blood coursing through his head. It was perfect! It would work! And he could help Agatha… "Here's the plan. I'll escape from this fool and then let everyone see me entering the castle!"

Krosp's jaw dropped. "Are you crazy?"

Vole nodded matter-of-factly. "Yez! He iz in de madness place! He iz capable uf ennyting!" He turned to the green behemoth. "Sergeant! Take him out qvikly!"

"Yes, this will work," Gil said with confidence, his voice rising with the excitement of a Spark working on a new scheme. "My father probably won't destroy the castle once he knows I'm inside! At least, not right away—OW!"

He turned to Krosp, who had dropped to the ground and was furiously scrubbing away at his mouth. "You bit me."

"We're about to get shot," the cat screamed. "Exactly how are we escaping?"

Gil looked up and saw the business end of two dozen rifles. "Stun rounds only," the green behemoth shouted. "Or I will personally eat your ears!"

Gil's face went blank. He'd been busy thinking about Agatha and Castle Heterodyne. Getting captured wasn't the part of the plan…"Oh. Um…"

And then he disappeared.

Moloch von Zinzer leaned against the faux doorframe and idly watched the fireworks taking place overhead, munching away at some dried apples that he'd stowed in a pocket of his apron.

Suddenly, a brick sailed up out of the darkness and smacked into the doorsill at his feet, causing him to jump. More followed. Dozens, hundreds of them, flying through space and creating an intricate latticework structure that quickly resolved itself into a beautiful, ornate bridge that curved out of the darkness.

Moloch nodded to himself. He wasn't surprised when, several moments later, Agatha came striding across the bridge. "So, you got the job, then?"

Agatha grinned. "Oh, yes."

A glint of red caught Moloch's eye and he saw that there was a deep cut on the back of Agatha's hand.

"You're bleeding! What happened?"

Agatha rolled her eyes as Moloch pulled a roll of bandages out of one of his pockets. "Let's just say that somewhere in this place there's a dial marked 'high drama' and it needs to be turned *way* down."

Moloch nodded as he expertly wrapped her hand and tied the bandage off.[48] "Probably next to the one marked 'Crazy.'"

"I like to think I have a certain flair," the Castle remarked.

Moloch only jumped a little, then snorted. He turned back to Agatha. "I'll bet. So now you're the queen and we're not gonna die, right?" From his tone of voice, it was obvious he expected to be corrected.

The Castle obliged him. "Not quite."

"It's not that easy," Agatha agreed. "The Castle's intelligence is fragmented, remember? As of now, I'll only be recognized as the

---

48 The status of minions is a tricky thing. It is calibrated, by those whose job it is to do so, using a complicated algorithm involving aspects of loyalty, coercion, and flammability. Experts agree that by being the first to spontaneously aid the new Heterodyne, Herr von Zinzer cemented his place as Agatha's Chief Minion. No one has ever had the heart to tell him this.

Heterodyne in areas that are subordinate to this fragment. Anywhere else, we'll still be in danger. I need to reconnect the whole system to get it working properly. For that, I need to know where the damage is, so I still have to get to the library for that map."

Moloch pondered this. "I thought you just went to the library." Agatha shrugged.

Moloch slumped, but didn't look surprised. "Hmm…well, the part of the Castle that controls the library is the one that sent you here, right? So it won't try to kill us…"

"Probably," said the Castle. It sounded a bit pleased with itself.

"Good point," said Moloch, thinking hard. "And this one knows you, now, so that's two relatively safe places."

Agatha brightened. "That's true. And as I repair the fragmentation, we'll gain more and more ground. We'll have Pinky and her thugs out of here in no time! And when I've got the whole thing running, the Baron will have to talk to me. Maybe I can finally convince him that I'm not a threat."

Moloch goggled at her. "Not a threat?" he asked incredulously. "Are you serious?"

"Well, of course. I don't want any more trouble with him."

"I don't think he's gonna believe that." He glanced upwards. "I think he's gonna be pretty mad, actually."

"Mad? Mad about what?" She thought for a minute, and a nasty suspicion grew to a certainty. Agatha addressed the Castle. "What did you do?!"

Moloch was looking at the sky and Agatha followed his gaze.

In the Northern sky, Castle Wulfenbach was fighting for its life. Patches of the great airship were burning. Squads of firefighter dirigibles hovered nearby, pumping streams of water and carbon dioxide foam, even while they themselves were trying to fight off attackers. Hundreds of torchmen still swooped and darted throughout the fleet, wreaking havoc indiscriminately. The flares and explosions were reflected off of the growing cloud of smoke that filled the night sky.

Castle Wulfenbach was already moving off as quickly as possible, but speed had never been part of its design specifications.

"I only did what you told me to do," the Castle responded, in a hurt tone of voice.

"You're attacking *Castle Wulfenbach?!*" Agatha screamed. I did NOT tell you to do that!"

"Of course you did."

The pain in her hand receded quickly as the great ivory jaws relaxed. "Welcome home, my lady," the Castle said, a tone of deference and relief in its voice. "How may I serve you?"

Agatha spared a moment to look at the injury on her hand. Apparently the Castle had been able to examine her blood and from that had determined that she was a legitimate member of the family. Fascinating.

She looked up. "So—that's it? I'm the Heterodyne now?"

"That appears to be so. Yes."

"I guess I expected something a bit more…I don't know…dramatic." She paused as she realized what she was talking to. "Not that I'm complaining, mind."

"Yes, well," the Castle conceded, "ordinarily, when a new Heterodyne assumes control of the town, the Doom Bell rings, there's a quaint little ceremony in the Red Cathedral, the populace parades about singing folk songs, and the princes of Europa offer you tribute and beg you not to plunder their lands."

Agatha nodded. "Sounds nice, but I don't think we have the time—"

The Castle interrupted. "But right now, I can't even kill the usurper for you! I am broken! She isn't even in an area where I can perceive her. Forgive me!"

"Uh—I don't think you need to kill her."

"YES I DO!"

Agatha sighed. "No, you don't. Just keep her away from me. If she comes where you can get her, just try to contain her. Once you're fully

repaired, she won't be much of a threat anyway. Seriously, I just wish
I could chase her stupid pink airship out of here—

"Really?" the Castle interrupted eagerly. "I can do that. I can keep
all your enemies out of Mechanicsburg airspace."

Agatha nodded. "There you go! That would make me very happy!"

"It is an enemy airship in Mechanicsburg airspace. I am merely
following your wishes," the Castle continued.

Agatha realized that her mouth was hanging open and closed it
with a snap. "I'm going to have to think carefully about everything
I say to you, aren't I?"

"It will be fun!"

"I'll bet." Agatha stared up at the fire in the sky and frowned. "All
right then…Don't kill anyone. Don't do too much damage. But…do
keep harassing them until they're…hmm…ten kilometers outside
of town."

"I believe tradition calls for two leagues."

"What's that in kilometers?"

"Ah…Let me get back to you on that."

"What are you doing?" Moloch asked, scandalized. "The Baron…"

"Has his flagship looming over my town." Agatha stood straighter
and a new note entered her voice. "In its heyday, Mechanicsburg
was an unbelievably strong fortress. It was one of the reasons the
Heterodynes answered to no one. The whole point of repairing the
Castle is to reestablish that strength. Clearing the skies is as good
a start as any."

"You…" The Castle sounded surprised. "You're not angry?"

Agatha's eyes narrowed. "Did you want me to be?"

"No, Mistress, but…" and here the voice echoed hollowly, "your
father and your uncle…nothing I did ever seemed to please them."

A number of thoughts tumbled through Agatha's head. First,
there was a burst of sympathy for the Castle, a warped intelligence,
certainly, but it had remained true, in its way. It was its masters
that had changed, changed to the point where it could no longer

please them, to the point where they had apparently abandoned it, and it couldn't even understand why. There followed the worrying realization that she had already developed a strange fondness for the thing. Apparently she was nowhere near as intolerant of evil as her father and uncle had reportedly been. She would have to watch that.

"No," she said gently. "I am pleased. You did good."

"Good." The Castle considered this. "Ah...Perhaps you could phrase it...some other way?"

Yes, Agatha realized, patting a wall, *this place was going to be a real "fixer-upper."*

CHAPTER 6

❧◎❧

For the jaded epicure, Romania's Mechanicsburg is a delightful respite in an area otherwise awash in excess amounts of paprika-saturated pork products, as it is the home of the ever-delightful Mechanicsburg Giant Snail *(Helix Quimperiana Mechanicsburg Gigantus)*.

Local legend claims that cultivation of these gastropods began almost two centuries ago during the Storm King's prolonged siege of the town. Since then, they have been embraced as a delectable homegrown resource. Within the last twenty years, it has, through clever marketing, been introduced to the outside world and the cuisine of Europa has benefited.

Most of my readers will be familiar with the familiar *Green Tri-horns*, the spicy *Red Pepper Snails*, the buttery *Golden Spiral*, as well as the now traditional Prester John Day's Eve favorite, the gloriously marbled *Double-Shelled Feast*.

But even the true gastronome might not be aware that these are but the snails that Mechanicsburg chooses to export. They may well be delicious, but, like the white wines of the Rhine Valley, the best are kept for the educated palates of the folk back home and never go farther than a hundred kilometers from their place of origin.

Thus, even the most ardent mollusk aficionado should prepare to be astonished at the scope and variety of snails available for

234 Phil and Kaja Foglio

consumption at the meanest Mechanicsburg inn or Escar-To-Go*
peddler's cart.

We suggest that you start with some of the favorite local varietals,
such as the *Carpathian Mauve,* the *Cerulean Giant, the Orange
Snap-Shell, the Variegated Spine-Tail,* or (from February to April)
the surprisingly minty *Phosphorescent Devil.*"

—*Go To Your Food: Local Delicacies and Culinary Secrets
for the Sophisticated Traveler* by the Lady Flora Alomari/
Constantinople Press

⤷⊙⊙⊙⤶

A gatha dusted her hands together. "So, let's get to this library,
shall we?" She waved her hand towards the glittering stone
confection that hung over the courtyard. "Back over the
bridge?"

The Castle chuckled and the bridge collapsed back into individual
bricks and tumbled lifelessly to the ground. "Oh, my, no." The wall
behind them crumbled to the ground, revealing a stairway that
descended into the earth. "*This* way, Mistress."

Guided by the ever-present red lights, Agatha and Moloch picked
their way down the winding stairwell.

"My Lady?" the Castle asked after a while. "Do you have a…
boyfriend?"

Agatha almost missed a step and it was only by grabbing the
banister that she refrained from pitching forward into the darkness
at the center of the stairwell. "A what?"

"A boyfriend," the Castle repeated helpfully. "A sweetheart."

Agatha made a strangled sound.

The Castle doggedly continued. "A swain. A beau. A lover. An
intended consort. A fiancé. A stud."

Agatha realized with horror that, unchecked, the Castle might
very well continue listing possibilities, like an increasingly salacious
thesaurus. "No!" she shouted.

"What?" Moloch was clearly shocked. "Are you serious? What happened to that thing with Gilgamesh Wulfenbach? You two have a fight or something?"

Agatha stared at him.

"O-*HO!*" the Castle boomed with obvious pleasure. "The young man who single-handedly stopped the invaders. A very good choice."

"We do not have a…a thing!" Agatha retorted hotly.

"Really?" The Castle sounded skeptical. "In my opinion he was certainly trying to impress *someone*. Yessss…he'll do nicely."

"Do for what?" Agatha demanded. "And don't you dare tell me. He sent a thug to try to kill me!" She paused. "Probably. Maybe."

Moloch whistled. "Wow, you two did have a fight. Back on Castle Wulfenbach, he wouldn't shut up about you."

"Oh reeeeally?!" The Castle was intrigued.

Agatha whirled and shook a finger at Moloch and then up at the ceiling. "Silence! Not another word!" They walked on for a while and then, despising herself, she asked quietly: "So…what did he say?"

Moloch was spared by the Castle's deep chuckle filling the stairwell. "Oh, this all takes me back. Four centuries ago, the Skull-Queen of Skral sent two hundred warrior homunculi to kill Dagon Heterodyne—just to pique his interest. I expect standards have slipped a bit since then."

Agatha looked puzzled. "What does that have to do with anything?"

"Why, you remind me of her. She was your ancestress, you know. So it obviously worked out rather well." The Castle's voice was nostalgic. "Lovely woman. Master Dagon and she were so happy together."

"Wait a minute," Moloch said. "My grand-nana used to scare us kids with stories about the Skull Queen of Skral if we got out of line. She's a…she was a real person? That whole 'souring of the mountains' thing…that really happened?"

The Castle sighed. "Very happy indeed."

Agatha looked tired. "Why am I not surprised?"

Moloch stopped briefly, and watched as Agatha moved ahead. He clutched his load a bit tighter. "Is she…" he whispered, "a *lot* like her?"

"Ah, it's too soon to tell," the Castle replied conspiratorially. "But

I *do* have cause for hope." It continued, "So, this Gilgamesh. He is Klaus's sole heir?"

Moloch shrugged. "That's what I've heard, but what do I know?"

"You would be astonished," the Castle admonished, "with what people 'like you' know. I know that I no longer am. The Wulfenbachs never were known for producing large families. A pity."

Agatha reached the bottom of the stair and spun around, her face almost glowing in the dim light. "I cannot believe this! I hardly know him!"

Moloch realized that she wasn't arguing with him, and wisely kept silent.

"What's to know?" the Castle asked. "His family is powerful. His Spark burns bright. He's already taken with you…"

"But—"

"And you cannot deny that he has a magnificent death ray."

Moloch had thought that Agatha couldn't possibly be any more embarrassed. He was wrong.

"That's…" She shivered and her voice came out in a conflicted little gasp. "That's hardly a basis for a stable, long-term relationship."

The Castle continued. "Heh heh heh. All of the Wulfenbachs have been known for their oversized machinery, you know."

Agatha had the feeling that the conversation was sliding out of control. "I'm *sure* I hadn't noticed."

"I mean, look at that Castle Wulfenbach. What *exactly* are we trying to say here?"

Moloch looked confused. "Well, it's *obviously*—"

"Is there a *point* to all of this?" Agatha shrieked.

The Castle paused. "Why, yes. A young gentleman and his attendant have just slipped in through the Phosphorus Gate. I was wondering if he was yours?"

Agatha's heart gave a thump. "Is it Gilgamesh?"

"I don't know. I haven't seen him. He's not throwing lightning around, but that's not—"

Moloch cleared his throat. "Tall. Fit. Aristocratic. Weird hair."

"*Nice* hair," Agatha snapped.

"It's hard to say," the castle confessed. "They are wearing stealth cloaks, and they are proceeding with extreme caution, which is why they are still alive. Well...barely alive."

Agatha felt her chest grow tight. "What did you do?"

"I? Nothing. They are in a dead zone. All I can do is observe. But there are independent guardian systems in the area."

Agatha looked wary. "Independent guardian systems? What, like those flying things?"

"Similar," the Castle confessed. "But I no longer control them."

Suddenly Moloch froze and dropped his bundle. "Wait! Are you talking about the Steam Cats?"

"Technically, they're called 'fun-sized mobile agony and death dispensers.'"

"Geargrit, no!" Moloch moaned. "Those things are almost impossible to kill!" He slid down the wall until he collapsed onto the floor. "We're finally in an area where nothing is trying to kill us and now she's going to drag me along while she commits suicide trying to rescue her crazy boyfriend from a bunch of unholy killing machines!"

Agatha sighed in exasperation. "He's not actually—"

"And if I don't go along," Moloch yelled, "you'll amuse yourself by squashing me like a bug! I'm doomed either way!"

"You have a remarkably astute grasp of the situation," the Castle said with a grudging respect.

"I've been around way too many Sparks," Moloch sobbed.

"And yet, even after dealing with them all, you are still alive," the Castle pointed out.

Moloch raised his head in surprise. "I...well, I...I guess I am."

"*Amateurs!*" the Castle sneered.

Moloch looked beseechingly at Agatha. "Come on—can't you just find a new boyfriend?"

But Agatha was already running. "Hurry!"

Almost five minutes later, they topped yet another stairwell. As they ran, Agatha's mind raced.

"So how do I beat these things?" she asked.

Moloch groaned. "You can't! All you can do is get to a place where they can't reach you. They're really strong, really fast, and really well-built."

Agatha considered this. "Are they really smart?"

The Castle answered. "Without me controlling them? Not very."

Agatha grinned. "Okay, I can work with that." She looked at the closed doors. "*You* could take them out, right?"

The Castle paused. "Yesssss…"

Moloch perked up. "Hey! I get it! Lure them out here and the Castle can smash them for us!"

"Destroy my own security systems?" The Castle sounded shocked.

Agatha cleared her throat.

"Oh, very well, but I'll want them repaired later."

"Holy smokes," Moloch marveled. "That is a good plan."

Agatha smiled as she slowly opened one of the doors. "Isn't it, though?" Beyond was a large open room, some sort of feast hall. In the dim light, they could see that there was a long open fireplace along one wall—and the rest were hung with musty tapestries. It was impossible to see what was actually depicted upon them, but from what Agatha could see, the artist had liked using a lot of red. Above was an impressive set of exposed ceiling beams. A row of tall windows, the glass long smashed out, allowed a breeze to blow through the room. The furniture had fallen into ruin due to rain rot and insects.

Agatha stepped through the door. Nothing moved. Moloch crept in behind her. She pointed to a set of doors located in a far corner. They moved quietly towards them. "Now we just have to find them," she said in a low voice. "Castle? How close to those things are we?"

A huge golden claw erupted from the shadows and slammed the door through which they had entered. A deep mechanical growl rose behind them.

Moloch closed his eyes. "Pretty close," he whispered. "Don't move!"

Agatha's eyes ached from strain as she tried to look behind her—but she froze in place. "Are you kidding me?"

A metallic sound, like a mechanism slowly walking, came from behind them. "They react to movement," Moloch said urgently. "So we want to get out of its line of sight, and then run like mad for someplace it can't get to."

Another step. Very close now. Agatha could hear poorly maintained gears grinding as it took yet another step towards them. Agatha frantically swept her eyes across the room.

"I don't think that's really an option here. I don't see anywhere we can hide."

A gigantic metal paw crashed to the ground between them. It was lovingly engraved with swirls and arabesques and had once been polished to a high gleam, but now it was encrusted with oil, dust, and what was very probably old blood.

Agatha felt her heart pounding so hard that she was sure her skin must be vibrating...But nothing more happened.

We can't keep this up forever, Agatha thought. *We'll get tired or get a cramp or an itch—just like the one that has magically bloomed on my knee.* Great. She realized that her breathing had sped up. She tried to remember the breathing exercises that Zeetha had taught her but they shot out of her head when a metal muzzle—festooned with cruel looking spines—eased into her peripheral vision. She saw Moloch close his eyes and heard a faint whimper. The head began to swing her way—when a boot sailed out of the darkness, bounced off the top of the automaton's head, and flew into a corner.

With a sound like a locomotive, the mechanical creature dived after it. As it passed between Agatha and Moloch, a woman's voice from the blackness above called out: "Sit down! Cover your mouth with your hands, and don't move!"

They did so, and could see the "steam cat" now. In Agatha's opinion, it did look like an enormous cat, but easily the size of one of the draft horses that had pulled wagons in the circus. Armored and covered in spines, hooks, and sharp edges, it had a large mouthful of jagged metal teeth which snapped open and shut in a idle mechanical reflex as it quested about the room.

Finding nothing, it swung about, red-lit eyes gleaming, and after a moment slowly padded back towards them.

"You can talk," the mysterious voice from above informed them. "Just don't let it see your mouth moving." The steam cat didn't react to this voice, just continued to slowly advance. It came up to Moloch and the red eyes swept over him once...twice... and then with a clank, the thing turned away and moved off back towards the door they had come in by.

Agatha swallowed the lump in her throat. "It—" she realized that she would have to speak loudly from behind her hands. "It can't hear us?"

No reaction from the device, which had begun a slow circuit of the room.

"Apparently," said the helpful voice, "it can't even see us unless we're actually moving. What? Like a *what*?"

Agatha heard murmuring and realized that there was at least another person above them. They must be up on the rafters, she realized.

"Oh, thank you, yes, like a frog." The voice was annoyed now. "Thank you for that piece of incredibly useless information. Now *shut up and if you open your mouth again I will gut you like a trout!*"

From behind her cupped hands, Agatha spoke up. "It's not supposed to work like this! It's another rogue system. It doesn't work properly if it isn't linked with the Castle."

The voice from above sighed in obvious exasperation. "You Sparks can't keep from running your mouths even when you have nothing useful to say. It doesn't *have* to be working right. All it has to do is stay here not seeing us—yes, okay, like a giant metal frog with claws—until we fall over from thirst and exhaustion!"

Agatha waited until the voice wound down. "I have a way to stop it," she said.

A brief silence. "You do?"

"Yes. I need to lure it through the door we just came through." The giant metal creature padded over to them and sank to its haunches, its glowing eyes fixed upon the door in question. Agatha took a deep breath. "But we need it…distracted."

The voice considered this. "Well…that should—what?" More low murmuring came from above. "I swear to the Mother of Knives, if this is more idiocy—all right! *All right!*" Another sigh. "You—what did you do to Vrin?"

Agatha was so surprised that she started slightly. Instantly, the automaton's attention snapped to her. Agatha held her breath while her mind raced.

"Vrin? I don't—"

The voice from above prodded her. "Lady Vrin. In Sturmhalten. What did you do to her?"

"Who are you?" Agatha felt a flush of sweat. The voice didn't sound like one of the strange warrior women she had fled from in Sturmhalten, but how many others even knew of Lady Vrin's existence?

"Please. This is very important." Despite this statement, it was obvious that the speaker thought it a waste of time.

Agatha didn't want to make an enemy of the owner of the voice, but…

"You won't be mad?"

"I'm already mad!" the voice growled, "But not about whatever stupid thing this is about. Please."

"Well, I kind of hit her with a broom."

Moloch interrupted. "A broom?"

"I…kind of hit her with a broom *a lot.*"

A different voice sounded above. "Thank God—it is you. Agatha…"

Agatha realized that she recognized the second voice. "Tarvek?"

"Okay, get ready to run!"

With a crash, Tarvek Sturmvoraus leaped from the shadows above and landed square on the back of the giant machine. He appeared to be wearing hastily wrapped sheets, and little else. "Run!" he yelled. Above them, the other voice shrieked in furious protest.

The automaton leapt into the air and gave a shrill mechanical roar. It then began a twisting set of gyrations, trying to dislodge its rider.

As Agatha and Moloch leapt to their feet, a girl dressed in deep shades of black and purple dropped to the floor beside them. She was staring at Tarvek with rage boiling off her. "What are you doing, you idiot?"

Tarvek, still hanging on to the monster, ignored her and called to Agatha, "The door! GO!"

The girl looked like she was about to leap straight into the fight. Both Agatha and Moloch grabbed her and began to drag her along with them towards the doors. "No!" she shrieked. "After all that trouble getting your useless butt out of that hospital, you are not going to commit suicide! Grandma will have me flayed!"

The automaton stopped its attempts to throw Tarvek off and lunged after the fleeing trio with a roar. Quickly, Tarvek threw his sheet over its eyes, and it stopped dead for a moment, as if puzzled. Then it shook itself like a dog and roared again, clawing at the fabric that hid its face.

Agatha shouted: "Everybody scatter!" If it doesn't follow you, get the door open!"

The three ran in different directions as the device cleared the sheet from its eyes.

"Don't follow me. Don't follow me…" Moloch's frantic voice could be heard as he pelted his way across the room. With a howl, the creature bounded off after him. "*I knew it!*"

Agatha forced herself to ignore Moloch's scream of rage and ran for the door. "I made it!" she called out exultantly, and she gave the great door a tug. Nothing. "And it's locked!"

"Oh, that's just perfect!" Agatha realized the girl in purple was at her side. She pushed Agatha away. Dipping a hand into one of the pouches at her waist, she extracted a slim, hooked rod. "Move! Highly trained Smoke Knight comin' through!"

The girl slid the rod into the keyhole and twirled it about. A look of surprise flitted across her face. "This isn't locked." Another twirl in the opposite direction. "This is jammed."

Agatha closed her eyes. "Yes, that happens a lot around here, apparently."

"Yeah, but I can't do anything about that. I'm not a weight lifter. How am I supposed to deal with this?"

Agatha glanced behind, and saw the creature, with Tarvek still astride it, galloping towards them. "Really quickly!"

"Violetta," Tarvek shouted. "Take her up!"

"You think? *Idiot*." In a single movement, the girl produced a chubby little air-pistol, pointed it straight up, and fired, grabbing Agatha around the waist.

Agatha felt a jerk as she was hauled upwards, the reel on the device screaming in protest. Centimeters below her feet, the automaton's jaws closed on empty air with a ringing snap.

A shove and a quick grab for support, and Agatha found herself hauled atop a thick wooden ceiling beam.

The girl examined the smoking device, then, with a curse, she tossed it towards the ground. The automaton leapt again, and snapped the little device out of the air, crushing it in shining metal jaws. Tarvek was still hanging on as the automaton dashed about, but his sheets were becoming more tattered and disheveled by the minute. He really wasn't wearing anything else underneath. Agatha tried hard not to notice. Instead, she concentrated on the question of what he was doing here, in Castle Heterodyne, and what she should do about it.

On the one hand, his family was mixed up with a shadowy plot to overthrow the Empire, and they had been working with Lucrezia—the Other—to do it. The Other's creatures and devices had been all over their castle. Tarvek himself had been working with Lucrezia and her servants—and had actively thwarted Agatha's efforts to warn the Baron about the Other's return.

On the other hand, Tarvek had rebelled—had tried to get Agatha away from Sturmhalten Castle before the Other's servants could catch her. When Agatha had been caught anyway, and it looked as if Lucrezia's presence in her mind would extinguish her altogether, he had helped her fight back. She was still alive because of him.

Plus—and there was no denying it—she had found him very attractive. Different than Gil, there was no question of that, but still…

It was all very frustrating, she thought. Definitely the sort of thing a girl needs to sort out…over time…with the aid of knowledgeable friends, a good wine, and several kilograms of good chocolate. None of which were now present.

"Okay," Violetta muttered. "So here I am, back where we started." She gave Agatha a sour look. "Without, I might add, the fool I'm supposed to keep alive. Great plan, my Lady."

Agatha tore her gaze from Tarvek. "Wait! Where's von Zinzer?"

"Over here." They looked up in surprise, to see Moloch sitting astride another beam. He waved at them amiably, and the tone of his voice conveyed a pleased surprise. "Thanks for asking."

Violetta stared at him in astonishment. Then glanced back down at the floor, which was easily five meters below. "You've trained in the way of the Smoke?"

Moloch shrugged and waved a hand. "Nah. My mother always said that stuff would kill you."

Agatha ignored them and looked around. Below them, the creature had changed tactics. It was by turns freezing in place and then suddenly shaking itself violently. Tarvek was managing to hold on, but Agatha knew it was only a matter of time. She had to try something.

The beam she was on was filthy. Encrusted with centuries worth of dust, grime, and cooking smoke. Luckily, it was also enormous, hewn centuries ago from some primeval oak tree, and was easily a meter wide. Agatha gingerly swung her legs up and eased herself onto her hands and knees. She eyed the doors she had spotted at the other end of the room and started forward.

"What are you doing?" Violetta asked from behind her.

"I'm wondering what's through that other door."

There was a soft whoosh through the air and the lightest of thumps, and Violetta was now standing before Agatha. "There's three more of those monsters on the other side. That's the way *we* came in," Violetta said wearily.

"Ah." Agatha thought about this. "Is there any other way out?"

Violetta shook her head. "No."

Agatha glanced about. The upper reaches of the vast room were shrouded in darkness. "How can you be so sure? It's pretty dark up here."

Violetta reached up to her brow. A strap ran across her forehead, with a small device attached. She snapped it on and an intense red beam blinked into existence. "Only got my hunting light, don't I?" She slowly began to pivot in place. "Let's have a look around."

The light drifted up, revealing a small square of darker black. "Air vent of some sort up there, but even if we could get you up to it, that hole is too small even for me." The light moved to the left and Agatha gasped as hundreds of small bright dots gleamed in the darkness. "But I guess it's big enough for those bloodbats.[49] The moon's coming up, so I figure they're almost ready to fly. We'd better get out of here soon."

The light now skittered up along the beam they were on. "Oh, and it's a good thing you didn't crawl much further." The light revealed a delicate lattice of threads. Dark shapes scurried away as they were illuminated. "If you had, you'd've got caught in that spiderroach web.[50] Once they know you're helpless, they'll pour out and strip the flesh from your bones."

Agatha slowly backed up, but stopped when she heard a meaty "thunk" near her left foot. Looking behind her, she saw a small creature squirming furiously, pinned by a slim black blade.

---

[49]   Bloodbat (*Desmodontinæ Extremum Sanguine Comedenti*) An interesting variety of blood-drinking bat said to have been introduced to the Mechanicsburg area by the Black Heterodyne, who discovered them on one of his adventures in the Subterranean Kingdoms. Apparently he was so enchanted by the thought of nature having produced something so dreadful, all by itself, that he wanted to share it with the world.

[50]   Spiderroach (*Loxosceles Blattella Stamina Telæ Heterodyne*). These creatures, on the other hand, were created by the Red Heterodyne, who was convinced that the works of Nature could always be improved. The Red and Black Heterodynes were brothers who were always involved in philosophical arguments that had horrendous real-world consequences.

"Look at that," said Violetta with a touch of surprise. "Venomous Rafter Toad.[51] I didn't know they were active at this time of the year."

Agatha tried to pull herself into the smallest amount of space possible.

Violetta sighed and sat down beside her, turning off her light. "See? Nothing up here that's of any use to us at all."

Agatha blinked and then smiled. "Actually, you're quite wrong."

Violetta frowned.

On the ground below, or rather, on the back of the rampaging automaton, Tarvek was coming to terms with his imminent death.

He had heard the stories about the castle, of course, but had assumed they were exaggerated. This had proven to be hubris on his part and the reality would have been challenging enough, even had he been fully fit and dressed. As it was, he was injured, practically naked, and depressed because he was about to die. He had always planned to die while ranting atop a tower or something—he had a very nice outfit all designed for the occasion and everything—and now all that effort would be wasted. Plus, he was worried that his mind might not be as properly focused as it should be.

But it would all be irrelevant anyway, at least to those people who wouldn't have to scrub his remains off of the floor, because now he was going rather numb and his hands were starting to slip and it was getting awfully cold and…

"Tarvek!" That was Agatha's voice. That opened another steamer trunk full of regrets… "Tarvek! Get ready to let go!"

Let go? Was she insane?

A bright red dot of light blinked into existence on the floor in front off them. The steam cat tensed. The dot wavered and then skittered off across the floor. With a roar, the creature leapt after it.

---

[51] Venomous Rafter Toad (*Bufo Venenatorum Trabe Heterodyne*) Actually, nobody is quite sure where these horrid little amphibians came from. They are only tolerated because they feed almost exclusively on bloodbats and spiderroaches.

Instead of letting go, Tarvek reflexively gripped harder and then realized his error as he saw the dot dancing merrily upon the jammed door.

He screamed as the steam cat plowed through the ancient wood like a battering ram and slammed into the opposite wall. It shook itself and spun about just as Agatha stumbled through the shattered door after it. "Castle! Can you hear me? Destroy it! Now!"

"Of course, my Lady." The Castle's voice was nearly drowned out by Tarvek screaming her name in panic and she quickly added:

"And don't hurt the person on its back!"

"Of course not." As the Castle spoke, parts of the floor rose up and crushed the clank with a squeal of metal and a shower of sparks. The crushed mechanism clattered over, sending Tarvek rolling to land Agatha's feet.

"Amazing," he breathed, staggering as he tried to stand. He felt a bit dazed. "And…and I'm completely unhurt!"

A thrown boot—the mate to the one on his left foot—smashed into his face. "Are you *done*?" Violetta shrieked. "Are you *finished*?" She strode over to Tarvek, who was dazedly trying to determine where the stars that drifted across his field of vision belonged on the Hertzsprung-Russell diagram. "No, wait, you can't be! You're still alive!"

Tarvek focused on her. "You know, I really hate you," he muttered.

"You hate me? How dare you!" Violetta began kicking the prone man in the head. "Feel my hate! *Feel it!*" Tarvek rolled over and feebly waved his hands in a parody of self-defense. "You aren't allowed to commit suicide," Violetta continued. "Only I must kill you!"

Agatha watched this with strong mixed feelings.

Since she had first met him in Sturmhalten, Tarvek had both supported and betrayed her in such quick alternating succession that she was unable to decide what she really felt for him. At the moment, impatience was winning out.

"Stop it!" Agatha's yell froze both combatants. "What is wrong with you two?"

Violetta grabbed Tarvek's hair and yanked his head up. "I'm responsible for this slug's continued existence."

Tarvek painfully pulled himself free from her grip. "And this useless nitwit is my loyal servant!" So saying, he delivered a sock to her sternum, causing Violetta to gasp.

Moloch strolled out the door and cocked an eyebrow. "Are you sure the two of you aren't married?"

Violetta looked like she was about to be violently sick. "Oh, eewww!"

Agatha turned to Tarvek, who was fastidiously fashioning an elegant toga. "This is loyal?"

Tarvek tucked in the final fold and bent to put on his boot. "It's not like she has a lot of choice. She's my cousin. Her branch of the family has served mine for generations. She's been trained since birth."

"And I hate it!" Violetta declared. "I'm awful at it! I'm so bad at it that I got posted way out here, where all I had to do was play secretary to the local Burgermeister! It was *easy!* He's such a fool that I *still* can't believe he's running this dump!"

She turned back to Tarvek, who flinched. "And then this fool gets captured! 'So what?' says me. 'Not my problem.' *Wrong!* 'Cause the moron they have positioned in the hospital gets herself killed while trying to off the Baron—and suddenly it's my job to drag the Royal Pain here out of the fire!"

By now, Violetta was punctuating her words by thumping Tarvek on the head with one fist.

"Not! My! Fault!" he wailed.

She gave Tarvek's head another smack. "Shut up!" She looked to Agatha with eyes full of weariness. "And then we're being chased by Wulfenbach troops *and* our own people and everyone's shooting to kill and there's nowhere to go, thanks to those flaming gargoyles, so Bright Boy here, *he* says," Violetta mimicked Tarvek's voice with the skill of long practice, "'We'll head for the Castle! They won't chase us in there!'"

"Wait." Moloch looked confused. "He wanted to come in here to be safe?"

Violetta grabbed Moloch's shirt and looked at him imploringly. "Yes! *Now* do you understand what I have to work with?"

"But why did you listen to him?"

"I *panicked!* I *told* you, I'm not very good at this!"

Moloch surprised her by gently patting her on the shoulder. "You're not dead. In here, that counts for a lot."

Agatha was eyeing Tarvek with an unnerving glare. "I want to know what all of these agents of yours were doing in my town." A thought struck her. "Flaming gargoyles… That pink airship! That pink *tart!* They're *yours?*"

Tarvek rolled his eyes. "The pink thing was not my idea."

Agatha grabbed the front of Tarvek's toga and leaned in. Her voice took on a dangerous harmonic. "This is all *your fault?*"

Agatha's eyes were only inches from his, and it was obvious she was furious. Tarvek's voice rose to match hers: "No! It's yours!"

She shook him so hard his teeth rattled. "You're trying to take over my town and it's *my fault?*" Suddenly, a cold metal blade was gently touching her throat.

"Okay, you, back way off," Violetta said from behind.

"My Lady?" The Castle waited for instructions.

"Alive and unharmed," Agatha said to the air.

A set of iron rods slammed up from the floor and Violetta suddenly found herself in a very tight cage. It was difficult to breathe. "As you wish, Mistress," the Castle said conversationally.

Agatha continued to glare into Tarvek's eyes. "Now. You. Talk."

Tarvek took a deep breath. "Okay. I'm sorry. It's not exactly your *fault*, but it is happening because you showed up. Yes, there was a plot to install a false Heterodyne girl. My father and his people have been working on it for a long time." He sighed. "They were nowhere near ready." He looked thoughtful. "I guess between your performance over Sturmhalten and the Baron's injuries, it must have seemed too good an opportunity to pass up."

Agatha snorted. "Did they really think that the Baron's son would do nothing?"

Now Tarvek was angry. "I didn't say they weren't idiots! *I* didn't tell them to go ahead. We know nothing about this son of the Baron's! I've never met him! No one has!" He paused. "Actually, from what you told us at dinner back in Sturmhalten, it sounds like *you* know more about him than anyone else in Europa."

Agatha sighed. Her initial anger had mostly passed, but she was still far from pleased. "He's a bossy, violent idiot who thinks he knows what's best for everyone, even though he can't even keep himself in one piece." She gave Tarvek a pointed look. "You'll like him."

Gil was peering between two shutters onto the busy street below. The crowd was dispersing and he was relieved to see that his father's troops were letting them go.

"Get away from that window, you fool!"

Gil closed the shutters and grinned. He had been astonished to see two of his dearest friends, Theopholous DuMedd and Sleipnir O'Hara, appear out of nowhere in the streets of Mechanicsburg.

Theo and Sleipnir were two of the students that Gilgamesh had grown up with aboard Castle Wulfenbach,[52] and they had fled, along with several other of Gil's acquaintances, during the chaos that had attended Agatha's own escape.

They had used an invisibility device he had given them back on Castle Wulfenbach to whisk him out from under Captain Vole's nose, leaving his new group of friends behind. Ha. Friends...he had his doubts about that cat...

"Well, excuse me for being concerned. There are people I know down there."

Theo paused, a bottle tipped upwards. He caught himself just before the drink he was pouring sloshed over the edge of his glass. "Anyone you want us to go get?"

---

[52] For assorted political reasons, The Baron had accumulated many of the children of various Sparks, rulers and troublemakers throughout the Empire—officially as hostages against their parents' good behavior. While they stayed on Castle Wulfenbach, he had them educated in political theory, business management, the sciences, the humanities, and charm and deportment. While history has shown that this resulted in an unprecidented sophisticated and well-rounded ruling class, Klaus frankly admitted that he had started the program "to keep them busy and out from underfoot."

Sleipnir looked up from the device she was tinkering with. "It wouldn't be any trouble. We can get at least another hour's use out of your little invisibility lamp dingus here."

"It's not a lamp." Gil's reply was almost automatic by now. Why did everyone think it was a lamp?[53] "No. Leave them be," he answered. "They'd only insist on coming along, and I don't want to take anyone into the Castle who doesn't deserve it."

Sleipnir tossed a screwdriver at him without rancor. "Nice."

Gil snatched it out of the air and threw it back. "I am not taking you in with me."

Sleipnir caught it and slid it back into the loop on her belt. "Of course you are." Gil opened his mouth to protest, but she cut him off. "And the last time you won an argument with me was…?"

Gil frowned, and changed the subject. "What are the two of you even doing here? Theo, you said you were going to search for your father's lost laboratory."

Theo looked uncomfortable and sipped at his drink. "Well…I still am. I mean, I will. We have some map fragments and I'm pretty close to cracking the cipher he used in his journal."

Sleipnir spoke up, "And I think I've got a pretty good idea of where the Eye of the Snake Eater is hidden."[54]

"But," Theo admitted, "I did promise Agatha that I'd catch up with her here."

---

[53]   Because it was a lamp. The device, which students will find first described in *Agatha H. and The Airship City*, was apparently looted from Castle Heterodyne, and, in addition to being a lamp, was both an energy source and a device capable of generating a small portable invisibility field. The Heterodynes liked to design mechanisms that had multiple functions, one of which was usually to cause surprise.

[54]   This sort of rigmarole is actually fairly standard when talking about "lost laboratories." Sparks are a secretive lot, and they keep their blasphemous secrets held close to their vests. On average, a good Spark will invest anywhere from one-half to two-thirds of his or her time and energy on the design and hiding of an elaborate lair, as they seem to have an instinctual understanding that people work best in an environment where the controls to all the deathtraps are right at their fingertips. This is a good thing, overall, as time spent digging an elaborate "Maze of Madness" is less time spent trying to find a way to turn the nearest city into a beautiful volcanic moonscape. Thus, it should come as no surprise to those who knows his *modus operandi* that it was Baron Wulfenbach who lavishly bankrolled a very effective advertising campaign that let people know that "You Can Judge A Spark's Strength By His Lair!"

Gil looked at Theo. "You promised Agatha…but why didn't you tell me that before you left?"

Theo and Sleipnir looked at each other. Then Sleipnir turned back to him. "I'm sorry, Gil. It was…well…it was because we didn't entirely trust you."

The awkward moment stretched out until Gil shrugged and turned away. "Can't blame you, I guess. You hadn't seen me in years and I suppose it was a bit of a shock, finding out who I really am."

Sleipnir snorted. "You think?"

Gil smiled mirthlessly. "If we're talking about trust, I guess I felt more betrayed than you did because I never got any mail." He raised a preemptive hand. "I'm still trying to find out what that was all about. But…I'm sorry I couldn't tell you. Really sorry, it would've been…nice to tell someone about it," he admitted. "Anyway, you were right. I probably would have made things worse. Agatha didn't trust me either."

Everyone was silent for a moment. Then Theo stepped forward and put his hand on Gil's arm. "For what it's worth," he said quietly, "I trust you now."

Gil looked surprised. "Oh?"

Theo gestured towards the street below. "I was standing right behind you when the soldiers found you. I listened. You really do want to help her. Out there? You sounded just like the Gil I grew up with."

"I'm not," Gil said flatly. "Too many things have changed. I'll never be that person again." He smiled and punched Theo in the arm. "But I can remember the important bits."

With that, it was like a switch had been thrown and the tension drained from the room. Minutes later, they were lounging about the room's settees, drinks in hand. Gil had protested but Theo had pointed out that they couldn't really do anything until the streets were clear of Wulfenbach soldiers.

Sleipnir leaned forward. "So Agatha is in the Castle and the Baron is going to destroy it. Why?"

Gil paused. "Because he thinks Agatha is the Other."

Both Theo and Sleipnir looked horrified. "Is she?"

"No!" Gil paused. "Well, yes. Sometimes..." He saw the two of them staring at him. "She's...possessed."

Sleipnir stared at him for another second, and then deliberately put her drink down. "Possessed."

Gil spent several minutes bringing them up to speed. He sighed as he finished. "I know it sounds crazy! It *is* crazy! But the important point is that if it's true, it's not actually Agatha who's the problem, and that means that there's got to be something I can do to save her!"

Sleipnir folded her arms together. "And if you can't?"

Gil drained his glass and slammed it down onto the table. "Then I'll take care of her myself. But, unlike my father, I'm willing to give her a chance."

Sleipnir and Theo glanced at each other and suddenly grinned. They turned back. "Listen to you!" Sleipnir snagged the bottle and poured Gil another drink. "That's why we can trust you."

Gil stared at them and suddenly slumped back into his seat. "I am so glad to see you guys again. My head is spinning. I..." He suddenly examined the drink in his hand. "What am I drinking?"

Theo grinned. "I cooked it up myself! It's a new recipe!"

Gil looked alarmed. "And you let me drink this?"

Sleipnir shrugged. "It's great. It helps you open up. Express your inner thoughts. *In vino veritas* and all that."

Gil frowned "Yessss... that sounds like one of Theo's. I remember his 'Electrical Acid Two Hundred Proof Jolly Sugar Doom.'" He carefully put his glass down.

Theo looked offended. "This from a guy who once concocted an aperitif from toothpaste and hedgehogs."

"They're still selling that," Gil said breezily. He caught himself. "Oh dear, it's still building, isn't it?"

Theo pulled out a pocket watch. "Relax, you just had the one, yes?"

Gil racked his brain. "I...I can't remember."

Theo waved a hand. "If you'd had more than one, then by now you'd be weeping maudlin tears over all those hedgehogs."

"Poor little hedgehogs," Gil whispered. Then he shook himself. "Yeah, that would be bad." He looked at them. "What were we talking about?"

Sleipnir smiled. "About how we were going to storm the Castle?"

Gil's head tipped back and he closed his eyes. "Riiight. Right, right, right. That's gonna be tricky. I should pick up some tools and... stuff. Tool stuff." He glanced at a clock on the mantle. "But it's late. All'a shops'll be closed." He turned to the two of them "Gunna have to build a mechanical shoplifter." A tear welled up in his eye and dripped off his nose. "Gunna be a criminal." His head lolled until he was looking at Sleipnir. "Agatha's not like you. She's not gunna wanna be in love with a criminal."

Sleipnir snorted. "It *is* an acquired taste."

Theo rolled his eyes. "Relax. Tools we have. We've been outfitting for an expedition, remember?"

Gil visibly brightened. "Excellent! Give 'em here!"

Sleipnir pushed him back into his seat. "Nuh-uh. We'll carry the supplies."

Gil frowned. "Why?"

"Because if we give them to you, you'll try to leave us outside."

Gil slumped back again. "Curses," he mumbled. "Another brilliant plan, foiled."

Sleipnir smiled serenely. "If you try to steal them, I'll have to fight you."

Gil recoiled. "No! You fight dirty!"

"A base canard."

Theo hiccupped and clapped his hands together. "I think we're as ready as we're going to get! Let's move out!"

A short time later, two Wulfenbach troopers were leaning on a balustrade outside one of Castle Heterodyne's smaller gates. There were troops at every entrance now. The Baron had acknowledged that it was unlikely that there were any more Heterodyne claimants waiting to push their way into the ancient deathtrap, but one never knew. At least with any luck, they'd be able to catch one of the ones already inside on her way out.

There had certainly been some excitement earlier in the evening when the Torchmen had activated and launched skyward, but since they seemed to have no interest in anyone on the ground, the troops had eventually relaxed and were gazing upwards, enjoying the show.

Castle Wulfenbach and its attendant flotilla had managed to outrun the Torchmen. Several smaller ships had fallen to Earth, some in more control than others, and at least a dozen more had successfully managed to contain the fires.

The Torchmen themselves had circled the town three times and even now the last of them were drifting back to their posts like flaming snowflakes. Every now and then, one of the aged mechanisms suddenly seized up and plummeted to the ground. At least two fires were burning, one in a small shop right below the troopers' post. Even as the two men watched, one of the great metal fire-fighting dragons of Mechanicsburg lumbered around a corner. The driver waddled the thing up close to the fire and the crew leapt off. They unreeled the canvas hose hidden in the tail and dragged it to the nearest of the many canals that wove through the city.

Then they signaled the driver. With a roar, pumps started, the metal neck swung up, and the mouth spat a highly pressurized stream of water. The attendant crowd cheered.

The two guards nodded in professional appreciation and returned their gaze to the returning Torchmen.

"The Castle is still flyin," the younger guard said with evident relief.

"Yup." The older man said. "And those flaming things are coming back home."

The younger guard thought about this. "Um…But we're still here… so who won?"

The older one clapped him on the shoulder. "Charge your gun and live in the moment, kid."

A murmur caught their attention. Three people were climbing up the stairway, a touch unsteadily. The older soldier instantly identified them as a bunch of tipsy kids. This wouldn't be the first batch of revelers to have climbed up the Castle stairs for a better look.

"Look," the kid in the lead said with exaggerated reasonableness. "You really don't have to come in. You just give me all the equipment, and—"

"No way," said a second young man. "This is our stuff. We collected it for our trip. If we give it to you, you'll just break it or use it to build twisted mockeries of science. Probably both."

"Yeah," the girl with them chimed in. "No way we're going to let you have all that fun without us."

The old soldier sighed. *Wannabe Sparks.*[55] There were a lot of them in Mechanicsburg. Time to send them packing.

"Halt!"

The group stumbled into each other at the top of the stairs. The old soldier was struck by the fact that they didn't look startled or even particularly guilty. This was ridiculous. Students were always guilty of something.

The lead fellow nudged his companion and murmured, "Here we go." Then he stood straight and bellowed, "Know that I—!"

"*Wait!*" The other one frantically tugged at the speaker's sleeve. The girl leaned in as well. "We forgot the crowd!"

The loud kid deflated and turned to them with a look of incredulity upon his face. "You are kidding me." He looked around and saw nothing but the two stolid soldiers. "I didn't think I could go three meters in this town without attracting a crowd." He waved at the soldiers and called out: "Hold on, we'll be right back!" Then the three of them clattered noisily back down the stairs.

---

[55] An interesting sociological phenomenon, usually found near colleges. Essentially, people who like to think that they are nascent Sparks. It was a conceit with varying degrees of dedication. At one end, you have those who play at what they think a Spark might be like, as an excuse to indulge in various recreational excesses, all the way up to those who desperately hope that they really are Sparks, usually because they didn't do the studying and hope to be able to turn their professors into weevils before finals. As seasoned professors, we can assure you that this hardly ever happens, so get back to your books.

The two soldiers waited for the regulation minute and then lowered their rifles. The older soldier turned to his companion. "See? That's what college'll do to you. Now go brew us up a mug."

Gil and Theo tried to ignore Sleipnir's giggles as they all clumped down the stairs. "Maybe we could just leave a note," she suggested.

"No!" Gil was emphatic. A part of his brain noted with relief that the fresh air seemed to be clearing the last of Theo's concoction from his head. "We need a crowd. A big crowd. They've got to see us going in." He rolled his eyes. "What's driving me crazy is that I *had* a crowd, and I let them get away."

Theo dramatically placed a hand to his forehead. "Ah, the fickleness of the mob. Their love, once gone, is gone forever. You are a has-been, my friend. Yesterday's news."

Sleipnir waited until Theo wound down. "We'll just have to build a new crowd."

Gil stopped dead on the stairs. "That would take weeks!"

Theo nodded, "And the graveyard is all the way across town."

Sleipnir nodded. "Stand a little closer so I can slap the two of you at once." With the ease of practice, the two stepped away from each other. "I mean," she continued, "that we have to do something exciting to get people's attention!"

Theo nodded. "Oh. Yeah, that would work, too."

They reached the bottom of the stairs, and Gil turned towards the tourist district. "Let's go."

They soon found that there were lots of people on the streets already—many of them drinking.

Theo looked around. "Standing out in this is going to be tough," he admitted.

Suddenly a familiar voice rang out. "There you are!"

Gil turned and saw Zeetha, a half-eaten honey-glazed "trilobite-on-a-stick" in her hand. Behind her stood Krosp and a bemused Airman Higgs, still cradling Gil's hat. "We knew you'd wander out here eventually. Still planning on going into the Castle?"

Gil nodded. "Yesss. But first we need a good fight."

Theo looked surprised, then nodded. "Oh. Yes, that would do it."

Zeetha's face went blank. Gil took a large step back and leveled a stern finger at her. "That's right, you brazen hussy!" he roared. A few of the people in the surrounding crowd turned towards them. "I, Gilgamesh Wulfenbach, will enter Castle Heterodyne! And if you try to stop me, I will fight you in a suitably noisy and crowd-gathering manner! Let all who gather see that I—*Gilgamesh Wulfenbach*—will defend the Heterodyne girl with my life!"

Zeetha's trilobite dripped honey onto her hand. "What?"

Gil opened his eyes wide and stared at her pointedly—willing her to play along. "No one will keep me from her side! She is my chosen bride and any who harm her will answer to me!" Gil stopped. "Whoa, did I really just say that?"

Theo nodded. "Yes."

Sleipnir nodded.

Zeetha stared at him.

Gil waved his hands. "Okay, nobody heard that."

"I heard it," Krosp said.

Zeetha stared at Krosp.

Gil gave up. "O-ho! So your vile cat slanders my good name! Now we must fight!!"

The crowd held its breath. Zeetha opened her mouth wider than one would have thought possible and stuffed the rest of the trilobite inside. She then spat the clean stick at Gil's feet and grinned. "You are such a dork. Fine. You want to get into the Castle?"

There was a shining blur and her swords were in her hands, glinting in the lights. The crowd moved back quickly and a clear space opened around the combatants. "I am going to kick your butt, hogtie you, and drag you to Agatha myself. She could probably use a good laugh right now."

Gil held a hand up and Sleipnir tossed an odd-looking tube weapon into it. Zeetha's eyes narrowed. Gil spoke to her, more quietly now. "I have a better idea. We'll fight, I'll win, and you'll stay safely outside."

The tube weapon began to whirr as it warmed up.

"Agatha will be mad at me if I let her friends get hurt. So come on! We've got to make it an *entertaining fight!*" His voice rose to a theatrical shout again and he looked comically alarmed. "Oooh. Swords! You're gonna beat me up? I'm scared!"

He aimed up overhead and pulled a trigger. In a lightning-fast series of soft explosions, he emptied the weapon towards the sky. "Scared it'll be over too soon, that is."

Zeetha had leapt back from the flash of heat from the weapon's muzzle. "Whoa! Hey! Watch where you're pointing the death ray, Madboy!" she yelled. "What exactly is your idea of 'safe'?"

Fireworks exploded overhead. Gil tossed the shooter away. "Ooh. The mean ol' swordswoman is afraid of a little boom!" he mocked. "Don't worry, I wasn't trying to hit you. I just wanted people to know there was a show."

Zeetha stared into the sky. "Whoo! Good job!" she sneered. "You found a target even *you* couldn't miss!"

"Kind of like your big mouth!" Gil returned. He flipped over the next device that was handed to him and turned a crank, ejecting a stream of what appeared to be forks. He raised his voice. "Now—face the terror of my hand-cranked runcible gun!"

Zeetha was having fun. Her swords moved in a swirling pattern—and she smirked as Gil found himself dodging his own forks. "Ha! Pathetic! Better a big mouth than a big empty space where my brain should be! *Nyeah!*"

"Oh, that's really mature—ow!" Gil shouted. He spun and weaved, but when he tossed aside the weapon and faced Zeetha he realized that she was nowhere to be seen. There were just Krosp and Higgs, standing there, gazing upwards wide-eyed. Gil threw himself backwards so that Zeetha's boots barely missed his head. He continued rolling, avoiding her kicks and lunges, until he doubled back and she sailed past him, giving him enough time to slap a small device onto her back.

Zeetha froze and then frantically tried to reach the small of her back. "What is that?"

"Nothing serious," Gil said, "Just one of Dr. Prometheus Bunbury's 'Jolly Fun Oxidation Enhancers.' You can buy 'em in any novelty store in Paris. Unless you toss aside those swords, in five seconds, they're going to go 'poof'!"

Zeetha glared at him and tossed her swords straight up into the air, where they spun in two glittering arcs. There was indeed a 'Thoof' sound, and Zeetha's clothing disintegrated in a small cloud of dust, fibers, and metal bits that clattered to the ground. The crowd "oooohed" appreciatively. Zeetha's swords dropped into her outstretched hands.

Gil's face went scarlet. "...Unless I used the 'Wacky Weave Destabilizer' instead, which is possible, since they all look quite similar...but!" He rallied quickly. "Well—um—well, now we're even. I guess you're staying behind after all. You can't go into the Castle like that! A pity the fight was so *short*, but—" Zeetha's foot caught him in the side of the head and he slammed into the pavement.

She stood over him laughing. "The Warriors of the Double Guard always train naked, little boy." She glanced about, "Besides, you wanted a crowd? You'll get a crowd." She waved to a group of soldiers, who responded with enthusiastic whistles.

"Not that kind of crowd!" Gil snarled.

Zeetha laughed and kicked him again, sending him sprawling, to the crowd's delight. "To an entertainer, there's no such thing as a bad audience." She sashayed towards him. "Besides what kind of Spark are you if you let something like *this* distract you?"

"The kind of Spark that lets other people get distracted."

Without thinking, Zeetha somersaulted backwards, which was why the cage produced by the little device Gil had slid towards her feet snapped shut on empty air.

Gil stared at her in admiration. "You're fast, I'll give you that..." A movement at the corner of his eye was all the warning he had. He dodged to one side and again the cage closed on nothing. As he scrambled back, Gil saw that the device had raised itself on a number of thin, spider-like legs. *I don't remember building those*, he thought worriedly. In his effort to escape, he ran into something soft.

"What is that thing?" Zeetha demanded.

"Well… It's a sort of automatic cage-trap…thing. It was supposed to pop up and grab you."

The device had seen the two of them, and now trundled towards them. "I based it on those little things that Agatha makes," Gil admitted. "But something seems a bit off."

The cage mechanism snapped out at the two of them. If they hadn't moved quickly, it would have trapped them both.

Gil looked down at it from the wall on which he perched. "Interesting. I guess it'll just keep going until it catches something."

"Idiot!" Zeetha smacked the back of his head and pointed. "You mean it could try to grab someone in the crowd?"

The device had been staring upwards at the two of them but at Zeetha's words, it paused, wheeled around and regarded the staring crowd. Its cage mechanism flexed and it moved off towards them.

Gil smacked the back of Zeetha's head. "Yeah, *maybe*." He stood and yelled at the crowd. "Don't let it get too close!" Unfortunately, the crowd had solidified nicely and things were so entertaining that they were loath to leave.

"Great!" Zeetha leapt towards it, "Can we stop it?"

"It should be easy," Gil said. Zeetha sliced through the clank's thin metal arms, then had to leap backwards as several dozen more unfolded and reached for her. Her next swipe cut halfway through one of the thin rods and stuck. She frantically tugged it free a half-second before she would have been trapped. The crowd applauded.

Gil stared. "It's…it's learning."

Krosp spoke up. "Yeah, Agatha's do that, too. Well done." Another set of arms unfolded. Several of these were equipped with tips that resembled policemen's sword-breakers. Zeetha swore and dodged a concerted attack by no less than five of them at once. The crowd cheered.

Gil turned towards Theo and Sleipnir. "A little help here?"

Their eyes lit up. "Really?"

Sleipnir pulled a large sack open and began tossing out devices. "I thought you'd never ask!"

Gil felt a sense of dread as he dodged a series of arms equipped with clasping pinchers.

Theo brandished a device with glowing orange lights. "I'll separate the crowd from the thing with my Stalagmite Gun!" He pulled the trigger and swept the resulting beam across the street. Wherever it touched, cobblestones melted and erupted upward into superheated glowing spikes, causing the crowd to shriek.

Sleipnir took a deep breath. She had a large oily bag festooned with glowing rods and pipes that began to pour out an acrid smoke. "And I'll get that beastie with my Hot Pipes!" She blew into a mouthpiece, spitting out an earsplitting shriek along with a thin stream of brilliant green flame. This enveloped a set of the device's arms, covering them with a sticky, burning coating.

Krosp took in the resulting chaos. "Great. Now the crowd is hemmed in by the stalagmites while the flaming clank advances."

Theo and Sleipnir looked abashed. "We can fix that," Theo assured the cat.

Zeetha dodged a set of metal hooks. "They *are* trying to help, yes?"

Gil sighed. "It's my fault, really. I make it look easy."

Another set of manipulators burst forth. "How many arms did you build into this thing?"

"It's making more," Gil told her.

"Hi! Are you a tramp?"

While they were chopping arms, neither one of them had noticed that a small girl had wandered up to them. She was obviously fascinated by Zeetha. "Mama says you must be a tramp 'cause of the way you're dressed." Zeetha frantically swiped away a set of arms that were reaching for the girl. "Either that, or you're an actress." The girl turned to Krosp. "You're a kitty."

Krosp grabbed the girl and swung her away from a large grasping hand. "Do you like cheese?" she asked.

"Hey!" Krosp yelled at Gil. "Prince Myshkin! This thing just wants to catch someone, right?"

"Yes!"

"Would it hurt them?"

"No!"

Krosp smiled. "Fine. I was hoping I wouldn't have to get involved, but if I don't, we'll be stuck here all night."

Gil looked alarmed. "Krosp, wait! Don't do anything dangerous!"

"Relax. I'll be fine." The cat shoved the little girl directly into the grasp of the device. Instantly it formed a cage. There was a "pop" and a small burst of confetti, followed by a few bars of victorious music. Then the clank stood still.

The girl's eyes went wide with delight. "MOMMA!" she squealed, "I'M INNA SHOW!"

The audience cheered.

Zeetha grabbed the cat by the scruff of his neck. "Krosp!"

"What? No one got hurt!" This was so evidently true that Zeetha could only glare.

Gil smiled charmingly as the little girl's mother strode forward. "Don't worry, ma'am, she's—*oof!*" He gasped as the woman sank her fist into his stomach.

"Hyu *peeg!*" the woman hissed. "Get her out, *now!*"

Krosp shrugged. "Well, no one important." He eyed the surrounding sea of faces. "So, showbiz girl, big enough crowd?"

"Yeah." Zeetha graciously accepted a robe from an admiring monk, who was having serious second thoughts about his current lifestyle choices, and donned it to a wave of collective disappointment. "This should be good."

Meanwhile, Sleipnir had twisted back enough of the bars that the little girl could wriggle free. "There you go, kid."

The girl twirled and curtsied at Gil. "Thanks! So long, funny man."

Gil gave a wan smile. "So lo—*gooorgh!*" Another sock to the gut caused him to drop to his knees.

"Hyu bad man," the woman hissed. "Hyu no talk to my leedle gurl."

Theo helped Gil to his feet. "Wow. Still the ladies' man."

"Will you give it a rest," Gil snarled. He looked around at the crowd and nodded. "Okay, I'm ready to speak."

Krosp and Zeetha glanced at each other. "Maybe you should let someone introduce you."

Zeetha nodded. "Yeah. On your own, you're too—"

Gil impatiently waved them off. "I can introduce myself." He turned to the crowd. "People of Mechanicsburg," he shouted. "I suppose you're wondering what this is all about?"

Actually, everyone in the crowd was already pretty sure. A shower of coins hit the ground around Gil's feet.

Gil waved his arms. "No! No! This isn't a show! I'm serious!"

The audience laughed. One wag called out, "So what's your name, kid?"

Krosp rubbed his forehead with his paw. "I knew we should've introduced him," he muttered.

Gil squared his shoulders. "I am Gilgamesh Wulfenbach. I'm the Baron's son."

The crowd stared at him. Then erupted with howls of laughter. The wag pointed to Krosp. "I get it! And that's the Baron's dog, isn't it?"

"And she's the Baron's daughter!" Zeetha's face went red.

"And those are your oafish minions!" Theo and Sleipnir looked around until they realized where the crowd was pointing.

"And you must also be the gol-danged Storm King!" The sight of Gil's face sent the crowd into such peals of laughter that many of them collapsed to the ground.

"What'll we do?" Zeetha hissed. "He's going to kill them."

Suddenly Gil threw his head back and laughed. Krosp and Zeetha jumped. "That's right, folks!"

Then Gil, lightning stick glowing, started back up the stairway to the castle entrance. "So follow me! The second act is just about to start!" And with that, he turned and bounded up the stairs.

Theo and Sleipnir looked at each other. "Uh-oh."

They rushed over to Krosp and Zeetha just as Airman Higgs ambled up. "Nice moves," he remarked to Zeetha.

For some reason, the realization that the airman had seen the whole performance—including her state of undress—caused Zeetha to blush furiously. That he had so little to say about it only annoyed her further. "Come on," she said brusquely. "We can't let him get too far ahead."

The two soldiers guarding the castle gate were gazing skyward again. Gil's fireworks display had died down but they were still hopeful and it provided a convenient hook for another of the old soldier's recollections. "And that was the last time Professor Phosphorous visited the fireworks factory." He thought for a moment. "Or anything else, really."

The younger soldier digested this. "Wow. So is that what you think we saw?"

The old soldier shrugged. "Wouldn't surprise me, kid." He waved a knowing hand at the brightly lit town below. "Lotsa loony Sparks come through Mechanicsburg."

The younger man, whose career as a raconteur was doomed by an unshakable respect for actual facts, pointed towards the East. "But they only got the one factory here and I don't see anything going on with it."

"In this town? It could've been an explosion in a coffee shop. I heard from one of the guys on the day shift that—"

This interesting line of discourse was silenced by the sound of footsteps at the top of the stairs. The soldiers looked down and recognized the three young people who had appeared before, now accompanied by a throng of townspeople and delighted tourists. Their voices grew louder as they drew near.

"Gil, you're making me nervous…"

"How can that be?" Both of the guards snapped to attention. There was something about the young man's voice now that made them uneasy. "A jolly entertainer like myself? A spreader of mirth?"

"At least…stop smiling like that. It's creepy."

"But everyone is having such a good time!"

"If you look like a demented idiot, no one will take you seriously."

This voice appeared to come from a midget in a cat costume. The guards looked at each other. Street performers. Simultaneously, they thumbed the safeties of their rifles off.

"But no one takes me seriously now!" Gil waved at the soldiers and took another step towards them, grinning maniacally.

"HALT!" The older soldier raised a hand while the younger ostentatiously cocked his weapon.[56] "You young'uns just turn around and head back to whatever tavern you came out of!"

Gil turned around and mugged at the crowd which began chuckling even before he faced back towards the troopers. He grinned. "Hi! I'm Gilgamesh Wulfenbach! Can I please go into the castle?"

"*NO!*"

Gil again turned back to the laughing crowd. "There, everyone! You heard me! I asked nice!"

The old soldier blinked. "Wait... You're who?"

But, of course, by then it was much too late.

The explosion caused the Castle itself to shudder. Agatha reeled as debris pitter-pattered down around her. "What was *that?*"

"The Gate of Lamps is under attack," the Castle replied.

"Who's attacking?"

"It appears to be a mob of some sort." The Castle sounded offended. "That's rather unfair, you haven't even done anything yet."

Tarvek was thinking. "The Gate of Lamps..." He grabbed Agatha's sleeve and hauled her down a different hallway. "Come on," he shouted. "We should be able to see that from the windows of the next gallery!"

Agatha was impressed. "You know a lot about the layout of this place."

---

[56] The Baron's Weapon Designers had demonstrated that the sound of a gun being cocked could instantly silence an entire room full of people yelling at each other. They had subsequently designed the Empire's guns so that this sound was amplified and engineered to convey even more menace. Klaus deemed the project a success when, in a field experiment, a single trooper was able to silence a stadium full of enraged football fans who had just watched a goalie obviously throw a game. To be fair, he then had the goalie executed. Klaus liked clean sports.

Tarvek dodged a hole in the floor. "Well, we have had people in here for years plotting on the best way to take it, haven't we? I did read the reports."

They stumbled past a shattered door and found themselves in a long airy room lined with windows. Broken glassware and dust-covered equipment littered the floor, almost obscuring the faded rugs.

"The Laboratory of Light," the Castle announced. Your great-grandmother was so very fond of it."

The lights here were dim and they had to step carefully past the machinery. The windows were filthy but an entire panel had been shattered at some time in the past so they clustered in front of the opening and peered out. The ground was easily three stories down and the excitement seemed to be taking place in front of a side entrance hung with glowing lamps. Far below, a crowd of tiny people was surging back and forth. Some were pouring down the long stairway that led back to the town proper. Many seemed to be just milling about in a panic. This was stopped by a lone figure gesturing towards the castle doors. A bolt of lightning leaped from his hand— no, from some sort of stick—and blew apart the great doors.

Tarvek gasped. "Was that lightning?"

Agatha leaned forward. "Is that Gil?"

Gilgamesh stood in front of the smoking entrance, flaming bits of doorway raining down around him. The two guards were huddled against the stonework of the castle itself, so terrified they couldn't even flee. The crowd that remained had also dropped to the ground, and now peered up at Gil, their eyes wide. This included Zeetha, Krosp, Sleipnir, and Theo, who at least were already rising to their feet. The only odd touch was Higgs. He alone remained standing patiently, Gil's magnificent hat cradled in one arm.

"Are we all paying attention now?" The madboy harmonics roaring through Gil's voice made sure that this was the case, even if he had not just blown down the castle door. "Good! I,

Gilgamesh Wulfenbach, am now entering the castle to aid the true Heterodyne heir!"

The older soldier stared up at him and dared to speak. "You... you're really him? But...but you can't be..."

Gil glared down at him. "I don't know what I have to do to prove it to you—"

At which point Airman Higgs stepped up behind him and gently placed the magnificent hat upon his head. Higgs lit the flame on its top with his pipe, stood back, and calmly struck a theatrical pose. Krosp, Zeetha, Theo, and Sleipnir—with somewhat more enthusiasm—followed suit. Zeetha added a hearty "Ta dahh!" as she gestured.

The crowd gasped in awe.

Gil felt a brief wave of sympathy for every rogue Spark who'd ever turned a town of peasants into squirrels.

High overhead, Violetta looked up from her spyglass. She had been giving the others a running report on what was going on below. "But where did he get that incredible hat?"

Agatha closed her eyes and took a deep breath. "I can guess."

Tarvek looked worried. "Let me see this guy." Violetta smacked his hand away. "No. Designed for my body chemistry, remember? If you try to use it, it'll send a spike into your eye." She paused. "Here you go."

Tarvek ignored her and turned to Agatha. "He says he's coming to help you. Do you trust him?"

Agatha blushed slightly. "Well...not really. Not yet." She looked at Tarvek frankly. "About as much as I trust you."

Tarvek frowned. "What did *he* do to you?"

From the crowd below, they could hear a tiny voice rising above the hubbub.

If Zeetha had learned anything during her travels with Master Payne's Circus of Adventure, it was how to shout coherently. "Yes indeed, ladies and gentlemen—the dangerously handsome young man who stands before you is indeed the son of Baron Wulfenbach!

Aaaand he has personally vowed to woo, win, and wed the Lady Heterodyne—and bring peace to all Europa!"

Gil's infuriated shrieks were nearly drowned out by a huge cheer from the crowd. "It's true, Ladies and Gentlemen!" she continued. "And never fear, folks, I'm sure he intends to wed her most vigorously!" This time, the colossal roar of approval completely obliterated Gil's screams of protest.

Agatha looked upwards. It was hard not to when addressing the Castle's invisible omnipresence. "Castle? You can kill me, now."

The Castle chuckled. "As if I hadn't heard that one before. Rest assured, my Lady, by this time tomorrow, I have every confidence that you'll be happy to still be alive." It paused. "If indeed you are."

"Ooh!" Violetta was glued to her spyglass again. "The guy in the hat is trying to kill the girl with the green hair." She looked up. "The others are holding him back but he's making them work at it."

"What an unspeakable cad!" Tarvek's face was almost as red as Agatha's. "Does he always have his lackeys announce his planned conquests?"

"Well, the crowd's for it," Violetta remarked, and indeed the sound of cheering had yet to die down.

Moloch snorted. "The crowd is always for *that*."

Tarvek dropped his voice. "Agatha, just say the word—and I'll do everything in my power to sort this fellow out for you—him *and* his uncouth minions..."

Agatha had a brief mental image of Tarvek trying to "sort out" Zeetha. Brief, because she figured it would be over in less than ten seconds, once Zeetha stopped laughing. "I appreciate the offer," she said, "because by the time I get through with him, I expect there will be a *lot of pieces to sort!*"

"What are you idiots trying to do to me?!" Gil shouted, waving the glowing walking stick he carried. "When Agatha hears about *that—Argh!* Not to mention that my Father will *level* this place because I've obviously gone *insane!*"

Zeetha looked like she was enjoying his misery. "Phooey. You *said* you wanted people to talk about it, and besides…it was *funny!*"

Despite his mood, Gil knew better than to ignore his surroundings. They were well worth the attention. Once they had entered through the now ruined gate, the architecture of Castle Heterodyne had proved impossible to ignore. The old Heterodynes had known the importance of architecture as a method of intimidation, and had used it well.

The effect was only emphasized by the ubiquitous red lights. The majority of the group stepped carefully, nervous about the traps that were supposed to be everywhere. The only exceptions were Gil, who was stomping furiously on ahead of the rest of the group, and Airman Higgs, who was apparently taking his order to stay by Gil's side as literally as possible.

Higgs spoke up. "Um…sir? I would like to point out that we are now inside Castle Heterodyne? A hideous uncontrolled engine of death?"

Gil scowled. "Now you're just trying to cheer me up. Well, it won't work. I'm still mad."

But Gil realized that he might be leading the loyal airman into danger and the thought brought him up short. He allowed the others to catch up and they proceeded more cautiously.

Zeetha caught him in a friendly headlock. She laughed. "Aww, you are so *cute*. Relax. Agatha is a smart girl. She'll be mad at *me*." Gil considered this. Zeetha continued, "And if she is mad at you, think of all the fun you'll have making up."

Gil growled at her. "I want you to know that, although I currently hate my life, I hate all of you more."

"Aw! So grumpy!" Zeetha rubbed his untidy hair with one fist and then allowed him to spin away from her. He harrumphed and again strode forward. Higgs scurried to keep up.

They heard a gasp from the doorway in front of them.

"Gil? Is that *you?*"

High above Mechanicsburg, the last of the Torchmen were beating their way back to their lampposts. Two of the last were working very hard. They had responded to signals while attacking Castle Wulfenbach, and the protocols had checked out. A passenger had been transferred to their care. They had actually been on their way back to the twinkling lights of Mechanicsburg with their new burden while the rest of the flock had still been driving the great airship and its attendant fleet towards the border.

At last the heights of Castle Heterodyne were coming into focus. A particular balcony lit up, torches puffing into explosive light one after the other, until a relatively undamaged area was clearly lit.

Wings working furiously, the Torchmen angled for the designated area. Once they were close enough, a great wood and iron door squealed ponderously open.

"Ah," the Castle said. "You've returned."

Their passenger, a tall woman sheathed in black leather adorned with a profusion of straps and buckles revealed her needle sharp teeth. Once they were over the balcony, she released her hold upon the strap held by the Torchmen and effortlessly dropped to the balcony. The clanks flapped off. She didn't bother to watch them go.

"Of course I've returned," Mistress Von Pinn hissed. "A Heterodyne has come home." She glided towards the open door. "And thus, so must I."

CHAPTER 7

HAVE *YOU* EVER WANTED TO HUNT *MONSTERS?*
THEN COME TO *Transylvania!*

The Valley of the Heterodynes, home to the fabled town of Mechanicsburg, encompasses less than fifty square kilometers, but within this space, the hunter who is looking for adventure will find *adventure aplenty!!*

For much of its history, the river Dyne was *poisonous.* The truth is that it was *worse* than poisonous! Animals that drank of the Dyne did not always die, but occasionally became *ravening monsters!* Those bloodthirsty devils, *The Heterodynes Of Old*, found this entertaining, and encouraged these monsters by using their own *monstrous sciences* upon them. Over time, these creatures began to *breed true!*

HARD CHEESE FOR
THE LOCALS–
GOOD NEWS FOR YOU!!!

The result today is one of the few places in Europa where TRUE Bloodsport enthusiasts with a genuine taste for adventure can hunt actual monsters, and less than fifteen minutes later, sit down to a hearty breakfast in a town with every amenity a Gentleman of Fortune could ask for!

And lest you think this some managed, mummer's play of a hunt using drugged chimeras bought on the sly from some university's 'Theoretical Zoology' Department
—*LIKE MANY OF OUR COMPETITORS*—
Be aware that in two out of three registered hunts, the hunters wind up *BECOMING THE PREY!*

BEWARE! IT COULD HAPPEN TO YOU!

But if this sounds like your sort of hunt, if you think you're ready to match wits with the crafty SHIFTING BOAR, successfully grapple with the deadly CONSTRICTING CATAMOUNT, or think you are man enough to take down the ultimate trophy, t he majestic EMPEROR SHARK–MAMMOTH,
then come to Mechanicsburg, Sir, AND PROVE IT!!!

Licenses can be obtained from August through March at the Mechanicsburg Rathaus on a strict First-Come, First-Served basis.

The smooth concrete walkways that wound through the Gardens of Mechanicsburg's Great Hospital were designed for the comfort of perambulating patients. Tonight, instead of patients, they were thronged with Wulfenbach military forces—taking advantage of the superior view that the hospital's elevated grounds afforded of the rest of Mechanicsburg.

Some were camped around impromptu fires, brewing mugs of something or other—or having a smoke and a rest. Others were gathered around long tables borrowed from the hospital, studying maps and lists by the light of field lamps. But most of them were leaning against the ornate concrete balustrades that encircled the area, looking down upon the rest of the town.

The hospital was constructed in an area of the town that is, by design, intended to shut down at night so that its patients can sleep in peace. The local businesses tend to be medical supply shops, hotels that cater to visiting families (who probably won't much feel like painting the town red), pharmacies, and the better class of resurrectionist.

That had all been overturned today. Every building in sight had been hung with the ornate, decorative trilobite lanterns that the townspeople haul out for festive occasions. Every courtyard and wide space in the road had been turned into an impromptu beer garden and dance hall.

One of the old Heterodynes had decreed that every Mechanicsburg child must learn to play a musical instrument.[57] The tradition has continued to this day, and the results filled the night with the distinctive Mechanicsburg stutter-step baseline that can be heard in the more bohemian cafes of Paris and Prague,[58] blending together

---

[57]   After the Incredibly Brief Rebellion (two minutes, thirty-six seconds), Queeg Heterodyne had faced a bit of a problem. Family tradition dictated that the people of Mechanicsburg were not to be indiscriminately slain—but a rebellion had to be punished. His decree, although directly harming none, would ensure that the townspeople suffered torture and misery for generations.

[58]   Stutter-Step, despite its obvious roots in Jewish Klezmer and African tribal rhythms, was, in fact, invented by a musically gifted construct named Two-Point-Five-Footed Fritz. Who was the house pianist in a Mechanicsburg brothel. Sadly, there are no known portraits of Fritz and thus the origin of his unusual name remains a source of pointless speculation.

into an infectious wave of music that had the far off watchers absent-mindedly tapping their toes.

A tall, grey-haired Captain of the Medical Corps smiled as he saw a portly little man instructing a mixed set of the younger ranks in a complicated pattern dance he himself fondly remembered from his days as a young rake in Plovdiv. He riffled through his brain until the correct name surfaced.

"Sergeant Scorp," he called out. At once the aergeant turned about, fired off a crisp salute, and then winced slightly as he trotted over.

The captain nodded, as he returned the salute. "How's the arm, Sergeant?"

"Good as new, sir." Scorp then realized that he was still rubbing it and gave a wan smile. "Well, good enough for the Baron's work, anyway. This hospital is a marvel, and no mistake."

Indeed it was. When the sergeant had been brought in two days ago, his arm had been dislocated with two bullets lodged in it. Balan's Gap had seen heavy fighting and, if the reports were to be believed, it was not yet pacified completely.

The captain prodded the sergeant's arm and nodded in satisfaction. "Excellent. We'll need every man we can get."

"And soon, I'm guessing," the sergeant sighed. "Though it's been quiet enough up here..."

Both men glanced over the railing. The situation was tricky. Officially, Mechanicsburg was a part of the Empire, but everyone knew that it was a slightly bent one. In any other town, seeing Castle Wulfenbach chased off might have had a few of the locals smiling quietly to themselves, but this public celebration was worrying. Especially since this unprecedented reversal was treated almost as an unimportant side-effect. The hoopla was really about the news that a Heterodyne had appeared.

Oh, it hadn't been confirmed by the castle or the Baron or anyone official, but word on the street was that this one was the real thing. Not like the fakes that turned up every now and then.

If that was true...well, neither soldier was privy to the rarified politics of the Empire, of course, but any fool could see that there was going to be trouble. For almost twenty years, wide-eyed naïfs and demagogues alike had declared that the return of the Heterodynes would bring about an end of the Baron and usher in a renaissance of plenty. Now one had appeared, and she was already up to her neck in trouble.

No matter how you looked at it, things were going to get interesting.

The captain sighed. "With any luck, they'll party all night. We're low on troops, so we've been concentrating what we've got on the city walls, the armory, and the hospital."

Both men glanced up at the sky. With those flying flamethrowers keeping the fleets away, fresh troops would have to come in overland, which would be a logistical nightmare. The Empire had grown accustomed to ruling the skies.

Scorp looked down on the celebrants again. They looked cheerful enough, but—"Shouldn't there be patrols on the streets?" He then looked abashed. There were numerous jokes about soldiers trying to second-guess old Klaus's strategies.

The captain politely ignored the faux pas. "He's got it covered. He's had a hundred hogsheads of double-fortified lingonberry snap distributed throughout the town, as a 'congratulations' sort of thing."[59]

Scorp stared and then started to grin. "If they hoist a noggin or two of that stuff to the Lady Heterodyne, they'll be too busy skipping through the streets tryin' to catch flyin' pink mimmoths!"

The captain nodded. "Still, there's no telling what this new girl will do now that she's in Castle Heterodyne."

Scorp's face went sour and he rubbed his arm again. "You're on target with that one, sir."

The captain failed to notice the degree to which this discussion affected the sergeant. "Personally, I just wish we knew if she was the real thing or a fake. Once we get some more troops—"

---

[59]   Double-Fortified Lingonberry Snap was possibly the most potent alcoholic beverage in Europa at this time. It was crafted by a complicated process that involved distillation, freezing, the application of mildly hallucinogenic fungi, and aging in specially seasoned stone crocks (which significantly cut down on the batches lost due to spontaneous combustion). Astonishingly, it was invented not by a Spark, but by a little old man in Switzerland who drank an Imperial Liter of the stuff every day, lived to one hundred and thirty-three, and whose funeral pyre burned uncontrollably for three days.

The sergeant swayed slightly. "Hey! You feel that?" "That" rapidly grew into a vibration underfoot which continued to grow in strength.

"It's an earth tremor," the captain exclaimed. "And it's getting stronger!" Shouts of alarm began to break out among the troops. "I knew it! She's going to kill us with some damnable earthquake machine!"

But the sergeant raised a hand. He heard a peculiar high-pitched squealing. One he was familiar with. "Everybody!" he roared in his best parade-ground voice. "Fall back to the walls!"

Instantly every trooper within earshot grabbed their gear and took off at a stumbling run over the shaking ground. In the center of the gardens, a mound formed and the raw earth continued stretching skyward until suddenly a spinning, metal drill point burst through, scattering dirt and plants for several dozen square meters. The point continued to rise, followed by the rest of the cylindrical machine erupting up and out of the ground. It wavered slightly and the great drill began to slow. Then slowly, majestically, it toppled onto recessed treads, which bounced with a springy jolt.

Everyone stared at it for a minute, as it cooled with a series of clicks and hisses. Then they all jumped again as the rear end swung open, spilling forth a red light and an excited young man in an abbreviated Wulfenbach uniform. He glanced around and then pumped his fist in triumph.

"Woo-hoo!" he crowed to the sky. He turned and yelled back into the machine—"Well done, Scopes! We're right outside the Great Hospital!"

A slim young woman appeared at the entrance and delicately wiped a sheen of sweat from her dark brow. "All it takes is an accurate 3-D sonar compass, sir."

"Good thing you built us one, eh?" He turned to the captain, who was frowning as he hurried over. "Never thought we'd get past all those basements." The captain opened his mouth and the young man snapped out a salute. "Ahoy! Major Resetti, First Subterranean

Mecha-Mole Brigade!" He jerked a thumb back. "'Scopes' here is Lieutenant Krishnamurti."

The lieutenant was already saluting, and the captain impatiently saluted back. "Begging your pardon, Major. But your worm-chaser's busted through a secure perimeter! Leaving a tunnel—" He broke off at the sight of the major's smirk. "Something funny, Major?"

Sergeant Scorp coughed delicately. "That's a Deep Six Model, sir," he said quietly. "Collapses the tunnel in after itself."

The captain shut his mouth with an audible click and nodded once.[60]

Major Resetti beamed. "Well spotted, Sergeant!"

The captain flushed. "Even so—"

Again he was interrupted. "Captain." The speaker had just emerged from the Mecha-Mole, and it must have been a tight fit. She was over two meters tall and her shoulders were almost two wide. She was dressed in no-nonsense leathers which steamed slightly in the cooler air. Across her chest were strung several bandoliers containing ammunition for the hand cannon hanging from her hip, as well as a thick baldric which held an enormous broadsword across her back.

Her face was broad and plain, her hair was black and cropped short, and her eyes were intense. "I have a package for the Baron." She patted an Imobilex jug that stood by her side.[61] "One that he ordered personally." Anticipating the captain's next words, she presented a sheaf of papers.

The captain ignored them and stared at her. "Who the devil are you?"

The woman merely jiggled her papers. Sergeant Scorp took them and perfunctorily checked them while he made introductions. "This is the Lady Grantz, sir. She's the Baron's monster hunter."

The captain blinked and stepped back. Grantz looked at the sergeant and raised an eyebrow. "Have we met?"

---

[60]   People who refused to listen to technical experts didn't last long in the armies of the Empire.

[61]   At this time, Imobilex jugs were state of the art portable containment units used to transport dangerous materials such as unstable chemicals or potential explosives.

The sergeant handed her back her papers and tossed her a salute of his own. "Sergeant Damien Scorp. Of the Baron's Vespiary Squad."

Grantz looked interested. "The Bug Hunters."

"Yes'm. Had the privilege of watching you work in Belgrade last year."[62]

Grantz looked pleased. "Good outfit," she conceded. "You'll do."

The sergeant's eyebrows rose. "Do for what, Ma'am?"

The monster hunter patted the Imobilex jug. "I need to get this bad boy to the Baron. I could use your help."

The sergeant grimaced. Imobilex jugs weighed a lot. "It'll take a while, Ma'am, but I could requisition a heavy caisson. Be a problem on the soft ground, but—"

Grantz interrupted. "No, no." She effortlessly hoisted the jug up onto her shoulder and indicated a leather grip at her feet. "I just want you to carry my bag."

The sergeant had worked with enough of the Empires' Special Units to know when he was seeing a show put on for the benefit of others, and indeed, the captain, the Mecha-Mole drivers, and the rest of the assembled soldiery were watching with clearly growing awe.

"Stand aside," he roared. "This lady is making a delivery!" Instantly a path towards the hospital gates opened and they set off.

"Do you know where the Baron is?" Grantz asked.

The sergeant shook his head. "Somewhere in the hospital, Ma'am. But I heard he's movin' around."

They approached the main entrance to the hospital, which was now behind a barricade consisting of at least two-dozen troopers, several of the large brass clanks, and an enormous green-furred ape creature. The soldiers saw the sergeant and Grantz approaching and the ape stepped forward.

"Grantz," he muttered cordially. Even though it was night, Nak wore a large pair of smoked goggles that glinted in the lights.

---

[62]   Empire records for the year in question do not show the Vespiary Squad active in Belgrade, but one of the sergeant's grandchildren does live there, so the chance that the sergeant was visiting during the incident of the Three Sewer Golems, which was highly publicized at the time, while coincidental, is not at all unlikely.

The monster hunter gave him a smile. "Sergeant Nak."[63]

The sergeant bared his fangs. "You have come for me."

The monster hunter shifted the Imobilex jug to her other shoulder. "In your dreams."

Nak stared at her. His fangs were still displayed, but the corners of his mouth turned up. "Yes—in the very best ones!" He then turned to Sergeant Scorp and his demeanor changed. "And who is this?"

The sergeant stared up at the large goggles and refrained from saluting with great effort. "Sergeant Scorp, Vespiary Squad."

Nak leaned down and examined him closely. Scorp felt the chemical-scented breath gust past him. Nak straightened up and waved them through. "Watch your back, little man," he growled.

Scorp waited until they were in the building's foyer. "What was that about?"

Grantz looked embarrassed. "Don't mind him. Nak gets jealous."

The sergeant almost dropped the bag. "But—wait—"

Grantz rolled her eyes. "He can't help it. Under those goggles? He's a green-eyed monster."

There was a lot left unsaid in that statement. Sergant Scorp was open-minded. He had to be. In the Armies of the Empire you worked with—and relied upon—any number of things that were, well, not human necessarily, but certainly people. And it followed that two people of any type might form the strongest of bonds. Scorp had seen it happen often enough. Hell, his daughter had fallen for an accountant, of all things, and after he'd gone to all the trouble of setting her up with a nice reanimated fellow from his old unit. No, nothing surprised him anymore, but...

"I thought you *hunted* monsters."

To his astonishment, the woman laughed at this. "Only the ones that cause trouble. Most of my work involves the shambling, mindless

---

[63]   When the Wulfenbach Empire had to take down a rebellious Spark, the official policy was to welcome the defeated Spark's constructs and experimental subjects into the forces of the Empire. Most of them leapt at the chance to be part of a large organization that actually saw to their well-being. Plus, it offered them a chance to punch Sparks, and get paid for it.

stuff. Rogue machines, beasts gone mad…Intelligent, sentient monsters are rarer than you'd think."

A sweet voice arose from one of the chairs in the lobby. It sounded amused. "About time you got here."

To his surprise, Scorp saw Grantz spin, slide the Imobilex jar to the ground, and whip her sword out in one smooth movement. The tip of the blade pointed at a curvaceous woman with dark skin and jet-black hair clad in the white uniform of the Baron's exploratory fleet. She was lazily unfolding herself from the chair and she was a beautiful sight. It wasn't until he saw the small skull-shaped bindi upon her forehead that Scorp realized they were standing before Captain Bangladesh DuPree. The bag dropped from his suddenly cold hands. *I never even heard her coming*, he thought, with a touch of panic.

Captain DuPree stared a moment, cross-eyed, at the sword held motionless centimeters from her nose. Then she grinned up at Grantz insouciantly. "Maybe someday, girlie." She moved the sword aside with the tip of a finger. "But not today. Come on, Klaus is waiting for you."

She turned and headed off with a light step. The monster hunter stared after her for a second, sheathed her sword, and bent to pick up the Imobilex jug. She only remembered Scorp when he moved to pick up her valise. She gave him a small smile, such as you'd see between two veterans who had survived an attack, and continued her conversation as if she'd never stopped. "But when you *do* meet an intelligent monster, you really have to be careful."

They followed Captain DuPree through the hospital corridors, which magically cleared of people as she approached. To Scorp's surprise, they passed through another lobby and he realized that they were again outside, in one of the hospital's hidden courtyards. This one was crowded with people, clerks, and functionaries, as well as a few of the higher brass. Scorp then saw that the tower of machinery they were clustered around was some sort of giant clank, which was currently at rest upon the ground. Seated at its apex was the Master of the Empire, Baron Klaus Wulfenbach. Sergeant Scorp had seen his share of battle injuries. The Baron looked like he'd decided to try a fair sampling of all of them.

Everyone was talking. Scorp resigned himself to a long wait, but Captain DuPree simply waded forward. "Hey, Klaus!" Everyone froze and again a space cleared out around her. She waved the two of them forward without looking at them. "Grantz is here, with that big jar of trouble you ordered."

The monster hunter stepped forward and swung the jar off of her shoulder. Her face was a mask of concern. "Herr Baron. I'd heard you were injured but I had no idea. Should you be up?"

Klaus smiled. "Despite Dr. Sun's histrionics, I can assure you that it looks worse than it is." He turned serious. "Your delivery?"

Grantz nodded. Taking a key from around her neck, she unlocked a panel, which swung aside. She flipped several switches and the lid of the jug squealed and slowly began to unscrew itself. The crowd pulled farther back. Sergeant Scorp would have liked to have done the same but instead he simply clutched the valise tighter.

The lid fell off and Grantz dipped her hand into the jar, hauling out a limp figure wrapped in a hunter's net. She pulled a small device from a pouch at her belt, touched it to the netting, and it fell apart, revealing none other than Othar Tryggvassen—the famous Spark and self-proclaimed hero—who glared defiantly at his surroundings before folding up and collapsing onto the floor.

Grantz held up her hand. "Please. Don't underestimate him this time. This is the second time I've had to bring him in."

She nudged Othar with her foot. "What's the matter with you? Are you trying to pull some kind of trick?"

"No!" Othar snapped. "My legs simply fell asleep! Have *you* ever been stuffed into one of those things?" He flexed his legs and grimaced. "You people certainly know how to ruin an entrance."

Klaus rolled his eyes. Othar lived his life knowing that, no matter the situation, he was The Hero, and thus tried to be as—Klaus searched for a word—dramatic? No—as *showmanlike* as possible. This made him a great favorite amongst the populace at large.

"Okay," Othar announced. "I'm good." He smoothly rolled, bounced to his feet, and struck a dramatic pose.

Klaus ignored the resultant smattering of applause.

"So, Tyrant, we meet again!" Othar said, "But know that Othar Tryggvassen—Gentleman Adventurer—remains unbowed! Though you hold all of Europa within your grasp, I am not afraid! Imprison me! Torture me! Try to break my will! You will fail!"

Baron Wulfenbach disliked dealing with Othar for so many reasons. Most of them had to do with the man's staunch determination to "right wrongs and fight injustice," while steadfastly ignoring the effects his often spectacularly destructive efforts had upon the delicate game of give-and-take necessary to maintain the fragile political structure that was the Empire of the Pax Transylvania. Still, probably the most personal reason was that, whenever he was in Othar's presence, the Baron invariably found himself acting like an over-the-top villain in a Heterodyne play, which was just embarrassing. Today was no exception.

"I suppose I really should just kill you," he said.

Othar paused in his dramatic speech. "Oooh. I didn't see that one coming."

Klaus smiled evilly, caught himself, and grimaced. "But, in fact, I won't. I have a job for you."

Othar considered this. "Why do I think I'd prefer to be killed?"

Klaus regarded him with raised eyebrows. "Good heavens. It's possible that you really are smart. The Heterodyne girl—"

"Ah! That would be the lovely young innocent who escaped your evil clutches—with some small assistance from myself." Othar interjected with a semblance of modesty. "Of course, I didn't know who she was then…"

Klaus nodded. "You *are* somewhat responsible for the current situation, but only somewhat. There are two Heterodyne girls at present. One is an obvious fake, part of a plot against the Empire that has already been crushed.

"But both girls are now inside Castle Heterodyne. In the fake I have little interest. But this 'Agatha Heterodyne'—as she calls herself at the moment—I have to believe that she has the potential to hold the Castle. The people will follow her. My own son has entered the Castle with the stated intention of aiding her. At this rate, all too soon she'll be securely entrenched within an impenetrable fortress, firmly established as a Heterodyne, and allied, in the mind of the people, with the House of Wulfenbach. She'll be able to do anything."

Othar mulled this over. "But… if she is working with your son…a loathsome concept! But…" Othar paused. "But why do you speak as though this is a bad thing? Agatha struck me as a good girl!" He shrugged. "Well, as good as a Spark can be, anyway."[64] He looked at DuPree. "Am I missing something?"

DuPree waved a hand. "Whenever he goes on like this, I just think of how many different ways I can spell 'eviscerate.'"

The Baron's voice rose until he was nearly shouting: "Because this girl, the girl you 'rescued' from me, is actually the Other!"

Othar's breath caught. "The Great Enemy!" He frowned. "But the Other hasn't been active in nearly twenty years!"

"Well she's active now! Her slaver wasps and her machines are responsible for the mess in Balan's Gap. I've talked to her. She didn't even try to hide it."

Othar shook his head. "I cannot believe that the innocent girl I aided is the Other! Her age! Her behavior—"

"Believe it, sir."

Everyone looked around in surprise at Sergeant Scorp. He was amazed at his own audacity, but determined to speak. "Your pardon, Herr Baron, but my squad's the one that found her at Sturmhalten." He turned back to Othar. "The city's full of revenants. A new type, not your usual mindless shamblers. Most of the time, they look and act normal."

---

[64]   Othar Tryggvassen has put forth the revolutionary hypothesis that Sparks are responsible for most of the war, death, and assorted chaos in the world, and wishes to test this by eliminating all Sparks and seeing if the world actually improves. The only awkward part of this is that Othar is a rather strong Spark in his own right, but he has promised that when he has eliminated all of the other Sparks from the world, he will also kill himself. Ironically, many Sparks are conflicted about this, as his hypothesis is compelling, his methodology seems sound, and many argue that it would be a valid experiment.

He paused. "I gotta tell you, there was something about that girl. I'd've trusted her with my life. And then…then she shot her friend point-blank in the back just because he was tryin' to warn us. She ordered the townspeople to kill us." Scorp looked ill at the memory. "And they sure as hell tried."

He looked up at them now, a fighting man talking to other fighting men. "I've been a soldier close to thirty years. I know how to…to read people, you know? I just got the knack. And I have *never* been as wrong about anyone as I was about her." His eyes met Othar's. "I know you don't got no reason to trust me, Herr Tryggvassen, but I was there and that's the truth of it."

Othar stared at the sergeant and nodded slowly.

Klaus blinked. There was a change in the man. The constant air of unspoken braggadocio was gone. *It…he can't* always *be…acting…can he?* The thought was chilling. Klaus had always considered Othar a clown. If this was all just a *game* to him…

"Assuming this is true," Othar asked the Baron, "what do you want from me?"

Inside Castle Heterodyne, Agatha, Tarvek, Moloch, and Violetta squeezed past a collapsed doorway into a large open atrium. Carved faces leered down at them as they picked their way through the rubble and dust.

Moloch looked back the way they had come. "Wulfenbach should be inside by now. Aren't we going to get him?"

"No," Agatha snapped. "I'm still mad at him."

Tarvek, who had been leading the way, stopped and hitched his toga up. "We should go get him."

Agatha bit her lip. "I really don't want to waste any time while you try to 'sort him out' for me."

Tarvek snorted. "Is that your reason? Trust me, while I'd love to, it would be prudent to defer that particular pleasure. Practically speaking, we're far better off if he's here working with us."

Agatha regarded him skeptically.

Tarvek continued, "Think about it. This place is broken. Its governing intelligence is fractured, and most of the sub-systems don't recognize you as the Heterodyne. The more Sparks we have helping, the faster we can get it fixed, and that can only help our chances of survival. I don't know much about this fellow but everything I've heard says that whatever else he may be, he *is* a powerful Spark."

Agatha's mouth twitched in annoyance. "I'm not terribly happy about having you here either."

Tarvek looked away. "Yes, I got that." He took a deep breath and looked back. "But I still think we should get him. You can always kill us both later if you must."

"No!" Agatha snapped.

"Your pardon, Mistress," the Castle chimed in. "But that is an accepted method of dealing with contractors."

"No! I want Gil out of here! Alive! Can you throw him out without hurting him?"

"Not in my current state. He is not in an area I can see."

"Don't be naïve," Tarvek growled. "You're obviously new at this, so let me give you some political advice. The only thing that might keep the Baron from leveling this place is the Baron's son being in here. If you want to deal with the Baron from a position of strength, you're going to need the legitimacy of being the Heterodyne. To get that, you need a functioning Castle. Gilgamesh Wulfenbach may be an ill-bred dog, but he can help you—if only by acting as a shield while you work!"

Agatha shook her head. "No! I won't use him as a hostage. This place is too dangerous. I don't want another—I don't want anyone dying on my behalf. Not even you."

Tarvek paused. "Why, that's the nicest thing you've said to me since I got here."

"Treasure it and get out!"

"I am not leaving. I *can't* leave. And, as much as it irks me, I'm betting Wulfenbach won't just leave either."

"I can't trust either one of you!" she shouted.

"So what? You don't have the luxury of trust. But if you're going to get us all out of this, you...you need to use what you've got." Tarvek swayed slightly.

Agatha looked at him with a touch of concern. Despite being clad in only a sheet, Tarvek was sweating profusely. "Are you all right?"

"No, I'm *not* all right. Violetta!" And with that, Tarvek folded up and collapsed to the floor. Violetta was at his side, swearing.

"I thought he'd be good for longer than that," she muttered.

Tarvek looked up at them. "Have Gaston bring the coach around," he said earnestly, "I think the eels are rising."

Agatha stared, "What's wrong with him?"

Violetta extracted a leather roll, which when opened, revealed a collection of small vials. "You were with this fool in Sturmhalten, right?"

Agatha considered this. "...Technically...yes?"

Violetta ignored the hesitancy. "Well, I don't know what happened, but apparently, after you took off, your evil twin—or whatever she is—went and shot him in the back."

Agatha gasped. "She did? But I thought he was working with her?"

"According to him," she nudged Tarvek with her foot, "that was just to keep you alive."

Tarvek nodded. "Imagine everything is made of pigs!"

Violetta sighed. "Then he gets captured by the Baron and he's brought to Mechanicsburg and put in the hospital under heavy guard." She snorted. "Not heavy enough, as it turns out. Here I go and infiltrate the hospital, knock out the guards and what do I find? He's been poisoned."

"Poisoned!"

Violetta looked troubled. "I think so. There was a dart. I...I don't know what it was, but I could tell that it came from another Smoke Knight."

Agatha looked confused. "Wait a minute, I thought the Smoke Knights were his...are you saying that his own people...?"

Violetta gave a bark of laughter. "If the Baron had made him talk, half of the Fifty Families would have had to leave Europa. Trust me, these guys take the 'Secret' part of Secret Society really seriously. Plus, from what little I heard, he was in trouble anyway." She glanced at Agatha. "There's a big plan involving a Heterodyne girl, but I'm betting you're not the one everyone had in mind. Him throwing in with you, no matter what the circumstances, would send them into a panic."

Agatha frowned. "But…it was an accident."

Violetta shook her head. "These people don't believe in *accidents*." She patted Tarvek's head. "And say what you will about this slug, they all know he can weave a plan that looks as natural as the sun coming up.

"No, they know him and our family too well. Everything they touch becomes a nest of snakes eating their own tails." Violetta was silent for a moment, obviously remembering something unpleasant. She shook herself and turned back to Tarvek. "So I had to get him out of there. I couldn't carry him, so I had to give him a dose of Moveit Number Six." She grinned at Agatha. "He was talking my ear off and feeling no pain all the way over here."

Tarvek jerked upright. "We must stop the moon from eating the mushrooms!" Then his eyes rolled up into his head and he fell back.

Agatha looked around. "Castle! Is there a medical lab anywhere we can get to?"

"The nearest medical laboratory is thirty meters behind you, down the hallway to the right."

Agatha blinked. "Well. That's a stroke of luck."

Moloch shook his head. "Not really. This place is lousy with medical stuff."

"Seriously?"

"Oh yes," the Castle confirmed. "When the urge took the Masters to do a little experimentation—say, upon an erstwhile 'guest'—they didn't like to have to drag the body very far."

"That's horrible!"

Moloch slung one of Tarvek's arms around his shoulders. "I think it shows a bit of respect for the working man."

Agatha stared at him.

"Oh, come on," he said. "Those old Heterodynes wouldn't have lugged their own bodies about."

"Not if they could help it," the Castle admitted.

They entered a small, but remarkably well-equipped facility. There was a row of stone topped benches, several walls covered in storage cabinets fronted with now-cracked laboratory glass, inside of which were rows and rows of jumbled containers. In the middle of the room was a top of the line medical slab. Although it showed obvious signs of disuse, it was still better than Agatha had dared hope to find.

"The Red Playroom," the Castle announced. "Iago Heterodyne's favorite."

Agatha shoved a small pile of rubble off of the slab and indicated that this was where Tarvek should be set down. "Twenty years worth of dust and neglect," she muttered.

Violetta shrugged. "Everything is still sealed up in jars and there isn't a lot of leakage."

Moloch wrestled Tarvek onto the slab with a grunt. Agatha and Violetta started examining him. Moloch found a tap and with a herculean twist, got a stream of filthy water going.

"I can't use that," Agatha declared.

Moloch was wetting down some rags and wiping down a table. "The cisterns on the roof are still working. They filter and aerate the water automatically. The pipes are kind of sludgy when they start running, but give 'em a few minutes and they'll clear out."

A little less than an hour later, Agatha slumped back, and found a stool positioned to catch her. Before them, Tarvek lay still, but now he looked more relaxed and was warmly swaddled in musty sheets.

"I don't really think we can do much more for him," she said flatly.

Violetta shook her head. "Yeah, I think we got him stabilized, but I won't know what we're dealing with until I see some more symptoms." She looked at Agatha with respect. "He never said anything about you being a doctor."

Agatha shook her head wearily. "I'm not. Oh, back at Transylvania Polygnostic I attended lectures. I observed hundreds of operations and other procedures, but they never let me do anything. I never had any hands-on training." She glanced over at Tarvek. "But even if I had, I don't think it would be doing me any good now. I never saw anything like this. He's still got a fever, that dart wound on his arm is draining green, and he smells terrible."

Violetta shrugged. "The smell's pretty normal."

Agatha stripped off her gloves. "Well I guess he's getting what he wanted after all. I'm going to find Gil."

Elsewhere in Castle Heterodyne, Gil stared at the barrels of the guns held in the sweating hands of the false Heterodyne's minions. It was obvious that, after some of the things that they had seen, they would have cheerfully started shooting at anything. Gil had been briefed on the false Heterodyne's coterie and he noted that there were now less than half of the number he had been told had entered.

The false Heterodyne herself, resplendent in a pink work outfit, pushed to the fore and glared at him. "Gilgamesh Holzfaller! It is you!"

Gil blinked. The incongruity of the circumstances had prevented him from recognizing her, but now he stammered: "Zola?"

This seemed to throw the girl into a rage. She stomped towards him and began furiously punching him in the arm. "You *idiot*," she screamed. "I *told* you! Didn't I? Didn't I tell you?"

Gil frantically tried to understand what she was talking about while blocking her punches. She switched tactics and smartly kicked him in the shins. "I told you to shape up, you dope!"

To his astonishment, Gil saw tears in Zola's eyes. "Even back in Paris I could see that you were heading for a bad end! And now—!" She waved her arm about. "Here you are in Castle Heterodyne! Caught like a common thug!"

"Actually," Gil remarked, "to get in here, you have to be a pretty uncommon thug."

Zola punched his arm again and smiled lovingly up at him. "Well I guess I finally get to help you out for once!" The thought obviously cheered her up immensely. "And I can do it, too! Because..." she paused, "I am the Lady Heterodyne! Surprised?"

Gil made an effort to close his mouth. "More than you can possibly imagine."

Zola clapped her hands. "Ha! And you thought I was just another chorus girl!"

Gil flashed back to his days in Paris. "No," he said, picking his words carefully. "I never thought of you as just a chorus girl."

Zola looked at him fondly. "Well, maybe not you. You were always so nice. But everyone else did! Little did they know that I had a secret!" She spun about in place and hugged herself in delight. "But now they'll all see just how wrong they were! When I rule Europa I'll—"

Suddenly she stopped, and examined the rest of Gil's party. "These people don't look like prisoners."

Professor Tiktoffen cleared his throat. "They're not, my lady. I've never seen any of them before."

There was a dangerous look in Zola's eye now. "Gil? What's going on?"

Gil threw up his hands. "All right! *All right!* Zola, you're not the only one who had a secret back in Paris." He looked at her. "It was one that I couldn't tell anyone! If it had come out, it would have caused a lot of trouble."

He looked away. "I especially didn't want you to know. I…I didn't want you to lose your good opinion of me. It's just that…" Gil took a deep breath. "I'm a pirate."

Krosp fell over sideways. Zola pounded a fist into her other palm. "Of *course!*" She stared at Gil. "It was so *obvious!*"

Gil frowned. "It wasn't *that* obvious."

"I can't believe I didn't see it! All those mysterious trips! And you always had money!" A knowing look came into her eyes. "And there was that crazy pirate girl you were *obviously*—"

"Yes! Yes! I should've just put a jolly roger on my hat!"

Zeetha leaned in. "Say…*Captain.* Are you sure we should be admitting all this?" Her hand delicately closed on Gil's shoulder and without seeming to move, delivered a painful squeeze. "And which *pirate girl* would this have been?"

Gil managed to pull free without ripping his vest. "You never met her. Sky krakens got her." He raised his voice, "But it's all right, me hearties, we're among friends!" Gil waved to the rest of his company. "Zola, this is my crew! We were in town fencing some machine parts when there was this huge uproar! We grabbed the chance and slipped in here when everyone was busy! I figure there's got to be something left in here worth stealing!"

Zola's eyes went wide. "Looting Castle Heterodyne? Are you insane?"

Gil looked contrite. "Well, I didn't know it was yours."

Zola shook her head. "No, you idiot! This place is a deathtrap! I'm astonished you're not dead already!"

Gil glanced around. "But I'm not, am I? It's obviously all hype. To keep people out."

Zola looked like she wanted to shake him. "I can't believe you! This is just like that abandoned toyshop off Place Maubert![65] You just waltz into these things without thinking! You don't even have a plan!"

"Plans," Gil rolled his eyes. "And I suppose you do."

"Of course I've got a plan!"

Gil sighed. "What is it this time?"

Zola gave him an unfamiliar look. She nodded. "I'll admit my plans in Paris never worked out. But this one... No. I think I'll just show you. And *this* time, I'll bet you're impressed."

So saying, the expanded group headed off. Zola consulted an intricate compass as well as a small, leather-bound book. She was obviously thinking. Gil knew her well enough to let her come to a boil on her own. And indeed, soon enough...

"So, Gil, what do you think about Baron Wulfenbach?"

This was the last subject Gil had been prepared for. "What, personally?"

Zola snorted. "No, of course not. His Empire. The way it's run."

---

[65] Deep within the Paris Department of Justice, there is a vault full of locked files under the personal seal of the Master of Paris. One of them is labeled "The Maubert Wind-Up Assassin Affair." It occupies a rather full shelf dedicated to the after-school activities of one G. Holzfaller.

Gil tried to consider the question as it would be viewed by someone who was not the Baron's son. "Better than most, I suppose."

Zola frowned. "An odd response, considering how they treat pirates."

Gil laughed. "Zola, there isn't a legitimate government in the Western Hemisphere that doesn't deal harshly with pirates. It's how they treat their own citizens that's important. The Polar Lords tax fire. The Gilded Duke hunted peasants for sport. To go against Albia of England's merest whim is literally unthinkable. I've been there, Zola. I've seen these things.

"The Baron demands taxes and deals harshly with peace breakers, yes, but he's kept the Long War at bay for years. He builds roads, schools and hospitals…" He saw the look on Zola's face and shrugged. "I raid elsewhere, but I choose to *live* in the Empire."

Zola pursed her lips in annoyance. "I'd forgotten how conversations with you never go like they should."

Gil grinned. "Oh yes, all those annoying, inconvenient 'facts.'"

Zola spun and shook her finger in his face. "Well here's a fact you can stick in your ear. The Baron's Empire is going down."

Gil rolled his eyes. "Oooh. I'll bet that's the first time he's heard that…*today*." Gil glanced at Zola's assistants. "And you're doing this all by yourself?"

Zola surprised him then. Instead of getting even madder, her face slid into a satisfied smile. *Now we're getting somewhere.*

"No, I'm not doing it all myself." She paused, glanced back at the others and drew Gil closer. "How much do you trust your crew?" she asked softly.

Gil spoke equally softly. "They give me lip, but they're loyal."

Zola looked back again. "I don't know…that green-haired girl seems…possessive." She regarded Gil coyly. "You and she aren't—?"

"No!" Gil didn't have to pretend to find the idea disturbing. "Absolutely not. I'm keeping things professional."

Zola smiled at him a touch wistfully and gently patted his cheek.

"Oh Gil, you never change." The look she gave Zeetha had a touch of sympathy to it. "And I'll bet you're just as clueless."

"What?"

"Nothing." She raised her voice. "Monsieur Zero?" One of her assistants raised his head. "Please allow us a bit of discretionary space?"

The tall man nodded and brought the rest of the group to a halt while Gil and Zola moved forward a few paces, then allowed them to move again.

"Everything is all very hush-hush, you know," Zola confided.

"You mean that this is information you don't want getting back to the Baron." Gil looked skeptical. "Which is foolish. It's going to get back eventually, and if it's that fragile…"

"If I can convince you, would you consider joining me?"

Gil was silent for a few moments. "Maybe." He raised an admonitory finger. "But I'll take a great deal of convincing. I *like* living here."

Zola nodded. "I trust your judgment. Gil." She collected her thoughts. "I'm the Heterodyne…"

Gil started a mental list: *Flaw Number One.*

"And I'm allied with…the Storm King!" When this had no obvious effect upon Gil, she continued. "A direct descendent of Andronicus Valois!"

Gil prepared to throw his list away. "Zola, if the stories about Andronicus are true,[66] half of Europa…"

"One that the Fifty Families will recognize."

Gil nodded. "Because he'll restore their full royal power, no doubt."

"Of course! The restoration of their traditional rights—"

Gil made a show of losing patience. "Please. They're fit to rule because their great-grandfathers chopped off more heads than anyone else did?"

"Oh? And how is the Baron any different?"

"Well…for starters, he doesn't chop off a lot of heads."

---

[66]   At an impressionable age, young Andronicus read a number of scholarly works that talked about a king being a fertility symbol. He thought this was a mighty fine idea.

Zola rolled her eyes. "Ha, ha. But what happens when he dies?"

This was unexpected. "Um…"

"His son takes over. So tell me how that's any different from the Fifty Families, Mister High and Mighty?"

Gil waved his hands. "Wait—this is about the Baron's son?"

"Don't tell me you haven't heard about him?"

"I know he's got the same first name as me, which has made things awkward once or twice… But other than that? Not much, no."

Zola shook her head. "Where have you been? Yes, the Baron has a son. He's kept him hidden away and no one knows who the mother is. The Baron has said that he'll hand him the Empire when he dies. So what do you think will happen then?"

Gil thought about this. "I don't know. What do people *say* will happen?"

"It could be the reign of a Neo Caligula!"

Gil frowned. "Oh, come on. Surely it couldn't be that bad?"

Zola shrugged. "Well that's the point. No one knows. He's an enigma. He was revealed four months ago—and then nothing until Beetleburg."

"Beetleburg?"

"Surely you heard about *that*. The tyrant of Beetleburg was messing around with a Hive Engine, so the Baron shut him down. Well, this Gilgamesh was there, and by all accounts, he was a complete lunatic. According to witnesses, he killed Beetle by throwing a bomb at him, and Klaus had to chase him down through the streets of the town with clanks and Jägermonsters no less. They say he was practically chewing the furniture."

Gil listened to this with growing horror. This was an understandable interpretation of that day's events. "No," he admitted. "That doesn't sound good."

Zola nodded triumphantly, "And the Baron's had him locked away on board Castle Wulfenbach ever since."

Gil looked at her bleakly. "There's got to be more to it than that."

Zola shrugged. "Perhaps, but that's what people have seen and heard. The Baron has never cared excessively what people thought about him; he was so powerful that he could just ignore them. That might have worked if he had heirs that were more like him, or even better, no heirs at all. But now that people think that the Empire is going to be given to a crazy person…"

"All right! I see your point." Gil thought quickly. "So, this plan of yours… Let's see if I can work out the basics. We have a Heterodyne girl…"

Zola preened. "That's me!"

"And then…a Storm King shows up." He smacked his head. "The old prophecy! Sure! They get married! Peace and free beer for everybody."

Zola clapped her hands. "Oh, I knew you'd see it! You were always so smart."

Gil didn't feel particularly smart at the moment. "But… You can't really think the Baron will allow you to just waltz in and do this?"

Zola looked smug. "You know how to boil a frog, don't you? You do it slowly. I'll get settled in as the Heterodyne. Surely there will be nothing wrong with that? Just one of those 'internal rule' things that the Baron can't be bothered with. Even better, I'm not a Spark! I'll be a safely *boring* Heterodyne. I'll busy myself with civic improvements, trade negotiations—my Mechanicsburg will just be good little client state of the Empire.

"A year or so from now, the Storm King's heir will be 'discovered' by a charming old man in Wurms whose hobby is heraldry. He doesn't know it yet, but he's about to make an amazing discovery in a used book shop our people run. The College of Heralds will reluctantly agree with his analysis, but the heir-apparent will modestly refuse to accept the crown.

"That will change when Mechanicsburg is attacked by an army of clanks while he is, coincidentally, here visiting a wounded friend in the Great Hospital. He will send out a call for help that will be answered by surrounding kingdoms, and he will defeat the invaders. I will ask to meet him, of course, and it'll be love at first sight!"

She fluttered her eyelashes at Gilgamesh and sighed. "It'll be so perfectly romantic that we will capture the hearts of all of Europa.

Then we will settle down and rule this little town so well that we will be the envy of the Empire and other kingdoms will beg us to move on to bigger things, which we will reluctantly do, and within ten years—sooner if the Wulfenbachs do something foolish—we will have all the Empire and no one has to die at all."

Gil considered this. He had to admit that he had never really looked forward to being handed the reins of the Empire, but…

He cleared his throat. "Except for young Wulfenbach, of course."

Zola rolled her eyes, "Well of course. We're not stupid."

Gil sighed with regret, "Yes, I suppose that was to be expected."

Zola frowned. "Oh please, who will even care?"

At that moment there was a strangled scream from Professor Tiktoffen. "Everyone," he shouted as he ran towards the door. "Out of this room!"

But as he approached the doorway, a massive steel shutter slammed down. "Welcome." The voice was barely a whisper. "Repairs…here."

Tiktoffen slumped to the floor. "We're doomed," he whimpered. "We're all going to die."

Zola strode over to him and kicked him in the leg. "What is happening, Professor?"

Tiktoffen didn't even flinch when her foot connected. "We've been pressganged," he said leadenly. "I didn't know where we were. The door we just came through, it's never led here before." He gestured towards the shadows and the others realized that the lumps they'd been stepping around were actually desiccated corpses.

"This is one of those rooms where things are too damaged, but the systems in charge won't accept 'no' for an answer. Anyone who comes here isn't allowed to leave."

Gil looked at the machinery that lined one of the walls. "Then we'll just have to fix it."

Tiktoffen snorted. "This isn't a broken rudder, young man. This needs a stronger Spark than we've ever had in here."

Gil smiled. "I like a challenge."

Agatha jerked awake as something sharp poked into her fundament. She was sprawled face down on a workbench. Someone had tossed a musty canvas sheet over her and there was a brisk breeze blowing. The sharp object was revealed as a toasting fork and it was being wielded by Moloch, who was cowering behind a makeshift barricade of assorted sheet metal. "Wake up," he growled. "C'mon, I thought you were in a hurry. It's getting light out."

This got Agatha moving. "It's what? How could you let me sleep?" It had been nearing midnight as she had put the finishing touches on. She glanced down and found herself clutching a cobbled together little device of some complexity.

From behind his barrier, Moloch flinched. "You said you weren't going out after Wulfenbach without some kind of defense and then you built a death ray. You conked out on the table, and then, every time I tried to wake you up, *you pointed it at me!*"

Agatha flushed. Her foster mother, Lilith, had always complained that it took heavy machinery to hoist Agatha from her bed on cold mornings. Luckily, her foster father was a mechanic. But threatening someone? That sounded a bit over-dramatic.

"I threatened you with this?"

"You totally did."

Agatha looked at it again. "Well I'm sorry this little thing worried you." At that moment, a strong gust of cold air blew hair into her face. Agatha blinked and turned in surprise. The source was a rather large hole that had apparently been melted through the castle wall. A little way off, she saw another hole through one of the castle towers. She squinted and thought she could just make out a circular chunk taken out of one of the looming mountains that encircled the town.

"...I did that?"

"You totally did!"

Agatha shivered and carefully put the little device down on a table. "What about Tarvek?" She tried to keep her voice neutral but Moloch caught her mood.

"Violetta said that the two of you were afraid that there might be gangrene but neither one of you wanted to say it."

Agatha swallowed. "I…yes."

Moloch patted her on the shoulder. "Well, the *good* news is that I've seen gangrene and this ain't it."

Agatha felt something inside her relax slightly as she walked towards Tarvek, who lay still and prone. "What's the bad news?"

Moloch raised the sheet covering him and Agatha gasped. Tarvek was still alive. He was panting and sweat poured off his body. He was a stunning shade of aquamarine.

Moloch shrugged. "He's definitely got *something* and I hope you know what it is 'cause we sure don't."

At this moment, Violetta came back, carrying a full bucket of water. She put it down, grabbed a cup, filled it, and poked it at Tarvek's mouth. "He's been slipping in and out of consciousness for the last hour," she reported. It was evident from the tone of her voice that she was worried, though she was trying not to show it.

Moloch nodded. "If you're gonna get Wulfenbach, you'd better do it fast."

Tarvek moaned.

Agatha leaned over him. "Tarvek?"

He opened his eyes and blearily tried to focus on her face. "Oh Agatha, I'm so sorry."

Agatha paused. "…For what, specifically?"

"For everything! All that in Sturmhalten! I was so worried. I knew you wouldn't trust me but the geisterdamen were everywhere and I had to—" He was really getting worked up now and Agatha gently but forcefully pushed him back down onto the tabletop.

"Stop it. You need to rest. I'm off to get Gil to help us, just like you wanted."

Tarvek surged back up and gripped Agatha's arms with a surprising strength. "No! Wait! I have to tell you! It's important! I'll never find anyone like you."

Agatha felt her face go red. "Tarvek…"

"I have all sorts of ideas for the most exquisite outfits! You'll be the envy of Paris!" Agatha blinked, then bent and planted a light kiss upon the top of his head. "Idiot. You're raving."

"You see?" Tarvek giggled as his eyes fluttered closed. "Oh, yes, it's all part of the plan. You're too perfect..." And he was again unconscious.

Violetta turned away. "Jeez. What a dope. What does she see in him?"

Moloch waved a hand dismissively. "Probably nothing. Now you want to see hot? Wait'll she meets up with Wulfenbach."

Violetta frowned. "Hey, don't let fancy boy fool you. He may want to dress her up but he can be just as interested in undressing her."

Moloch shrugged. "Yeah? Well, you haven't seen Wulfenbach when he really loses it. He'll have her over his shoulder thirty seconds after he sees her. Your boy won't stand a chance."

Violetta narrowed her eyes. "You think she'll put up with that? You wait and see. Tarvek's a pig but he's great with the sweet talk."

"Sweet talk, huh? You got me there. She gets Wulfenbach so worked up he can't remember his own name. But he's smart, he'll learn." He leaned in and dropped his voice. "'Specially since, when she punches, she puts her hips into it."

Violetta grinned and leaned in herself. "Ouch," she breathed in delight. "This should be good. Say...you wanna make a bet on who she'll pick?"

Moloch assumed the air of a man possessed of a sure thing. "A bet? Might be interesting...but hey... she's the Heterodyne. Maybe she'll take them both."

Violetta went pink at the idea. "Oh please, a boyfriend is an accessory. You don't go around wearing two hats."

"Oh yeah? I saw this Jägermonster—"

Hands like steel claws clamped down on both of their throats and lifted them bodily into the air. Agatha, her face scarlet, shook them like a terrier shaking a pair of rats. "WHAT IS THE MATTER WITH YOU TWO?" she screamed. "ARE YOU *TWELVE*?" She flung them to the ground. "Boyfriends? *Seriously?* I've got more important things to worry about! The Baron wants me dead! An imposter is trying to take my place! Armies are trying to take over the town! The Castle is broken and the Other is still inside my head!

"Now, when all that is taken care of, we'll have a great big fancy party and I'll wear a pretty dress and I'll dance with all the boys, and everything will be sugar hearts and flowers, but until then—" She took a deep breath and shouted, "FOCUS!"

Moloch and Violetta huddled on the ground and nodded in unison. Violetta tentatively raised a hand. Agatha glared at her. "What?"

Violetta twisted her hands together and looked imploringly up at Agatha. "This party...Can I have a pretty dress, too?"

Agatha's fury stopped cold. She looked surprised. "Well...well of course." Then she turned grim again. "Assuming you're still alive."

Several minutes later, Agatha was scrambling over the rubble of what appeared to have once been a trophy hall. The walls were tilted at alarming angles, and the floor was strewn with bric-a-brac and the contents of broken cabinets.

"So...Castle? Gil's been inside for hours by now. Is he even...I mean, is he all right?"

The voice echoed from all around her. "I am sorry, Mistress. I don't know."

Agatha's mood was still sour. "Why is nothing easy with you?" she growled.

"You want easy? Go live in a yurt," the Castle said.

Agatha stared blankly at the nearest wall. Not having a physical face or body—at least, in the usual sense—made the Castle a very difficult person to read. "A what?"

"A yurt!" the Castle repeated "A type of portable shelter made of wool felt. Used by the Mongols!"

Well, at least it wasn't speculating about her love life. "How... fascinating," Agatha said.

"Yes! The Mongols!" The Castle was getting excited now. Bits of broken metal floated into the air in front and formed a rough tent-like shape. The Castle went on, "Those extraordinary fighters who swarmed out of the East, subduing all that lay before them! Your ancestors learned so much from them!"

"Really." Agatha didn't know what to say.

But the Castle did. "Yes! The tactics of battle! The use of superior technology! The art of *ruthlessness!*"

The makeshift model yurt clattered to the ground. An iron statue of a mounted warrior shot out of a pile of rubble and took its place—hanging in the air in front of Agatha's nose. She took a quick jump backward. "Ah…" she said. "No kidding…"

The Castle was not finished. "Oh, to see such glorious carnage!" it enthused, its voice rising. "My greatest dream is to be remade as a *yurt!* To travel! To see the world as a series of battles! To eschew stairways and windows—"

Agatha couldn't take any more of this nonsense. *"What on Earth is the matter with you!"* she screamed at the ceiling.

There was a brief silence. Then the Castle spoke again, in a more subdued tone. "I…I…forgive me, mistress." It sounded confused. "I do not know."

Elsewhere, at that very moment, Gil was arm deep in the Castle's machinery. He pulled a small component out of the wall and held it up for Professor Tiktoffen's approval. "Aha! And here's *another* problem!"

They had already made substantial progress. Professor Tiktoffen had proven himself to be an extraordinarily strong Spark in his own right, who had apparently dedicated the last few years to an exhaustive analysis of the Castle's systems—while Theo and Gil were old friends, and knew how to bring out the best in each other when they worked. Sleipnir was an exemplary mechanic in her own right and was used to working with Sparks. She had also proved invaluable in finding ways to keep Zola, Zeetha, and Zola's tall men too busy to get in the way or succumb to despair. Even Krosp had proved useful, as his small size had allowed him to squeeze into spaces the others could not.

Still, they had been at work for several hours and, one by one, the others had retired to the other side of the room to get out of the way. Now, only Gil and Professor Tiktoffen crouched before the disassembled panels as the others slept.

"You were right, Professor, we have got everything else connected, but if you look here, you can see a bit of rubble has sheared through a cable! No wonder we couldn't make it work!"

Tiktoffen looked and then slumped to the ground. "All of those mechanisms are interconnected." He looked up at the bank of controls. "We'll have to disassemble the entire wall!"

Gil tapped a dial face. "Maybe not." He popped open one of his leather waistcoat's many pockets and pulled out what appeared to be a large watch fitted with little brass arms and legs. "I picked up a little thing in Sturmhalten that might be useful. It's something a…a friend made." He thought it prudent not to mention that the friend who made it was, in fact, Agatha. He wound the stem on its top and with a springing noise, the little device jerked into movement. A shutter that should have concealed a watch-face clicked open, revealing a mechanical eye that swiveled up to stare at Gil's face.

Gil smiled engagingly. "Hello. Do you remember me? I don't know how much you can understand, but—"

Quick as a flash, the little clank leapt from Gil's hand and jerked to a halt, swinging from the end of a watch chain. It flailed briefly as Gil hoisted it to eye level, then it simply hung limp, glaring.

After a moment, Gil spoke to Professor Tiktoffen. "This may take a minute, Professor. If you'd like to get something to eat?"

Tiktoffen looked at him blankly. "I'm not sure what we have," he muttered, "but I confess that I am hungry enough that if I find a particularly soft socket wrench, I'll take it."

Once the man was out of earshot, Gil lowered his voice. "Do you want to help your mistress?"

The device looked everywhere but at Gil's face, but Gil was patient. Eventually, it gave a mechanical click, glanced back at him, and jerked in an attempt at a nod which set it swinging.

Gil lowered it so that its diminutive feet touched a tabletop, but the chain was still attached to his waistcoat. He leaned down until his face was mere centimeters away. "Good. So do I. But if we're to do that, you have to help me."

The little clank considered this, then bounced forward and kicked Gil in the nose.

Gil again hoisted it into the air while rubbing his injured face. "There is no question as to who built you, you troublesome gizmo," he muttered.

"Oho!" Zeetha's voice mocked him over his shoulder. "Are you saying this thing's creator is...troublesome?"

Gil frowned. "What? No! Shhhh!" He looked around and saw that they were alone. "Where is everyone?"

Zeetha grinned. "Tiktoffen fell asleep with his head on his tool bag. You work your subordinates hard. Everyone else has been asleep for hours."

Gil blinked. "Oh. I wondered why it had gotten so quiet."

Zeetha looked at him curiously. "Yes. Don't you ever sleep?"

Gil waved a hand. "Oh, my father taught me some mental exercises. I'm good for a couple of days when I have to be." He glanced up. "You?"

Zeetha shrugged. "I'm good. Ancient Skifandrian warrior discipline—hardly ever taught to outsiders." She was watching him closely as she spoke, mischief in her voice.

Gil considered this. "My father never said where—"

But Zeetha had already moved on. She pointed over at Zola. "Seems like you knew a lot of girls while you were in Paris." She made a stern face. "You aren't one of those Don Casanovas, are you?"

Gil had been called a lot of things, but that had never been one of them. "Um...definitely not."

"So what's Pinkie's story?"

Gil shrugged and sat back, idly twirling the little clank on its chain. "She was a dancer."

Zeetha looked unimpressed. "A 'dancer', eh?"

"That's what it said on her card."

"Uh-huh." Zeetha continued to give him a stony look.

"She sings, too," Gil added, always helpful.

"Ooh, I'm *sure* she *does*."

"She's *also* a decent actress and she was very good at looking interested while people talked and bought rounds of drinks. She was always getting mixed up with some Sparky sap she met in the clubs."

"Ah. So that's how you met her. You hired a lot of these 'dancers'?"

Gil looked pained. "Please. I met her on my first day in Paris, when a giant squid burst up out of the sewer and flung her into the café where I was *trying* to *relax*." Gil sighed. "She was always getting involved with some Spark's idiotic scheme that was going to change the world. That particular one involved raising calamari steak for the restaurant trade.

"A few weeks later, I rescued her from the Comte de Terracciano's 'Ultimate Endgame' chess set, then the unsettlingly large, acid-spitting snails of Professor Yungbluth, and then some overly-dramatic maniac who was living underneath the Paris Opera House." Gil paused. "That last one wasn't even her fault, really." He shrugged. "Well, after that, she was just someone I knew."

Zeetha stared at him. "Who had to be rescued a lot."

Gil shrugged. "Well, she wasn't boring."

"She sounds annoying."

Gil nodded. "Annoying I'll give you. Then one day, she was gone. Bills paid, all her stuff taken away, no forwarding address…" Gil smiled. "I'd seen that happen before with some of the other girls. They finally hook a rich guy from out of town and get married. The last thing they want is people who knew them coming around to talk about 'old times.' They just disappear. If you see them, you're supposed to pretend you don't know them and they'll return the favor. So yeah, I thought she'd got married. But apparently, she turned into 'the Heterodyne.'"

Zeetha nodded. Actresses and other girls who had worked in the circus had a similar code. Then a thought struck her and her eyes went wide. "You…you don't think she really is a Heterodyne, do you?"

Gil shook his head. "*I* don't, but I'm afraid she might. Every single scheme Zola got caught up in, she was *convinced* that she was indispensable.

"That fairy tale she spun us? Sure, I'll believe that's the plan as she knows it, but there's a lot more going on here and I want to know what it is. I want to find out who's running her, if only because I fully expect them to try to kill her."

Zeetha blinked. "Kill her? But she's their Heterodyne!"

Gil snorted. "Not any more, she isn't. This plan of hers is in shambles. My father knows about it. I'm betting those fools that I blew up were her 'attacking army'—jumping the gun by a couple of years, no less, and Agatha is here, in the castle. There's no way she'll let Zola take her place."

A gentle tug on his hand made him look down. The little clank raised its hands over its head and stared at him woefully. "Oh, you're ready to help? Good." He lifted the little device up to the hole in the wall. It squeezed itself in and Gil began feeding out its chain as he continued.

"No, it's over, and while Zola may not know it, the people at the top undoubtedly do. She's become a liability. She knows things my father will want to know." He sighed. "Besides, this place is dangerous all by itself. I'm not going to just leave her to die in here. I'm not thrilled about having one more thing to worry about, but I don't see what else I can do."

Zeetha drummed her fingers. "She sounds like an idiot."

Gil shrugged. "Well…yes, but she was never a malicious one."

"Is that important?"

Gil made an odd, angry face. "Heavens, yes. If I let *everyone* I thought was an idiot die, there wouldn't be many people left."

Zeetha thought about this and shivered. "Oh."

Meanwhile, within the panel in the walls, the little clank had successfully resolved a problem involving force and pressure. It emerged, proud of itself, dragging a sliver of the stone wall.

"Ha!" Gil examined the rock chip. "I knew you could do it!" He put his eye up to the gap and examined the scene before him. "Yesss… That debris sheared right through the cable. We got everything else, so…" He turned to Zeetha. "Go wake up Higgs, Theo, Sleipnir, and Krosp. Quietly."

"What for?"

"You're leaving."

"Oh really? How?"

Gil raised a finger. He set the little clank on his palm and addressed it directly. "I'm stuck here for a while but I want my friends to go find Agatha and help her. They can't leave until we get that door open. You can do that. Follow those red cables to the left and you should be able to access the door mechanism."

The little device stared at him and then tugged pointedly at the chain.

Gil continued. "I realize that the chain will be a problem. So it's a question of trust."

The little clank gave a drawn out clicking that sounded to Gil like a raspberry.

"You don't like me? Fine." Gil snapped open a hook and the chain came free. The little clank was all attention. "But this *will* help Agatha, if you do it quickly. Do you understand?"

The little clank lashed out and biffed Gil in the nose before leaping off his hand. Quick as a flash, it vanished back inside the huge mechanism inside the Castle wall.

Gil rubbed his nose and leaned in close to the opening. "Does that mean you'll do it?" He turned to Zeetha and shrugged. "I'll take that as a 'maybe.'"

Zeetha nodded. "The others are up and moving. You're really not coming?"

"No. Tiktoffen did a lot of talking tonight. Zola's got…something. She thinks it will shut down the castle. That's the last thing we want, so I'm going to find out what it is and disable it. Plus, Zola's giving me more information than she thinks she is, so it's worth keeping an eye on her."

Zeetha smirked. "Old habits die hard, eh?"

"Yes, yes." Gil paused. "Um…Look…when you see Agatha, please tell her…" Zeetha looked expectant. "Um…tell her I am…ah…anxious to speak to her so that we can overcome our mutual obstacles."

Zeetha looked like she was experiencing actual physical pain. "No."

"What?"

"That sounds moronic. Try again."

Gil looked lost. "Um…Then…Then tell her that I'm pretty sure that I'm fond of her, and that if it's mutual and she's not too evil, perhaps we can—"

"NO!" This was delivered with a sharp slap to the side of Gil's head.

"Ow! Why are you hitting me? I love her and I want to help her!"

Zeetha lowered her fist and smiled. "Now *that* I'll pass along."

Gil frowned. "But…that's so imprecise!"

"I'm going to hit you again."

"Hey!" Krosp tugged his trouser leg and pointed. "The door is opening!" He darted under the slowly rising gate and stuck his head back in. "It's clear!"

"Get moving," Zeetha told Theo and Sleipnir. "I need to get something."

Airman Higgs ambled up to Gil and considered him for a moment. "Sure you don't want me to stay with you, sir?" He jerked a thumb over to the remaining sleepers. "That lot might get kind of mad when they see we're gone."

Gil smiled. "Why, thank you, Mr. Higgs, I appreciate the offer. But this will work better for me if you're all gone."

"Okay." Zeetha reappeared. "I'm all set. Let's go." She was wearing one of the long coats and tunics worn by Zola's assistants.

"Where did you—?"

"Oh, I smacked goon number three with a wrench. I can get a guy undressed really fast."

"Why would you risk—?"

"Cold." Zeetha hoisted the edge of her tunic. "You wanna see these goosebumps?"

Gil's face went scarlet. "No! Get going!"

Zeetha grinned and gave him an affectionate hug. "Good luck, kiddo." And a moment later, she and the others were gone.

Gil rested a while, examining the exposed machinery of the wall. Really, all that was left was to repair that sheared cable. He selected a tool and reached into the wall, muttering to himself: "Okay, I just have to hook this end here…argh, this is tricky—onto this bit… and—" An electrical crackling split the air and a blinding flash of energy knocked him back several feet where he landed with a crash against the decorative metal wall panels that had been laid aside. Zola and all her men were instantly awake.

The Castle made an appreciative noise. Agatha looked up. "Ah! My Lady, I believe I have found your other young man."

"How is he?"

"He appears to be slightly singed. Ah, but never fear, I see there are other young men as well. My my! I shall reopen the old harem quarters!"

"Not you, too! Will you please—" Agatha realized that the Castle was quietly chuckling. She paused. While mechanisms advanced enough to posses a sense of humor were extremely rare, they were not unheard of.[67]

"Ha, ha," she said, giving up. "Just keep them…contained until I get there. All right?"

"I cannot. A connection has been made which has extended my awareness, but that is all."

"How annoying."

"You have no idea," the Castle complained. "I will guide you part of the way, but beyond the Serpent's Gallery, I will be unable to talk with you."

Agatha sighed. "Another dead area?"

---

[67] There was an appreciable gap between what fragile, organic humans and cold, crystal intelligences found "funny." This problem resulted in a great deal of death and destruction until the Spark Simon van Stampfer created the Stroboscope and produced the first electro-magnetic kinetic-projection of a cat attempting to catch its own tail. Once a baseline for humor appreciation was established, human/machine relations improved greatly.

"Oh, no. It is quite active. I am currently attempting to take control, but there is a fragment of my personality already occupying the area. Because I am damaged, that part of me will most likely not recognize you as the Heterodyne. In addition, I fear that it may be quite insane."

Agatha tried to keep her face neutral. "*You* think so? That's… worrying."

"There is one bright spot though; I believe I can reassimilate it, and during the process, it will probably be too busy fighting back to hinder you much."

"'Probably'? 'Much'?"

"I can't guarantee your safety, of course." The Castle sounded completely unconcerned. "I recommend that you retrieve your young man and return to a safe location as quickly as possible. Still, it should be all right…as long as nothing else goes wrong with my mechanisms."

Deep within the castle's walls, the newly-freed pocket clank surveyed the expanse of inert machinery and rubbed its little brass hands together. So much to be done! And so much to do it with!

Gil opened his eyes. His head was filled with that familiar tingling he always got after contact with ungrounded electricity. The first thing he saw was one of Zola's minions, clad in short pants and a simple grey singlet, rubbing a bump on the back of his head. He was pointing a nasty little black pistol in Gil's general direction. "I say we kill him," the man was snarling.

Zola stood before him, unarmed but without fear. *Playing the adventuress to the hilt,* Gil realized with a touch of admiration.

"Don't be absurd. He hasn't done anything wrong. Besides," she waved a hand, "he's obviously useful. He got the door open, didn't he?"

They both noticed that Gil was awake and Zola frowned at him. "Your 'loyal crew', on the other hand, appears to have deserted you. Why?"

Gil rubbed his head. "How should I know? I guess they're just not as tough as your guys."

As he'd thought, this statement mollified the angry man slightly. "At one point, I got the door open halfway. They wanted to leave you behind, and when I wouldn't go, they got mad." He ruefully rubbed the back of his head. "I didn't think they were *that* mad, but after that, things went black and here we are. We should get out of here as quick as we can."

Professor Tiktoffen spoke up. "He's right, we should get moving. I wouldn't worry about those fools. They were too far back to hear anything when the two of you were talking and I'll be surprised if the Castle doesn't crush them, if it hasn't already."

He leaned in. "It was that Zeetha girl, I'll bet. She must've seen how it was between you and young Gil here and realized she didn't have a chance, if you know what I mean."

Instantly Zola's trepidation vanished. "Of course!" She turned to Gil. "You always were completely clueless when it came to women. And this certainly isn't the first time its bitten you, is it?"

Gil would have liked to argue, but he really couldn't. Zola nodded in satisfaction. "I could tell she had her eye on you. I knew it as soon as I saw her." She clapped her hands. "All right everyone, grab your equipment and let us be off!"

Gil slowly packed his equipment back into his satchel. When he looked up, Professor Tiktoffen was handing him a wrench.

"Thank you, professor."

"It's the least I could do...sir." The sudden use of the honorific caused Gil to pause and look closely at the man.

Tiktoffen nodded slightly. "I like to think that I'm rather good at knowing what to do—or say—in order to keep things moving smoothly."

Gil realized this was not about handing him the wrench. "Is that so?"

Tiktoffen nodded again as he stood up. "Oh yes, sir," he said quietly. "It's one of the reasons why I was chosen to be the one to report to your father."

Gil blinked and glanced over towards Zola.

"Have no fear, sir," Tiktoffen breathed. "I'll keep your secret. I'm very good at that, I assure you." And with that, he turned away.

Gil, not reassured at all, stared after him until Zola took his arm and led them all out. "I knew you could do it," she said. "You're always so handy to have around."

"I'd probably be even more useful if I knew more about what you're doing in here."

Zola nodded. "That does make sense." She called out to Tiktoffen. "What am I going to do, Professor?"

The professor fished a small device from a pocket and consulted it. His eyebrows rose. "Have a party, I think," he said in a distracted voice.

Gil wasn't sure if he'd heard correctly. "A party?"

"Oh yes! A party!" Zola smiled dreamily as they moved off down the hallway. "Once I'm settled in as the Heterodyne, I shall have a big, fancy party! I shall wear a beautiful gown and I shall dance with the heads of Europa and all the handsome men—" She tightened her grip on Gil's arm. "But mostly with you, of course."

Gil wondered if she had gone mad. None of the others seemed to think this conversational turn an odd one, which was surprising, and Zola prattled on nonstop for almost ten minutes until they entered a new corridor and Tiktoffen, who had been monitoring the device in his hand, interrupted a nuanced description of her plans for Gil's party outfit, down to the number of pearl buttons on his cloth-of-gold pants. "We're safe, my lady."

Instantly, Zola stopped talking. She took a deep breath. "Thank goodness."

With a start of surprise, Gil resurfaced from the pit of abstract mathematical conundrums into which he had long ago retreated. "Safe? Safe from what? The fashion police?"

Tiktoffen chuckled. "The Castle. We're in a dead zone now. Before, there was a distinct possibility that it could hear every word we said."

A prickle of uneasiness flowed through Gil's mind. He turned to Zola. "You mean—all that party stuff…"

Zola gave him a patient look. "I want the Castle to underestimate me. Surely you didn't as well?"

Gil kept his mouth shut and looked guilty.

This delighted Zola, who patted Gil's cheek. "So here's what's going on. For a long time my associates have been trying to figure out how to get control of Castle Heterodyne."

"Wait," Gil interrupted. "Who are these associates?"

"Oh, the Storm King's Loyal Order of the Knights of Jove."

Gil snorted. "Right. And England's Knights of the Round Table are right behind them, I'll bet."

Zola laughed. "You can't imagine! They are so old-fashioned! But they're deadly serious!"

"And you're telling me that the Knights of Jove have stuck around all this time."

"Oh yes! They're a secret society, you know. It's very exciting. They've been seeking out and keeping track of the royal lineage, but the time was never right."

"Uh-huh. Let me guess. A long line of sots, imbeciles, and—God forbid—*females*, right?"

Zola laughed again. "As well as at least one reported werewolf."[68]

"Well that's the problem with monarchies, isn't it? They just never can make 'em like they used to."

Zola shrugged. "Yes, well, that was before the Mongfish family took a hand in things."[69]

Gil was surprised. "Mongfish—like the last Heterodyne's wife?"[70]

"Of course. The qualities of candidates aside, for a long time the order itself had…stagnated. It became an excuse for the old boys to get together, drink brandy, and go on about 'the good old days of yore.' Completely fossilized. No fire at all."

---

[68]   It happens in even the best families.

[69]   The Mongfish family, rich in Sparks and steeped in evil as a means to an end, have woven their schemes behind the scenes throughout Europa's history.

[70]   Certainly the capper to the Heterodyne's meddling in the affairs of the House of Mongfish had to be Bill Heterodyne's wooing and marrying Lucifer Mongfish's favorite daughter, Lucrezia. At the very least, the holidays were an awkward time for all concerned.

Gil bit his lip. Now that he thought about it, he *had* seen the Knights of Jove on a list of assorted drinking clubs and fringe cabals that the Empire knew existed. Obviously, this list was in desperate need of a reevaluation. "And the Mongfish family?"

"They got the Order whipped into shape, and then, well, they are very gifted, especially when it comes to the biological disciplines."

Gil nodded. "So I've heard."[71]

"Well, they just made sure that there was an appropriate heir."

Gil made a face. Zola shrugged. "Oh, nothing *too* unnatural, they just insisted on things like arranging marriages that produced family trees with actual branches."

Gil nodded. Royalty did tend to have its little traditions.

Zola continued. "Anyway, these days the High Council has Sparks working for the Order on all kinds of things—and one of the biggest is this place." She waved a hand indicating the Castle. "If I'm going to be acknowledged as the Heterodyne, I've got to hold the Castle. But it's broken and insane. It won't listen to anybody. We've had brilliant people working on it for ages, trying to find a way to control it, but nothing has worked."

She turned and faced Gil. "Well recently, they made this huge breakthrough. The Castle isn't just one entity."

"What?" The look on Gil's face satisfied her. "Yes, I thought a clever boy like you would find that interesting. As best they can determine, it's split into something like twelve different minds, each of which controls a small section, thinks that it alone is the 'real' Castle-mind, and they are all working against each other at cross-purposes."

"Fascinating," Gil breathed. His brain was working furiously.

"Isn't it?" Tiktoffen chimed in. "This is a priceless opportunity!"

---

[71]   Zola is understating things. Cain Mongfish's masterpiece, *A Reasoned Diatribe Regarding thee Methods and Required Madnesses Towards the Manipulation of ye Stuffe of Life and thee Entertaining Consequences Thereof and How Best to Avoid Them* is regarded as the seminal work that gathered and codified all of the then-known processes for reanimating, bending, warping, and subjugating life as we know it. Cain died while researching a sequel, which according to his notes was to be entitled *How to Promote and Manipulate thee Natural Fealty and Gratitude That Thine Creation Will Express Towards Thou, Their Creator.* For some reason, that never works.

"I'm sure," Zola said dismissively. "But now we're out of time. I have to take over as Heterodyne quickly. We no longer have the luxury of trying to control the Castle, but we have found a way to kill it."

"That is a mistake!" Professor Tiktoffen burst out. "We need more time, yes, but we have made progress! With this information we could—"

Zola cut him off. "Yes, yes, I know. I've read your reports. 'A priceless antiquarian thinking engine that could teach us about the very nature of consciousness and rational thought—blah blah blah.'"

"But it *is*," Tiktoffen screamed in frustration.

Zola turned and regarded him fondly. "You Sparks are all alike. I promise you, Professor, when this is all over, you can take whatever parts you want and build yourself a chatty little gazebo somewhere." The smile left her face and her voice hardened. "But today, Castle Heterodyne dies."

Gil raised his eyebrows. "And you're going to do this, how?"

Tiktoffen sighed and led them through a thick wooden door. They stepped into a large room filled with people and the sound of activity. The largest group was gathered around a brass pedestal set with blue glass spheres. It was slightly taller than the men who stood beside it and surrounded by a nest of cables and tools. All of the people in the room paused to stare at the newcomers as they entered. With a shiver, Gil realized that several of the more exceptional Sparks that his father had sentenced to service in the Castle were gathered in this room.

Zola indicated the device. "How will I kill the Castle? Simple. With this."

Gil examined the device and felt another jolt of unwelcome surprise. Many of these parts would have required sophisticated manufacturing processes. He turned to Professor Tiktoffen. "Surely some of these components weren't manufactured in the Castle. How did you get them in without anyone noticing?"

The professor shrugged nonchalantly but it was obvious that he appreciated the chance to brag a bit. "Patience, mostly. Now, some parts were here already—the old Heterodynes kept all sorts of useful machines—but it was easy enough to slip a little something extra in occasionally with the supply shipments. It wasn't particularly difficult, since the Baron allows almost everything we ask for anyway."

Zola now addressed a tall, intense man. "What is our status, Professor Diaz?"

The man scowled. "It is not yet ready, Señorita."

"That is not what I wanted to hear."

The professor made an exaggerated expression of dismay with his hands. "¿No? My heart, it weeps."

Zola narrowed her eyes and her voice grew cold. "It might. What is the problem?"

Diaz snapped his fingers and a minion dragged another prisoner out from a side room. Despite the fact that he had obviously been worked over by someone who knew what they were doing, the man in manacles wore an arrogant smile. A long scar marred his face. "This cucaracha," Diaz snarled, "has been intercepting the shipments. Not all of them, but he has managed to collect several of the parts that we need."

The man's grin widened. "That's right, girlie. And that means that you gotta deal with me to get them!"

Zola's expression was cold. "I see." Smoothly, she took out her little pistol and fired a round through the man's kneecap.

He screamed and dropped to the ground. Zola strode over to him and kicked his hands away from where they clutched at the wound. She placed her foot squarely on the shattered knee, leaned in, and tapped the barrel against the man's head. "The question is, just how much of you will I have to deal with before I hear what I like?" She ground her foot down.

"In the cistern," the man shrieked. "There's an oilskin bag in the cistern!"

Zola straightened up and waved her hand. The man was dragged off, whimpering.

As Zola holstered her gun, she caught the look on Gil's face. She looked grim. "My patience only stretches so far," she said.

CHAPTER 8

After Faustus Heterodyne finished his Great Work, the waters of the river Dyne ran clean—at least beyond Mechanicsburg's famous "mouth of the Dyne" sculpture through which it leaves Castle Heterodyne and falls to the base of the pinnacle from which it springs. Previously, the waters had been possessed of unusual and generally poisonous properties and had wound through the landscape, killing or mutating man and beast alike.

Once the waters of the Dyne were cleansed and the Castle and its defenses improved, the Heterodyne began the task of fully establishing his town.

Faustus liked the idea of ruling his own city, but—aside from his own band of reavers, the occasional oppressed servant, and the extremely odd camp followers that favored his men—the area was sorely lacking in people. The Heterodyne was forced to create a thriving population from next to nothing. He threw himself into the challenge with a will.

From that point on, across Europa and Asia, indeed, wherever he raided, Faustus was seen consulting what his men jovially called "The Master's Shopping List." But it was not a list of stores, treasure, or materials—it was a list of people.

Like a hausfrau at market, the Master of Castle Heterodyne browsed the World and carefully selected farmers, carpenters, engineers, stonemasons, and a half a hundred other professions, all lured or looted to populate the town that was to become Mechanicsburg.

317

As a result, while there are many other adjectives that can be used to describe the Heterodyne's creation, the first and foremost one must be *cosmopolitan*.

—*Mechanicsburg: Economic Principles of a Town That Should Not Work* by Professor Isaac Horowitz/ Transylvania Polygnostic University Press

～ଔଓ～

gatha had set out by herself, following the Castle's directions, and she now found herself toiling up a tilted floor. There were cracks throughout the stonework. She climbed upward gingerly as the cracks became wider. The Castle had assured her that this broken hallway was the quickest, safest way to Gil—but it had been quiet for a while, now. She wondered just how much perverse amusement it was getting from watching her clamber around, puffing with effort. She briefly considered turning back and demanding another, easier route. Then she realized that it could probably always find someplace worse—and more entertaining—to send her.

As she pulled herself to the top of the incline, she realized that she was now standing upon a giant saw-toothed gear. Faintly gleaming in the darkness around her, she saw several more, equally large. Agatha marveled at the sight. She again moved forward, but carefully. She didn't want to damage anything else.

The Castle broke in on her thoughts with a wracking, metallic cough. "Oh, now this is interesting. I really do have to thank your young man, my Lady. I can now observe several areas formerly closed to me." It made a sound remarkably like a fussy professor clucking his tongue. "I really do need dusting."

"What about Gil?" Agatha felt a flash of annoyance at the eagerness she heard in her own voice.

"Ah. He is with our imposter."

"That pink fake? What's he doing with *her?!*"

Gil slammed a hand down on a countertop. "You shot him in cold blood!"

"I'm the Heterodyne," Zola said in a low, furious voice. She glanced at the prisoners. "People have expectations. I had to!"

"Had to? You didn't even hesitate!"

The Castle paused, processing the conversation. "He is complimenting her."

Agatha felt a pang in her heart. "Really?"

Zola stomped her heel and leaned in. "If I show weakness, these scum will defy me!"

Gil shook his head. "But you didn't even try anything else."

Zola rubbed her temples. "I'm not as clever as you," she muttered, "and I don't have a lot of time."

"Generally, shooting people is the last resort!"

"He is impressed with the way she does things," the Castle said. Agatha's eyes narrowed. "And she thinks that he is clever," the Castle continued, helpfully.

"For a normal person, yes! These people are animals! They have to fear us, or else they'll turn on us!"

"Of course they will!" Gil's voice was sarcastic. "So how about we just shoot them all now and get it over with? Then we can build a nice doomsday device and wipe out all of Europa!"

"He has asked her out on a date."

Agatha took a slow, deep breath. "I see." She blew a lock of hair away from her eyes. "Well, I don't care what he's getting up to with the sugarplum airship princess. He can jolly well put it on hold until he's had a look at Tarvek." She kicked a fragment of rubble that lay at her feet—hard enough to send it smashing through a nearby window. It seemed to activate something. A warped wooden wall panel juddered aside and a large clank, armed with a rusty polearm, swiveled towards her.

"Die!" it rasped.

An instant later, its head and most of its torso boiled away into super-heated vapor. "I never said he was my boyfriend," Agatha snarled as she stomped past. "That's just what the rest of Europa seems to have decided!"

"Er...My Lady—" The Castle sounded slightly worried.

Agatha ignored it. "After all, let's not forget why I'm risking my neck trying to find the idiot. I've already got a perfectly good 'suitor' on the slab—assuming I can keep the treacherous, duplicitous weasel alive!"

A faint sound came from above. Agatha kept walking—she merely raised her weapon and pulled the trigger. The rain of javelins directly above her exploded into a metallic mist along with an entire section of ceiling, upper stories, and roof, as the rest thudded to earth around her.

"Of course, my Lady, but..."

"And you know what *really* gets me angry?"

"Er..."

"I actually do like Tarvek. I mean, I can't *trust* him, but that doesn't mean I want him to *die*." She paused. "Or even stay that weird color."

The Castle tried again: "Ooh, but could you just—"

She came to the end of the hallway and glanced at the giant door before her. Agatha saw an intricate locking mechanism connected to a series of copper dials cunningly inscribed with alchemical symbols. She frowned.

"Behold!" a voice boomed. "The Puzzle of the Philosopher's Conscience. If you can—"

Agatha raised her gun and a hole three meters in diameter burned into existence, its edges glowing red. She stepped through it.

"And the *really* annoying thing is that even if you completely misinterpreted the situation—which I wouldn't put past you, by the way—Gil has still managed to get himself tangled up with

Miss Pinkie Psycho Pants. He's such an idiot! It's just a good thing *one* of us has a death ray!"

Agatha glared around and seemed a bit put out at the lack of further obstacles to incinerate.

"Yes, my lady!" the Castle spoke quickly now: "It is indeed a *lovely* death ray! But… could you perhaps lower the power just a *little* more?"

Agatha made a moue of disappointment. "Aw, but I already turned it way down."

"Which is probably the only reason I am still standing." When it spoke again, there was an odd quality to its voice. "Er…Please?"

I've scared it, Agatha realized. A feeling of guilt swept through her. She knew she was being unreasonable, and the thought aggravated her more. "All right. Fine. I'll turn it down. Anyway, it's not like we can't rebuild everything when—"

"Oh dear."

"What? Am I about to be amusingly dumped into lava or something? Because at this point—"

"No, my lady, it is the Imposter. She is now showing your young man the device with which she intends to shut me down."

Agatha gasped. "Oh no. Already?"

The Castle paused. There was a slight gloat in its voice when it spoke again. "Ah. It seems they are missing some essential parts. Good. But…do act quickly." It paused. "Also, please be careful, you are about to leave the area under my direct control."

Agatha swiveled about and stared back at the corridor she had just come through. "I thought I already had! What were all those traps about, then?"

"My apologies. But many of the more sophisticated traps currently have minds of their own. I do not control them."

The Castle's unconcerned attitude was not helping Agatha's mood. "Tch. When I get around to redesigning you, it'll be with a hammer." She sighed. "So, what am I heading into now, then? More of the same?"

"Oh, dear, no. It's much worse from here."

"Lovely. It's not more of those fun-sized tiger things, is it?"

"Oh, yes. There's one of those directly ahead of you, as a matter of fact—" Agatha stopped dead. The Castle continued, "but it has been incapacitated."

Warily, Agatha peeked around the doorway. The hulk of one of the fearsome mechanisms was stretched out on the floor before her. Its carapace gleamed in the light that poured in through tall stained glass windows. The reason for its incapacitation was clear—several of the javelins that Agatha had encountered earlier had pierced it. Dried puddles of fluid crusted the rug beneath it.

Agatha frowned. "Wow. What happened?"

"I have said the controlling mind here has gone mad. Here is the proof. It has begun to destroy Castle systems. The Serpent's Gallery is beyond this room. I will not be able to communicate with you when you leave."

Agatha leaned down to examine the prone machine. As her hand passed before one of its eyes, the device shuddered and a massive paw flexed. She leapt back. "You said it was incapacitated!"

"That is not the same as deactivated."

Agatha knelt down and reexamined the machine. An idea flickered. "Hm. I can use some of this…" she muttered. "Fine. I'll stop here for a moment and you can tell me how to get to Gil.

"How many of Pinkie's people are with him?"

"The Imposter has three minions with her. They are armed, as is she. There are also five prisoners. Four Sparks, one minion. They are all dangerous."

Agatha pondered this. As she thought, she began to hum, the strange, faint sound rising and falling through the empty halls. Suddenly she stopped, a gleam in her eye. "Oh yes," she said under her breath. "I can use some of this."

"My Lady…while I realize the futility of trying to dissuade you from acquiring greater firepower, could you please try not to hit anything…er…structural?"

Agatha had to smile at this. "Oh, stop whining. You'll be fine," she told the Castle. "You're incredibly overbuilt."

The Castle was pleased. "Oooh! Do you really think so?"

As the Castle preened, Agatha pulled out a little pocket clank—the near twin of the one Gil had sent into the Castle walls—and began winding it. With a whir and a snap it clicked to attention.

"What is *that?*" the Castle asked with a touch of alarm.

"It's a little clank," Agatha explained. "I like to have assistants when I work, so I make them."

The little device gave her a salute. Agatha brought it down to the broken fun-sized tiger clank. "Let's see what we can do with this thing, okay?" she told it.

"I don't like it," the Castle boomed.

Agatha rolled her eyes. "Oh, for goodness' sake. It's just one little clank."

The little clank examined the mechanism it had been offered and its gears squeaked with glee. There were lots of parts here.

A short while later, Gil let out a deep breath and settled back onto his heels. "And then all I have to do is hook this lead up to this connector!"

"¡Ingenioso!" Professor Diaz rubbed his jaw. "Superb."

Gil waved a hand. "You're too kind, Professor."

Diaz snorted. "I assure you, young man, I have never been noted for my kindness."

Zola came up behind them. "What are you two doing here?"

Diaz tapped the device before them. "Your pirata, señorita. He has reworked the device! How, I am not quite sure, but he has eliminated the need for all but a few of the stolen pieces."

Gil shrugged. "Give me a machine shop and a few days and I'll replace those, as well."

Zola smiled with delight. "Another day is simply too long, and the men I sent should be back with the parts soon enough. But still," Zola patted Gil on the cheek. "That was very sweet of you." She took his arm and pulled him away from the device. "Now you should come, sit down, and get something to eat. I'll bet you've forgotten again, haven't you?"

A gurgling sound from his midsection confirmed this and Gil allowed himself to be led to a seat. Zola handed him a bottle of homebrewed beer and a sandwich made from some sort of crustacean that apparently could be eaten whole, much like a soft-shelled crab. It was savory and unexpectedly tasty. He had his suspicions as to its origins[72] but realized he was so hungry that he did not particularly care.

Zola silently watched him eat, which was unusual behavior for her. When Gil took a final pull from the bottle and sighed in contentment, she leaned forward and wiped a spot of mustard off his nose.

"You know, Gil," she said fondly, "I have to say, when I first saw you, I had some very mixed feelings."

Gil blinked. "Zola, I *told* you, that money was a gift, not a loan."

A wistful smile flitted across Zola's face. "No, I meant that usually, back in Paris, when you showed up it meant that something had gone wrong." She shyly glanced at Gil, who was desperately trying to keep his face neutral. "And I was…I was going to need rescuing. Again."

Gil looked guilty. "Oh, well, I…"

A new voice cut in: "Oh, something's *certainly* gone *wrong*."

There, in the doorway, stood Agatha. She was very pointedly ignoring Gil—instead glaring furiously at Zola. In one hand, she held something that looked like a repurposed soldering gun. In the other, she gripped the handle of an ornate lantern-sized battery cylinder—the kind one might find in a medium-sized clank. A short cable connected the two devices.

Agatha pointed the gun-like part of the device directly at the astonished people in the room but continued talking to Zola: "But whether or not you're going to need rescuing? That's up to you."

---

[72]   These suspicions were fully justified. These creatures are apparently a mutated form of louse (*pediculus humanus gargantua heterodyne*) sold throughout Mechanicburg as "Deep Fried Crunchy Castle Crabs." By all accounts they are incredibly delicious, but no native of Mechanicsburg has ever been able to bring themselves to eat one.

"You!" Zola rose, baring her teeth in a fierce snarl. "*Kill!*" She screamed to her men. The order was drowned out by a hellish crash, as the stained glass window beside her shattered. Through it leaped a roaring nightmare built like a huge metal tiger.

As he leapt to push Zola out of its path, Gil saw that one of its huge glowing eyes had been smashed and in the socket rode one of Agatha's little pocket-watch clanks. He found himself wondering if it was the one he had released into the Castle wall or another one entirely—and then one of the monster's great forepaws caught him and slammed him to the ground. One of its padded toes was planted firmly over his mouth—and to his chagrin, he found that he couldn't call out to Agatha. All he could manage were muffled, inarticulate noises.

The other paw had trapped Zola, who stared up at the creature's teeth in horror. "…Nothing." She whispered. "Kill nothing. Nothing at all."

One of Zola's minions apparently didn't hear her. He pulled an odd little pistol from its holster and shouted: "NO! Take her down!" Agatha frowned and raised the weapon—blowing a hole in the wall above his head. Debris rained down upon him, knocking him to his knees. His weapon went skittering away as he ducked behind a bench. "Don't just stand there," he screamed at the Castle prisoners. "Don't you know who that is?"

In one smooth arc, Professor Tiktoffen swung his arm, scooped up a nearby piston, and slammed it across the back of the man's head. The Tall Man dropped unconscious to the floor. The professor then deliberately tossed the weapon aside and executed a formal bow towards Agatha. The other prisoners followed his lead.

"Of *course* we know who she is," he said with an evil grin. "We are at your service, Lady Heterodyne."

Zola's other two minions stared back and forth between the Castle prisoners and Agatha, then simultaneously dropped their weapons. Agatha nodded once, then strode over to loom over Zola, who was still held firmly beneath the huge mechanical paw.

"I am Agatha Heterodyne. You are in *my* town. In my Castle. And *in my way*. This little play of yours is over." Agatha's voice had taken on a dangerous edge that Gil recognized as that of a Spark. An extremely displeased Spark millimeters away from unleashing unholy vengeance upon a hated enemy.

Zola made a valiant effort: "But…but *I* am—"

Agatha stepped back and the tiger clank brought its nose down to brush Zola's face. Even the little pocket clank—who appeared to be controlling the larger one from inside the eye socket—looked angry.

Agatha tapped her foot. "I *said*, it's *over*." The great jaws opened and a burst of hot metallic steam washed over Zola's face. Agatha continued through clenched teeth: "One way or another."

Zola thrashed and shrieked. "Yes! I yield! Please!"

Agatha briefly closed her eyes. "Good. Now…" She opened her eyes, and her expression grew colder as she spun toward Gil. "As for you—" Gil winced. *An extremely hated enemy,* he thought. *I've got to do something. She's—*

"Wait!" Zola called out. "Don't hurt him! He doesn't know about any of this!" Her voice broke. "He's my only friend! The only one I can trust. *Please don't hurt him!*"

Agatha turned her glare back to Zola. "The only person you can trust is *Gilgamesh Wulfenbach? He's* all you've got? I'm almost starting to feel sorry for you. Wasn't that *your* army of clanks that he completely *destroyed* yesterday?"

"I…He…He's…Gil? You're—" Zola was stammering with shock. "He's Gilgamesh Wulfenbach? The *Baron's son?* But—"

Gil rolled his eyes back into his head with frustration. If he ever got a chance to speak, he had no idea what he was going to say… to either of them.

"Oh?" Agatha still sounded like she could level an entire hapless town at any moment. "You didn't *know?*"

Agatha glanced back at Gil, who looked away. Then she nodded slowly. "I see. You *didn't* know. Well, then. I guess he didn't trust *you* all that much. Mind you, I can see why… He was probably judging you by his own standards—"

Now, Gil felt his own Spark rising. *If she would only stop bullying Zola long enough to get her monster off his mouth so he could speak to her...* He made another attempt to wriggle free, and the clank bore down ever so slightly to hold him in place.

Zola made a peculiar sound in her throat. Her eyes filled with tears. "But I...he's always been there...I've known him for so long!" Zola's voice was breaking. Her head slammed back against the floor and she erupted into deep, wracking sobs.

Agatha stared down at the weeping girl in astonishment. Professor Diaz sidled up and clapped his hands. "De*light*fully done, my lady!" He shook his head in admiration. "Your enemy is thoroughly crushed. You are indeed a true Heterodyne!" His voice was ghoulish and nasty and reminded her a bit of the Castle, but he clearly meant it as a compliment from one villain to another.

"But..." Agatha looked back at Gil. He was glaring up at her. A wave of horror washed over her as she imagined herself through his eyes. Then her shame exploded into fury. "Oh, I can't believe this!" she shrieked, her rage growing with every word. "Fine! Just...fine!"

She held up a hand. Her voice grew quiet, but the deadly tones of an enraged Spark still resonated. "*I* get it. I *see* where this is going." She pointed at Zola. "*She* came in here, claiming to be the Heterodyne, with her stupid pink airship and her pretty perfect clothes and her cheap theatrics, trying to steal *my* town and *my* Castle—" Gil continued to glare silently and Agatha leaned in towards him: "Not to mention that she tried to *kill* me as soon as she saw me, and probably is the one responsible for that army of clanks at my gate—but *I'm* the big meanie because I made your little psycho princess cry!

"Sure, I'm the bad guy, because—for whatever reason—you didn't tell your nasty little friend who you are, and now she's sad! So you're mad at me, because now she's all sweet and teary and needs rescuing—"

Agatha knew she was shouting again but she was so angry, she didn't care. And *I'm* the evil madgirl with the death ray and the freakish ancestors and the town full of minions and the horde of

Jägers and the homicidal Castle full of sycophantic evil geniuses and fun-sized hunter-killer monster clanks and *goodness knows what else—*"

She stopped, panting. A thought had just struck her. A wonderful, terrible thought. She *was* that madgirl and she *did* have all those things.

"And you know what? *I can work with that!*"

Agatha turned to the prisoners, who were staring at her in awe. She stood tall and addressed them. "So listen up, all of you. I am armed, extremely annoyed, and the mistress of this Castle. You will follow my orders, and I will tell the Castle not to *squash* you. Everybody okay with that?"

One of the prisoners, a tall, corpse-pale man with a battered metal console implanted in the center of his bare chest, stepped up and nodded enthusiastically.

"Oh, absolutely, my lady."

Agatha blinked but remained poised. "Good. I expected a bit more of an argument."

The man laughed merrily. "Normally? You'd be quite correct! Those with the Spark are constantly engaged in a dance of dominance! There is a delicate balance between crushing one's enemies and being crushed. It takes an excessive amount of time and mental effort."

He ran his gloved hand through his thick, snow-white hair and again grinned. "But you—you are a Heterodyne deep within your own lair. There is no question as to who is in charge here." He took a deep breath. "Socially, it removes a great deal of pressure."

Agatha stared at him. "Who are you?"

The man grinned and came to attention while clicking his heels together. "Herr Doktor Getwin Mittlemind. University of Vienna. MD, Psychology, PhD, Sociology, at your service."

Agatha nodded. "I...see. You don't meet many mad social scientists."

Mittlemind snorted. "Of course not! All the funding goes towards building those flashy clanks and death rays! It's so unfair!

"I *told* the Baron: 'Give me a thousand orphans, a hedge maze, and enough cheese and I can give you the Empire of the Polar Lords within three years!' But noooo..."

Agatha had had enough of this. The man was working himself up toward a full-blown Spark rant.

Agatha interrupted him. "You are not reassuring me."

A short, solid young woman dressed in protective gear sidled up to Agatha. "Your pardon, my lady, but you probably *can* rely on most of us. Hexalina Snaug, at your service, my lady."

Agatha looked at her. "Oh?

Snaug nodded. "Sure. If you *are* the Heterodyne and the Castle gets fixed..." She spread her hands. "Then the Baron won't be using the Castle any more. We'll be free to go. It's even one of the conditions of our sentences."

Agatha glanced over to Gilgamesh and raised an eyebrow inquiringly. "Really."

Gil, still pinned under the tiger clank's paw, made affirmative noises.

Agatha turned back to the prisoners and smiled happily. "Very well. Cross me, and die."

The prisoners beamed. Mittlemind rubbed his hands together. "You won't regret it, my lady!" He then pulled a battered notebook from his pocket and began flipping through pages. "Now, if I might make a suggestion? I couldn't help but notice that with the addition of just a very few added walls, your town will make an excellent maze!"

Agatha shrugged. "Let's get the Castle repaired and I will listen to any scheme—um—proposal that you want to submit."

The others gasped. This was largesse on an unexpected scale.[73]

---

[73]   Agatha had no idea what she was in for. As the largest supplier of money, resources, and personnel in Europa, the Wulfenbach Empire received hundreds of proposals for insane schemes every day. What made it truly maddening was that all-too-often a scheme might be horrifying, insane, counter-intuitive...and the perfect solution for a current problem. Thus, Klaus insisted that every one of these ideas had to be fairly evaluated. It was challenging, infuriating, and occasionally dangerous work. The clerks assigned to the Department for the Containment of New Ideas were bureaucrats who regularly earned Hazard Pay.

Agatha couldn't put it off any longer. "All right, I'm going to let them up. Take their weapons and get ready to hold onto Pinkie."

When the clank finally lifted its paw, Gil raised himself on one arm and looked up at Agatha, an unreadable expression on his face. Agatha's Spark rage had passed and now she felt slightly ill. It was so hard to see him again. She reminded herself that she still hardly knew him...yet...he had cared for her and she had let him think she was dead...and now, here he was—unexpectedly close with this scheming rival...She knelt next to him and the two stared at each other, silently.

When she spoke, her voice was even and calm. "Look, I'm sorry I can't cry and let you rescue me, but it looks like I've got to be the big bad Heterodyne for a while. I've got a lot of people counting on me, starting with someone who's really sick. That's why I need you to come with me now, even though I'm really mad at you." She bit her lip. That would have to do—she didn't have time for any more explanations right now.

Gil nodded and with a single fluid movement was on his feet offering her his hand. She looked up at him and noticed—for the first time—the ring he wore on a thin metal chain around his neck. Her ring.

The ring he had given her on Castle Wulfenbach. The ring that she had left on poor Olga's burned corpse. He'd kept it. He...

He spoke. "All right, then we'd better get going."

Agatha felt relief wash over her. Maybe things weren't so hopeless after all. She took his hand and pulled herself to her feet. Her heart was pounding. She didn't let go of his hand. Instead, she pulled him toward her and leaned in until their faces were only centimeters apart. "And later?" she told him, a hint of the Spark still in her voice, "*We* are going to have a *long talk*."

Gil took her other hand in his. He leaned in even closer, glaring down into her eyes. "Yes," he growled, "Yes we are."

And then they stood there. He continued to hold her hands and gaze into her eyes. His expression softened. Agatha realized that her breathing was accelerating. "Well...um...good." She couldn't move. His eyes were so beautiful—deep and golden brown... "Uh... so that's settled, then."

"Um...yeah. That's settled." Gil spoke softly, pulling her toward him

Just as she was about to shut her eyes, Agatha glimpsed a sudden motion in her peripheral vision. Her mind's rosy fog vanished in a flash and she thrust Gil away as hard as she could. They spun away in opposite directions as a burst of mechanical gunfire chewed into the wall next to where they'd been standing.

It was Professor Silas Merlot. He was looking down on them from behind the controls of a heavy walking transport which sported two arm-like guns. "Finally! It's just too perfect! Now the *both* of you can die!" he cackled maniacally. Once again, a double stream of metal pounded into the wall, swinging toward Agatha.

"Everybody scatter!" Agatha screamed.

The guns stopped. Merlot deftly slapped a new ammo feed into the intake hopper. "Oh, I don't care about the *rest* of them, Miss Clay! But *you* are going to die!"

Another spray of bullets chased her as she darted away, leaping over furniture and around debris until she slid, gasping, behind the relative safety of a thick stone wall.

Professor Diaz was already there, staring at her with wide eyes. "That was an amazing display of agility, señorita."

"Thank you, Zeetha! Thank you, Zeetha!" Agatha panted. She looked around frantically. "Where is my stupid death ray?"

Merlot snapped another ammo belt in and then engaged the controls. The machine began to walk forward, Merlot laughing wickedly. "You can't hide forever!" he called.

With a thump, Gilgamesh leapt onto the back of the walker—scrabbling toward its driver. "She doesn't have to!" he shouted.

"Guh. How Romantic," Merlot sneered. He smoothly pulled an efficient looking little zipgun from his pocket and fired a shot into Gil's shoulder—knocking him back off the machine.

Then he spun and yanked the controls about, just in time to

unload both gun barrels into the huge, clawed tiger-clank, which was leaping toward him. The bullets caught the mechanical beast at point-blank range, blew it back against the wall, and pinned it there while they ripped it apart.

At last, the guns ran dry, and the clank finally collapsed to the floor with a crash.

Gil's groan filled the silence as he stirred on the floor. "Gil!" Agatha called—fear in her voice. "Get out of there!"

Merlot let out a giddy laugh as he reloaded. "Oh my, so many potentially interesting experiments present themselves! Is killing his only son and heir a fitting revenge upon the man who sent me here? Or is he too much of a coldhearted despot to care? We shall see!" He swung about to face Agatha. "But I do find it amusing that *you* care, Miss Clay. It would be fascinating to find out how much. But…it is the fascination one has when dealing with *any* monstrously dangerous creature. And if this place has taught me anything, it is caution—so I shall just have to satisfy myself with your immediate death!"

He slammed the controls forward, and the walker stumbled. Apparently the left leg had seized up. Merlot swore. "If it's not one thing, it's another." He threw open a hatch cover and attacked the mechanism inside with a screwdriver and pliers.

Behind the wall, Diaz eyed Agatha. "Our Doctor Merlot is an intense and bitter little man, yes? But what is his grudge against you?"

Agatha shook her head. "I don't know! I never knew! He was just one of my teachers at the University!"

Diaz held up a hand, his expression knowing. "Ah, say no more. I too, have had students."

On the other side of the wall, Merlot was raging as he fussed with the machine. "It was *all you!* Everything that went wrong was because of you!

"Doctor Beetle's notes were in some sort of fiendish code. The Baron assigned a team of the finest cryptographers to examine them. I never expected them to crack it—*I* never could!"

Agatha risked a look from behind the wall. Gil was still out in the open. She could see her weapon lying in the middle of the floor where she had left it. It was across the room but she would have to try to get to it while Merlot was working.

"But they did! They found everything! Beetle knew who you were! Knew who your construct guardians were! Knew who your real parents were! I had always wondered why he kept an incompetent fool like you around!"

Agatha motioned to Diaz to keep silent. Then she left her hiding place behind the wall and crept softly across the room. Merlot's voice became more shrill and hysterical as continued to rant.

"It was all there—and I had never known! And I—I had expelled you! I tried to find you, but you had vanished. The Baron was going to crucify me!

"So I burned it all. Beetle's notes, every one of his secret labs that I could find, the entire hall of records, and all the cryptographers—

"And I *still* wound up in here! Is that unfair or *what?*"[74] He slammed the cover closed and the walker shuddered forward. "But *now!*" he shouted. "Now, I will—NO!"

Merlot had seen her. And she was still too far from the weapon. Agatha made a dash toward her death ray, but a volley of bullets smashed into the stones in front of her, and she jumped back, lost her footing, and fell, directly in the path of the walking machine.

Merlot was savoring his victory. "At last!" he cried. He swung the tips of the walker's guns around until Agatha could look directly into their barrels.

---

[74]   To a chronicler of the life of the Lady Heterodyne, the tragedy of the destruction that Doctor Merlot claims credit for cannot be overstated. Tarsus Beetle was evidently enough of a confidant of Barry Heterodyne that he was entrusted with his niece. Although historical records show that Barry was a prodigious diarist and notetaker, none exist after the date of the destruction of Castle Heterodyne up through his time in Beetleburg (which may have lasted as long as a year). It is not unreasonable to assume that any and all writing that he generated, which would certainly have covered or at least mentioned tangentially, where the brothers had been and what they had been doing since their disappearance, had been deposited with Dr. Beetle for safekeeping before Barry left town. So, in answer to Merlot's rhetorical question, no—it was *not* particularly fair, but the Baron did not permit torture.

She was gathering herself for a desperate leap between the walker's feet when Gil slammed into the side of the machine so hard that the foot nearest him briefly left the ground.

Agatha stared up at him as he stood between her and the machine. One of his sleeves was caked in blood and raw fury was on his face. "You shot me!" he roared. "And it *hurts!*" He took hold of the walker, and, through sheer strength, lifted it a few inches off the ground before flinging it to one side.

He then staggered and clutched at his shoulder. "Oh. Oh dear." His voice was weak. "...and *that* hurt, too..."

The second Gil tossed the machine aside, Agatha leapt to her feet and dived for the death ray. She spun back to Gil in time to see him sinking to his knees.

"I...I seem to have overdone it..." he whispered. His eyes were losing focus and he looked like he was about to faint.

"No!" Merlot frantically slammed at levers as he tried to right the machine. One of the gun barrels was smashed. "No! No! No! I'll not be cheated again!" He gave a cry of triumph as the walker rolled to its feet, then swung the remaining gun back toward Gil—

But Agatha stood in his path, her death ray purring ominously. "You warped, nasty little buffoon!" Her voice had once again taken on the full tone of an angry Spark. "You're blaming *me* for all that? Fool! You deserve everything you got!"

The audacity of this gave Merlot pause. Students, even Heterodynes, were not supposed to speak to their professors like that. "How dare you?"

"Idiot!" She was shouting at him now. "Do you know *why* you couldn't find me? I was on Castle Wulfenbach! I was already the Baron's prisoner, *but he didn't know who I was.* If you'd told him before I escaped, you probably would have been rewarded! You killed all those people for nothing!

"So if you don't stop this stupidity right now, I will have no qualms about putting a hole the size of the Castle in you!"

Agatha was panting with rage. She saw the truth of her words percolating through Merlot's enraged brain. It was apparently too

much for the man. His face went blank. "No," he whispered. Then
he yanked back on the controls and the cannon began to spin as he
screamed inarticulate defiance. Agatha heard the Castle's calm voice
cut through the shrieks: "Oh dear."

A block of stone easily four meters on a side slammed straight
down from the ceiling. There was a flash of blue light and a contained
explosion that sent a shudder through the floor.

"We can't have that," the Castle finished.

The prisoners gawped. "Castle?" Agatha asked in disbelief.

"Impossible!" said Tiktoffen. "This is a dead room! I know it!"

The Castle gave a ghoulish titter. "Hello, Professor. Surprised?
I found a group of nice young people—not any of yours—just
wandering around. They were ever so helpful, and they were able
to repair several previously inaccessible areas."

It sounded pleased with itself. Agatha felt cold. Were Zeetha and
her other friends also in the Castle? They had been with Gil when
she saw him outside…

"Of course, my lady, I was only able to direct their repairs because
of the work that your young man had already done."

Agatha started. "Gil!" He'd been hurt…she turned to find him,
and froze in shock. Gil lay on the ground, sitting up slightly with
his head pillowed on Zola's bosom. She was kneeling behind him,
holding him against her with one hand on his bare chest. With the
other, she was pouring something out of a small vial onto a nasty
looking bruise on his shoulder. She was admonishing him in a tone
that Agatha found unnecessarily familiar. *You'd think he was her pet
or something*…Agatha ground her teeth in fury.

"Don't move, you fool," Zola was saying. "You always try to move
around too soon after you get hurt." She paused as she stroked the
skin next to the bruise. "Huh. It looked like he shot you point blank,
but this doesn't look that bad…"

Agatha briefly considered blowing them both to dust. Then she
caught herself and slowly set down her weapon. *She doesn't own
him and neither do you*, she told herself silently. She hardly knew
him. She had no right to be angry…it was just the Spark in her

that made her think so strongly of things—and even people—as "hers." Agatha swallowed hard, and moved to stand at Zola's side. If she loomed again, just a bit, she thought, it was only because she *was* the Heterodyne…it was hardly even her fault if she was a little intimidating, really.

"How is he?" she asked Zola, coolly.

Zola looked up at her, paused, and then answered carefully. "Um…not that bad, actually. The shot must have been deflected somehow." She dabbed tenderly at Gil's sweating brow with a pink handkerchief. "But he's really out of it. I think he's in shock."

Agatha nodded. She felt like her heart had stopped beating—like she no longer even inhabited her body. She spoke like some ancient spirit long separated from the concerns of the living. "Mmm. You seem to…care for him."

"What? Yes, of course! He's always been there when I needed him! He's saved my life dozens of times!"

Agatha glowered down at Zola, who had the sense to ease Gil carefully off her lap and scoot back on her heels slightly. "And now that you know who he really is?"

Zola didn't even hesitate. She stared at Agatha, wide-eyed and sweetly terrified, while she answered. "He…Well…I guess it makes sense that he had to hide it…"

Agatha nodded. She liked terrified. "All right then." She spoke clearly and slowly, with a controlled tone that still marked her as every inch a Spark. She wanted to make sure Zola was paying attention. "Listen carefully. You are now *mine*. Your only job is taking care of Gil."

Zola started to protest but Agatha overrode her. "I have a *lot* of things to do. If I have to drop everything in order to make a girly fuss over him, we could all wind up *dead*.

"So you make sure nothing happens to him, don't even *consider* giving me any more trouble, and stay where I can see you. If you can manage that, I *might* be persuaded to let you both live when this is all over. Do you understand me?"

Zola only stared at her goggle-eyed and gurgled.

Agatha blinked. "What was that?"

Zola gave a loud wordless moan.

"I am doing my best to be *calm*, but—"

Zola's face was turning red.

Then Agatha realized that she had her hand around Zola's throat. She let go with a start and flushed. She wondered what she was becoming, here in this place.

Zola gasped as she drew in a huge breath of air. "Yes! I understand! I'll do it!"

Agatha retrieved her death ray and turned back to the Castle prisoners, who had been watching with evident approval. This was already taking far too long. She needed to sort them out fast and get back to Tarvek. She pulled herself together and gave her audience a cheery smile. "Well!" she told them. "I feel better now that's all sorted out. Back to work. Show me this 'Castle killer' machine."

A dark-haired man, whose lower body had been replaced by a set of six mechanical, insect-like legs, stepped forward with a smart clack.

"Ah, 'Fra Pelagatti's Lion'![75] Right this way, Lady Heterodyne. I am Professor Caractacus Mezzasalma." They approached the device, a thing of warm, shining metal adorned with blue glass globes.

"This is it," Mezzasalma said. "Capable of generating a low-pulse ætheric 'roar', punctuated by short bursts of trans-dimensional dissonance harmonics." He stepped back and watched Agatha closely.

She nodded. "Hm. All right, I've got it."

Mezzasalma blinked. "You...you what?" His metal feet made a syncopated clicking sound upon the floor. "Young Wulfenbach took

---

[75]   Fra Pelagatti was an Abbot of the Corbettites, a monastic order based in Ireland. Whereas many orders raised a little pocket change by brewing up various alcoholic beverages, the Corbettites ran a railroad system that united Europa and was making inroads into Asia and the Middle East. While it welcomed and sheltered Sparks, the order also attracted quite a few of the overlooked mechanics, engineers, tinkerers, and self-taught inventors who were not Sparks but didn't feel like working for the Wulfenbach Empire. The order gave them a home and a greater purpose. It also gave them access to tools, workshops, and large, dangerous things that went very fast.

only thirty minutes to figure it out—but you—you've just *glanced* at it. How can you *possibly—?*"

Agatha raised a hand to forestall him as she selected a stout monkey wrench from a nearby bench. She raised it behind her shoulder and, with a powerful swing, shattered the largest of the blue glass spheres.

"To be fair," she said as she turned back to the horrified man, "what I was after was a lot simpler."

"YAY, MISTRESS!" the Castle cheered.

Agatha tossed the wrench back onto the bench. "Oh, quiet, you." She pointed to a section of the mechanism. "But really, it didn't look like it would have worked anyway."

Professor Diaz picked up a long shard of blue glass, "Oh, well, some of the parts *are* missing…" he admitted. Regretfully, he tossed the shard into a waste barrel. "We've sent some men to get them. But the theory was *quite sound!*"

"Ah," the Castle interrupted. "Those parts, they were in the cistern?"

"Why, yes." Diaz said.

"The one with the giant electrified squid clanks?"

Diaz waved a hand. "Tch. Those are deactivated." He froze. "Oh."

The Castle chuckled. "Oh, I *do* feel good today!"

Diaz glowered. "Those parts…it is good we won't be needing them, yes?"

"Actually," Agatha said. "I *am* going to want those parts."

"What? *What?!*" The Castle was outraged. "Why?"

"Don't worry. I…have my reasons. I don't suppose any of those people they sent *survived?*"

"Now you're just being unreasonable," the Castle huffed.

Doctor Mittlemind stepped forward with an eager grin. "Oh! Do allow *me* to assist, Mistress."

Agatha was surprised. "You're volunteering to go get them?"

"But of course!" He then swept out an arm and pulled Fraulein Snaug to his side. "Even though I am incarcerated here, I still have my best minion! Fraulein Snaug, go fetch those parts!"

Snaug closed her eyes and whimpered in resignation. "Yes, Doctor."

Agatha spoke up. "Castle, not only do I not want you to hurt her, I want you to help her get me those parts."

"Hmf. How *dull*."

"Cope."

Snaug's eyes shone as she gazed at Agatha. "Wow! Thank you, Mistress!"

Agatha waved a hand. "It's nothing."

Mittlemind gave a conspiratorial chuckle. "We are alike, you and I."

Agatha eyed him with alarm. "Er—and how do you figure that?"

"I too tend to be overly softhearted." He beamed.

"Really?" Agatha was doubtful.

"Oh, yes! Why, back when I was conducting research at the University, I always *insisted* that the children be allowed out of their containment tanks for Christmas!"

Everyone in the room stared at him.

Mittlemind flushed with embarrassment and waved a hand. "Oh please, what do you all take me for? I'm *obviously* not talking about the Control Group!"

The other prisoners relaxed, chuckling.

Agatha stared at Fraulein Snaug, who dimpled into a nostalgic smile. "I love Christmas," she sighed.

"All right! Enough!" Agatha shouted. "I don't have time for this!" She pointed to the prisoners. "You lot stay here and keep an eye on things." She waved a hand around the dilapidated lab. "You can clean up a bit while you're at it. And don't go wandering off or the Castle may get testy."

"It's true…I sometimes do, you know."

The prisoners glanced helplessly at one another. Mezzasalma spoke for them all. "But for cleaning, we'll need to get squeegees and mops and…" he shrugged, "…and minions."

Diaz nodded vigorously. "Oh yes! There must be minions. Although Doctor Mittlemind does share…" at this he and Mezzasalma bowed slightly to the genial doctor, who nodded in appreciation, "…but if you expect this to be done while we Sparks are disassembling 'The Lion'…"[76]

Agatha paused. "No, don't disassemble it yet…Guard it, and get all the bits together so that I can have a look at them later."

"My lady," the Castle wheedled, "I really don't like—"

Agatha cut it off. "Look, you can just squash anyone who actually tries to activate it, okay? Other than me, of course."

"But I still—"

"HETERODYNE!" Agatha screamed.

The Castle gave in. "Yes, Mistress."

"That's better." Agatha turned back to the prisoners and pointed to Zola's remaining Tall Men. "You will assist the professors. If you survive, you'll be free to go." The men looked dubious.

Agatha continued. "Without Pinkie here." With a sigh of relief, the men picked up brooms and got to work. Agatha nodded. "Professor Tiktoffen? You'll come with me. From what the Castle has told me, you probably know this place better than anyone."

The professor grimaced. "Enough to know that I'd rather stay here."

Agatha looked interested. "Permanently?"

Tiktoffen stood up and dusted his hands together. "I'll get my notes."

Agatha turned to Zola, who had once again pillowed Gil's head on her lap. "We're going. Get him on his feet."

Zola gave her an imploring look. "But—you can't make him walk around the Castle like this! It's dangerous out there. He's hurt! He's not even coherent!"

"Making him the only one here who won't give me an argument. It'll pass, but I'll take it while I've got it. Now get him up."

---

[76]   As it may be inferred, most Sparks have much in common with small children in that they may be cheerfully breaking the laws of physics one minute and be astonished that their room has not been cleaned in the next. For many Sparks, the most heinous part of being sentenced to Castle Heterodyne was that they were stripped of their minions and found that they were expected to do everything for themselves, from preparing their own meals, to seeing if a pair of wires are, in fact, live.

Gil stirred. "Um…Zola? Did Professor Belette get away? We've got to stop him before he steals the Moulin Rouge."[77]

Agatha ignored him. "We're going," she told Zola. Then she called to the room: "All right! Now, did I forget anyone?"

"Oh, yes," hissed a chillingly familiar voice from behind her.

It was Von Pinn. Agatha stiffened, then, with preternatural calmness, turned to face her.

The construct hadn't changed. She towered over Agatha, blonde hair pulled back hard into a severe bun, a ruby monocle covering her malevolent, inhuman left eye.

"If you'd wanted to kill me," Agatha said, "you could have done it ten times over."

Von Pinn's mouth twitched, briefly revealing beast-sharp teeth. Perhaps she *had* changed, somewhat, after all. She seemed…almost subdued.

"I am not here to kill you. You are the Heterodyne girl. I must keep you…safe."

This was too much. A wave of fury fueled by grief, stress, and the Spark washed through Agatha. "Safe? From my parents? You tore Adam and Lilith to shreds while I watched!" Agatha's voice rose to a maniacal scream. "*DIE!*" She raised the death ray and fired it, point blank, blasting a hole through the wall in front of her.

"Tsk." Von Pinn was, somehow, behind Agatha. The construct lifted Agatha into the air effortlessly, pinning her arms to her sides. Agatha could feel the pointed claws digging into her skin through their protective gloves. "I see I must *also* teach you *manners*," Von Pinn said.

She studied Agatha's face and a slight moue of puzzlement crossed her face. "You are…genuinely upset about the deaths of the

---

[77] This comment may explain a curious and heretofore unexplained incident when the famous cabaret briefly disappeared from its usual lot on the Boulevard de Clichy. A month later it was just as mysteriously returned, unharmed. No perpetrator or motive was ever revealed. The only evidence of the theft was a series of postcards sent to the Master of Paris showing the iconic structure standing in front of the Taj Mahal in Agra, the Emperor's Palace in the Forbidden City, the Kaaba in Mecca, and the Hofbräuhaus in Munich.

constructs back on Castle Wulfenbach. I am surprised to find you so sentimental."

Agatha thrashed uselessly. She was vaguely aware of the Castle's voice, making conciliatory noises, but she was too enraged to listen. "Those constructs were my *parents!*"

An expression of regret stole across Von Pinn's face. "You know as well as I that they were not. They were merely expendable caretakers. As, in many ways, am I.

"But I have waited over two hundred years to fulfill my purpose. My beloved King charged me with the solemn duty of protecting you." Von Pinn gave Agatha a brief shake. "He was a romantic fool in many ways, but I can not—" Another shake. "*Will* not—disobey him."

"I don't want your protection," Agatha snarled. "You stay away from me or I will find a way to kill you!"

Infuriatingly, Von Pinn smiled. "Ah, that is where it becomes... interesting." She made a low sound in her throat. "Truly, I serve too many masters. My *creator* did *not* charge me with your protection. My *creator's* last orders to me were to keep you 'safe.' He meant 'safe for those around you.' He *knew* what you were. *He* knew what would happen if you were not watched. I once thought I could render you harmless by killing you, and still 'protect' you by guarding your tomb..."

Agatha was still furious. Her struggles had done nothing. All she could do was listen as Von Pinn continued.

"Sadly, due to the interference of my last mistress—may her bones burn green—I am instead compelled to defend *your* unworthy life with my own."

Agatha's eyes narrowed. Her fingers found the trigger of the death ray that she still clutched in one hand. She couldn't see it, held as she was. "Really." She said. "You're prepared to die to protect me."

"Whether I want to or not," Von Pinn said.

Agatha grinned nastily down at her. "Fine. Then now's your chance." As the Castle howled in protest, she pulled the trigger on the death ray, and a large circle of floor boiled away beneath Von Pinn's feet.

"Truly you are your mother's child," Von Pinn shrieked as she flung Agatha away from her. Her voice grew fainter as she tumbled away into the depths of Castle Heterodyne, screaming with rage.

Agatha hit the floor in an ungraceful roll, coming to a painful stop against one of the stone lab benches. Professor Tiktoffen and Snaug were at her side instantly, helping her to her feet. "Are…are you all right, my lady?"

Agatha rubbed her left shoulder as she peered into the hole that she had created. Neither Von Pinn nor the bottom of the shaft could be seen. The blast had cut a perfect hole through floor after floor of the Castle below them. Even as Agatha watched, the final bit of illumination provided by the molten edges of burnt stone faded back into darkness.

"That was hardly necessary, my lady," the Castle complained. "I can assure you that Mistress Von Pinn poses you no threat."

Agatha glanced back at the hole she had made. No wonder the Castle was upset. "Is—is she still alive?"

The Castle took a moment to answer. "An interesting question. I do not know."

"How deep does this thing go?"

"Deeper than The Great Movement Chamber, which is as far down as I know. Also, you have now damaged several of my systems. By some miracle, you hit nothing essential, but I am still fond of them."

Agatha nodded. "Ah. I'm sorry about that. No more death ray then."

"Thank you," said the Castle.

"It's nearly out of power anyway," she told it.

"Such a shame."

Agatha turned to Tiktoffen. "And now, we are getting out of here before anybody else shows up."

Tiktoffen nodded enthusiastically. "I am completely in agreement with that plan."

Agatha turned toward Gil. She had rather expected him to say something about Von Pinn, or at least, well, would it kill him to compliment a girl's death ray? But she saw now that he hadn't been paying attention to anything that had been going on. In fact, he was still flat on his back.

"What's wrong?" she asked Zola. "That wound doesn't look bad enough to keep *him* off his feet."

"He won't get up," Zola said defensively, "and I can't carry him."

Agatha took a closer look and bit her lip. Zola had bandaged the wound expertly. Gil's skin was flushed and he was sweating. His breathing was deep but quicker than if he was simply resting.

"Well he can't stay here, especially if there's something weird wrong with him." *He may not be much use like this, but at least I'll have both sick idiots in one place*, she thought.

Gil was mumbling in French: "Sorry, Professor, my latest experiment ate my lecture notes."

He thinks he's in Paris, does he? Agatha had an idea. She leaned down to shout in Gil's ear. "Hey, Gil! All of Paris is about to go up in flames and Zola has her head caught in a bucket! Up and at 'em, hero boy!"

It worked. Gil's eyelids fluttered and he jerked up into a sitting position. "A bucket?" He shook his head ruefully. "Again?" With a sigh, he swayed to his feet. "Okay, I'm comin.'"

Agatha glanced at Zola's expression of rage and nodded in satisfaction. "Yessss, I suspected as much."

When they had been walking for a while, Agatha looked up from the map of the Castle. She had borrowed it from Professor Tiktoffen and it was hand-drawn, much marked and tattered. She looked down the long, enclosed stone corridor, checked the map again, and nodded. She tapped the vellum with a fingertip. "We're here. And…I'm afraid that the way we're going is through one of these red marked areas."

Tiktoffen took his map and nodded matter-of-factly. "Ah. We are indeed in uncharted territory." He carefully rolled the map back up and placed it in the satchel he carried. "I will scream like a little girl now," he informed them.

"Please don't," Agatha said.

"No, no—I insist."

"Oh, do let him, Mistress," the Castle said. "It's very funny."

Zola interrupted them. "Are we anywhere near this medical lab of yours?" She glanced back, worry evident on her face. "Gil's still pretty much out of it."

This was clear. Gil was ambling along the corridor as though he was enjoying a garden stroll. As Agatha watched, he approached an empty suit of armor and politely addressed it. "*Pardonnez-moi, Monseiur, mais où est la catastrophe?*"

"And what is that noise?" Zola asked.

Agatha had been trying to calculate their best route back to the lab and Tarvek. When Zola spoke, she realized that there was a noise, and it was growing louder. A terrible banging and clonging noise, like a half-full water tank being dragged fast behind a team of oxen.

A spiked ball of steel, easily the height of two men, came hurtling around a far bend in the corridor. It rumbled toward them, apparently under its own power.

Agatha stared at it in astonishment and asked no one in particular: "Why do I even *have* one of those?"

Tiktoffen shrugged. "I'd always wondered where that thing went on Tuesdays."

Zola stared at the onrushing ball and then screamed for help. "GILLLLL!"

This jolted Gil from his distracted mood and he snapped into action. He leapt forward, scooped Zola into his arms and without breaking stride, ran directly toward the ball. Agatha's heart stopped as she watched. There was no way around. With its spikes, the ball filled the corridor neatly from side to side.

Fortunately, the hallway was higher than it was wide. With Zola shrieking in his ear, Gil spun and jumped towards the wall. Hitting it, he instantly pushed off and bounced towards the other side of the corridor, then back again. As he made his highest leap, the spikes of the ball swept past centimeters below his feet. As the ball rolled on, Gil bounced them back to the floor.

As his feet touched the ground, Gil blinked with the look of a man awakening from a particularly absorbing daydream. "Wait. Back there…" He spun in place and watched the ball crashing away down the corridor. "Was that…Agatha?"

Zola tightened her arms around Gil's neck and stared at the twisted wreckage of Agatha's death ray, scattered across the floor where the ball had passed. "Oh dear," she said breathlessly, "How tragic! I guess my Castle is even more dangerous than I'd imagined!"

"MY Castle!" Agatha's voice rang out from above. Gil nearly dropped Zola as Agatha drifted down towards them. Professor Tiktoffen was clutching frantically at the arm she had slung around his chest. With her other hand, she held tightly to a small device that looked like another of her little pocket clanks. As she was about to touch down, the little clank burst with a loud crack, and everyone ducked as a barrage of short propellers ricocheted off the walls and into the darkness.

As he ducked, Gil set Zola on her feet and covered her head with his arms. When the clattering died down, he raised his head. "My Castle," Agatha repeated, glaring at Zola. "And don't you forget it."

Gil beamed at her happily. "Agatha! What are you doing in Paris?" Agatha just looked at him. "Are you going to Professor Goodwin's freestyle reanimation demonstration?" A hopeful thought entered his head. "Afterwards, let's get some coffee and—"

Agatha grabbed hold of Gil's shoulders and gave him an impatient shake. "No! You are coming straight to my lab so I can look you over properly!"

Gil felt a blush work its way up his face. That had gone even better than he had hoped! "Wow. Really?"

Agatha just looked at him. "Let's go," she said and stalked off.

Gil started to follow her and ran the toe of his boot into the remains of the little clank. As the metal casing clanged across the floor, he looked around him. Suddenly, he had a realization. "Hey! This isn't Paris!"

Agatha blew out a sigh of relief and kept walking.

"This is Castle Heterodyne!" Gil tried to catch up to Agatha, but Zola took his arm and lightly squeezed his shoulder. "OW!" Another memory surfaced. "And I got shot!"

"Yes," Zola said. "But don't worry, I'm taking care of you."

Gil stared at her, glanced at Agatha as she hastened away, and then turned back to Zola. He felt he should make things clear right away. "Listen, about Agatha, you should know—"

Zola waved a hand. "Oh, *her*. She's taken us prisoner, you know." Zola dropped her voice. "She's been acting all crazy and violent and she talked mean to me."

Gil looked at her. "Well, you *did* try to kill her," he reminded her. Zola rolled her eyes and snuggled in closer. A thought hit him. "But—she's really mad, huh? Hmmm…" Agatha had a lot of reasons to be angry with him.

The group continued on their way. Zola kept her arm locked with Gil's, and Tiktoffen stopped frequently to check his maps and instruments.

Agatha said nothing, staring fixedly ahead. Every so often, Agatha stole a look at Gil and Zola out of the corner of her eye. She could tell that Gil wanted to talk to her but she was not going to have any kind of conversation with him with Zola clinging to him like a newlywed.

Agatha knew she wasn't being completely fair to him. Back on Castle Wulfenbach, they had been friends, of a sort. They had worked together, fought slaver wasps together. He had believed in her. And, in the end, she had left him and lied to him. What was she going to say?

Things might have continued this way but Professor Tiktoffen cleared his throat and engaged Zola in consultation about the types of traps that might await them ahead. Zola had reluctantly released Gil's arm and the two of them now paced on ahead.

Gil glanced at Agatha's profile and his breath caught. Here she was, less than a meter from him. Alive and whole and…if the firming of her jaw was any indication…extremely annoyed.

He had to speak to her. Had to find out if she cared for him at all. He didn't have much hope—all she had done was run from him. She had let him think she was dead, and she had pretty obviously never meant to see him again. But Zeetha had been encouraging, and the green-haired girl *was* her friend...

By sheer force of will he opened his mouth. "So..." Gil coughed and tried again. "So, Aga—" *Was he being too familiar? She wasn't his lab assistant anymore.* Gil switched gears. "Miss—um—" *No, you idiot! She isn't Miss Clay anymore!*

"Lady Heterodyne," he said. She turned to look at him. Yes! This was working! And then the yawning chasm of conversation loomed bleakly before him. *What to say? "I'm so glad you're not dead?" Moronic! Of course you're glad she isn't dead! Who wouldn't be glad about that? That's patently obvious! Saying that would make you look like a fatuous simpleton! She's smart! Say something smart!* "So who's this...sick...person?" Gil closed his eyes. *People who pay attention in medical school call them "patients," he reminded himself. Maybe she'll—*

"The patient?"

Gil died a thousand silent deaths while Agatha considered this.

"He's a...friend."

"A friend."

Agatha sighed. "Well, as long as I keep an eye on him, anyway."

"And...'he'?" Gil couldn't help himself. He tried to get a look at her face as she answered, but she kept walking just ahead of him, avoiding his gaze.

"Yes. He's sick and injured, and you're a much better doctor than I am."

Gil felt gratified that she thought so. He also felt Zola clamping once again onto his arm. He almost screamed in frustration. This was the last thing he wanted. But he was torn. Zola was obviously in way over her head. If he pushed her away, she might break down altogether and that would just delay things more. He couldn't run the risk. Surely Agatha would understand.

Agatha glanced back at them and her eyes hardened. "It was his idea," she said. "I wanted the Castle to throw the both of you out."

Gil tried to step forward but Agatha was striding ahead and Zola was too much of an anchor. He ground his teeth. "Well excuse me! I can help you, you know," he snapped.

Agatha was unimpressed. "Yes, that's what *he* said, too."

Gil narrowed his eyes at this. "Well, I can't wait to meet him." *And possibly kill him, kill him, kill him,* he thought.

"He's a sneaky, manipulative, fast-talking smoothie," Agatha said tartly. "You'll like him."

This conversation was proving extremely unsatisfying. But then, what *did* she want to say to Gil? That she still dreamed of him at night? That she never wanted to see him again? That maybe they could work out something in the dark?

She cut *that* thought off with a savage inner snarl. She mentally braced herself to speak, and found she couldn't look straight at him.

She began hesitantly: "Look…Gil, I really—"

"EEEEE! GIL!"

The scream made her jump. Zola had been ensnared by a rusty set of mechanical arms that had descended from a set of holes in the ceiling. They were dragging her toward a gaping pit in the floor.

"HELP!" she squealed.

Gil jumped on cue. "Coming!" With the aid of an old iron curtain rod, he pried the arms apart and dragged Zola to safety. He then left her to walk by herself while he returned to Agatha, brushing broken pieces of machinery out of his hair.

"Sorry about that. You were saying?"

Agatha was torn. She didn't like the way he leapt to Zola's rescue as though it was his sole purpose in life. The idea that the two apparently shared a long history of adventures together before she had even met him annoyed her. On the other hand, watching him in action had perhaps been worth the interruption. The evident strength and speed he displayed sent a shiver down her spine.

She carefully examined the tips of her boots while she tried again. "Well, it's just that—"

"GIL!"

This time, Zola had ventured too close to what looked like an elaborately framed picture of a large fanged mouth and had been pulled halfway inside by some unseen mechanism. Once again, Gil dashed away to pull her out, leaving Agatha in mid-sentence.

By the time Gil stumbled back, Agatha had been examining a large painting of Mechanicsburg's Red Cathedral long enough to count all five hundred and fifty one gargoyles on the façade, none of which dared return her gaze.

"You were about to say?"

Agatha turned away from him. She couldn't do this now, after all. It was too ridiculous. "Oh, *never mind*," she said.

Then Gil's hands were on her shoulders. He spun her firmly around and glared directly into her eyes. His voice was intense. "No. No 'never mind.' Listen, you—"

"GIL! HELP!"

One of the many clocks in the corridor had unfolded itself into a vaguely human-shaped clank and had grabbed Zola with one great, articulated hand. Zola thrashed and squealed in terror. Professor Tiktoffen was pulling on one of her legs, trying to get her free but had only succeeded in removing her boot.

Agatha was on it in an instant, ferociously smashing it to bits with a heavy wrench. She reminded herself that this…whatever it was… was her property and part of the Castle, but she didn't care. It felt good to smash something. Zola dropped to the floor and stared wide-eyed. Agatha thrust the wrench savagely back into a loop on her belt and stalked back to Gil.

They came to the end of the corridor. Agatha recognized the area. "Um…I'd have…" Gil began.

"Oh, no," Agatha snarled back. "It was so *very* much *my turn*."

Gil nodded approvingly. "Mm. Good job. You've been practicing."

"Well, the place is all full of monsters and traps—and if *I* stood around looking all pink and pretty and squealing for help, I'd never get anywhere."

"Agatha—" Gil gently tilted her chin upward. They looked at each other for a long moment. "You—"

"AIEEEE!"

Both of them sighed.

Gil held up a hand. "No, no! Relax! I'll get this one." He turned towards the noise and froze.

Agatha came up behind him, and there was Zola, pressed into a corner, shivering and hugging herself in fear. Advancing toward her was brightly colored spider, easily as large as an adult hand. When Gil and Agatha arrived, it paused long enough to make a small lunge toward them, audibly snarling, before turning back to its original prey.

Gil stepped back. "Wow. You know, on second thought, you go ahead."

Agatha shook her head. "What? No way. She's your...um...your whatever she is. This one's yours."

Gil made a face. "Are you kidding? *Look* at that thing! Anyway, it's in your house—"

"Yesterday you took out a whole army of clanks!"

"That was a small army. This is a big spider!"

"Well, those things'll jump on your boots, run up your leg, and bite your butt!" Agatha shuddered. "*You* get it!"

"No way! When you stomp one that big, it makes this horrible crunching noise—"

"Ugh! *Stop!*" Agatha went pale. "That's *disgusting!*"

Gil nodded. "I know!"

During this exchange, they had recoiled away from Zola and the spider and closer and closer to one another. Now, their shoulders were pressed up against each other, which both seemed to find reassuring. "Well..." Agatha whispered, "We've got to do *something*."

"I know," Gil whispered back. Zola's eyes were now staring at them from within a silk cocoon. The spider was brandishing something that looked unsettlingly like a knife and fork.[78] "This is just embarrassing everybody."

At that moment, Moloch von Zinzer walked in through a door carrying a sturdy pole with a trigger mechanism built onto one end. The other end sported a large mechanical hand. This he closed hard upon the shrieking arachnid with a sickening crunch.

"Ooh, nice." A small woman dressed in shades of grey and purple had followed him and was admiring his work.

Von Zinzer shrugged as he retracted the mechanical hand-on-a-stick. He examined the green slime that now coated its palm and tossed it away. "Yeah, you don't want to touch those things."

"Poisonous?"

Von Zinzer shook his head. "Nah, just really, really *icky.*"

Zola had fainted, apparently from sheer disgust. Gil decided to leave her tied up for now. He turned back to her rescuer. "Von Zinzer! *You're* the patient?" Gil beamed, relief flooding through him. He had known the mechanic briefly back on Castle Wulfenbach and was confident that the man was no rival. "Well, that's—"

Von Zinzer blanched. "What? No! Am I changing color?" He examined his hands.

Gil drew back. "Changing—is that what this is about?"

"Well, yeah." Von Zinzer and the purple girl nodded.

"Sweating? Fever? Delusional?"

"Yeah."

Gil rubbed his jaw. "Vericus Panteliax's Chromatic Death," he pronounced. "Interesting."

"Chromatic Death?" the girl looked alarmed. "As in *dead* death?"

Gil waved a hand. "Don't worry about it, it sounds worse than it is. Did the patient get anything weird into an open wound?"

---

[78]   The Variegated Knife & Fork Spider (*Theraphosidae Cultro Furca Mechanicsburg*) is a species endemic to the Mechanicsburg Valley. Like many other spiders, it cocoons its victim, paralyzes them and injects them with eggs, which hatch into young that feed upon said victim's liquefying, but still living, flesh. The difference is that the Knife and Fork Spider does this with impeccable table manners, which is why it was selected as the mascot for the Mechanicsburg Restaurant Association.

She nodded. "Yeah, he was poisoned. Someone tried to kill him with a dart while he was in the Great Hospital. And then we knocked over a whole rack of stuff and he fell on the broken glass and then—"

Gil frowned. "Poisoned in the hospital? Sifu is going to love hearing that." He thought for a second. "Chromatic Death seems a bit…"

"Flashy?"

"No, actually, it's a bit of an imprecise choice for an assassin. It's too easy to spot and cure, especially if you're already in a hospital. Do you have any open wounds? Swallow anything? Hold still, you." Gil took the girl's hand and checked her fingernails, then pulled up her eyelid to get a close look at her eyes.

"No!" she said quickly. "And I'm Violetta, by the way, not 'you.'"

"Violetta. Good." He looked around the room. "This is a medical lab? Fine. See if you can find me…let's see…a large syringe, some Ichor of Somnia, at *least* one hundred grams of Hesperidial Salts, some kind of disinfectant, oh, and a hammer."

Von Zinzer jumped to attention. "Oh, yeah! On it!"

Gil turned back to Violetta. "And stick Zola here in a safe place for a while, okay? In another room, if possible."

Tiktoffen stepped forward. "I think I can handle that, sir." He lifted Zola, sticky web and all, and carried her out of the room.

Agatha put her hand on his arm and he turned.

"Okay, let's look at this friend of yours," he said to her.

Agatha held her other hand up to stop him. "No."

Gil was surprised. "What? But you said—"

"First *I'm* going to have a look at *you*." She steered him toward a nearby workbench. Violetta disappeared through the door she and von Zinzer had come through. She returned with a small, standard-issue Wulfenbach medical kit—*probably something von Zinzer had been carrying*, Gil thought—and a basin of water; then disappeared again, leaving Agatha and Gil alone together. Agatha turned her back to him while she washed her hands.

"Now, remove your shirt, please." Her voice was brisk.

Gil cleared his throat. "Look, I'm sure I'm fine. Shouldn't I be looking at this person who's *really* sick?"

Agatha half-turned toward him. She was picking through the medical kit. "You just said he's not as bad as we thought. Whereas you just got shot, threw a clank across the room, were severely disoriented, and are now insisting you're fine. Don't you think that's a bit *odd*? If it was *your* patient…"

Gil considered this. "I'll get my shirt off." He turned away to hide his embarrassment and searched for something to say. "So…you've had medical training?"

Agatha glanced over her shoulder and quickly turned back to the workbench. "Took a lot of classes. Observed a lot of procedures. Did a lot of assisting in the university labs…" she said.

"But they never let you practice."

"Nope." Agatha tried not to sound bitter. She stole another glance at him over her shoulder; then turned fully around, her eyes lowered pointedly to his wounded shoulder. She was clearly avoiding his eyes.

When Gil had removed his shirt, he had felt the ring around his neck turn on its chain until it hung down his back and now he wondered if she had noticed it. He wondered if she recognized it, and what she felt if she did…

"Well, you're pretty smart," he said, finding it difficult to speak, "so…so you'll probably be fine."

"Thank you," she said, and began to examine the bandaging Zola had applied. Her hands were cool and every touch sent an electrical jolt through him. Her fingertips were slightly rough. *She likes to work with machines.* He thought of the devices she had built in his lab, the times they had spent working together under the influence of the Spark. It was all he could do to hold still while she examined him. He wanted to sweep her into his arms…

Her hands brushed the chain around his neck, and he heard her breath catch. She tentatively touched it again, like she was reassuring herself of its existence, then she moved on.

The silence stretched out for several minutes. Gil stared at the ceiling. His cheeks were burning. Finally he stole a glance down, just as Agatha glanced shyly up. Their eyes met, and held. He caught her upper arm and pulled her closer. He could feel her hand resting gently on his chest and his breath stopped.

Finally, she looked down again, and spoke. "Gil—you…you were right."

This was not what Gil had expected to hear. "What?"

"You were absolutely right. And I felt so bad and I'm *really sorry.*"

Gil was confused. Right about what? Wanting to marry her? Bringing her to his father? Entering the Castle? "Ah—What about, exactly?"

"Othar." Agatha stepped away and waved her hands in front of her. "I was so mad at you—you threw him out that window—and then, within the hour, I threw him out of an airship, *too!*"

Gil waited. "And you felt bad for throwing him—"

"I felt bad for yelling at you!"

Gil understood. "Oooh. Yeah, it's okay. Othar does that to people." He pulled her toward him again. "And listen, while we're talking about annoying people, let's talk about Zola."

Agatha tried to pull away. "Oh. Yes, I suppose we *should* go and—"

He held her firmly and tried to look her in the face. "No. What I mean is, she's just someone I knew in Paris. I came into the Castle to find *you.* At least—I *hoped* it was you."

Agatha kept her head turned away from him, looking at the floor. "I really want to believe that…" she said.

Gil pulled the ring back around his neck and tapped it. "I thought you were dead." He felt his hand shaking. "And there was so much that I wanted to say to you. Needed to say…and I thought I never could." Agatha turned to meet his eyes again, and he put one hand to her cheek. She wasn't trying to get away, now. "And then my father told me that you were alive…and I just—when I thought you were dead, I just—"

His voice faltered. "Please. You've got to believe me. *Please.*"

"I…do believe you," Agatha said. She threw her arms around him and hugged him tightly, resting her cheek on his bare chest.

Gil had more to say but it all flew out of his head as he wrapped his arms around her. He buried his face in her hair. His lips were close to her ear and he whispered to her. "But it *is* you! I'm so glad. I know about the Other—your friend, Zeetha, told me some of what's going on. She said…"

He remembered the green haired girl's sharp-toothed grin. "The best thing to do is get it all out of your system first, so you can start talking to each other intelligently."

Gil closed his eyes. "…She said a lot of things. But I'll help… somehow, we'll find a way to—" he faltered. He just wanted to stay that way—to lose himself in the scent of her hair.

Agatha's breath was warm against his chest as she spoke: "I'm sorry I…upset you—I wouldn't…*couldn't* risk getting captured again and I was so scared." Gil tightened his arms protectively around her. "Tricking anyone who came after me into thinking I was dead was the only thing we could think of. And then…then it was *you* who came to get me—and with that crazy pirate girl—and all those clanks—and I didn't know what to think."

Agatha lifted her head. Her hand brushed the ring lightly. Gil saw tears in her eyes. "But if you were really unhappy when you thought I was dead, then you'll understand why you need to leave. Now."

Gil's entire body had been awash in a growing bliss but at this pronouncement, it changed to cold shock. "Leave? But I'm here to help you!"

Agatha hugged him tighter. "You can help me. This place is too dangerous. I need you to get yourself and Tarvek, somewhere safe. Away from the Castle."

Gil stared at her in horror. "Tarvek?" his voice rose to a shout. "Tarvek *Sturmvarous?* That smug, condescending snake?" Spark harmonics were creeping into his voice.

Agatha looked up at Gil in surprise. "You know him?"

"I most certainly do! Of *course* someone tried to kill him! Who *wouldn't* want to kill him? Where is the little toad? *I'll*—"

Gil realized that Agatha was now bent backwards, trapped against the workbench while he leaned over her, ranting. Before he could let her up, a voice rang out behind him: "Gilgamesh Holzfäller! It *is* you!"

Gil turned where he was, still pinning Agatha to the bench. And indeed, there was Tarvek Sturmvoraus himself, standing in the doorway. He was wild-eyed, swaying, and a vivid turquoise all over his mostly naked body. "I knew I'd heard your degenerate bleating! You get away from her, you swine!" He lunged forward and would have fallen to the ground if von Zinzer and Violetta hadn't darted forward and caught him. Gil and Agatha stepped away from each other and stared.

"Sorry," von Zinzer grunted. "Couldn't stop him!"

Violetta nodded. "We couldn't find a hammer!"

Tarvek was glaring at him. "I can't believe you! Every time I see you, you're…you're en déshabillé and up to the same tricks! Have you no shame?" He shook von Zinzer and Violetta off and staggered forward, waving a trembling fist at Gil. "You stay away from Agatha! She…she is a nice girl! Not part of your harem of nightclub tarts and pirate doxies!"

Gil wasn't really listening. Tarvek was blue. That wasn't right…

"Agatha," Tarvek was saying, earnestly waving a finger under her nose, "If this cad insults you with his lewd advances again, just give him a good smack with one of these lovely fish and I will—I will—" his voice weakened as he collapsed face-first to the ground.

"Tarvek!" Agatha's voice was frightened. She fell to her knees at his side. Gil knelt beside her and laid a hand on the back of Tarvek's neck. He was out cold. "This is not good," Gil muttered.

Agatha was frantic. "You said it sounded worse than it was!"

"I was wrong!" He grabbed Tarvek under one arm. "Help me get him up off the floor! Hurry!"

Agatha helped him move Tarvek onto a weathered table that looked as if it had once been used for patients or—considering their location—victims. "This isn't Chromatic Death! What did this idiot get himself *into?*"

Agatha bit her lip. "Then, what is it? You sounded so sure."

Gil stepped back. "This is Hogfarb's Resplendent Immolation. It's similar, but a lot more rare."

Tarvek was rambling. "I'm...I'm sorry, Agatha. Um—I'll thrash him later, 'kay? ...don' feel so good..."

Agatha looked worried. "Resplendent Immolation...what on Earth is *that?*"

Violetta was looking over his shoulder. "Um—this is another 'sounds worse than it is,' right?" She didn't sound very hopeful.

"Ah, no," Gil said distractedly. He walked to the workbench and started to clear a space. "The name's a bit of an understatement, actually."

Agatha followed him. "He's going to burst into flames?"

Gil swept piles of long-unused debris off the bench. "Well, probably. There's a small chance he'll just *melt.*"

Agatha made a choked, miserable noise deep in her throat.

Gil winced. "Of course, there's always a chance that he'll be perfectly fine," he added.

Agatha looked at him hopefully. "Really?"

Gil nodded confidently. "Oh, yes. If we assume that this is an infinite universe, then theoretically, anything, no matter how unlikely, has to happen somewhere."

Agatha looked sick. There were tears in her eyes. Gil was puzzled... that always comforted *him*...

"Castle, could he have contracted this here?" Agatha asked.

The Castle's voice echoed around them. "Hmm...possible. There is Vipsania Heterodyne's Cabinet of Contagion, and, of course, the Ghostmaker Mice..."

"Well," Agatha said, "knowing my ancestors, there must be a poison pharmacology around here somewhere." She turned to Gil, "I assume most poisoners have antidotes to hand."

"Your ancestors weren't terribly concerned about antidotes..." the Castle said, "but you may certainly search for one, if you think you have *time...*"

"See?" Agatha pounded the table with both hands and shouted at Gil. "This place—this is why I want you *out* of here!"

Gil wasn't budging. "No way. Anyway, there won't be an antidote, it's more of an illness than a poison. But he didn't get it by mistake, not even in here. Violetta is *right*. Someone got him with this on *purpose.*"

"Sir?" Von Zinzer and Violetta stood in the doorway, carrying a canvas sheet full of jumbled bottles and tools. "Found the stuff you wanted, except the hammer."

Gil glanced at Tarvek. "Pity." He turned back. "See if you can find some Hypatia's Clove. The red kind."

Von Zinzer nodded and ran back out. Agatha, Gil, and Violetta began setting the bottles out on the bench. Von Zinzer appeared again, a glass canister held in his hands. "Bad news, sir," he said simply. "There was a jar marked 'Hypatia's Clove," he held it up, "but the stuff inside is yellow." He glanced at it. "Nearly white, really."

Gil pinched the bridge of his nose. "Well, of course. Everything here is nearly twenty years old. Most of it won't be any use at all!" He groaned. "This isn't good."

Agatha shook her head. Even though Gil seemed to hate Tarvek so much, he wouldn't just let him die...would he? "Gil—you've *got* to take him back to the hospital. I...I don't think I can *stand* losing any more friends." She laid a hand on his uninjured shoulder. "Please."

Gil clenched his jaw. "He is *not* going to die." He swung around to von Zinzer and Violetta. "Have either of you ever assisted in a *Si Vales Valeo* system-transferal procedure?"

The two stared back at him blankly. "I'm a mechanic," von Zinzer said. "If he was a clank, I could maybe change his oil..."

Violetta gently shoved him aside. "Never heard of it, but we can follow instructions if you tell us what to do."

"Wait." Everyone looked at Agatha. "I've heard of that..." She thought furiously. "*Si Vales Valeo...*" Her eyes went wide. "That's that horrible reanimation process from Krakow! That *kills* people!"

Gil waved his hand dismissively. "Only if you do it wrong."

"But at the very least, you'll get whatever this is that Tarvek's got."

Gil shrugged. "Quite probably, but I wouldn't worry about it."

Agatha stared at him, sure in the knowledge that *somebody* should worry about it.

Gil continued. "My father figures that a ruler should be hard to kill. So whenever a new disease is found, we're inoculated against it or simply infected with it. Same with building up a resistance to poisons. I'm probably proof against almost anything."

Agatha was dubious. "That…seems a bit risky."

Gil smirked. "Most people just know my father as the despotic warlord who rules Europa, but he does have his amusing Sparky quirks. Did you know he really loves waffles?"

"Wait! I see it now!" Tarvek announced, clutching at Agatha's wrist.

Agatha frowned as she thought. "Don't try to distract me, either of you. No—we studied this. Doctor Beetle said that even under ideal conditions, most of the people who tried it died, or at least came out of it raving mad." She paused a moment. "*Really* mad. Worse than when they *started*. Gil, you're talking about trying this on a living person. The systemic feedback could short out your entire nervous system."

"True, it *could*…" Gil conceded, "but as long as he stays relatively calm, there shouldn't be any major problems."

Tarvek suddenly flung himself upright. "I am the prettiest frog in this entire pond!" he shouted triumphantly. He then rolled off the bench onto the floor with a crash.

Gil shrugged again and bent to lift him back onto the table. "And, of course, I'd hate for it to be *boring*."

Once Tarvek was off the floor, Agatha took a sheet and tucked it tightly around him so he wouldn't fall off again. She spoke as she worked: "And let's not forget how that sort of thing—even if it works at all—has a good chance of leaving the subject an out-of-control *monster* that has to be hunted down and shot."

Gil flung his hands into the air. "Well, there you go!" he shouted. "In that case he'll be *right back to normal!*"

"Gil! I'm *serious!* Even if we wanted to do this, we don't have *any* of the right equipment. I've already checked. Everything here is useless!"

"Surely not all of it." Gil waved a hand and indicated the machines scattered throughout the room, the piles of discarded components and shelves and drawers full of tools. "I mean, this was some powerful Spark's workroom! *Look* at all this stuff! What about this thing?" He gestured to an intricate copper lattice.

"That one will electrocute him in one of eight amusing ways." She pointed to another. "That one can transplant his mind into a wide variety of household pets, and *that* one will drain all of his blood and artistically replace it with molten brass."

Gil paused, and pointed to a small metal box. "Oh. Well, what about this one? It sort of looks like a toaster."

Agatha nodded. "It sort of is a toaster."

Gil waited. "Sort of?"

Agatha sighed. "Oh, yes. It could toast the whole town. Look, Gil, my family...they weren't nice people."

Gil stared at it. "How did you figure all this out so quickly?"

"Apparently the Castle moonlights as a set of instruction manuals."

"You should be more grateful," the Castle said. "When you're standing in the body-washing rain simulator trying to decide which knob activates the scrubbing powder dispenser and which the boiling water, I'm sure I will have quite forgotten."

Gil leaned wearily back against a cabinet and ran a hand through his hair. "Agatha, listen. I...I can see that you really like this toad." He looked at his boots and waved vaguely at Tarvek.

Agatha blushed. "What? How—I mean—why would you say that?"

Gil gave a humorless snort. "Listen to yourself. You're a strong Spark, but you're holding back. You're so afraid of *hurting* him, you've gone all sloppy and helpless."

This was just insulting. "How dare you?" Agatha snapped.

"This isn't like you!" Gil snarled back. "You haven't even *tried!*"

Who did he think he was? "What do you know about it? About me? You hardly know me!"

Gil swept a hand around the room. "I know you well enough! You're *better* than this! *Look* at this stuff! 'This isn't what we need'? Are you serious? Do you think molecular destabilizers show up in pork pies? Of course not! You have to build them out of sausage grinders and automatic bootjacks just like everyone else! With the machines in this room alone, you could cannibalize enough material to make *anything* if you weren't all frozen up worried about killing him, which is *stupid!*"

By this time, Gil was shouting in full Spark voice, and Agatha's tones matched his. "Gil, this stuff is dangerous! It would be easier to just kill him and *then* revive him!"

The two of them stopped and stared at each other round-eyed as amazing possibilities began to blossom in their imaginations.

"It…it would greatly simplify the procedure," Agatha breathed. "But…there's still the danger of catastrophic mental breakdown for both participants…"

Gil put his hands on her shoulders and looked up at the nearest machine. "Nonsense!" he said. "Once we cure him, sorting out the minor side-effects will be *simple!* Come on, if we try to get him to the hospital, it will be too late. We've got to act fast or we'll lose him for good. I think, if we're creative, these machines might actually be useful."

Agatha turned to face him. She could feel her blood roaring through her veins. "Ah! Yes! We may be able to reconfigure that blood-to-brass thing to act as a filter!"

Gil's eyes were wide. "Oh! Yeah! And it may be possible to eliminate death-trauma memory loss entirely if we shunt him out of his body while we work—"

Agatha slapped the copper lattice. "And we even have something that can generate the nuanced current!"

Gil was actually hopping in place. "Ooh! Ooh! And if we keep high voltage running through everything the whole time, *while* applying—"

Agatha squealed and clapped her hands. "Exactly! Then the cascade effects that usually kill everyone and set the lab on fire probably won't even have a chance to begin!"

The next few minutes saw the two of them dashing about the laboratory, excitedly producing bits of arcane technology and figuring out how they could be repurposed. At the end, they were laughing and yelling, clutching each other's hands, and jumping up and down while finishing each other's equations. Finally they both simultaneously shouted out a final "Zero!" and stood panting, staring at each other with shining eyes.

Agatha gripped Gil's shoulders. "This has a small, but fascinating, chance of actually working. Let's *do* it!" she growled.

Gil wiped the sheen of sweat off of his brow and stared back at her with smoldering eyes. "This will be *great!*" he said fervently. "I can get killing Tarvek out of my system *and* give him a hard time about it later!"

At the mention of his name, Tarvek stirred and let out a small groan. Agatha flew to his side. His eyes fluttered open. "Agatha," he whispered. "I don't think I'm at all well."

"No, no!" Agatha brushed his long bangs out of his face and patted him happily. "It's all going to be all right! We're just going to kill you and then you'll be *fine!*"

Tarvek goggled up at her. Agatha wasn't sure if he understood or not, but—

Gil stepped in. "Agatha… Okay, my turn." He clutched his forehead. "Tch. You have a *lot* to learn about talking to patients."

Agatha was confused. "Oh, but—Science—"

Gil put a finger to her lips and she paused. He then sat on the table next to Tarvek, who continued to look horrified. Gil was, apparently, something much worse than a simple nightmare. Gil leaned in. "Shut up," he told Tarvek.

Tarvek, who hadn't actually said anything, blinked, and continued to be silent. Gil took a deep breath. "Okay. Listen up. Because you are an idiot, you've somehow managed to get yourself infected with

Hogfarb's Resplendent Immolation. If you were paying attention in Professor Fauve's lectures,[79] which I rather doubt, you'll know that once the second stage begins, you're going to go up like a torch. We're going to try to prevent that by destroying the chroma igniters that have invaded your system.

"Now, we've got a bunch of old Heterodyne torture machines here, so we're going to tear them up and try to cobble something together with the parts. It looks like we might have to drain all your blood and run it through an improvised filter—but we're thinking we'll combine everything with a modified *si vales valeo* which, yes, means that we're going to have to kill you for a while. Unless…huh. Interesting. Actually, it's possible that instead of a single moment of death, you'll experience a continual rolling death for as long as we run the current. Still, that's only if we can't transfer your mind into a rat, or something…either way, *do* try to pay attention so we can take notes later.

"Also we think we probably *might* have a way to keep you from becoming a ravening monster but we'll keep you chained down just in case."

Agatha gently put her hand over Gil's mouth. "Okay," she said. "Thanks. I think I've learned a lot."

Gil raised his eyebrows in pleased surprise. Agatha turned to Tarvek and took his hand. It had turned lime green. Her heart was pounding. He looked so terrible…what could she say to him… "Tarvek, I—"

"It…It's brilliant!" He pressed both her hands in his. "Oh, Agatha! You really *do* care!"

Agatha wondered if he was still hallucinating. "Well, of course, but—"

---

[79]   Professor Tybalt Fauve, MD, PhD. Became renowned for his lecture series about esoteric diseases. One of his more memorable teaching aids was to randomly infect various members of the audience with some of the diseases that he was discussing in that session. Extra credit was awarded to students who could correctly diagnose these various illnesses (either in themselves or in others) before the lecture ended (or before the victim died, whichever came first). Due to the perversity of human nature, Professor Fauve's lectures were always packed to capacity, which made things really interesting when he covered some of the more contagious pathogens.

Gil snorted and stalked off, taking von Zinzer with him.

Tarvek gazed at her adoringly. "It'll work! I know you can do it! You're so amazing! Yes, let's start right away!"

"Wait—but first," Tarvek said. He looked around cautiously. "Where is Violetta?" He asked in a low, serious voice. "I need to talk to her. Now."

Violetta, who had been, frankly, cowering next to Moloch while watching Agatha and Gil rant around the room, calmed herself using the secret Smoke Knight technique of biting her tongue, and stepped up. "Well, talk! I'm right here! You Sparks get all into your freakish, twisted courtship rituals and completely forget that you have an audience, don't you?" She scowled at him. "Have you also forgotten that *I'm* supposed to keep you *alive?*

Tarvek was overjoyed. "Yay! There you are!" He grinned up at her. "I really am sorry for all the trouble I've caused you—" Violetta looked like she had a bone caught in her throat. Tarvek blithely continued, "but I'm going to make it up to you!"

Violetta turned to Agatha. "Did you already swap out his brain and I missed it?"

Tarvek settled back onto the table and gazed upwards, contemplating infinity. He spoke in a whisper that Violetta had to bend over him to hear: "Since I'm going to die, I hereby release you from all duties to the family and to the Order."

Violetta gasped.

Tarvek nodded. "And I'm sending you into the service of the Lady Heterodyne."

Violetta clutched at her head. "Oh no," she moaned. "I'm sick too! I'm starting to hallucinate!"

"You'll do fine," Tarvek assured her. "You're like a faithful hound, with your cold little nose…"

"Oh my gosh!" Violetta was starting to hyperventilate. She turned to Agatha. "Oh my gosh! If…if I could stick with you—And…and do girl things…and I…I could go to your party and wear a pretty dress…"

"She's always wanted to, you know," Tarvek confided to Gil, who was walking past with an armload of syringes, tubes, and bottles. Gil gave him a blank look and continued across the room to where von Zinzer was setting out a selection of bizarrely shaped glassware and connecting it with pipes.

"ARRGH," Violetta scowled. She leaned in again to whisper furiously: "But it…it won't work. You don't have the authority!"

Tarvek raised his eyebrows. "I'm the King!" he shouted cheerfully to the whole room.

"Stupid!" Violetta smacked him. "Not if you've been killed and revived!" her voice dropped to the barest whisper. "The Order will throw you out!"

"Not if we don't tell them," Tarvek whispered. "It'll be a secret!"

"But I'm sworn to…" She stared at Tarvek. "This is how you do it," she said faintly. "This is how you get people to…to betray their vows and perjure themselves and commit blackmail and murder for your schemes—"

"Murder?" Tarvek closed his eyes and wearily held up a hand. "Baby steps, Violetta, baby steps." He cracked open an eye. "Well?"

Violetta sagged. "I'll do it," she whispered.

Tarvek's voice returned to normal volume, and he playfully waggled his finger at Violetta. "Excellent. So you obey Agatha. Keep her safe." He waved a regal hand toward Gil, who was lifting jars off the workbench and checking their contents. "And don't let this Lothario bother her. After all, she is my future bride!"

"What?!" Gil shouted. The jar he had been holding smashed on the floor, scattering iridescent green powder across his boots. "I've changed my mind," he informed them all at full volume. "Let's just kill him!"

"Oh my," Violetta marveled. "For the first time in my life, I don't actually want to."

Agatha crossed her arms and frowned at them. "Stop it. We're going to kill him properly."

Tarvek nodded sagely and smiled. "I hear birdies," he chuckled.

Agatha nodded. "Great. Then that's settled. Let's get started."

Gil raised a hand. "Oh. Wait. I've just remembered something I have to take care of first." He turned to von Zinzer. "Did you find that Ichor of Somnia?"

Von Zinzer nodded. "Yessir. The jar is still sealed, so it might even still be good?" He found the correct jar and handed it to Gil, who examined it, nodding in satisfaction.

"Excellent. Come with me." Gil said, and led von Zinzer out of the room.

Once they were in the hall, von Zinzer cleared his throat. "Ah… sir? Can I ask you something?"

"Of course."

"What was all that about messing up this guy's being king? King of what?"

Gil rolled his eyes. "Tarvek is in the direct line of descent for at least three thrones that I can think of off the top of my head." He waved a hand. "Oh, a bunch of his relatives would have to die first, but let's just say *I* wouldn't sell any of them insurance."

Moloch considered this. "But—all that about being dead and revived?"

Gil waved a hand. "Oh, well—Sturmvoraus is a Prince. You know—traditional royalty…they're all about succession, right? That's why the dying thing is important."

"I guess."

"Well someone who's been waiting twenty or thirty years to assume power doesn't much like it when their predecessor goes and gets reanimated. So they've come up with all kinds of rules about that sort of thing. As far as the Fifty Families are concerned, once you're dead, you're dead. Even if someone zaps you back later."

Von Zinzer looked worried. "But, the Baron…there's rumors that he's….I mean, um…no offense, but…"

Gil laughed. "None taken. My father doesn't choose to play by their rules and they can't make him.

"But he knows them. And, every so often, some blueblood succumbs to the lure of resurrection and then desperately hopes no one ever finds out." Gil lowered his voice conspiratorially. "But my father always does."

Von Zinzer nodded. "I'll bet."

Gil held up a hand. "Hold that thought." He opened a door and found Professor Tiktoffen stripping the last vestiges of spider silk off of Zola. "Ah! Professor! Zola! And how are you doing?" he asked cheerily.

Tiktoffen waved a hand gummed with spider silk. "Very well, thank you! I've just managed to get the Lady…er…*Zola* loose!"

Zola was livid. "Gil! Are you seriously going to—AAH!…and *why is your shirt off?*"

Gil smiled and poured a small amount of Ichor into his hand. "Yes, yes. Now, I need you to test something for me!" He raised his hand and blew a cloud of powder at them just as Zola was drawing in a deep lungful of air. She and Tiktoffen collapsed to the ground.

Zola began to snore gently. Gil nodded. "Still good." He turned to von Zinzer. "—and, of course, my father believes that it's best if we're the *only* ones who find out."

Von Zinzer knew an implied threat when he heard one and accepted this one with remarkable equanimity. "Find out what, sir?"

Gil nodded. "Good man."

CHAPTER 9

"Mechanicsburg: A thousand years old and crazy
to the bone."
—*Graffiti originally discovered on the Tower of the
Doom Bell and subsequently adopted as an unofficial
town motto.*

⁓⦿⦿⥱

ilgamesh strode back to the main room of the medical lab,
von Zinzer at his heels.

Von Zinzer was shaking his head. "…and it doesn't
bother you at *all* that her house even *has* all those big iron cages?"

"Why should it?" Gil asked. "This way, even if Zola and
Tiktoffen wake up, they'll be completely out of the way while
we work—"

They froze in the doorway. Agatha stood in the center of the
room with her back to them. She had found an old split-tail lab
coat, gloves, and a pair goggles that sported an array of dials and
special lenses. The lab coat had evidently seen some use—both
arms appeared to have been burnt away to the shoulders. The
machines that had been scattered about the room had been
collected, partially disassembled, and hooked together into a
huge installation centered around two heavy, ironbound medical
tables. Pipes, cords, and machinery wound around everything,
and alarmingly colored substances bubbled through twisted glass
tubes. Little helper clanks like the ones Agatha had left infesting
his labs back on Castle Wulfenbach scrambled everywhere.

Tarvek was strapped to the left hand table, his skin a softly glowing teal. A complex helmet covered with lights and meters hid most of his head, with only his mouth showing.

Violetta was dangling overhead, her knees thrown over an exposed beam. As she connected a final cable, the entire bank of machinery shuddered to life. More lights began to glow. Agatha checked a dial and then nodded. Violetta dropped, spun elegantly in midair, and landed lightly on her feet.

Agatha turned and saw Gil and von Zinzer. Her face lit up. "Ha! *There* you are!" She sounded delighted, energized, and terrifying, all at once. Gil felt his heart rise in his chest and try to soar away. She was glorious—an angel of creation. He had known she was a strong Spark, but here she was, practically crackling with power. And the way she had rearranged everything while he was gone was nothing short of miraculous.[80]

"Get on the slab." She pointed to the empty table. "I want to get to work!" The harmonics in her voice sent thrills down his spine, and Gil just stood where he was, awestruck.

Von Zinzer gave him a sharp poke in the small of the back. "Spooky girl's all yours, pal."

Gil pulled himself together. Agatha took his arm and drew him forward. He examined the machinery, and felt a little disappointed. "Is there even anything left for *me* to do?" he asked.

"Sure! Lots! Don't worry," Agatha told him. "But we need to move quickly…and you were *right!* There's *tons* of great stuff here, if you're willing to try non-traditional methods!"

"I helped! I made some suggestions, too!" chimed the Castle.

"Oh. Good." Gil wondered what kind of suggestions the Castle would think up. Best not to dwell on it…he stopped to check the

---

[80]   Just how Sparks are able to warp the laws of time and motion (among others) has never been successfully analyzed. People who try to carefully watch them report suffering a sort of cognitive dissonance where they simply cannot remember what happened even though it happened right in front of them. These, as it turns out, are the lucky ones, as most people who get too close to a Spark who is happily building something tend to wake up and realize that they have become components.

instruments attached to Tarvek.

"I see, yes, he's getting worse," Gil told Agatha. "We'll have to start the *Si Vales* right away and work on the rest as we go."

"Well, you didn't want it to be boring," she reminded him.

Gil turned to the empty table. "Strap me in, then."

Agatha began the process of connecting him with the rest of the array, and Gil couldn't help himself. He began to fuss. "Um…did you connect all the feedback switches?" he asked her.

"All except the cardiac sequence."

"Ah. Yes. Good. Er…did you key the pump sequence to stutter?"

Agatha swung a control panel around to show him. "Two-two on the cranium. Three-seven on the extremities. Four-five on the torso."

Gil nodded reluctantly. "Right. Perfect." A set of arms equipped with large steel needles swung down and positioned themselves above his arms. Large glass bottles rotated into position.

"Ah! The whole brass infusion thing! How did you solve—" Agatha placed a gloved finger across his lips.

"Gil. You're going to have to trust me."

Gil nodded. "Well, of course. But I *am* letting you strap me into a refurbished pile of torture machine parts and then mix me up with a guy who's full of virulent pathogens and no brains. So, of course I'll want to be extra careful about the variables that I *know* could kill me."

Agatha smiled sweetly and bent toward him. She touched her nose to his.

"Very wise. But I am *not* going to let you die," she said. She then reconsidered this statement. "…Or at least…If I do, not for very long. Now—good luck."

"What?"

And then she kissed him. It was a light, unsatisfying brush of her lips against his.

"Don't worry, that wasn't for good-bye," Agatha said matter-of-factly. She lowered the apparatus over Gil's face. A thought surfaced in his brain.

"Hey!" he called to Agatha. "Did you kiss him too?"

"Don't you worry about that," she said, ensuring that Gil would worry about it quite a bit.

When von Zinzer and Violetta had scrambled to their stations, Agatha took a deep breath and threw the first switch. "Gil," she called, "Give me a count back from...from eighty-three!"

Gil began: "Eighty-three. Eighty-two..."

"Violetta," Agatha called. "Start the bellows!"

With a grunt, Violetta threw her weight onto a leather strap and began pulling on an accordion-like mechanism that towered over her. She released it and it pulled back up. She pulled it down again, and then, with a cough, it began moving on its own, sending great waves of air through several large pipes.

"Seventy-nine..."

"Von Zinzer! Get the resonance accelerators up to speed!"

With a grimace, von Zinzer stooped and began to turn the great crank. "I hate this stuff. Hate it, hate it, hate it..." He chanted through gritted teeth, in perfect time with his movements.

"Seventy-seven..."

Agatha raised her hand to a massive knife-switch and addressed Gil. "Okay. This'll probably hurt a little," she said.

"It'll hurt a *lot!*" Gil corrected her, still counting. "Seventy-five..."

Agatha threw the switch. Gil screamed as he was wreathed in a glittering web of electricity.

"Gil! Keep counting!" Agatha shouted.

He kept going: "S...seventy-three..."

The electricity now enveloped Tarvek, who simply spasmed once and then went limp.

"Seventy..."

A high-pitched ululation filled the air as a pressure-relief valve burst open, jetting steam into the air. The generators began shuddering as the pitch of their whine continued to cycle upwards.

"Tarvek's reading are going crazy," Violetta called out nervously. "They're jumping all over the place!"

"Good," Agatha called back. She wrenched open a shunt, and a container of boiling red liquid drained away into a set of glass pipes that sent it flowing through the system.

"Sixty-seven…"

"Wulfenbach's readings are crashing," von Zinzer yelled. "Everything is in the red! We should hit the cutoff!"

"NO!" Agatha shouted back. She was hunched over the control board, her thick gloves smoking whenever they touched one of the crackling controls. "This *must* work! Increase power!"

Von Zinzer stared at her. "Increase—No! Are you crazy?" He thought a moment and began throwing switches one by one. "Oh wait, of course you are," he grumbled.

"Sixty-three…"

Violetta paused.

"Sixty-two…"

The voice… it wasn't coming from Wulfenbach…

"Sixty-one…"

Or rather, it wasn't coming from *just* Wulfenbach.

"Sixty…"

With a shudder, Violetta realized that the countdown was coming from both Gil and Tarvek simultaneously.

"Fifty…nine…"

Violetta now saw Gil's skin shift to a royal blue. "Lady Heterodyne!"

The lightning crackled around the two prone men as they changed from blue to purple. "Yes!" Agatha pounded her fist upon the board in triumph. "Yes! They're in synch!"

A tug at an overhead chain, and a pair of enormous glass globes encrusted with tubes and cables dropped down, their apertures pointed directly at the hearts of the two men on the tables below them. A light began to glow within them.

"Fifty-seven…"

"Cover your eyes!" Agatha pulled down her goggles and grabbed a large red switch. "I'm releasing the lightning!" With a shriek of exultation she slammed the switch home. Everywhere the lights dimmed and—

A small spark cracked briefly at the end of the tube nearest Gil and Tarvek's chests.

"Fifty-Five…"

Von Zinzer looked surprised. "Huh. I expected a bit more… kaboom."

"Oh dear," the Castle said.

"No!" Agatha screamed. "NO!" She stared upwards. "What's happened? *Where is my lightning?*"

"Ah…This is very embarrassing," the Castle answered. "I do not know."

"You don't *know?*" All around them, the machinery was beginning to wind down. Some smoothly, some to the accompaniment of small internal explosions and the smell of burnt insulation.

"I will attempt to execute a quick Dio-Gnostic routine," the Castle said. Its voice sounded detached—as though they were hearing some mechanically prerecorded message. "In the meantime, please enjoy this musical selection: *Divertimento for String and Garrucha.*" There followed what Agatha guessed to be the melodic sounds of cats being swung from the Castle walls by violin strings.

"What? No!" she howled, tearing off her goggles. "I'm talking to you!"

Von Zinzer put a hand on her shoulder. "Forget it," he advised her. "It's locked up until it finishes whatever it is that it's doing."

"It does this a *lot?*" Agatha roared. "How long does it take?"

Von Zinzer shrugged. "Dunno. You should ask Professor Tiktoffen. I *do* know that it's been happening more and more lately." He listened to the music with a critical ear. "This one probably won't take too long. Now, if you'd gotten an opera…"

"NO!" Agatha stalked away and stared at the gently smoking slabs. "We haven't got time! Gil and Tarvek are fully integrated!" She threw a switch and the machinery covering the young men's faces retracted. Gil was unconscious. "It wasn't supposed to last this long! The strain on Gil's system will be enormous!"

"Don't panic," Tarvek said. Agatha gasped and turned. From his slab, he looked back at her with the clear, intelligent expression she remembered from Sturmhalten. "We're actually doing fairly well." He glanced about at the clamps holding him down. "After all, I'd expect Gil to mess things up. On the other hand, much to my surprise, my brain doesn't appear to be inside an otter, so I suppose I can't really *complain*."

Agatha set his glasses on his nose and mussed his hair affectionately. "Listen to you. You sound like Gil." She smiled. He frowned.

Agatha continued. "Well, good. That means there's still a chance this can work."

"Agatha—" Tarvek began, but she cut him off.

"Shh. You sit tight. I've got to have a look at the lightning generators." She tapped the tip of his nose with one finger and moved off.

After a minute, von Zinzer and Violetta wandered over to stand by him.

"So…sounds risky. What do you think? Should I disconnect you?" Violetta asked.

"No!" Tarvek said. "At this stage it would kill me!"

"Weren't you listening?" Von Zinzer asked. "It'd kill both of them."

"Yeah?" Violetta didn't seem too worried. "Well, I guess it *would* be kind of a shame about Mister Gil, there."

Tarvek tried to sit up and only slammed his head against the restraints. "Good Lord. She hooked me up with *him*? What did she do? Knock him on the head?"

Von Zinzer frowned. "It was *his idea*."

Tarvek blinked.

Violetta nodded. "Yeah. He insisted. That's when we knew he was crazy."

Tarvek looked appalled. "But…but that makes no sense. He hates me! He's always hated me!"

Violetta shrugged. "Hey, I didn't say he was smart."

"And…and what's he even doing here, anyway? The Baron's son was the one who entered…" Tarvek's eyes went wide with shock. He stared at the ceiling for a moment; then his head sagged back against the slab. He shut his eyes and winced as if he were in pain.

"Oh. Of course. He's really Gilgamesh Wulfenbach, isn't he?"

Violetta clapped her hands to her cheeks and squealed. "Oh, wow! She's right! This thing really is working! You already sound smarter!"

Tarvek glared at her. "You *knew*?"

The real venom in his eyes caused Violetta to step back. "Well… yeah." She glanced at von Zinzer uncertainly. "Who was I supposed to think he was?"

"Gilgamesh Holzfäller! A conniving, backstabbing, amoral weasel, that's who! I can't believe he tricked me *again*!"

"Oh, yeah. I remember. You knew him in Paris."

"Paris? He's the one who got me sent home from Castle Wulfenbach!"

Violetta rolled her eyes. "Tarvek, they found you in one of the Baron's top-secret security vaults. You were caught red-handed."

"Yes, and who do you think got me in there? When I was first sent to Castle Wulfenbach, Gil was already there. He was a total nobody. He had no family. No friends. No nothing. The people on the Castle ignored him, when they weren't bullying him.

"Well, I thought he might be useful. He seemed pathetically grateful for any kindness, and one can always use people like that…I thought I'd make him my lackey. But he was brilliant—and he was always coming up with really fun ideas."

Tarvek made a disgusted sound. "I actually *liked* him. I *thought* we were good friends." He glanced at von Zinzer. "I'd never really had any of those, before."

He continued. "And then, one day he told me that he had found out where the Baron kept the family records for all of the students aboard Castle Wulfenbach—"

Violetta interrupted. "Whoa. Hold on. You're telling me that you knew this guy by *name* on Castle Wulfenbach, and it never occurred to you that this guy, *with the same name,* might be the mystery son the Baron had been hiding all these years?" She smacked him on the side of the head. "Idiot!"

Tarvek flinched. "No! Well, yes, okay, I am an idiot; I'll give you that. But…We broke into the vault. We *found* Gil's family records."

Tarvek sighed. "You have to understand. On Castle Wulfenbach…in the schoolroom…lineage was a big deal to us. It was one of the major things we students used to torment each other.

"Gil was at the bottom of the pecking order because nobody knew who his people *were*. The other kids thought he was just ashamed, but he honestly didn't know anything.

"We figured out how to crack the security on the vault. He was desperate to get in and search. Not knowing was terrible for him. He had all kinds of wild ideas about what we'd find: that he'd turn out to be a lost Heterodyne, or—heh—the Storm King, or a…a Martian Prince or something. *Anything*."

Tarvek slumped and was silent for a moment. "I was secretly hoping we'd turn out to be related."

More silence.

When he continued, he spoke slowly. "Unfortunately, that was not what we found. The records showed that Gil's father had indeed been a Spark, but he was one of those rustic buffoons you hear about in bad jokes and tavern songs.

"The creature he constructed from farm machinery and pork products terrorized a small village for the two hours it took the Baron's men to hear about it, show up, and blow it apart. Unfortunately, by that time, the creator and his family had already fallen victim to the thing's built-in sausage maker.

"All, that is, except for the late Spark's infant son; Gil. As there was no other family, the Baron placed him with the other children aboard Castle Wulfenbach.

"Well, he wasn't the only one on the Castle like that, but until then, even the kid whose father built the Perpetual Molasses Fountain ranked higher than Gil, who didn't even *know*.[81]

"Even so, Gil was devastated. I tried to stop him, but he ran off in tears."

Tarvek paused again.

"Now, the thing was…the Spark with the sausage monster? We'd

---

[81]   Herr Tyldon Üglemaach of Belarus could never quite believe, even right up until the very end, that not everyone liked molasses as much as he did.

all heard that story…"

Von Zinzer interrupted, "They still tell it, back where I come from."

"I'm not surprised. But I'd never heard about there being a son… and I didn't believe it for a moment."

Violetta was slowly nodding in agreement.

"You don't last long in our family unless you've got a good nose for intrigue," Tarvek said. "I've never had the luxury of believing everything I read.

"The story was *perfect*. All the details were right. There were secondary reports that confirmed everything and orphaned children of careless Sparks were taken in by the Baron all of the time. But…" Tarvek shook his head. "But they were usually placed with trusted vassal families—people who knew to watch them carefully—in case they exhibited signs of the Spark themselves. Gil, on the other hand, was *already* aboard Castle Wulfenbach. Was *already* being educated along with future rulers and the children of powerful Sparks. Why? Why did Wulfenbach think he warranted such close supervision?

"I started to dig further, but I got caught. Gil had been caught, too. His running off blindly like that is probably what got us *both* caught. When I was dragged before the Baron, Gil was already there. He looked awful. It was obvious that the Baron had told him something that had shaken him to his core.

"The minute I had the chance, I tried to reassure him. I told him that I thought the story we'd found was a fake. That I was determined to get to the truth about him, no matter what.

"I was just trying to make him feel better, but I'll never forget the hatred in the look he shot me. I didn't understand. What had I said?"

Tarvek closed his eyes, exhausted. Several seconds passed in silence. "Well, I never found out, but now I can *guess*. That must have been when the Baron told him the truth. He probably also warned him that I was a person that couldn't be trusted. That was true enough too, really…or that I would try to unearth his real identity."

Tarvek gave a humorless chuckle. "And then I immediately went and told him that was *exactly* what I was going to do."

"The Baron accused me of spying for my family. I denied it, of course. And then Gil betrayed me. He told the Baron to look behind the light fixture in my room. He knew that I had a cache of notes there. He had helped me put it there. He'd even helped me install the secret compartment. The Baron found everything and I was shipped home the next day."

Von Zinzer looked puzzled. "Wait—so you really were spying?"

Tarvek snorted. "Of course I was spying. All of us were spying! In retrospect, it's obvious that we were being fed tailored information. Things that the Baron wanted our families to know."

Tarvek smiled. "We all thought we were so clever because no one ever got caught. He just didn't *want* us to get caught.

"But I *did* get caught, and everybody knew it. So I was made the Object Lesson. I was the only one who ever got sent back home." Tarvek closed his eyes. "It was so unfair."

"But…" von Zinzer really looked confused now. "But I thought all those kids on the Castle were there as hostages—to keep their families in line. Weren't you glad to go home?"

Tarvek shrugged. "Leaving aside the fact that the only way to keep *my* family in line would be to bury them in a row, Castle Wulfenbach was the place to be. The Baron was collecting and educating us as the future rulers of Europa. We had access to teachers, diplomats, scientists, and adventurers from all over the Empire—all over the *World*. It was the center of the universe. To get sent away from all that—not to mention back to Sturmhalten and my father's obsessive work—was the worst punishment ever.

"To me, it made no sense. It was too harsh. I thought the Baron had to be hiding something. Eventually, trying to find out *what* became a sort of hobby. And years later, I found it. I discovered why the Baron had overreacted.

"My research revealed that 'Gilgamesh Holzfäller' was the son of Petrus Teufel, Leader of the Black Mist Raiders."

Von Zinzer and Violetta gasped. Tarvek smiled. "See? Of *course* his family was kept secret. Every power in Europa would have cause to kill him. Only the Other has caused more fear, death, and devastation. Teufel was a Spark so strong that even Wulfenbach had trouble taking him down.[82]

"No wonder Gil was brilliant. No wonder Klaus wanted him under his eye. The discovery was too much—it turned me sick just to think of it. I shut it all away and tried to forget the whole thing.

Tarvek paused, and took a deep breath. "Eventually I managed to convince my father to let me go to Paris. I felt like I was back in the center of the world. I found freedom! Culture! New Ideas!

"—And Gilgamesh Holzfäller; a debauched, amoral wretch who spent most of his time in the local nightclubs and bordellos. Nature had obviously triumphed over nurture.

"Well, our friendship was long over, so—at first—I was determined to ignore him and get on with my life. I had my *own* work to attend to.

"But Gil had a way of showing up where he was least wanted—and it quickly became obvious to me that he was involved in something nefarious. I was never able to discover exactly what but, because of him, I wound up dealing with an endless stream of monsters, pirates, and what seemed like every half-baked Spark who wandered through Paris, never with good results. By the time I was called back home, I wasn't terribly sorry to go. Whatever Gil was up to, someone else could sort it out."

Tarvek stared into the past for a moment. "It's so obvious now. He's the Baron's son. Of course that's what he was hiding! And all that about Petrus Teufel—I see now that the Baron had merely concocted yet another layer of false identity to hide his son." He smiled ruefully. "I wonder how many more I would have discovered if I had kept digging? Probably scoundrels all the way down…"

He snorted and shook himself. "Well, fine. It serves me right. I'll just have to be less trusting from now on!"

---

[82]   Empire records show that the battle against the Black Mist Raiders, which military historians have called "The most dangerous game of chess in history," took over three years and led to the death of almost a hundred of the Empire's Intelligence officers. The scene of their final battle, the shadow-town secretly built by Klaus to lure Teufel in for their final battle, East Zagreb, remains uninhabitable to this day.

"Tarvek! Hold still and let me put this on your head! I have a great idea I want to try!" Agatha had bustled up with an armload of instruments, topped by a pair of bulky metal skullcaps connected by wires and hoses.

Agatha settled Tarvek's cap in place, and turned to von Zinzer. "Okay, get them both up!" she called.

Von Zinzer began to snap open his restraints. "Uh…they're not going to go all monster-y, are they?" he asked.

Agatha considered this. "Well, that's still within the realm of possibility, of course… But probably not."

Tarvek relaxed slightly.

Agatha frowned. "Not yet, anyway."

Tarvek sat up and tried to look at the device strapped to his head. She was clamping one of its cables to an exposed terminal on the larger apparatus. "Agatha, what exactly is this thing going to—"

"Here goes!" she called, as she flipped a small switch.

A wave of nausea hit him, and he toppled into Agatha's arms. "Uergh. I feel terrible. Again. What is this?" he asked her.

"It worked!" She sounded delighted.

"Oh dear." Tarvek tried to stand, then leaned heavily on Agatha. "Violetta must be right. You do hate me. I'm crushed. Eurgh…"

Agatha tucked herself under his arm and lifted him to his feet. "Idiot." She smiled at him.

"Hey! Hey! Sturmvoraus! Hands off, you!" Gil was getting up off his slab, the other skullcap strapped to his head. His skin matched Tarvek's, which was currently a delicate shade of lemon. Suddenly, he clutched at the helmet and swayed as if he had been struck. Then his face cleared. "I…I feel better." He blinked, and swayed sideways. "In a horrible, slowly dying as my life energy is sucked out through my pores kind of way." Gil wobbled. "I think I'm going to fall down, now."

He toppled, and was caught by Tarvek, who had been falling the other way. They staggered around until they got their arms around each other's shoulders for support. Then Gil noticed whom he was leaning on.

"You!" Gil snarled. "I'm going to kill you!" He winced. "Ugh. Later. When I can…when I can stand."

"Oh, yeah?" Tarvek waved a finger under Gil's nose. "Listen, you, you've got a lot of explaining to do, you…" he wobbled drunkenly. "Erk. Yeah. Later." He agreed. "When you can stand."

"Yeah. 'Cause I sure can't stand you now." Gil returned. They broke into identical pathetic giggles.

Violetta was checking the readings on a set of dials. "Well, they're both back in the safe levels."

Agatha watched as their skin, in perfect unison, changed to a light, robin's-egg blue. She nodded in satisfaction. "They've integrated even better than I'd dared to hope."

She held out two old-fashioned chest-mounted system monitors. She had clearly modified them. They sported extra dials, lights, and wires. Like the skullcaps, they were connected.

"Put these on," Agatha ordered. She then proceeded to do it for them. They watched curiously as she pulled straps that set the little devices snugly against their chests.

They kept their arms around each other's shoulders, partially so they wouldn't fall down again and partially because the cables that connected the little machines didn't allow them to get very far from each other.

"Okay, pay attention," she said as she finished the last few connections and finally removed the skullcaps from their heads. "With these things, I was able to stabilize the *Si Vales*. But it won't last.

"If we don't complete the procedure, you're both…um…well." She paused. "Anyway, we *have* to see this through.

"But there's a big problem. This place functions by means of some kind of huge power source. It's way down deep underground in the cellars.

"The Castle says it isn't sure exactly what's wrong, but the central core is no longer generating power.

"Apparently, this place has been running on stored energy since the Other's attack, and, after all this time, and with the extra energy we've been using since we came in, it's running low.

"That's enough to maintain sentience and minor systems, but something like this—" Agatha patted the lightning generator. "This needs a lot more than the system can supply all at once."

She tapped a fingernail against the device strapped to Gil's chest. "These units will keep your systems linked and the *Si Vales* connection intact while we make our way down there.

"We may be able to fix the generator, or at least tap directly into one of the storage devices."

Tarvek looked like he was in the midst of a terrible dream. "Um— that could kill us."

Gil gave him a disgusted look. "Really? Deader than a *Si Vales Valeo* decay? Or deader than Hogfarb's Immolation?"

Tarvek's expression did not change. "I like fixing generators," he told them.

"Good," said Agatha. "Now I'm going to calibrate the stimulators. This is kind of delicate." She fiddled with a handheld meter and stared at its dials. "Try to act lively, but not *too* lively, okay?"

"Lively?" Tarvek asked Gil in a weak voice. "I'm amazed we're standing."

"No kidding." Gil poked him. "Just, I don't know, flap your hands or something."

"You first."

"Nuh-uh. You first."

Violetta walked up and shoved a bundle at Tarvek. "All right, you buffoon—I dug around in the back room and found you some old clothes, so get dressed!

"She may be too busy saving your worthless life to notice, but you're not going to walk around in front of *my* lady without *pants!*"

Gil and Tarvek stopped arguing and looked down in horror.

"Oh, now, that's *way* too lively." Agatha told them, frowning at the meter she held. All that shouting was making the readings jump all over the dials.

Finally, Agatha was satisfied that the stimulators were working properly. Gil and Tarvek sat side-by-side as she bustled about, collecting tools and discussing with the Castle the best route through its basements.

They sipped at scrounged beakers full of what von Zinzer called "Best Not Ask."

Tarvek shook his head. "The Castle's power source! Amazing! Our spies never could find it."

"So Tiktoffen wasn't just holding out on us," Gil said. "From what I heard earlier, I thought maybe—"

Tarvek was surprised. "Wait—Hristo Tiktoffen? But he was *our* inside man."

"Oh really?" Gil thought about this. "I see. That explains a few things. But didn't you wonder if…er…if someone else had spies here?"

Tarvek took another sip. "Sure. We knew about all kinds of spies. According to Tiktoffen, there were agents and observers from all sorts of organizations, but he could never identify the Baron's insider. Fancy that."

Gil took a sip. "So he wasn't telling your side everything either?"

The Castle began to chuckle. It sounded as though a third person was sitting with them.

"Ah, the light dawns!" the Castle mocked.

Tarvek made a wry face. "Huh. It sounds like he's on nobody's side except his own."

The Castle practically crowed: "Actually, the professor is on *my* side! Heh, heh, heh."

Tarvek frowned. "Your side? You have a side?"

"Wait—" Gil said. "I can see this. Tiktoffen's university dissertation was on 'The Autonomy of Architecture.'"[83]

"That was *him*?" Tarvek rolled his eyes. "Sweet Science, he must

---

[83] In *the Autonomy of Architecture* (Rupert-Karls-Universität Heidelberg Publikationen), Hristo Tiktoffen laid out reasons why some buildings should remain pristine, as designed by their architects. Many great buildings, designed by geniuses, are subsequently remodeled, for a plethora of bad reasons, to their detriment. Tiktoffen dared to dream of buildings equipped with defenses, much like the immune systems of living bodies, except instead of antigens, these would eliminate poor aesthetic choices. There are those who think this idea insane. These are people who have never walked through a Renaissance palace infested with shag rugs.

love this place."

"And what is not to love?" the Castle said smugly.

Gil and Tarvek remained silent, sipping their drinks. Finally, Gil spoke. "So you're involved in this whole 'Storm King' farce, are you?"

Tarvek looked guilty. "Well, yes, a bit. Did Agatha—"

"No. Your tame Heterodyne girl told me all about it…and *she* was a bit of a surprise, let me tell you."

Tarvek clutched his forehead and groaned. "She is not *my* tame Heterodyne girl. This whole debacle was not my plan. *Mine was much better.*

"And even though a real Heterodyne girl appeared, they panicked and rushed into it anyway! I swear, those fools couldn't topple the corrupt government of a sandcastle."

Gil shrugged. "Well, what with Agatha's performance in Sturmhalten, I can see how they thought it was now or never."

"So this girl's in the Castle, is she? What's she like? Will she be any danger to Agatha?"

Gil stared at him. "Wait—you don't know?"

"Well, no. I've never met her. I *said* this wasn't my plan."

"Um, well, let's just say I don't think much of this Storm King guy's taste."

Tarvek was stung. "Oh, really? That's encouraging, considering the kind of girls you preferred in Paris."

Gil raised his eyebrows. "True. *They* didn't like to play dress-up much at all."

"That's because they were *hardly ever dressed!*" Tarvek sniped.

"Jealous?" Gil answered.

Agatha interrupted them. "It's time to go. We'd better not leave Professor Tiktoffen and Pinkie here, they'll have to come with us. Where are they?"

Tarvek was surprised. "They're *here* here? Both of them?"

"Yeah. I knocked them out with some Ichor of Somnia." Gil selected a small jar from a shelf and tossed it to von Zinzer. "Here. Wave this under their noses. It'll wake them up fast."

Von Zinzer eyed the jar suspiciously. "What is it?"

"Vitrium of Mustard. It's harmless enough, just don't try sniffing it yourself, it's really pungent."

He was too late. Von Zinzer had opened the jar and taken a sniff. He shrieked and clapped the lid back on, his eyes watering furiously. Violetta followed him out the door and just managed to keep him from walking himself into a wall. Together, they went to fetch the prisoners.

When they had gone, the Castle made a strange sound. "My lady! There is something moving within my walls. It...it appears to be heading this way, and it seem to be...quite large."

Agatha looked at the door they had come in. "Seems large? You can't tell?"

"No. It is...amorphous, I think. I cannot halt, destroy, or contain it...and...and...*it tickles!*"

"How close is it?"

The wall next to them cracked and a portrait fell to the ground.

"Very close!"

With a rumble, the wall collapsed into fragments, revealing a dark space. Within, something moved. It stepped out into the light. One large, central eye blinked.

"Oh!" Agatha looked down with astonishment. "It's one of my little clanks."

Gil and Tarvek bent to examine it. Gil grinned. "Yes! It's the one our people found at Sturmhalten. I activated it earlier and it actually came to help you, just like I told it to! It's actually a very smart little—OW!" Gill yelped as the diminutive clank lashed out and punched him in the nose.

Tarvek chortled. "You're right! It is really smart! So—this is one of the ones she built in Sturmhalten, eh? I helped with some of those, you know—YEEE!"

The clank had found a mallet and brought it down hard on Tarvek's toes.

"I see it remembers you, too," Gil said with a smirk.

"That's enough of that," Agatha told it sternly. "Stop picking on my—er—my experimental subjects."

The small clank managed to look contrite.

There was a sound behind them. One of the pocket-watch clanks already in the room had wandered over. It had evidently just dropped a wrench and was now staring fixedly at the newcomer, which was staring back.

"Er, my lady?" the Castle asked nervously. "Just how many of those have you built?"

"Oh," Gil said with interest, "that must be another primary. It looks a lot like the other one, doesn't it?"

Suddenly both clanks began to chime angrily. From the lab behind them and out of the hole in the wall, swarms of small clanks poured into the hall. They paused, each group assessing the other, and then flowed towards each other, apparently eager for battle.

Agatha brought her foot down hard between the two tiny generals, the sole of her boot ringing against the stone. She flung out her hands. "STOP!" she boomed. "I am your creator and I command you to stop!"

For a moment, the two primary clanks stared upward. Then, in unison, they brought their heavy tools down upon her foot. Agatha shrieked and began hopping about, swearing like a professor with tenure. The two primary clanks ignored her and leapt at each other, doing their best to disassemble one another.

Tarvek watched critically. "Seriously. Does that ever work?"

Gil shook his head. "No. She *is* ahead of the game, in that she didn't try it on a giant wolverine/snake thing with poisoned tusks."

Tarvek nodded. "Oooh, yeah. I heard about that."

"You're lucky. *I* got it on my shoes," said Gil.

Tarvek nudged Gil. "Hey. Look at that. The other ones obeyed her."

It was true. The remaining clank armies had frozen in place and seemed content to watch the glorious single combat of their leaders.

Gil stroked his chin. "Another difference between the first and second generation."

Tarvek looked at him inquiringly.

Gil continued. "You don't think Agatha built *all* those, do you? I watched her working back on Castle Wulfenbach. She builds some of them herself, like those two there. Then *they* go and build more, and so on."

Tarvek was impressed. "Oh. She didn't tell me that, but it explains a lot. When I was working with her in Sturmhalten, I was kind of distracted…"

"Yeah. I'll bet." Gil scowled. "Anyway, the secondaries build tertiaries and so on, but subsequent generations get simpler and more crude. It's like the later ones just don't have…"

Tarvek stared at Gil wide-eyed. "The Spark," he said. "She's built a machine with the *Spark?*"

Gil shook his head. "No, it can't be! Is that even *possible?* In some ways they're very simple devices…"

Tarvek massaged his forehead. "But they can plan and carry out such complex functions! I've seen them do it!"

"I don't know…" Gil said, "…if they acted like Sparks in other ways…"

With a clang of triumph, one of the pocket-watch clanks smacked the other across the floor. When it had skidded to a stop, the second clank pantomimed just how it would rain lightning down upon its tormentor. The first clearly indicated how its opponent's springs were wound too tight. Their chimes shrieked as they leapt towards each other in diminutive fury. Gil and Tarvek glanced at each other and slowly nodded.

Finally Tarvek couldn't stand it any more. He grabbed both of the little clanks and held them up. "All right," he said sternly. "Enough of this! You two stop this right now. You're supposed to be helping—"

Simultaneously, the little clanks pinched Tarvek's thumbs. Hard. He gave a whoop of pain and proceeded to bang the two errant machines together several times.

Their eyes spun wildly for a moment, and then both clanks focused fearfully on Tarvek.

"I'm not enjoying this," he lied, "but I can do it all day. Do you understand?"

The two devices looked contrite and clicked at him submissively. Gil chuckled.

Tarvek turned angrily. "What's so funny?"

"That's a really good impersonation of my father."

Tarvek glared at Gil and then again addressed the two machines in his hands in a deeper, mock-serious voice. "And now I will establish an illegitimate government based on brute force, which will eventually leave you under the heel of my debauched libertine of a son, so be sure to hide all of your booze and women!"

This was the first time the little clanks had been aware that they had either booze or women. They stared back with interest.

"Hey, now, wait a minute—" Gil scowled.

Violetta burst into the room, followed by von Zinzer. "They're gone!" she announced.

Von Zinzer looked worried. "Wulfenbach and I locked them up, but it looks like they've escaped."

Tarvek looked sideways at Gil. "Wait. She was here and you left her unguarded?"

Gil was defensive. "I knocked her out with Ichor of Somnia!"

"And then left her unguarded."

"And I locked her in an iron cage!"

"Unguarded!"

Gil threw his hands up. "Yes! We had work to do! On *you!*"

Agatha was shocked. "Gil? You put her in a *cage?* But I thought you…um…but she's completely useless!" She looked thoughtful. "At least, she *seemed* useless…"

Tarvek clutched the sides of his head. "I can't believe this!" He stared at Gil. "A powerful secret organization, one capable of hiding an army from the Baron, has been planning a slow-motion coup for years—and you completely underestimate the girl they groomed to be the *Heterodyne?* Practically the linchpin of the *whole thing?*"

"You obviously haven't met her," Agatha said.

"Oh, yes he *has!*" Gil said. "Your fake Heterodyne was Zola la Sirène Dorée!"

Tarvek snorted. "What? No, that was that idiot back in Paris—"

The look on Gil's face stopped him dead. His jaw dropped.

"She is good," he whispered. "Agatha, she's going to be real trouble."

They decamped quickly after that. Tarvek was still protesting. "I'm telling you, we've got to kill her as soon as possible." He glanced over at Gil. "You'll be sorry if we don't."

Gil and Tarvek, still wobbly on their feet, had gone back to leaning on one another. Each had his arm across the other's shoulders, keeping the tubes and wires that connected them safe.

Agatha strode on ahead. "No. If she's really that dangerous, I want you two fixed up as soon as possible."

"You can't seriously think Zola is any kind of threat?" Gil insisted.

"In Paris, I would have said, 'Only if you let her sing.' But if she's the Order's 'Heterodyne Princess', then there's a lot more to her than she ever let on."

"Good point," Gil said. "But still, Zola…I just can't see it…" A thought struck him. "They'll have a Storm King, too, I imagine. I *can't wait* to meet *him*."

Tarvek looked carefully over at Gil's face for a long moment. Gil didn't *seem* to be toying with him…

Finally, Tarvek said: "Hmf. Watch out. He's probably your manservant."

"Nah. He's a spy for the British. You know him—Ardsley Wooster."

"Really?" Tarvek was interested. "I thought the British spy was Ludmilla—you know—that grad student from the Pie and Phlogiston club."

"No, no. She was the last keeper of the Lost Key of the Red Pyramid of Bishara," Gil said.

"Red Pyramid—" Tarvek thought a moment. "Oh, right! I read about that in the Journal of the Société Archéologique de L'Étrange! Some adventurer won the key by defeating Bishara's champion."

"Yeah!" Gil grinned. "Remember Thegon Ba'Kont? Big guy? Wrestling team?"

"What? He was the adventurer? Really?"

"Of course not! He was their champion! He and Ludmilla got married last month."

"Oh. Yeah." Tarvek said, "I sent them a toast rack."

"We're there!" called Agatha.

Professor Mezzasalma looked up in pleased surprise as Agatha appeared in the doorway. "Lady Heterodyne! You're still alive!"

"Indeed I am. How are things here? Has Professor Tiktoffen shown up? We lost track of him."

Diaz shook his head. "I'm afraid not, Señorita, but that one? The Castle will watch over him."

Mittlemind nodded. "And my minion has returned from the cistern with the stolen parts for the 'Lion.'"

Fraulein Snaug sat huddled on the floor clutching a large oilskin bag.

"I kept her safe, *and* gave her a tour!" the Castle reassured Agatha.

Agatha was not reassured. "Are you all right?" she asked Snaug.

Snaug stared back at Agatha. "Spiky trapdoors," she whispered. "Torture chambers…man-eating bats…impertinent mechanical squid…" She shuddered.

Mittlemind tousled her hair affectionately. "Oh, there's some minor psychological damage," he said cheerfully. "But I always wipe her memory afresh for her birthday!"

Snaug began slowly rocking back and forth. "Happy birthday to meeee…" she crooned softly.

Agatha nodded. "Right." She strode over to the large hole she had burned into the floor and looked down into the darkness. "I have to get to the bottom of this hole."

Professor Mittlemind clapped his hands together and rubbed them as he joined her. "Nothing simpler!"

"—And survive."

Mittlemind paused. "Ah. Tricky."

The other prisoners peered down into the depths. Diaz raised a finger to the ceiling. "I will strap a series of shaped charges to your chest, and then you will detonate them just before you land!"

Professor Mezzasalma snorted in derision. "Bah! I have a secret procedure of my own devising that will—probably—give you many properties of the noble spider! You can simply *leap* to the bottom!"

"No, no, my lady," Mittlemind interrupted. "My hydrophilic attractor could—theoretically—be modified to fill the Castle with water! Assuming your drains have been properly maintained, it will gracefully lower you to the bottom as it subsides!"

The three scientists reared back and regarded one other with rising scorn. Von Zinzer raised a hand and indicated a large industrial winch. "This thing looks like it has enough cable, and it should be strong enough...we could knock together a platform and lower everybody down with some tools and everything. Nice and safe."

Every Spark in the room glared at him. Then Agatha looked sheepish and cleared her throat. Tarvek and Gil shook themselves. Diaz, Mittlemind and Mezzasalma continued to glower at him.

Von Zinzer wilted under the Sparks' gaze. "And...and then at the bottom," he mumbled, "it could unfold into a...a giant caterpillar or something..."

"No, no," Mittlemind snarled. "You've already taken all the joy out of it."

Agatha rifled all the toolboxes in the room—searching for anything that looked like it might come in handy later. She asked the Castle if it had been able to find Zola.

"No, my Lady. She escaped while I was checking the power, and she is most likely keeping to my dead zones."

"Well, pay attention, this time," she told it.

Von Zinzer checked the cable, hooked it up and, soon enough, declared the platform finished.

Violetta threw a switch, and the engine on the winch chugged to life. Von Zinzer climbed aboard the platform and gently moved a sliding switch. With a gentle jerk, the platform rose into the air. Von Zinzer nodded and moved the switch the other way. Nothing happened. He frowned, reset it, and tried again. This time the platform dropped and bounced lightly against the ground. He raised it again and gave Agatha a thumbs-up. "I think we're good to go."

"No, no, *no!* Absolutely not!" Mezzasalma declared. "The controls obviously need work!"

"The gearage looks loose to me!" Mittlemind said.

"I want all the weight-bearing areas double reinforced!" Diaz chimed in.

Agatha blew a lock of hair out her eyes. "We don't have a lot of time—"

They weren't listening.

"I need to install an entirely new backup system!"

"Maybe triple! Even quadruple!"

"The linkages—they should be rebuilt!"

Von Zinzer touched Agatha's arm. "Leave this to me." He turned to the three scientists. "I'm going, you're staying here."

They stared at him.

"Oh, well then," Mezzasalma shrugged.

"It should be fine," Mittlemind admitted.

"Let us get started!" Diaz said.

Violetta and Snaug watched with interest. As they helped load the platform, Snaug leaned in. "So. Your boyfriend is really good with dealing with Sparks. Has he served the Lady Heterodyne long?"

Violetta shrugged. "I don't know." For some reason, her face was suddenly bright red. "Um…and he's not my boyfriend."

Snaug regarded her in surprise. "Oh, reeeeally…" She turned her gaze back at von Zinzer and gnawed gently at her lower lip. She glanced back at Violetta and smiled. "I'm so glad we had this little talk."

Violetta sat down hard on a box, her eyes slightly crossed.

Agatha handed a box of tools up to von Zinzer. "We'll make a preliminary trip to make sure it's safe, then we can bring everyone down."

Von Zinzer nodded. "Who else is going?" he sighed deeply. "Besides me, of course."

Gil and Tarvek stepped up. "*We're* coming."

Agatha spun to face them. "*You?* Don't be absurd! You're—" She paused. Aside from their exotic, ever-changing pigmentation, they were both practically glowing with good health.

Agatha's eye's narrowed. "You're looking pretty good, actually."

Tarvek grinned. "Aren't we, though?"

"...*Suspiciously* good." She bent to examine the device strapped to Tarvek's chest. Her eye's widened. "You—what have you done?" She examined Gil's device. "These settings! You've rerouted the entire—" She stared at them, appalled. "You've cut your time in half! At least!"

Gil and Tarvek tightened their jaws. "Yes!"

"You need us functioning!"

"We're not going to stay up here—"

"While you go into possible danger—"

"And do all the work!"

"Even if you can't cure us—"

"If we all work together—"

"A few hours should be all we need—"

"To get the Castle repaired enough to keep you safe!"

This had all been delivered by Gil, then by Tarvek, back-and-forth at an escalating pace that seemed spoken by one person with two throats. With a jolt Agatha realized that they were now speaking in perfect unison.

"I thought you were dead! After losing you like that once, I'm going to make sure that you're safe even if it's the last thing I do!"

They fixed her with identical, challenging stares.

Agatha threw her arms around both their necks and hugged them to her fiercely. "I am going to save you both," she whispered. They stood together for several heartbeats, and then she tightened her grip.

"And then I am going to kill you!" she shouted.

When they climbed onto the platform, Agatha looked over at the other Sparks. "Actually, it would be helpful if one of you came along."

Diaz shrugged dramatically. "¡Que mala suerte! I have just remembered that I must see to my knitting! If it escapes, I shall have a devil of a time finding it again. Also, my narcolepsy, it is suddenly returning!" He dropped to the ground.

Professor Mittlemind regretfully pulled forth a small calendar. "Today is the Feast of Saint Bunge: My religion forbids excessive vertical travel today, and I really should polish the spikes in the pit trap!"

Mezzasalma watched their antics, his lip curling. "The two of you disgust me." With a clatter of mechanical legs, he stepped aboard.

Agatha regarded him with respect as von Zinzer threw some levers and swung the platform out over the shaft. "Professor Mezzasalma, you actually want to come?"

Mezzasalma snorted. "Of course not, but they took all of the good excuses, and crying is undignified."

Von Zinzer rolled his eyes. "Brace yourselves! Here we go!"

With a shudder, the platform began sinking down the shaft. To von Zinzer's satisfaction, the platform descended slowly but smoothly, and the bright disk of light above them shrank and faded. Agatha flipped a switch and a jury-rigged set of lamps crackled into brightness, allowing them to examine the interiors of the rooms they were lowered through.

"So, I hate to spoil the party," von Zinzer began, "but have any of you Sparks actually thought about what we're going to find down there?

"I mean, what kind of power source runs a place like this?"

Tarvek spoke up. "Tiktoffen said he never discovered it." He peeked over the edge, down into the darkness. "I'm now tempted to believe that it was something he didn't actually know."

"I asked my father about it once," said Gil. "He told me that even Barry Heterodyne didn't know. I found that a bit hard to believe—"

"Master Barry did not lie." The Castle's voice was subdued. "By order of my creator, Faustus Heterodyne, my power source is one of the most closely guarded of family secrets."

"But," Agatha frowned, "Uncle Barry was family."

"Technically, that is correct. However while he was a Heterodyne, he was never *the* Heterodyne. That was your father, the eldest brother. As it happened, he did not know either. Both Master William and Master Barry spent very little time within my halls. They were poisoned against me by their mother.[84] As a result, we had...philosophical differences."

"It never became necessary for the last Heterodyne—your father— to know all of my secrets and thus he never bothered to learn them."

The Castle paused. "It was a shame that he never fully embraced the family legacy. There was a refreshing *simplicity* to him. If he had been born two hundred years ago, I do not think that even the Storm King would have been able to stop him."

"Philosophical differences...yes, I can see that...Well, it's necessary now," Agatha sighed.

"Under the circumstances, I must concur. I'll of course have to kill most of your companions, to limit the knowledge of my workings and their location."

Everyone on the platform shot Agatha a worried look.

"Don't you dare," she said sternly.

"Well, of course, we must preserve your consorts. For the good of the line, you know. And for spare parts..." The Castle gave another chilling laugh.

Mezzasalma glanced at Gil and Tarvek and turned to Agatha. "I...I think the two eyes you have are...are beautifully spider-like?" he said weakly.

---

[84]   The Lady Teodora Vodenicharova. She was married to the Heterodyne Boys' father, Saturn Heterodyne, as part of a deal to save her kingdom from being exterminated, which was typical Heterodyne courting behavior. An astonishingly strong-willed and capable woman, she managed to defy Saturn Heterodyne on an almost daily basis. Not only was she allowed to live, but by all accounts, he was still in love with her to the end. She refused to live within the Castle, and insisted on raising her sons outside of its day-to-day influence as well. She waged a never-ending campaign to prevent Bill and Barry from being molded to their father's ways, with astonishing success. When it became obvious that she had succeeded, Saturn swore to kill them both and try anew. Teodora killed him and was herself subsequently killed by the Castle, but died knowing that her sons were safe. Volumes have been written about her charisma, strength of will, nobility of spirit, and simple courage. Sadly, they are written by shoddy pretenders to true academia and are rife with inadequate research, unattributed sources, faulty indexing, and poor spelling, and thus are not included in these classes. Less than twelve years after her death, five of the seven recognized Popes concurred, and she has been declared a Martyr, canonized as Saint Teodora of Transylvania, Patron Saint of Those Who Fall Afoul of Sparks.

Agatha patted him gently on the arm. "Stop talking now."

She addressed the Castle. "I realize that you're just amusing yourself at our expense, but even so, I want to make this very clear. These people are under my protection and you will honor that. Do you understand?"

The Castle grumbled with a sound like gears grinding together. "Oh, very well, then," it said sullenly.

"Very well then—*what?*"

"Very well then. *Mistress.*"

Agatha nodded in satisfaction. "Don't forget that."

"Hey!" Von Zinzer was peering over the edge of the platform. "We're coming up on something big! What is that stuff?"

"Indeed," the Castle informed them. "You are approaching the Great Movement Chamber, wherein is hidden the source of the river Dyne. This is where your ancestors learned how to harness its power."

The platform cleared the ceiling and descended into a vast cavern. Everyone gasped in astonishment.

Higher than a cathedral, the cavern was filled with massive gears and ancient machinery. The nearest wall was a towering relief of worked stone. Its design was only dimly visible near the bottom, which was lit by a flickering pool of clear blue light. It was a semi-enclosed spring, from which a glowing river of water burst forth. It flowed through an elaborate series of ancient iron gates and rushed down a central channel and off into the vastness of the cave. It flowed past the paddles of a titanic waterwheel that lay off-kilter and motionless, its axle splintered. The great pillar of rock that had caused the break still lay amongst the wreckage.

"That's not a new break," Gil muttered as they all stepped off of the platform. "I'll bet that big piece broke off the ceiling and smashed it when the Other attacked."

When everyone else had left the platform, von Zinzer threw a switch. He leapt off the platform as it slowly began to rise back to the top of the shaft. "Hope that was a good idea," he muttered.

The others were still mesmerized by the scene before them. "You— All of this is powered by *water?*" Agatha asked the Castle.

"The Dyne is more than just water." Deep as they were, the Castle's voice was still with them. It echoed through the deep chambers and sent shivers through the listeners. "A bit of family history, my lady. When your ancestor first came to this place, there was only a small spring, sacred to the local Battle Goddess."

Tarvek interrupted. "When was this?"

"How should I know?" the Castle replied. "It was long before I was built, and I measure time differently than you."[85]

It continued. "The spring's guardians claimed that immersion in its waters brought insanity and death—except on those rare occasions when it pleased the Goddess to grant miraculous healing instead. To actually drink from it was *unthinkable*.

"But your ancestor never had much use for other people's rules. He drank from the spring. He should have died screaming. Instead, it granted him unearthly strength and stamina. He became greatly feared as the chosen consort of the Goddess and built his fortress upon this spot.

"When Vlad the Blasphemous first brewed the Jägerdraught, he used water from the spring as a key ingredient.

"Egregious Heterodyne decided that the spring was too small and set out to increase its flow. That was when the river Dyne came to be. It was also when the first Castle was destroyed."

"The years when the Dyne flowed unchecked placed the family's mark on this area for all time." The Castle paused for a private chuckle, then continued. "It was Faustus Heterodyne who learned to spin a powerful energy from the waters. He was able to use this energy to create marvels undreamed of by earlier Heterodynes. His crowning achievement was, of course, myself.

"I am afraid I require everything that can be wrung from the spring. Beyond this chamber, the waters of the Dyne no longer produce any interesting effects at all. Now the water can be drunk and safely harnessed by practically *anybody*. Ah, well, but that is outside. Here at the source, I would advise you to stay clear."

---

[85] This is the sort of thing that causes Heterodyne scholars to drink heavily whenever nit-picky scientific journals insist on things like "dates" and "authentication".

Von Zinzer leaned on an ornate, trilobite-decked rail and watched the water as it flowed through the channel. "So—drink the water here and you become a Jäger?"

"Oh, dear me, no," the Castle laughed. "Drink the water here and you *die!*" It laughed again. "Of course, drink the Jägerdraught and you'll most likely die as well. But, even if you don't, the water is only the start of the process. You should ask my lady to try it on you, once she's got the time."

Von Zinzer stared at the water below. "No, thanks."

The Castle broke into another nasty laugh.

Professor Mezzasalma stood near a row of ancient vacuum tubes that stretched off into the darkness. "And all of this bric-a-brac is necessary to extract the power from the waters?"

"Of course not. The systems in the Great Movement Chamber serve many functions. There are thousands of systems and devices whose motive force originates here. Or did, rather, when everything was functioning…why, the bird baths alone require several dedicated steam turbines. All those little brushes, you know."

Gil and Tarvek had found a good spot and were, together, slowly pivoting in place as they looked around. When they returned to their starting place, the two men glanced at each other and scowled.

"I don't even know where to start," Tarvek confessed.

"This can't be all of it," Gil said. He waved towards the broken paddlewheel. "This thing has been broken for quite awhile, yet the Castle still has power."

"There's obviously some sort of voltaic pile, but to run a place like this…"

Gil grinned. "Oh yeah, I can't wait to see it." They walked back to Agatha. She had her back to them, staring at the hole in the floor and dabbing her cheeks with a handkerchief. "It's your Castle, Agatha. Where should we go next?"

"Hm?" She turned towards them, blinking. Gil and Tarvek gasped. Agatha's skin was a bright emerald green. "Sorry," she said. "I'm feeling a bit—" She saw their stares and glanced at her hand. "Ooh. That's bad."

Tarvek turned to Gil. "No! She wasn't hooked up to us! How is this even possible?"

Gil crossed his arms. The purple of his skin deepened. "I knew it. You did kiss him."

Tarvek looked surprised. "She—what? I don't remember *that!*"

Agatha's blush turned her skin slate-grey. "What would that have to do with anything?" she asked hotly.

Gil indicated his now magenta skin. "I'm just replicating symptoms because of the *Si Vales Valeo* process." He pointed at Tarvek. "But he's actually infectious! You put your mouth on his dirty, diseased skin!"

Tarvek glared at Gil. "I would have used better words than that." He turned to scold Agatha. "But he's right. You've shown a shocking disregard for basic medical safety."

Gil pointed to Tarvek. "What he said!"

Tarvek continued in a gentler voice. "I can't say I'm not touched, but when in the lab, it can be very dangerous to yield to one's romantic impulses—"

Gil rolled his eyes. "Oh, you're definitely 'touched' all right," he told Tarvek.

"—No matter how difficult it is to resist."

Gil shook his head. "Before we die of this," he said conversationally, "I *am* going to kill you."

"Stop it," Agatha said. "We're not beaten. We can still do this. We'll find a sufficient power source, and finish the *Si Vales Valeo.* I'll just hook myself into the circuit as well."

The two young men stared at her. Tarvek glanced at Gil. "Well… theoretically…"

Gil shook his head. "I don't think anyone has ever made something like that work."

Agatha poked him in the chest. "We'll make it work."

"LOOK OUT BELOW!" The scream was followed by the crash of the lift platform against the lip of the shaft. Fraulein Snaug held onto the controls, even as she was thrown about. Quickly, the others rushed in and grabbed hold of the lift. They dragged it more firmly onto the floor beside the shaft and Snaug shakily got to her feet.

"Here's the equipment! S-sorry about that, Lady Heterodyne," she said breathlessly. "I sort of came in a little fast and..." She looked around and worry filled her face. "Violetta was with me! She was!"

"I'm right here."

They looked up in time to see the Smoke Knight slide down the last meter or so of cable and land delicately upon the roof of the platform.

"I'm fine," she declared airily. "When Snaug lost control, I simply—"

Von Zinzer ignored her. "Are you all right?" he asked Fraulein Snaug, as he half-carried her to a bench. "You should sit. Better yet, lie down while I get you something to drink." He paused. "Not water."

Snaug smiled gamely at him. "How sweet," she whispered.

Violetta stared at them sullenly until Tarvek derailed her thoughts. "Come, come, Violetta, let's get this stuff unloaded."

Violetta swung smoothly down from the top of the platform, bringing her face-to-face with Agatha, who was currently orange.

"What have those pigs done to you?" Violetta screamed. She rounded on Tarvek and Gil. "I can't believe it! I hardly let you out of my sight and you morons violate enough medical protocols to get her infected? I'll kill you both!"

Agatha put a soothing hand on Violetta's arm. "Mistakes were made," she said vaguely, "but please don't kill them. I need them alive, for the moment, and I *am* somewhat fond of them."

"What? Why?" Violetta began a full catalog of Tarvek's faults, Gil's probable equality of malfeasance, and a detailed suggestion about the benefits of taxidermy.

Gil tried to get Agatha's attention, but Tarvek shook his head. He waved Gil to a seat. "Don't bother trying to ask Agatha anything, she'll be busy until Violetta's done ranting." He turned towards Gil with a serious look on his face. "Just as well, actually. Listen, about these devices she built..." he patted the unit strapped to his chest.

Gil gave Tarvek a wicked grin. "Well, we could get started right now if you'll let me take *yours* apart to see how it works!"

Tarvek nodded. "Good. I'm glad we're on the same page."

Gil looked startled. "What? Hey, no, I was just—"

Tarvek was serious. "You're hooked up to me so you'll keep me alive. Now you're expected to manage for both Agatha and me? Ridiculous. The stochastic variables will start degrading the system almost immediately."

Gil looked away. "Yes, of course. But…"

"I really don't see this working," said Tarvek. "If things even *start* to break down, we're going to cut me loose."

"That won't be necessary! If we do this quick enough—"

Tarvek held up a hand, cutting him off. "If we do, that's great, but, if not, no heroics. We save her. Right?"

Gil nodded slowly. "Well…right. Of course."

Agatha came back to them, frowning suspiciously. "Are you two fighting again?"

"No," they said in unison.

Professor Mezzasalma gave a shout and waved excitedly from a dark archway. Everyone else hurried over. He had discovered another cavernous room filled with long orderly rows of glass spheres. Each sphere was almost two meters in diameter and rested on squat little stands made in the shape of rather sullen looking lizards. Their red eyes glowed dimly in the dark. Inside each sphere was a strange column of metal and crystal, rising from a pool of liquid. Each was capped with a dull metal lid, and each lid was hooked into an elaborate swirling net of wires that connected and interconnected in a dizzying tangle that stretched off into the shadows.

Tarvek gave a shout of recognition and dragged Gil to the nearest sphere. "Baghdad Salamanders![86] An entire room full of them!"

He turned to Agatha. "I did a whole thesis on these!" He turned

---

[86]　The Baghdad Salamander is one of most fascinating archeological finds of the last hundred years. Tentatively dated from somewhere between 250 B.C to A.D 500, chemical and metallurgical tests have definitively shown that the device was a functioning battery built over a millennium before anyone else produced anything even remotely similar. While its true purpose is unknown, across the device's base was a contemporary inscription which dared those "of an unbelieving and barbarous nature, who would mock the mental abilities of the device's creator, to kiss the lizard."

back and regarded the room in awe. "But this isn't a corroded, broken ruin in a buried tomb! These are active! Functional!" He stared around the room. "Blue fire," he whispered. "There's got to be over a thousand of them!"

Gil nodded. "At least a thousand." He turned to Agatha. "He's right. These have got to be the power source."

"There's so many of them," Agatha whispered. "No wonder this place could run for so long."

"I'm astonished it's running at all," Tarvek declared. "See the eyes? Those are supposed to be blue. This place is almost done." He turned back to them and rubbed his hands. "The good news is that I'm pretty sure I can recharge them."

Agatha considered this. "I think our best bet would be to find one in good shape—maybe two—and see if we can drain the power from a bunch of the others into it."

Tarvek bit his lip. "That sounds fun, but we are pressed for time."

The Castle interrupted. "There is a maintenance shed nearby. There should be tools and supplies. I believe you should also find a set of blueprints as well as a current flow diagram." There was a different quality to its voice. Agatha suspected that it wasn't quite the same part of the Castle they'd been dealing with earlier.

Gil beamed. "Why, that should help us tremendously! Lead us to it!"

Agatha nodded. "Good. While you're working on that, I'll start working on one of those chest pieces for myself. Then, we've got to start on something to channel the current through us."

"Yeah, we…um…" Gil stopped. "Wait." He said, turning slowly to Agatha.

"Channel the current through 'us'?" Tarvek finished, worried. "You, too? But—"

The Castle rumbled softly. The lights flickered.

Agatha sighed. "Yes. To cure Tarvek, we were going to kill him, clean him out and then revive him. Obviously I'll require the same treatment. That's why we need to find sufficient power. I can hook myself into the system, and we'll zap both of us at one go. It'll be very efficient."

"Hold on!" Gil said, "I know I said this was a good plan, but that was when Sturmvoraus was the one to fry!"

Tarvek raised his voice. He was making small, frantic "stop talking" motions with his hands. "Heavens, yes, Agatha, this is for me, your loving consort! We could never do something like this to you!"

Agatha was annoyed. "What are you—" Too late, the pfennig dropped and she turned her eyes upwards. "Oh."

"I agree!" the Castle howled. "I will not permit this!"

"What do you mean, 'you won't permit it,'" Agatha shouted back. "I'm sick. This procedure can cure me!"

"You cannot die!" The Castle sounded, if possible, more unbalanced than ever.

"I assure you, I most certainly can!"

"I must have a Heterodyne in residence! Until you produce an heir, you are not expendable."

"I don't really see that happening any time soon."

"Why not? You have two fine, strapping—"

Tarvek stepped in. "There is insufficient time for the viable gestation of an heir, as technically, she is already dying."

Agatha stared at him with a sour look on her face. "Yes, obviously that is the only thing stopping me from producing an heir for you in the next five minutes."

Tarvek rolled his eyes.

The Castle was not deterred. "Troublesome, yes. However, with a little effort, you should be able to get your great grand-uncle Zagnut's Corporeal Duplicator built before it is too late. With a little tweaking, you could have a disease-free copy of yourself. Several, if you desire."

Tarvek and Gil looked at each other.

"Intriguing…" Gil murmured.

"How *many* more?" Tarvek asked.

The Castle continued. "The prototype merely tore him in half, but he did leave excellent notes."

"This is crazy," von Zinzer said from the archway. "By your logic, you shouldn't have let any of your Heterodynes out of their bedrooms! Ever!"

Everyone stared at him.

"Oh," the Castle said in surprise. "Yessss…that *was* a mistake. I see that now. Well spotted, minion."

Von Zinzer blinked. "I…" He looked at Agatha.

"Thank you," she said, "for your help."

"I'll just…"

"Shut up?"

"Yes." Von Zinzer shut up.

Agatha shook her head. "Enough of this. I know it's dangerous, but I think it'll work, and it's not as if you can stop me."

"You are incorrect." The section of floor under Agatha's feet sank into the ground. A slab thudded into place over her head. "In any situation where the succession is at stake, I am permitted, even required, to disregard your commands. You are not the first Heterodyne to be more concerned with destruction than with the continuation of the family. But even at low ebb, as I am now, I have more than enough power to keep you from doing anything foolhardy."

Agatha pounded a fist against the stone wall. "But Gil and Tarvek will die!"

"They are potentially valuable, but ultimately replaceable."

"No they are not!" Agatha screamed. "Besides, *I'll* die!"

"If you truly are a Heterodyne," the Castle said smugly, "You'll think of something."

Agatha stared into the darkness and then finally sagged back against the wall. "All right," she said finally. "Fine. You've made your point. I'll come up with another plan." She took a deep breath, "In fact, I believe I have one already."

"Excellent." With that, the floor rose and the stone unfolded around Agatha, revealing the anxious faces of her companions. The Castle continued smugly, "I'm so glad we had this little talk."

"Anything else you want?" Agatha asked it sarcastically.

"Well, one simply can't have too many weathervanes…"

"Okay," Gil looked grim. "We all heard it, so what are we going to do?"

Tarvek nodded. "You said you had a new plan?"

Agatha shrugged. "The Castle isn't giving us a choice. Now I've got an idea I want to work on, while you two—" She leaned in and breathed the words "distract it," before straightening up and continuing in a louder voice, "find us a place to set up!"

Tarvek looked thoughtful.

Gil muttered, "Wait, so you still want us to—"

The blow caught him completely by surprise. "You!" Tarvek roared. Then he paused and thought for a minute. "Um—Do what she says! Don't argue!"

"Hey! What was that for?" Gil yelled.

Tarvek rolled his eyes in exasperation. "I tire of this charade!" he screamed to the air. "The Lady Heterodyne is mine! And I will prove it, by stomping this lout into the dirt!"

Gil gave a slow grin. "Oh. Yeah, I guess we can do that."

"Oh. Oh, my. Can it be Christmas?" the Castle asked in wonder.

"Nah," Tarvek told it. "I'm just going to senselessly pound him."

"Ah!" The Castle thrilled. "Mindless violence! What a good boy!"

"Ho, yeah. Merry Christmas to me." Gil gloated. His eyes were wild and his voice was resonant with the Spark. He crouched and stared at Tarvek. "It is so on."

"Yesss! That's the spirit!" the Castle cheered. "Oh, well done, my lady! They will *both do nicely!*"

A vision of Gil tossing aside Doctor Merlot's clank flashed before Agatha's eyes. "Tarvek! No! You don't want to do this!"

Tarvek grinned. "Agatha! Oh, I really do! Now come! Before you flee to spare your delicate sensibilities, bestow a final favor upon your chosen warrior!" He pulled her backwards against him with one arm. "That's me!" he stage-whispered.

Agatha whispered desperately. "You don't understand! Gil—"

Tarvek pecked her on the cheek and whispered into her ear. "Tell Wulfenbach I won't really hurt him. Not permanently."

Agatha tried to turn in his arms. "No! He—"

Tarvek gallantly spun her into Gil's arms. "Now, bid this churl farewell!" he cried.

Gil held her against him and laughed. "I'm going to turn you inside out, Sturmvarous," he vowed. "It'll be an improvement!"

"No!" Agatha whispered. "He says he won't hurt you!"

Gil looked momentarily impressed. "Wow. I guess he *is* smart!" he growled. "Yessss! If I rip his heart out, it will solve all our problems!"

Agatha stared into Gil's maddened face. "Ah, Gil, please don't kill him."

"Shh. It'll be a great diversion!" Gil whispered.

He tossed Agatha out of the way.

"Gil!" she shouted. "You're the one who said you're supposed to stay calm!"

"I said *relatively* calm! Now stand back! I don't want to get his blood all over you." Gil took hold of the largest cable that connected him to Tarvek, and began to pull it toward him.

Agatha gave up. She turned to Violetta and Fraulein Snaug, who appeared to be settling in comfortably to watch the show. "Snaug, where are those parts you ferried down?"

Snaug was disappointed. "Aw…Now?"

Agatha grit her teeth. "*Right* now!"

Snaug dashed off. Before Agatha followed, she faced the fighters. "Don't forget, you idiots! If you break those cables, I won't *have* to kill you!"

Tarvek ignored her, and assumed a ridiculous boxer's stance. "Ha!" he called out. "Come now, thou villain, and receive the thrashing you so richly deserve!"

Gil grinned at him lazily, and strode toward him, only to land in a crumpled heap on the ground.

"For *shame*, sirrah," Tarvek said with exaggerated horror. "What are you doing? Must you always make a spectacle of yourself?"

Confused, Gil sat up. "Uh…"

Violetta blinked. "What the…"

Gil got to his feet. "I must've…"

"Tripped over your great clumsy feet?" Tarvek executed a mincing little shuffle step as he shadow-boxed. "Tch. At least *try* to face me like a gentleman." He turned away haughtily, "Although why you should be expected to start now, I—"

Gil lunged, and his foot skidded out from under him. He crashed over a toolbox.

Tarvek looked embarrassed and offered Gil a hand up.

"I don't believe it," Violetta breathed.

Von Zinzer had made himself comfortable next to Violetta. He frowned. "Am I missing something?"

Gil batted Tarvek's hand away. He spun to his feet and immediately folded back down, clutching his stomach.

"Ow!" Tarvek bleated, "My elbow! You ran right into it! Oooh! That smarts!"

Gil paused. "*Wait* a minute…"

"All through our training," Violetta said in wonder, "That useless lump just sat around doodling girls and clockwork. But…those moves…" Her voice sharpened in outraged accusation. "He was paying attention after all!"

Gil looked at Tarvek as though he were seeing him for the first time. "You! You're doing this on purpose."

Tarvek gave a final little clownish skip and then settled into watchful stillness. "Aw! You figured it out. Much faster than I thought you would, too."

Gil shook his head in admiration as he climbed to his feet. "Well done. You really had me fooled. I completely underestimated you." He clapped his hands together. "And now, it's your turn."

Tarvek continued to grin. "What? I already got you three times! But I'll cheerfully do it—" As he spoke, his foot snapped upward to where Gil's face had been. But Gil had vanished. Tarvek felt a tap upon his shoulder. "No, no, no," Gil said.

Tarvek whirled in place, his hands and feet scything through empty air.

"It's your turn…" Gil said from near the floor.

Tarvek leapt back.

"…to underestimate…" The sound of Gil's voice came from directly overhead.

Tarvek looked up while dropping into a squat.

"…me!"

And suddenly, there was Gil, also squatting, his grinning face centimeters from Tarvek's own. He tapped Tarvek's forehead with his forefinger. Tarvek went tumbling over backwards.

Gil rose to his feet and smiled down at him. "And that's four. So now that we've got *that* all settled—"

Tarvek reached up and grabbed hold of Gil's arm. "Forget finesse," he growled, his own voice finally rising into the tones of the Spark. "I'll just pound you, after all, like the worm you are!"

Suddenly, Gil was flying through the air. He twisted and his feet smacked into the wall. "That was surprising," he admitted. He then launched himself back and sent Tarvek sprawling. "But then, I shouldn't really be surprised, should I? You always were an underhanded fake."

Tarvek's foot connected with Gil's jaw. He wrapped the cable that connected them around Gil's neck. "Oh, and I suppose wallowing in the gutters of Paris was your idea of authenticity?" he snarled with a nasty grin. "*Sooo Bohemian.*"

Gil spun himself free. His fist barely missed Tarvek's nose. "I had my reasons," he roared.

"Well, sure!" Tarvek had to leap to avoid the leg sweep Gil aimed at him. "*All your lowlife friends were there!*" he roared back.

They collapsed, panting and glaring.

"Snitch," Tarvek huffed.

"Sneak," Gil wheezed back.

They rose to their knees and feebly tried to attack again.

"Libertine!" Tarvek growled weakly.

"Fop!" Gil shot back.

Tarvek's head thudded to the floor. "I…I'd heard you could fight…I don't feel so good…"

Gil tried to sneer, but realized that he lacked the strength to curl his lip. "You…you're…pretty good…for a…a spoiled aristo…but this is…"

Suddenly, their chest devices were hooting urgently. Red lights flashed.

Tarvek looked worried. "Uh-oh…"

Gil poked weakly at the dials. "Maybe this wasn't…um…the best plan we ever…"

The Castle had apparently been following their every move. "Plan?" it asked suspiciously. "What plan?"

"My plan!" Agatha shouted. She eyed Gil and Tarvek. "Or, at least, a small, inelegant, poorly thought-out part of it."

Tarvek looked contrite. "Sorry."

"I think we overdid it a bit," mumbled Gil.

"Maybe just a bit, but it worked," Agatha said.

She looked back to Snaug, who stood beside a new device, its belts spinning and coils glowing. Snaug gave her a thumbs-up signal.

She handed Tarvek a chest device similar to the ones he and Gil wore. "Here. Hook this up for all three of us."

"NO!" the Castle screamed, "I told you! I forbid it!" The scream was broken into mechanical stutters, rising and falling in volume.

"Listen to you!" Agatha fumed. "You're falling apart!"

"I see I must. Remove the problem. At the source!" the Castle sputtered. The instability in the voice was getting worse.

"That doesn't sound good…" Tarvek began…

"Such. A pity…" it mourned.

There was a shudder in the stones around them. Gil grabbed Tarvek and rolled them both aside, just as a ceiling block crashed to the ground.

"They really are…" The Castle sent another stone dropping toward them as they dodged furiously,

"So entertaining…but ultimately…" A bolt of energy struck the ground as Tarvek grabbed Gil and leapt aside. "…they are replaceable."

The Castle's voice had deteriorated to a broken, echoing whisper. It sounded like three Castles, whose speech was overlapping slightly.

"NO!" Agatha screamed, as she threw a switch on the new machine. "They are *not replaceable!*" She threw a second lever. "But *you*—you are!"

There was a roar of electrical discharge. The Castle gave a ghastly, drawn-out shriek, shook to its deepest foundations, then abruptly cut off into silence.

CHAPTER 10

When Saturn Heterodyne died and William Heterodyne assumed his seat as Master of the Castle, it took a while for the City of Mechanicsburg to reinvent itself. The town needed time to adjust to the idea that it was now a citadel of evil…without the evil.

Saturn's sons—known to the World as the Heterodyne Boys—had not been raised in the Castle. This is an important factor to consider when examining their reasons for abandoning the long-held traditions of the Heterodyne family. Even before their father's death, attentive townspeople had been aware that, soon enough, a new wind would be blowing.

But talk is one thing, and action another. Contemporary written accounts show that the razing of the flesh yards, along with the beginnings of the Great Hospital in their place, came as a rude shock to a large part of the populace.

There was grumbling. Resistance. It was the fear that members of any group will experience when a familiar, established order comes to an end for reasons they cannot understand. Never, in the long history of Mechanicsburg, had the populace come as close to outright rebellion against their Masters.

But the linchpins of the Heterodyne's power held. The Jägermonsters stayed loyal. The Dyne still flowed. The von Mekkhan family stood with the new Master. And above them all, the Castle loomed, waiting to crush any who disobeyed.

Mechanicsburg evolved.
—*Nurture Over Nature: The Story of the Heterodyne Boys (Part 1) What Went Right?* by Professoressa Kaja Foglio/ Transylvania Polygnostic University Press

❦◦◉◦❧

Agatha waited a moment, listening in the silence. "Yes, I think that did it," she finally said, with a sigh of relief.

Professor Mezzasalma clattered over to the device Agatha had activated and studied it intently. He looked up in amazement. "It's the Lion," he said. "But you smashed it!"

"I only smashed one big showy bit. Once I had the other parts, it was easy enough to rework the design and reassemble it in such a way that the Castle didn't realize it could still work."

"You shut down...the whole Castle?" asked Tarvek.

Gil's eyes went wide. "Agatha! The Castle was the only thing keeping my father from just coming in here and grabbing you!" A fresh wave of weakness hit him, and he sank to the floor. Tarvek followed him and the two sat there, breathing hard for a moment.

Agatha bit her lip and signaled von Zinzer and Mezzasalma to help them back up. "It was keeping us from getting ourselves cured. It's a broken mad automaton, remember? And it was becoming more and more irrational. I suspect that I was putting too much stress upon its cognitive faculties, and since they weren't sufficiently integrated, it just couldn't handle it. In my opinion, it was dangerously close to deciding that killing us all would have kept us 'safe.'"

All the Sparks nodded. It was a problem endemic in the field of artificial intelligence.

Agatha continued. "We'll just have to get the repairs done before the Baron realizes what's happened."

Gil waved his hands weakly. "We don't know how long that could be! For all we know, there's a giant red light flashing on the main tower right now!"

"That's…unlikely," Tarvek said grudgingly. "But we can't count on having much time."

Agatha sighed. "Tarvek, Gil, we're already out of time," she said. "We'll work on getting the Castle back once we're no longer *about to die.*

"Don't worry. As far as the Castle goes, I'm reasonably sure that we can revive the whole thing, assuming we can get enough energy running through it."

Von Zinzer stood by the lift, frowning down into the shaft. "I thought this was supposed to be the lowest level of the Castle," he said. "What's down there?"

Agatha stood by him and stared down into the darkness. There were lights down there. They were very faint, but flickering, and growing brighter. An odd look crossed her face, then she shook herself abruptly and turned away, knocking a chip of broken rock over the side. "One thing at a time. We've had too many distractions. First we cure ourselves, then we fight the World, *then* we get to explore. No more delays!"

Far below, the stone landed with a faint, bell-like ring. Seconds later, the lights flared, and a wild, mechanical scream of triumph echoed from the depths.

"FREEE!"

Agatha leaned over the edge and screamed back. "I *said,* 'no more delays!'"

There was a crowd in the apartment. When Vanamonde arrived, the leaders of Mechanicsburg society paused in their whispered conversations and stepped aside to let him pass. In one corner, a smaller knot of close friends had gathered around Arella.

Van hurried to her side. "I came as soon as I heard, Mother. How is Grandfather?"

Arella smiled gamely. "He seems all right. He's been asking for you."

"What happened?"

Arella shrugged. "No one is sure. He just suddenly gave a shout, and collapsed in the middle of the Poisoner's Market."[87]

The doctor stepped out of the bedroom, rolling down her sleeves as she walked. "He seems more embarrassed than anything else," she said to Van and his mother. "But he's positively frantic to see you, so the sooner you get in there, the sooner he might actually rest."

Van thanked her and stepped into his grandfather's bedroom.

The seneschals of Mechanicsburg tended to live simply and Carson von Mekkhan certainly continued that tradition.

The main features of the room were an elegantly carved bed frame and two matching wardrobes. A small shrine—one of the few personal touches evident—held a single votive lamp before portraits of the old man's late wife and son.

The former master of the city was propped up in the center of an enormous goose-down mattress. A fresh set of bandages covered his head. He was distracted, staring into the distance, nervously stroking the belly of the cat.

Van cleared his throat. "Grandfather?"

"Finally!" Carson looked relieved and shifted, sending the cat off in a resigned huff.

Van removed his frock coat and carefully sat down on the edge of the old man's bed. He had to admit that the Doctor's assessment matched his own. "So what happened?"

"That blasted heap of rubble!" Van knew to whom, or rather to what, his grandfather was referring. "All these years it must have had some kind of hold on me..."

Or maybe not. "Grandfather, what are you talking about?"

"The Castle," the old man said flatly. "They've killed it." He tapped his head. "I felt it die." He stared back at his grandson defiantly.

Van considered this outrageous statement. "The Castle is...dead."

---

[87] Despite its colorful label, the Poisoner's Market, like most of Mechanicsburg, has scrubbed almost all of its authentically horrible past. It has maintained its original name because the tourists like it. Thus, alchemists no longer transmutate on the Street of the Goldmakers, resurrectionists no longer raise the dead on the Boulevard of the Blasphemies, and the infamous Dream Rendering Plant sells incense. This is known as gentrification. The original businesses still exist, of course, they just had to move to cheaper parts of town.

"Yes."

Vanamonde regarded his grandfather. "And you felt it die."

"Yes!"

Van sighed and rested his elbows on his knees and allowed his head to sag forward. "Well," he muttered. "That explains some things."

Carson stared at him amazement. "You *believe* me?"

Van didn't bother to open his eyes. "Oh, yes."

"What's happened?"

Van sat up straight and peaked his fingertips together. With a shock, Carson recognized the gesture as one that he himself used whenever he had to make a report.

"All the town clocks have stopped," Van said quietly. "All of the fountains have stopped flowing. The bridges over the rivers no longer work, nor do the street and traffic signals." He turned to face the old man. "Grandfather, where does the Castle end and Mechanicsburg begin?"

The two men stared at each other in silence. Van turned away. "Never mind. I think I'm beginning to guess..."

Carson looked at his grandson and allowed himself to sink back into his pillows. Awkwardly, he reached out and patted his grandson on the arm. "You were so young. You never really knew what it was like when the Castle was fully operational. You never saw the town really...really *running*." Van raised his eyebrows. Carson snapped out of his reverie. "I'm sorry, my boy. The girl...she must have failed." He closed his eyes. "I had...allowed myself to hope..."

Van looked at him in surprise. "Failed?" He seemed genuinely taken aback at the idea. "Agatha? Failed? No, I don't think so."

Carson's eyes popped open and he regarded his grandson with interest. Van shifted upon the bed. "I...No, I can't really explain it, but..."

Carson began to smile. "But you can't imagine her failing."

Van thought about this, and began to look slightly alarmed. "No, I can't."

Carson nodded. "She's your Heterodyne, all right."

"But—"

"You'll make a fine seneschal," Carson declared with satisfaction.

Van snorted. "If I get the chance! We still don't know what the Baron is doing. He's kept most of his troops outside the walls. It's obvious that he has some plan in motion to get his son out before he flattens the place, but we don't know how that race is going." He leapt to his feet, strode over to the window, and stared upwards at the Castle it framed.

"If he knows about this, he'll…" Van began. "But does he know? Surely, if he knew that the Castle was dead, he'd…" He spun about and faced his grandfather. "But how could he *not*? He must know! It's so obvious! And if he knows, then why hasn't he already attacked?"

In the elegant gardens of the Inner Courtyard of the Great Hospital, a battle was taking place. Orderlies and nurses scurried frantically through the building, evacuating patients from rooms facing the open area.

The Baron's enormous clank stood alone. Within the cockpit, smoke poured from a control panel, and one of the operators wiped a rivulet of blood from her eyes. She blinked at the console, which was covered with urgently blinking red lights.

"Status?" the Baron asked.

"Not good, Herr Baron," she answered. "The hydraulics have ruptured, and we're losing pressure in the left leg. I'm trying to shunt cooling fluid to—"

"INCOMING," screamed the other operator. A massive blow landed upon the central torso. With a whine, the last of the gyroscopes spun into shards that ricocheted away across the lawns.

On the ground below, Bangladesh DuPree nodded grimly. "That did it! He's going down!" She dashed forward, followed by a terrified squad of soldiers and medical technicians.

With a final groan of tortured metal, the great walker toppled backwards and crashed to the earth, throwing up a shockwave of soil and vegetation for several meters in all directions.

In the cockpit, The Baron struggled for consciousness. "No!" His speech was slurred, but there was no mistaking the desperate iron in his voice. "You can't do this! There's too much I have to do! I have to save my son."

The center of a cloud of swirling smoke and dust seemed to coalesce into a shadowy figure, which leapt onto the fallen machine's chest.

"You're dooming all of Europa," Klaus croaked. "I'm the only one who can do this. I have to save everything before she gets to me."

The smoke cleared to reveal Dr. Sun. His elegant coat was tattered, and smoke curled up from his beard.

"Fool," he declared scornfully. "You are saving nothing! Your delusions will kill you and destroy the Empire!" The Baron started to speak, and was cut off as Sun jabbed a large hypodermic deep into his chest. He shuddered once, and collapsed.

"The Empire does need you!" Doctor Sun raged.

"But you never listen to your doctor! I said strict bed rest!" He stood up, panting, and made an effort to straighten his ragged coat. "—And I *meant* it!"

Aboard the great airship Castle Wulfenbach, Boris Vasily Konstantin Andrei Myshkin Dolokhov stood in the Empire's war room and listened to a report of the events at the Great Hospital. He sighed and used two of his four hands to clean his glasses. Another ran through his hair. Being the Baron's second-in-command was never easy, but today... Today, he desperately wished that his free hand held a tall glass of vodka. Preferably some of that stuff that the fuel chemists in engineering brewed up—the kind that tended to spontaneously ignite when exposed to strong sunlight.

"I should have known he'd pull something like that," he muttered. He glanced at Dr. Merrliwee, the head physician on board the Castle. "And now?"

"Dr. Sun has placed him in an armored, high-pressure healing engine."

Boris winced. Healing engines were effective, but that efficiency came at a painful price. He tried to imagine what a full-body engine would feel like, and then wished he hadn't. He took a deep breath.

"It's what should have been done to begin with," he conceded. "But it's dangerous and now he'll be incommunicado."

The thought flashed through Boris' mind, *I'll have to run his адский Empire for him—again.*[88]

Out of the crowd of assorted military officers that swarmed around Boris, the Master of the Ætheric Vapor Squad cleared his throat. His voice rang hollowly from within his refrigerated suit. "Sir, the deadline for the destruction of Castle Heterodyne is approaching…"

Boris glared at him. "Is Master Gilgamesh still in there?"

The Master's eyes could be seen to roll. "…Yes."

"Then you will hold off! I will not be the one who kills the Baron's heir! Next?"

A Captain dressed in the white leather outfit of the Empire's Intelligence Offices stepped up. "We're getting reports of rioting all across the Empire." She picked up a pointer and strode over to a hanging map of Europa. She flicked the pointer across the map, tapping delicately several times, and each place it touched, a soft red light glowed. "These areas are reporting outright revolts."

Boris frowned. "I'd expect that, what with the news about the Baron being in the hospital. But…"

The Intelligence Officer nodded. "Yes. But this is…too quick. Too coordinated." She slapped the pointer across her palm. "We're looking into it."

Boris nodded.

---

[88] As Baron Wulfenbach's second-in-command, Boris was burdened with the running of the Empire on more than one occasion. While others would have been tempted by the almost unlimited power this entailed, Boris always complained about the extra paperwork. This is disingenuous, as Boris always did all of the paperwork anyway, but now he was in charge. It has often been stated that Boris' priorities revealed him to be the most boring man in the Empire. This does Herr Dolokhov a disservice, as our research indicates that he was, in all likelihood, the most boring man in the world.

There was a sudden disruption at the doorway, and a crowd cleared to allow a Jägermonster officer to saunter in. "Hey dere, Meester Boris bug man," he called out cheerfully.

"Oh, this is all I need," Boris said under his breath. He paused. "Wait a minute…" He began flipping through the papers before him. "What are you even doing here? All of the Jägers are supposed to be up North."

The Jäger carefully collected and straightened a stack of paperwork, then sat on it. "Heh. Yez, vell, sveethot, ve gots a message for hyu." He smiled at Boris. "Ve quit."

Agatha tightened the last connection and threw a switch. There was a brief shower of sparks, and the bank of machinery before her shuddered back to life as, deep within, tubes began to glow. She nodded in satisfaction, leaned back on her heels, and looked up. "How are Gil and Tarvek doing?" she called out.

"Not well at all, my lady." Violetta sounded worried. Agatha hurried over to where both men lay stretched out upon the floor, their skins a ruddy reddish orange. "They just collapsed," Violetta said, "and their fevers have gone up. It's really bad!"

Fraulein Snaug waved a wrench to catch Agatha's attention. "But they did keep going until they finished their work," she said approvingly.

Worried as she was, Agatha had to admire the woman's grasp of priorities.

"That's good, I suppose." Agatha raised her voice. "Herr von Zinzer? Do you see anything?"

Von Zinzer gripped his broom handle a bit more tightly. He sat perched upon the edge of the hole in the floor, watching. "Whatever is down there is keeping quiet now. I heard some clanking and saw a big green flash of light about an hour ago. Nothing since then." He peered back down. "Still, I really think we should hurry, you know?"

Agatha knew. Suddenly, there was a shout of triumph. Professor Mezzasalma clattered over, a pleased look on his face. "I have successfully finished splicing the power connectors!" he announced. "I predict that hardly any of them will explode!"

Agatha nodded. "I'll take that. Violetta, wind up the dynamos." She turned back. "Professor, you haul Gil and Tarvek into place, and Snaug, you help me get myself connected to the system." A sudden wave of dizziness caused her to sway and her skin shifted towards a deeper shade of purple. Mezzasalma winced and stepped forward in concern. Agatha held up a preemptory hand. "I'll make it, let's get this done!"

Agatha removed her outer garments and Snaug began to buckle her into a device-encrusted harness. "Are you sure about this, my lady? You're taking such a terrible risk." She paused as she tightened a strap and meticulously set the buckle. "I mean, being an assistant, I'm kind of used to it being me who gets hooked up to things…"

Agatha adjusted herself to ease a bit of pinching. "I don't see that I have much choice," she said frankly. She glanced over to the array where, with a casual display of strength, Professor Mezzasalma was tossing Tarvek onto a metal slab. Tarvek's head bounced slightly as he landed, and Agatha winced. "Besides, the one taking the biggest risk is Gil. He wasn't even infected when we started this."

Snaug nodded glumly. "True, but now…well, he's so sick…Do you think he'll be strong enough to pull you both through full resurrections?"

Agatha adjusted her shoulder straps. "I really don't know," she finally admitted.

Behind her, Professor Mezzasalma cleared his throat. "Prince Wulfenbach and Prince Sturmvarous are in position. The connections are made and will probably hold. All we are waiting for is you, my lady." He glanced in her direction, blushed, and looked away. "Are you all right?"

Agatha glanced down and saw her skin color shift to a bright cyan. "Well, no, Professor, I'm not."

Mezzasalma looked flustered. "Yes, of course…I knew that…"

Fraulein Snaug slid her wrench back into one of her belt loops.

"I'm finished," she announced. "I'm hooking you into the circuit—" She flipped a switch. "Now."

Suddenly, Agatha pitched forward. "They're sicker than I thought," she groaned. With effort, she straightened up. "We'll start with Tarvek," she muttered.

Snaug looked alarmed. "Weren't we going to do you all at the same time?"

Agatha shook her head. "At this point both Gil and Tarvek are too worn out. The *si vales valeo* procedure hasn't got a chance of working without someone stronger in the donor position." Agatha noticed that her hand was trembling and dropped it to the console. "At the moment, the strongest person is me."

"But…" Snaug frowned, "if you use all your energy on them, then won't you all be drained when it's time to revive you? It's just, well, I'm as big a fan of perpetual motion machines as the next girl, but they hardly ever work."

"Well spotted. Yes. It's possible there could be some problems at that point, but I've got a few things set up that will fix that." She poked at her devices and fiddled with a dial. "Probably."

Snaug frowned. "Oh, *that* fills me with confidence."

Agatha didn't bother to argue further. "To your station, Snaug," she ordered.

"Yes, mistress," Snaug moved to her place.

Agatha looked around, her gaze lingering first on Gil, then on Tarvek. They lay still, strapped in their arrays on the slabs that flanked her, and took a final deep breath. They were all as ready as they were going to get. "Good luck, you two," she whispered. She then wheeled about and unhesitatingly threw a large lever. "First switch!" she called.

There was a crackle of electricity and Tarvek shrieked and strained against his restraints.

Violetta went pale. "He…he sounds like he's dying!"

Agatha rolled her eyes. "Well of course he is. That *was* the point." She sat herself down in an elaborately constructed chair. "Now come on, it's time to get me strapped in." Violetta tore her eyes from Tarvek's thrashing form and fumbled at the first of a series of straps and buckles. "Make sure those are really secure," Agatha admonished.

"I know! I know," Violetta mumbled.

Agatha studied a bank of readouts next to her chair. "Hurry! Tarvek's readings are almost terminal!" She raised her voice. "Professor! We're getting power fluctuations!"

Mezzasalma swore. He scuttled over to a smoking cable, ripped it apart, and slammed a new connector into place. "We're burning through fuses faster than expected," he shouted back. "But I can deal with it!"

"Sturmvarous is flattening on all meters," Snaug sang out.

"Good!" Agatha hunkered down in place. "Keep the power running as smoothly as you can!" She glanced towards Violetta—

"This is the last strap," Violetta said.

"Then start the countdown—Now!"

Numbers started flicking down on the board. "Professor!" Snaug shouted, "My controls just went dark!"

"Sorry," Mezzasalma returned, "this thrice-cursed fuse has melted! I'm shunting to number four array!"

Agatha ignored them. "Violetta?" she asked nervously, "did you remember to strip all the metal off them?"

"Yes. Of course." Violetta assured her, settling a heavily-wired crown of lights onto her head and strapping it on.

"Even Gil's...ring?" Agatha whispered.

"Sheesh! Yes! You only told me three times!" said Violetta, connecting wires in the crown to the rest of the array.

"You're nervous," Violetta said. "If you don't relax, this is really going to hurt like crazy."

Agatha gave her a grim smile. "Oh, I certainly hope so."

"Prince Sturmvarous is prepped for revivification!" Snaug announced.

Agatha closed her eyes and grit her teeth. "All right—Do it! And then get back!"

Violetta nodded. She took hold of Agatha's locket and held it in place while she undid the clasp. Then, all at once, she leapt backward, taking the locket with her.

Agatha's head slammed back against the headrest of the chair and she screamed, initially in agony, but midway through it changed into a scream of triumph. The blue lights on the crown device went red, and Lucrezia opened her eyes.

"Why, I'm back!" A wicked smile crossed her face. "What a lovely surprise!"

Then her eyes widened in panic and she tugged at her restraints. "Wait—What is this?" She looked up and saw Violetta watching her intently. "Release me at once!"

Violetta licked her lips. "Wow. That really is weird."

Instantly Lucrezia looked scared and vulnerable. "Yes! There's something very wrong! There's been a terrible mistake! Quickly now, untie me!"

Violetta shook her head in admiration, never removing her eyes from Lucrezia. "So, you're the...evil twin thing, eh? Tarvek said you could be really convincing."

Instantly Lucrezia snapped out of her helpless routine. "Oh, did he? Did he also say that he's neck-deep in a plot to steal my work? Release me now, and I'll show him—!"

Violetta backed away with a small laugh. "Tempting, but you already had your shot at him." She glanced at the nearby panel, where a green light flashed. "No way." She grasped a large handle and threw it triumphantly. "Second switch!"

Nothing happened. Frantically Violetta jiggled the switch back and forth a few times. Still nothing. She glanced back and saw Agatha's body, strained almost to the breaking point, as Lucrezia tried to tear free of the straps, regardless of the physical consequences. "Professor," she screamed.

Mezzasalma jammed a screwdriver into a partially melted panel and brutally wrenched it open, exposing the cracked unit behind it. "Useless, inferior, coprolithic components!" he snarled, as he yanked the unit free and slammed a new one into place. Orange lights blossomed around him. "I wouldn't electrocute my mother with these!"

Lucrezia screamed and collapsed back, panting. While she marshaled her strength, she examined Violetta. "You," she hissed. "You're one of the Order's Smoke Knights! You fool, you people have sworn yourselves to me! Do your duty! Release me! I demand it in the name of the Holy Child!"

Violetta paled. "Whoa!" she said, nodding. "I'd heard the Order was in thrall to some secret cabal...so that's you, eh?"

Lucrezia stared at her. "You refuse to honor the First Command?"

Violetta shook her head. "Noooo...I think you'll cause a lot less trouble by staying right where you are."

Lucrezia screamed with all the power of the Spark. "Release me!"

Violetta folded her arms. "Nope."

Lucrezia stared. "You're...you're a *Smoke Knight*..." Her voice rose to a shriek of frustration. "But you're not *wasped?*"

Violetta shuddered. "I'm *supposed* to be?" She was so shocked at the idea that she almost didn't catch Snaug as she attacked from behind.

"I'll release you, Mistress!" Snaug seemed mesmerized. Her eyes were glassy.

Violetta slammed her fist across the woman's jaw with no small satisfaction. "Oh great," she muttered as Snaug collapsed. "PROFESSOR?"

A bank of lights went from orange to green. "Soon," the Professor called back.

Lucrezia seemed to swell as she screamed at the top of her lungs. "RELEASE ME OR I WILL GRIND YOU TO DUST! CAN ANYONE LOYAL HEAR ME? HELP!"

A voice shrieked back from deep inside the shaft in the floor. "*I HEAR YOU, LUCREZIA! AND I AM FREE!*" The unearthly voice echoed throughout the huge chamber.

Lucrezia froze, and then rolled her eyes toward Violetta. "Um... Perhaps I should have asked, but...where are we, exactly?"

Violetta had finally taken her eyes off Lucrezia, and was staring at the shaft. "Hm? Oh. A big power chamber under Castle Heterodyne. Your 'friend' is in a...well, I guess it's a secret room or something we opened underneath."

Lucrezia screamed again, this time her eyes wide with terror. "Get me loose!" she cried frantically. "Get me loose NOW!"

There was a terrible laugh from the shaft, and the thing spoke again: "I'll get you loose! Oooh, yessss..." intensely bright light flared at the bottom of the shaft. Von Zinzer shut his eyes in pain. When he opened them again, there was *something* silhouetted against the glare, laboriously making its way up the side of the shaft.

Von Zinzer stared at his broom and gripped it tighter. "You guys really need to hurry up with the zapping, 'cause whatever is down there, it's coming up here!" he yelled.

Lucrezia's voice was a frantic whisper. "Release me!"

Violetta idly clicked the switch again. "Are you still going on about that?"

"Fool!" Violetta caught something different in Lucrezia's voice and turned to listen. "If that thing reaches me, this girl will die! And I *know* that will spoil your Master's precious plans!"

"Violetta," Mezzasalma called out. "The power should be restored! Hit it!"

Violetta nodded. She shrugged apologetically to Lucrezia. "Sorry, you'll have to come up with a better threat than that."

Lucrezia looked wary. "Oh, really? But—"

Violetta narrowed her eyes. "Tarvek's not my master, and the Lady Heterodyne was planning on dying today anyway. *Second switch!*"

This time Lucrezia's scream was one of agony as the current roared through her. Violetta resolutely spun about and examined the console. "All right!" she shouted. "Her *Si Vales Valeo* connection is now fully engaged! Tarvek's revivification sequence should start any second!" Silence answered her. "Hey! She's really gonna be mad if I blow him up after all this trouble, so I need his readings, now! Professor? Answer me!"

There was a flare of blue light from the banks of controls. "I dare not leave this junk unattended!" Mezzasalma shouted. He was holding two sparking components together with both hands. "Where is Miss Snaug?"

Violetta glanced down at Snaug and bit her lip. The woman was still unconscious at her feet. "Moloch!"

Von Zinzer stepped back from the lip of the shaft, panting. He'd so far managed to keep the impossible thing he'd seen in the shaft from climbing out, but it was hard work. All he had to hand was a broom. "Kind of busy here," he yelled, prodding the thing back down with the bristled end. It giggled.

"Snaug's...she's been knocked out! I need you on Tarvek's system!"

Von Zinzer shook his head. "Forget it! I'm—"

What looked like an iron reaping hook arced up out of the pit and sliced von Zinzer's broom handle in two, centimeters from his hand. He leapt backward. "On my way!"

He lunged to the controls and, not liking what he saw, slammed his fist against the side of the machine. Instantly the readouts swung wildly and then snapped back to more satisfactory positions. Still, he frowned. "Sturmvarous's readings are at eighty-three percent! We're gonna need more! Can we increase the flow on this thing?"

"Not from the Lady Heterodyne," Violetta said, she's already at her limit. She bit her lip. "I...I'm bringing Wulfenbach's connection back to full strength!"

Mezzasalma called out, "But didn't she say that we shouldn't?"

"No choice! He's the only other source we have! In three...two... one...NOW!"

She slammed home a knife switch, and Gil shuddered in place. Lights blossomed across von Zinzer's board. "Hey!" he said beaming. "That did it! It worked!"

Tarvek's eyes snapped open. With an inhuman scream, he tore himself free of his restraints.

Tarvek grabbed von Zinzer and roared. "I *LIVE!*"

Von Zinzer felt Tarvek's hands tightening painfully upon his arms.

428

-◦⟨◦⟩◦- Phil and Kaja Foglio -◦⟨◦⟩◦-

"Whoa! Worked a little too well!" he squeaked.

Tarvek's face twisted into a maniacal scream. "And now I will—"

"Hey!" Von Zinzer interrupted, distracted. He was staring over Tarvek's shoulder and pointed, "Check it out."

Tarvek turned and stared. He dropped von Zinzer and reached for his glasses, which he adjusted carefully—never taking his eyes from the thing emerging from the shaft in the floor. "Good heavens." He said, apparently shocked back to semi-sanity.[89]

It was an angel. A mechanical angel almost three meters tall. Its wings had once been elegant, elaborate constructions, but now they were nothing but a twisted framework, dangling a few threadbare and grimy metal-lace feathers. Once, it had been dressed in some kind of tunic but this was also worn to a few tatters. Although there was an enormous cracked leather scabbard chained to its back, it was armed with a twisted girder and a rusty bladed hook.

A pair of blazing, pitiless green eyes stared from its stern face. Matted hair framed its features, partially obscuring the golden fleur-de-lis of the Storm King that adorned its brow.

"Aaaaahhh...Little rats..." The angel's voice was harsh and strained—and hauntingly familiar. "Little rats busy in my cellar. Where is your Queen, little rats? Where is Lucrezia?"

Von Zinzer saw the look on Tarvek's face. "You know what that thing is?"

"Otilia," Tarvek whispered in awe. "The Muse of Protection![90] She's been lost for over two hundred years!"

The Muse straightened from its crouch and took a tentative step

---

[89]   Still a Spark.

[90]   Andronicus Valois, the Storm King, possessed a set of nine mysterious, oracular clanks known as the Muses. They were constructed by the Spark artificer Van Rijn and were designed to help the Storm King rule by teaching him and advising him on the various disciplines that a monarch needed to hold together a large, disparate Empire. Anecdotal evidence suggests that while Andronicus appreciated their abilities, he didn't like them much. This is hardly surprising, as any student of human nature will tell you that kings usually have no patience with being schooled. After the fall of the Storm King, the Muses disappeared from history. Many thought they had been destroyed, but the truth is that they had hidden themselves in order to safely await the appearance of a legitimate heir to the Lightning Crown.

forward. Both Tarvek and von Zinzer noted the stiffness of its joints. "Where is Lucrezia? She has betrayed the House of Heterodyne." Another step. "Give her to me, or I will crush you all."

Von Zinzer swallowed. "This is bad." He whispered to Tarvek. "She'll kill Agatha."

"Not if I can help it." Tarvek whispered back. He strode forward, trailing the tubes and wires that still connected him to the great array. By the time he stood before Otilia, he stood as a Prince, radiating power and authority. "Stop! I am Prince Tarvek of the House of Sturmvarous. I am the direct descendant of Andronicus Valois and heir to the Lightning Throne. I am the Storm King, so acknowledged by your sisters Moxana and Tinka, who have sworn their allegiance to me.

"You were created to serve me and I demand your fealty."

The casual blow from the girder that caught him across the chest threw him back into the machinery where von Zinzer cringed. "That never works, you know," von Zinzer said sympathetically as he helped Tarvek back his feet.

Tarvek brushed him aside. "No! That *should* have worked! Something is not right!"

"Tarvek!" Violetta's voice held the beginnings of panic. "Lady Heterodyne's readings are starting to crash! I need another Spark over here!"

Tarvek rolled his eyes. "Get her ready for the next step," he called back, never taking his eyes from the giant clank. "Disengage the *Si Vales Valeo* circuit, then begin reversing my settings!" He shoved von Zinzer towards Violetta. "You! Hook her up to the electricals. I'll be right there."

"Yessir!"

The clank had paused to listen and was now slowly looking about the great chamber. "Sparks…" It mused, "What are you people doing down here? Where is the Lord Heterodyne? Which of you bellows pumpers is his Chief Assistant?"

"I am!" Tarvek again strode forward. "Now listen to me! You did not hear Lucrezia!"

The clank stared down at him and lazily twirled the girder around her fingers as she spoke. "I know who I heard." The girder froze, pointing at Tarvek's face. "And you? I see the resemblance, and can well believe you to be a degenerate whelp of the Valois." Again the girder moved around its hand. "You are no assistant to the House of Heterodyne and I have no patience with your obvious lies."

The girder arced down and Tarvek caught it in his hands. The momentum of the great piece of metal drove him several steps backward, but he remained undamaged, and held it firm.

"I am not lying," he said in a strained voice, "Look about. Do you see Lucrezia here?"

"You…are surprisingly strong." The clank paused. Its head moved slightly with a whine of servos, and it was obvious that it was examining the others.

Violetta's jaw sagged down. "That's a steel girder. How—?"

Von Zinzer grimaced. "Post-revivification rush.[91] He'll feel it later."

Meanwhile, Tarvek fought to bring his mind to speed. He'd pay for everything that happened to him later, but here and now… he felt the pressure on the girder relax, minutely. He spoke again.

"Yes. I am. Now listen. The person you heard was Lucrezia and Bill Heterodyne's *daughter*, Agatha. The current Lady Heterodyne. Yes, she sounds like her mother, but she's the last person who would help Lucrezia in any way." His voice lowered to a menacing growl—"And I will not let you touch her."

The girder was pulled back abruptly as the eyes of the clank flared bright. "The current Lady Heterodyne?" The clank began to vibrate. "Then the old Lord is dead?"

Tarvek nodded slowly. "Dead and gone for many years. Agatha is the last of the Heterodyne famly."

---

91   The Post-revivification rush (PRR) is a well-documented phenomenon. When a construct is bequeathed the sudden gift of life, everything goes into overdrive, as it were. The senses are sharper, reflexes are faster. Strength and stamina are increased to alarming degrees, and thus the body is capable of astounding feats of destruction and strength. Naturally all of this has to come from somewhere, and so the higher brain functions are noticeably diminished during this time. It's why constructs wake up in chains, which naturally freaks them out, beginning the entertaining feedback loop long celebrated in song and story.

"The...the last? But his brother?"

"Also gone. Agatha is the last, I tell you."

The clank looked off into some mechanical infinity. "A girl child..." it mused. "If true, I could work with that...but..."

Next to Violetta, Lucrezia groaned as she regained consciousness. "Miserable lackeys," she whispered. "I'll feed your flesh to the spiders. Grind your bones to powder to sweeten my tea..."

Von Zinzer slapped a hand across her mouth. "Violetta! Hurry!" He searched for the last couplings and yelped. "We're all prepped here! Really, really prepped! Ow! And she's biting me!"

Violetta resolutely tried to ignore him and keep her attention focused on the tortuous sequence scrawled on the paper before her. She flipped another switch. "Going as fast as I can," she shouted back.

The clank focused again upon Tarvek. "The last of the family... and she is a true Heterodyne? You are sure?"

Tarvek nodded. "Absolutely. She has even been accepted by the Castle."

The girder smashed into the floor at Tarvek's feet. "Oh, no, she has not!" the clank screamed.

At this, Lucrezia roused enough to look at what was happening around her. At the sight of the angelic muse, she squealed in fear and froze, allowing von Zinzer to slam a final restraint across her mouth. "Now!" He turned and yelled even as he tightened the last buckle. "Hit it now!"

With a roar, the generators spun faster, and bolts of electricity began flowing through Agatha's body.

Violetta shielded her eyes against the glare and stared at the console. "Power readings—" She paused in surprise. "Um...the power readings look pretty good, actually."

Professor Mezzasalma strutted up to her side and shrugged self deprecatingly. "Well...a circuit is like an elegant lady, spot–weld her enough and—" He caught sight of the angel for the first time. "What the hell is *that*?"

As the machinery crackled, the angel looked up and nodded approvingly. "I will speak with your 'Lady Heterodyne.' Release her from this array and I will judge her worth."

Tarvek made a placating motion. "Not yet. She's sick. We're treating her right now. If we decouple her before we're finished, she will die."

"That's done it," von Zinzer sang out. "The readings are flattening aaaand…There! That's it! She's dead as a doornail!"

He looked up to see Tarvek glaring at him. "What?"

"*Ix-nay* on the *ead-dey!*" Tarvek hissed. Of course, it was too late.

The angel turned its head towards Tarvek. "Wait. You're telling me that this girl was the last of the family, and you fools have just killed her? Before *my very eyes*, no less?"

"Oooh, sorry about that…" von Zinzer whispered, his eyes widening.

Tarvek smiled desperately. "Well, only a little." He took a deep breath. "Look, it's very simple. Yes, she's *technically* dead, but it's a kind of rolling death thing, so she's *dead*, yes, but still *dying*, so you can't really say that she's all the way dead, which is important, because—"

Von Zinzer slammed Tarvek out of the way. The girder smashed down hard enough to crack the stone floor where he'd been standing. Tarvek sighed. "Yeah, okay, I could've put that better."

Mezzasalma screamed at him. "Get it away from the machines, you idiot!"

"Moloch! Don't just stand there cringing!" Violetta added, "Get Lady Heterodyne ready for the final stage!"

Tarvek was trying to dodge the Muse's two-pronged attack. "And you!" Violetta shouted at him, "We're going to need you to help revive her."

Tarvek spun, dodging a sweep of the bladed hook, which struck a blur of sparks off a pipe. "Oh, sure, no problem. I'll be right there."

He grabbed the angel's weapons and held them at arm's length as he shouted over his shoulder. "You all are aware that once the revivification process begins, someone else is going to have to do the fighting over here?"

Violetta looked at von Zinzer—

"Forget it," von Zinzer said flatly.

Tarvek looked back at the enraged clank. "Please. Let us reason together. If you'd just let us finish undisturbed…"

The angel paused. "This miserable excuse for a cognitive engine." Its metal fist slammed into the side of its own head. "Situational dissidence has exceeded operating parameters." It straightened up. "Killing you will not solve anything."

Tarvek let out a sigh of relief. "Good. Then we can—"

The angel continued. "Go to fallback interaction sequence: kill everyone anyway. Masters will sort out remains."

Again it lashed out with its weapons, but now there was a new purpose to Tarvek's reactions.

"I was afraid of this," he told the clank. "It appears that your mental processes have suffered severe deterioration." He leapt to one side and snatched up a thick pipe. "You may be one of Van Rijn's masterpieces, and it's a shame to damage you further, even in self-defense…"

He leapt in and delivered a brutal blow that snapped the clank's head back and caused it to drop the hook. "But I told you. I won't let you hurt Agatha." Another blow and the clank went down on one knee, its internal gyroscopes screaming with effort. "If we're both lucky, I can take you down quickly, and repair you later."

The clank looked like it was about to topple, but instead used the momentum to snap the girder around, surprising Tarvek, who had but scant moments to dodge.

Mezzasalma stared in admiration. "He's doing remarkably well." He smiled nostalgically. "Nothing like a good Post-Revivification Rush."

Violetta snorted as she quickly replaced a rack of burnt out tubes. "Otilia is the one that's doing surprisingly well. The Muses were toys! They weren't supposed to be heavy-duty fighting clanks. Otilia had some fancy sword flourishes that she would perform to entertain visitors, but she was built for teaching, not bludgeoning people to death!"

The Professor looked at her, impressed. "You sound like you know a lot about the Muses."

Violetta looked at him from under lowered eyebrows. "If I had a Belgian chocolate mimmoth for every hour I've had to listen to Tarvek blather on about those stupid Muses, I'd weigh a thousand kilos."[92]

Mezzasalma looked impressed. "Really?"

She nodded. "Oh yeah, I worked it out once."

She was roused by von Zinzer's shout. "Agatha's clean! Let's go!"

Violetta slammed the lid down on the console and saw that all of the lights were green. She called out, "Tarvek! Hurry up! I'm hitting the switch in three…"

Tarvek stared up at the mechanical angel and desperately held up a hand. "Please! Stop! You *have* to *listen* to me! You're a Muse! I—"

"…Two…

The clank threw its head back and laughed at him. "Stupid little king," it hissed. "I am not one of your pretty Muses." It drew itself up.

"…One…"

"Even trapped in this miserable shell, I *am Castle Heterodyne!*"

Mezzasalma paused in shock. His face went pale. "The Castle?" he breathed. Then he jerked back to action. "Hit the switch! Hit it now!"

Violetta hesitated. "But she…it…when he stops fighting, it'll kill him…"

Mezzasalma's fist crashed down upon the switch. "Without the Lady beside us, it will kill us all!"

A fresh surge of power ripped through Tarvek and Gil. Tarvek froze in agony and the clank nodded and raised its girder triumphantly.

"And now, little king rat, you are—"

A wild battle cry split the air. "You are SUUUPER LUCKY!" Zeetha shouted cheerfully as she slammed her foot into the back of the angel's head, sending it crashing to the floor.

---

[92] Belgian Chocolate Mimmoths. One of the more famous products of the Odalisque Chocolate Company of Antwerp. Interestingly enough, the original recipe was for chocolate covered peanuts, but, as everyone knows, mimmoths will bore through concrete walls in order to obtain the tasty groundnut, and so it should not have been a surprise that they wound up in a chocolatier's peanut vat. The serendipitous result was hailed as a gastronomic wonder, as long as you don't think about it too much.

Professor Mezzasalma looked like an irate opera patron who had lost his program. "And who the devil is *this?*"

"Who cares?" Violetta answered as she got to work. "She's bought us time! Get to your places!"

Von Zinzer paused, and yelled over to Zeetha, "Hey, you! The clank says it's the Castle! Give it a kick for me!" He then turned back to Gil's console and involuntarily sucked in his breath in dismay. "Wulfenbach's readings aren't looking too good!"

Mezzasalma smoothly swapped out a series of fuses in-between power sequences. "That would be because he was tapped to help revive Sturmvarous and has not yet had a chance to regenerate his élan vital.[93] As long as the red meter stays above thirty-three, he should be fine."

Von Zinzer observed the needle bouncing erratically between thirty-four and thirty-two and rolled his eyes.

"Probably," amended Mezzasalma.

Violetta began to look worried. "I need someone to monitor Lady Heterodyne!"

"I can do it."

Violetta spun in surprise and saw a handsome, dark young man with a pince-nez peering over her shoulder with interest. He introduced himself with a grin. "Theopholous DuMedd. What are we doing?"

Mezzasalma swung over, enmeshed in a web of spitting electrical cables. "Modified *Si Vales Valeo* rolling resurrection chain between the three of them!" he shouted.

Theo stared at him in shock. "But that…that's…" He grinned again, a mad fire lighting his eyes. "That's amazing!"

Violetta rolled her eyes and then flinched as a board spat sparks and a dial-face exploded in a small ball of flame.

---

[93]   Élan vital, also known as the "vital force" is the theoretical "life energy" that a being uses to live and move. There is some dispute amongst scientific circles as to whether this life energy actually exists as a measureable thing. For a long time it was confused with electricity, but as any backwoods dabbler will tell you, just pumping electricity into a corpse gets you nothing except disturbing ideas about barbeque sauce.

Theo flinched. "Sleipnir! We've got a fire—I need you!"

"You'd better believe it!" A red-haired girl with goggles sprayed the burning console with a quick blast of carbon dioxide. "I'm on it. Looks like an overloaded junction router." She glanced at Violetta. "Do you have any butter?"

Violetta looked at the girl blankly. Sleipnir raised a hand reassuringly. "Never mind, brought my own!"

Violetta nodded uncertainly. "Well, then I guess everything is going to be fine then." She turned around and found herself face to face with a large white cat wearing a gaudy red coat.

"You're new to all this, aren't you," Krosp asked sympathetically.

"WHO ARE YOU PEOPLE?" Violetta screamed.

With a shriek of triumph, Lucrezia pulled herself free from her chair. "Oooh, Yes! Look out world!"

"She's loose!" Violetta blanched. "But how? I strapped her down with—"

Theo gave a laugh and waved a hand self-deprecatingly. "Oh, I got those. After all, we're going to need Agatha to—"

"THAT'S NOT AGATHA!"

Theo felt a fist close on his shirt and haul him up and forward. He stared down into Lucrezia's triumphant visage. "She's not?"

Lucrezia examined him with appreciation. "Ooooh, aren't you a cutie," she crooned. "Hello."

At the sound of Lucrezia's voice, Zeetha spun around, turning her back on the clank. "You took her locket off? Coming!" she called, dashing past Airman Higgs. "Deal with the clank!" she told him.

Higgs watched her go and then turned to look at the clank, which was climbing to its feet. He sighed and released a small puff of smoke from his pipe.

The clank saw him and pointed at him with a shaky hand. "You-You-You—" It stuttered as it lurched toward him. "You are all intruders and I-I will squash you into j-jelly!"

Higgs took his pipe from his mouth, absently crushed out the coal with a callused thumb, and slipped it into his pocket while giving the towering clank a sympathetic look. He spoke. "Hey."

The clank paused in surprise. He continued, "I don't want to fight you."

The clank clashed its jaws in fury. "That's too-too ba-ad!" It raised the girder high and swept it down faster than the eye could follow, shattering the stone floor.

The clank refocused its eyes with a click. The man had been standing right—

From the side, Higgs gave the clank's elbow a knowledgeable prod. "Tsk. Look here. These joints are out of alignment."

Gyroscopes squealed as Otilia spun in place, the girder sliced through the air—"DIE!" Otilia screamed—But Higgs was gone.

A fingernail tapped against Otilia's spinal array. "Huh. Looks like all these load-bearing structures are out of kilter..."

This time the clank moved so fast that it actually connected. The fist holding the girder slammed into the airman's face, sending him into the nearest wall so hard that it left cracks.

The angel shuddered in pleasure and turned, joints faintly smoking, towards the others. "And now-now-now I'll kill the-the rest of you—"

"Huh," a mildly surprised voice came from behind the angel. "But those galvanic relays are still working." The angel spun back in surprise as Higgs pulled himself from the slight dent in the wall. He brushed his sleeves off thoughtfully. "That's good," he said to the clank sincerely. "Be a shame if you got too messed up."

Lucrezia was gaily laughing as she waved Theo about at arm's length. "You thought you were aiding my daughter, eh?" She gave him a playful shake. "How very droll!" The laughter cut off as if by a switch. "But now..."

"Wait!" Theo gasped. "You're...you're *Aunt Lucrezia?*"

Lucrezia almost fell over in surprise. "Pardon?"

Theo feebly waved his hands about. "I'm Theopholous DuMedd! Your nephew! Your sister, Serpentina Mongfish? She was my mother!"

Theo's feet touched the ground. "Little Theo?" She stared up at him and shook her head admiringly. "Oh, how you've grown! I haven't seen you since..."

"You came to my christening!"

Lucrezia gave a fond smile and put a hand to her cheek. "Why... So I did!"

Theo nodded. "And you brought me a clockwork snake!"

Lucrezia went misty-eyed. "Mr. Hissyfit! He used to be mine, you know," she confided.

"Yes! He tried to eat my father and knocked the bishop into the punchbowl!"

Lucrezia smiled nostalgically and gently took Theo's face in her hands. "Oh, let me look at you! My, yes! You do take after your father."

Theo smiled. "Really?"

Her hand clamped around his throat. "Oh, yesss. You know, when we first met, he blew up my favorite lair, and then he had the temerity to leave *me* behind while he escaped with my sister, dear little goody-goody Serpentina." Her fist tightened.

"Really," Theo choked out.

Lucrezia's eyes narrowed. "And I never liked her much, either."

Stars slowly swam before Theo's eyes. "Really?"

Lucrezia's fist tightened again. "Really."

The angel clank stared at Higgs, then glanced again at the damaged wall. "You-non-possible-you..." it said haltingly. It focused again on Higgs and new lights came on behind its eyes. "Accessing non-essential core memories..."

A set of lights flashed green. Higgs held up a hand. "Wait..."

Tarvek shivered back to consciousness and rose on one elbow. "What's happening?" he mumbled.

The clank straightened and stared at Airman Higgs. "I know you," it whispered. Tarvek coughed, and the clank pointed to him. "You must help me. By the terms of—"

In a single smooth motion, Higgs stooped and grabbed a large hammer off the floor. With a sideways blow, he hit the clank so hard that its top half tore free and smashed into a wall several meters away.

He then dropped the hammer and turned to Tarvek, who was staring at him in terror. "You..." His eyes clicked to the angel's twitching legs. "How…" He then looked up into the airman's bland, indifferent face. "Don't…"

Higgs's hand moved. Tarvek flinched—and then saw that the man was simply reaching into his coat pocket to pull out his pipe. Higgs continued to silently regard Tarvek as he slipped it into the corner of his mouth. He then pulled it out and pointed at the broken clank with the stem while his eyes never left Tarvek. "More messed up than I thought," he sighed. "All this fighting must've been too much for it." He put the pipe back into his mouth. "Not really made for fightin', you know?"

The two men stared at each other for a timeless moment. Then Higgs squatted down until his face was a few centimeters from Tarvek's own. "Don't you agree?" He paused. "Sir?"

Tarvek stared up into Higgs's eyes, and without the man shifting, or even changing expression, Tarvek was suddenly all too aware of the rock by his side, the one that *could* have fallen and smashed his head; The live wire sparking a meter away, the one that could easily have touched his foot; The great fists of the Muse, still twitching faintly, that *could* have, all too plausibly, crushed his throat just before it fell apart…

"Goodness, yes," Tarvek said reasonably. "Why, it's a miracle that it was still functioning at all!"

Higgs nodded once, almost imperceptibly, as his eyebrows rose with interest. "Is that so? Guess we got lucky." He straightened and offered Tarvek a friendly hand up. "I'll tell 'em you said that, sir."

Meanwhile, Zeetha bounded towards Lucrezia. "Okay, spooky girl," she sang out. "Time to go back to sleep!"

Effortlessly, using Theo as a blunt object, Lucrezia swatted Zeetha backward into Violetta's arms.

"Ah…I meant you, not me…" Zeetha mumbled. Then she rallied. "She seems healthy, anyway. That's good. I guess. Ouch."

Violetta nodded glumly. "She's riding the Post Revivification Rush. She'll be faster, tougher, and stronger for a while. Also meaner." She peered at Zeetha. "You—I saw you in a circus once, right?"

Zeetha blinked. "Uh…probably…"

Violetta firmly pushed her aside. "Okay, you listen up. This thing inside the Lady Heterodyne is a killer. Stage clowning will only get you killed, so you just stay back here out of the way while we sort her out."

Zeetha's blinked. Then her eyes narrowed. "Oh, I've got news for you. That harpy inside Agatha? She's only the second most dangerous thing in the room."[94]

Violetta nodded. "Well of course. There's all this half-baked madboy stuff lying around."

"I am Zeetha! Daughter of Chump! Royal princess guardian of Skifander!"

Violetta rolled her eyes. "Oh jeez—seriously?"

"Silence!" Lucrezia shouted. "I am leaving! If you want this fool to live, you will not impede me!"

"No," Theo protested. "You can't!"

"Oh don't worry," Lucrezia assured him. "Killing you will be simplicity itself."

"Um…That's not actually what I meant…"

Lucrezia shook her head affectionately. "Silly boy."

"You're not killing anybody," Violetta announced. "Because I won't let you."

Lucrezia looked at her with contempt. "Oh, just look at you. You're one of the Order's Smoke Knights. With your pathetic attempts at misdirection and your silly sleight of hand. But I am Lucrezia Mongfish, and whether you acknowledge it or not, your order serves me."

Violetta crossed her arms. "Oh this is sweet. Okay, two things: First, like I told you, I no longer serve the Order. And second, I *specialize* in misdirection and sleight of hand." She grinned.

Lucrezia stared at her. "…And that's supposed to impress me how?"

Everyone was staring at her now, and Lucrezia suddenly realized that she was clutching, not Theo, but a Theo-sized bundle of cloth tied up with twine. She screamed and flung it aside.

Theo looked at Violetta with new respect. "Wow!"

Zeetha closed her mouth and tried to look unimpressed. "Not bad," she allowed.

Violetta made an elegant "after you" bow. "Your turn, 'princess.'"

Zeetha snorted and strode forward. Lucrezia looked wary. She backed away, shrugging off the harness that bound her to the array. "I know better than to fight you, Skifandrian!"

Zeetha almost stumbled with surprise, but caught herself and a grin slowly spread across her face. "You do?" She ostentatiously cracked her knuckles. "Now that's interesting."[95]

"Stay back," Lucrezia demanded.

Zeetha's grin grew more predatory. "Or what? You'll hurt Agatha? So what? She's tough, she'll get over it." Zeetha gave a feral grin. "You'll kill her? I don't think you could do it hard enough. Not here."

Lucrezia's eyes narrowed. "Then I'll just have to settle for a distraction." And with that she swept the heavy crown of lights off of her head and flung it towards the array. It tore into the machinery near Gil's slab. Lightning and exploding droplets of molten metal erupted and the air filled with smoke.

Zeetha didn't bother to look. She lashed out with a looping right cross that snapped Lucrezia's head to one side.

"How is that supposed to distract me," Zeetha sneered. "That's a problem for the Sparks. My job is to take you out so they can work." She paused to deliver a neat backhand punch to Fraulein Snaug, who had been sneaking up behind her. "Although that was a nice try."

Lucrezia rubbed her jaw and visibly rallied. "Wretched girl! Did you think I would fold with one punch?" She swayed slightly. "Or... or was that two?"

---

[95]   On her initial voyage to Europa, the Princess Zeetha had been abducted by pirates, who slaughtered the rest of her shipmates. When she got free, she returned the favor. This left her stranded in a strange land with no clue as to where her homeland was. In the subsequent three years, she traveled Europa trying to find anyone who had ever heard of her homeland, Skifander. By the time she encountered Agatha, who had heard stories of Skifander from Barry Heterodyne, Zeetha had almost become convinced that she had made the place up.

Her teeth snapped together with an audible clack as Zeetha danced in and delivered a quick uppercut.

"Nah," Zeetha said judiciously, "It'll take twenty punches. Maybe thirty—you're wound pretty tight."

"That's right, I am!" Lucrezia snarled as she leapt forward. "Which means I only have to hit you once!"

Violetta slammed a boot into the side of her head, then stood over her, peering down into her face. "Oh, like I'm going to let that happen."

Zeetha looked offended. "Hey! Hey! I'm working here. You got DuMedd out, I'm wearing her down."

Violetta snorted. "As far as I can see, you're just waltzing around and playing with her. You'd better let up, or you're really going to hurt her. She's *already* worn down."

Lucrezia uncoiled from the floor and caught Violetta with a punch to the jaw that lifted her feet from the floor.

Zeetha shrugged modestly. "See? She's not 'worn out', I'm just really good."

Violetta waved a hand from where she'd landed. "Okay, yeah, got it. Thanks."

Professor Mezzasalma stared in horror at the lightning that enveloped Gil. "The controls are fused," he cried. "I can't shut it down! He's going to fry—and no power on Earth can stop it!"

Suddenly, the lightning storm vanished. There was popping and the cooling of metal. Mezzasalma turned, astonished, to see von Zinzer holding up the plug end of the cable that had connected the main array to the power generators. Mezzasalma stared at von Zinzer a moment, then smacked him on the back of the head.

Tarvek took control. "Get Gil out of there!" he ordered. "Clear off that table and find me a medical bag!"

Gil was unconscious. The four men decoupled him and hauled him to a clear bench. Tarvek examined him and bit his lip in frustration.

"Hey!" Von Zinzer poked Gil's arm. "His color is back to normal." He looked at Tarvek. "You too."

Tarvek stared at his own hand in astonishment, then glanced at Lucrezia. She was also back to normal.

"DIE!" Lucrezia screamed.

Sort of normal. "So how is Wulfenbach doing?" Von Zinzer asked.

"Not good," Tarvek reported. "We haven't finished the last part of the process yet." He gave Gil a gentle slap. "Hey! Gil! Hang on! The system's been damaged!"

Mezzasalma grabbed von Zinzer and Sleipnir. "The two of you, come with me. I want a full diagnostic!"

Tarvek leaned in and muttered, "If you die before it gets fixed, I swear I'll kill you!"

To his astonishment, Gil's eyes fluttered halfway open. "Afraid you won't have time," he whispered.

Violetta sprang back to her feet. "So if you're so hot, why are you still fooling around with her?"

Zeetha looked offended. "I'm not 'fooling around', I'm learning." She waved towards a swaying Lucrezia. "For instance, she's lousy at hand-to-hand combat."

"I will crush you," Lucrezia snarled.

"Probably she's used to batting her eyes and wiggling her hips and getting other people to do her fighting for her."

Lucrezia's face went red. "SILENCE!"

Zeetha grinned. "Plus, she's pretty bossy."

Lucrezia kicked a hammer that lay on the floor, sending it flying at Zeetha's head. As Zeetha ducked, Lucrezia rushed her. Zeetha casually stepped to one side and held out an arm, sending Lucrezia crashing onto her back. "She is pretty good at dirty fighting, though," she said admiringly. "It might help if we knew where Agatha's locket was."

Violetta gave a guilty start. "Oh, I've got it. So you knock her down and sit on her and I'll slap it back on."

An embarrassment flitted across Zeetha's face. "Ah. Well…all kidding aside, she's a little too strong for me one-on-one. She's ignoring blows that should bring her down. Agatha is going to ache all over when she gets back." Zeetha shrugged. "I mean, don't get me wrong, I could hit her harder but that might kill her. It's all I can do to keep her from escaping." She gave Violetta a look. "If you're so good at sneaking, why don't you—"

Violetta shook her head. "I've been trying, but she's too fast, and she knows my moves. She's ready for them."

Zeetha frowned. "I didn't see you do anything."

"I should hope not."

Von Zinzer dashed up. "Why are you two still fooling around with her?"

Violetta scowled with irritation. "Don't distract us. All we can do is dance with her until her revivification edge wears off."

Von Zinzer rolled his eyes. "How long will that be?"

Violetta shrugged. "Ask the Sparks. Could be an hour. Maybe two."

"Can you speed it up? Sturmvoraus needs her."

"Well, he'll just have to be patient."

Von Zinzer rubbed his neck. "I don't think he can. Wulfenbach's dying."

This caught Zeetha and Violetta by surprise, and they both turned to look toward the array and Gil. Lucrezia saw her opening. She sprang forward, both her fists connecting solidly with her opponent's jaws. "Thank you for the distraction," she sang out to von Zinzer. She jerked Zeetha up by her hair and gloated as she prepared to drive her fist in through the dazed girl's eye. "I'll be sure to tell dear Klaus that his boy was ever so helpful!"

She stopped. There was confusion in her eyes. "*NO!*" she shouted. "What?" Her head began to jerk from side to side, and she seemed to be arguing with herself. "He's dying!"

"I don't care!"

"NO!"

"I won't…"

Zeetha, Violetta and von Zinzer stared as the shouts became more and more frantic.

"He's dying!"

"How dare you!"

"HE'S DYING!"

"Give up!"

"NEVER!"

Lucrezia rocked back, then toppled to the ground. She curled into a ball on the floor, and then Agatha opened her eyes, panting. "And that is not going to happen in my Castle!" she finished.

Von Zinzer stared at her and gingerly began to help her up. "Hey... Are you..."

"My locket!" Agatha's voice was strained, and sweat poured off of her. "Get it on me! Quickly!"

Violetta was already beside her. The clasp shut with a snap.

Agatha slumped and would have fallen if Violetta and von Zinzer hadn't supported her. She was gasping for breath.

Zeetha watched as she slowly got to her feet. "Good girl. That was... impressive. Remember you can do that. Preferably sooner next time."

Agatha nodded. "Gil. It was..." She looked at von Zinzer. "He's in trouble?"

"Prince Sturmvarous says he's dying."

Gil lay on the table and stared upwards. He felt things beginning to close in on him. He was so tired, and really, what had it all been for? Perhaps it would be a...a relief to let go and—

Agatha slammed her hands onto the table and screamed in his ear. "DON'T YOU DARE!"

Gil was instantly shocked back to awareness. Agatha's face loomed before him, her eyes filled with fury. "Is this supposed to *impress* us? 'Oooh, all my friends went and died, so now I have to do it too.'"

The sheer absurdity of this gave Gil's brain a kickstart and he tried to answer. He made a soft gurgle of protest.

"Oh, no you don't! Don't even try to justify it," Agatha said hotly. "You do not get to die just because 'everyone else did!' Do you hear me?" She pounded the table next to his shoulder.

A small flame of outrage awoke in Gil's mind and began to grow, fed by sheer frustration. He stirred, and began to formulate a devastating reply to Agatha's unfair accusations. He then realized, with even more frustration, that he was unlikely to get a chance to deliver it.

Tarvek had been frozen with horror at the scene before him, but finally sputtered to life. "Agatha! What the devil are you doing to him?"

He was about to stride forward when a hand grabbed his harness and jerked him back. Tarvek turned and saw Sleipnir staring at the medical readouts. "Whatever she's doing—don't make her stop. Gil's readings are improving." She gave a quick grin. "He always loved a good argument."

Elsewhere in the silent castle, a small group of prisoners huddled at the bottom of a deep stone pit. They were the last survivors of the group Zola had driven into unknown parts of the Castle in pursuit of Agatha and now they were trapped by the Castle, waiting for death in the dark.

Sanaa still hoped for rescue. She could see the slight opening several meters above them where the floor had tilted and thrown them all down here. Nervously, she ran her hand through her pink tinted hair and screamed up at it. She had been calling for help for hours and her voice was hoarse.

The others watched her with varying levels of apathy and annoyance.

Snapper clashed his metal jaws together. They gleamed in the semi-darkness. "That is really getting on my nerves," he declared.

Normally this statement would have caused a sudden cessation of any activity within his extended vicinity, but this time the others merely shrugged.

"Quit yer mewling," Dr. Wrench told him.

He was an older man who was never seen without a thick set of work gloves and he was known for his stoic calm. "Someone findin' us is our only chance."

The immense construct, R-79, raised his head and grimaced. When he shifted, the intricate webwork of stitching that crossed and recrossed his body creaked softly. "We have no chance," he rumbled. "Never did."

Squinaldo, the tall, tattooed man sitting beside the construct, did what few other people on Earth would dare, and smacked the creature on the arm. "Don't talk like that, *paesano*. It's bad luck. Talk about something else."

The hulking brute pondered this advice. "Oh. Okay." It searched for a topic and as usual, settled on the most inappropriate one for the moment. "You think maybe human flesh taste like chicken?"

Snapper got a dreamy look in his eyes. "Oh no, it's more like pork," he crooned. "Sweet, succulent…" a thin bead of drool ran down his metal jaw.

"You are not helping," Wrench snapped.

"Hello," a cheerful voice called from above. "Is someone in there?"

Instantly they were all on their feet, shouting. "Yes! We're trapped!"

"Yes, I see. Hold on!" With a grinding sound, the top of the trap began to shift to the side, letting in a wan light. All of the prisoners flinched.

"Who's there?" Wrench called out.

"Why, I am Othar Tryggvassen! Gentleman Adventurer!" Silence greeted this revelation. Othar chuckled. "Now I don't expect any thanks from lawless, murdering scum like yourselves, but as long as I'm here, the least I can do is rescue you and hope that incarceration has allowed you to reconsider your dissolute ways! Just to keep my hand in, you understand."

Within the pit, the prisoners stared up at him, paralyzed.

"*The* Othar Tryggvassen," Snapper said hoarsely. "Oh, fry me!"

"He broke up the Slaver's Guild," Squinaldo muttered.

The giant construct nervously bit his fingers. "He just broke R-78 and R-76."

"He broke my master's Doom Ships," Wrench sighed.

"He broke his *word*," Sanaa said firmly.

Everyone paused at this, including Othar. "I assure you, Miss, that Othar Tryggvassen does not break his…" Suddenly Othar gave a start and peered down at the girl. "Good heavens," he said. "Sanaa? Is that *you*?"

Squinaldo gaped at Sanaa. "Wait—You know him?"

The pink-haired girl rolled her eyes. "Oh, yes. He's only my stupid brother, isn't he?"

"What do you think you're doing here, young lady?" Othar thundered. "And what have you done to your hair?" He pointed at her dramatically. "You stay right where you are while I get a rope!"

Everyone in the pit stared after him in shock.

"You're...you're really his sister?" Wrench asked.

Sanaa shrugged. "Oh, yes."

"But...your last name? Wilhelm?"

Sanaa looked at him evenly. "And how long do you think I'd've lasted in here as a *Tryggvassen?* The old guy who sent me in here suggested I change it, so I used his."

Wrench nodded. Many of the prisoners sought anonymity.

R-79 cast a worried look upwards. "I think maybe Mister Othar will not be our friend."

Snapper clacked his jaws thoughtfully. "Oh, I wouldn't worry about that." In an instant, he was behind Sanaa with his arm encircling her throat. "Not if he wants his tasty little sister back in one—"

Sanaa slammed her head back into Snapper's nose with a soft crunch. Snapper screamed and released her. Sanaa spun and delivered a kick to his jaw that audibly snapped his neck before throwing him into the wall.

The other prisoners stared at the dead man and looked at each other in embarrassment. R-79 summed it up for everyone. "Even I knew that was stupid."

Wrench nodded matter-of-factly. "*Requiescat in pace* and all that. Dibs on his boots."

Squinaldo just stared at Sanaa wide-eyed.

"I *said* I'm his sister," she said.

"I can see the resemblance."

Soon enough, a workman's ladder thudded down into place and Sanaa scrambled up it. The others followed, then quietly slipped away as the siblings began to argue.

"I left you at home," Othar said with annoyance.

"Yes you did," Sanaa replied. "After you *said* that we would go adventuring!" Othar paused and a vaguely guilty look crossed his face. Sanaa soldiered on. "You *promised!* I was going to be your spunky girl sidekick!"

"Unthinkable! You're my sister!"

Sanaa stared at him. "What's that got to do with it?" A thought crossed her mind. "Oh, ewww! Othar! You're supposed to be a *gentleman* adventurer!"

Othar's face went red. "No, no, *no!* I mean it's too dangerous!"

Sanaa stared at him in disbelief. "You want to hear about dangerous? A week after I left home—following you—our ship was attacked by a mechanical narwhal full of pirates!"

She paused, and it was obvious that the memories she was trawling through were not all pleasant ones. "It's a long story, but I kind of got elected their queen and we wound up running weapons to student revolutionaries in Venice."

Othar interrupted. "Wait, the ones who tried to overthrow the Chancellor of Ca' Foscari—"

"—And his semi-invisible hand. Yeah, that was me. Well, after Venice sank, we wound up in the middle of the Aegean, which is where we discovered that our new ship had one of those Ulysses Engines, and what with all the time-traveling, it would take us thirteen years to go twenty-five kilometers!

"I was just sorting things out with the Spark who sold it to us, when Wulfenbach troops showed up. Everything got pinned on me, which got me sent here to Castle Heterodyne!"

She poked Othar in the chest. "So, you tell me. How can traveling with you be any more dangerous than that?"

Othar stared at her and then sighed deeply. "When can you start?"

Sanaa squealed and threw her arms around him. "Yay! You're the best!"

Embarrassed, Othar looked around. Aside from the two of them, the hallway was empty. Sanaa straightened up. "So, how are we gonna get out of here?"

Othar scratched his head. "Well…actually, we can't just yet."

"Why not? You're the one who's always coming up with the sparky plans."

"True enough. But I am here to rescue the Baron's son."

Sanaa looked interested. "Whoa! So it's true? Old Klaus really does have a son?" She paused. "Wait—and he's in here? Jeez, what did he do?"

Othar raised his eyebrows. "I have a list, if you're interested."

Sanaa stopped. "Wait—and you know him? You're here to get him out?"

Othar sighed. "Yes."

A light dawned in Sanaa's eyes. "Oooh, I get it." She put a supportive hand on Othar's sleeve. "He's your boyfriend, right?"

"WHAT!"

Sanaa squeezed his arm. "Othar, please. It's totally okay. I've been hanging around with *pirates*. Anyway, there's nothing wrong with—"

"Gilgamesh Wulfenbach is a foul villain!"

"Got it bad, do you?"

Othar rolled his eyes. "He is not even a *friend*, let alone—"

Sanaa interrupted, "Oh yeah? Then why did you leave Grimstaad to avoid Helga Gootergund?"[96]

Othar flinched. "Helga? She vowed to brain me with a marlinspike if she ever saw me again!"

Sanaa shook her finger. "Mom says that just means you should have tried harder! Helga is smart, rich, and beautiful! Plus she can kill a frosted cave bear with her bare hands!"

"Believe me, I took that into consideration," Othar sighed. "Anyway, she said I was crazy!"

Sanaa drew herself up furiously. "You are not crazy! You're my brother and you're a hero!"

Othar straightened up and gently ruffled her hair. "Why, thank you, little sister! I am touched!"

---

[96] Grimstaad, Norway. The ancestral home of the Tryggvassens. A tidy little Northern village of fishermen and farmers, who were periodically terrorized by semi-sentient sea lions, laser crabs, exploding oysters, flesh-eating sea gulls and the occasional Polar Lord raiding party. In light of this, Othar's antagonism towards Sparks is not particularly surprising.

"Yeah, you sure are." Sanaa smiled. "Now, let's go save your—" Sanaa glanced sideways at Othar's frown. She shifted gears. "Um… your hated enemy who is not your boyfriend at all in any way?"

Othar actually stamped his foot in frustration. "I said Gilgamesh Wulfenbach is no friend of mine, 'boy' or otherwise! How you could even think I could be friends with such a—"

"Okay, okay! Jeez!" Sanaa interrupted. "I get it!"

The area they were in was in rough shape. The disaster that had shattered Castle Heterodyne had toppled walls and left furniture and enigmatic machinery scattered everywhere. As Othar scrambled over a tilted floor, Sanaa tried again. "So, if this Gilgamesh guy is such a villain, shouldn't you be taking him out? I mean, instead of rescuing him?"

Othar shrugged. "Ordinarily, yes. But I have a rather 'under-duress' agreement with the Baron." He pulled aside the fabric of his sweater to reveal a metal collar with a trilobite set at the throat.

Sanaa's breath hissed between her teeth. She herself wore a matching device—all the Castle's prisoners wore them—and all the Castle's prisoners knew that the collars would explode if removed or taken beyond the Castle walls.

"So you've got a 'splody collar too, huh?" she said. "But you can crack it, no problem, right?"

Othar rearranged his collar. "Well, possibly. But I would have to do it perfectly the first time, yes?"

Sanaa bit her lip. She'd certainly seen her share of smart people who had guessed wrong about that. Usually spread out over several meters.[97]

Othar continued. "Besides, that would take time. The fastest course is simply to grab young Wulfenbach and get him out of here. The Baron is a tyrannical fiend, but they say he does tend to keep his word in cases such as this.

"Probably only to look good in the public eye, of course," he added.

---

[97]   Only one person had successfully circumvented this system; Herr Doktor Felix van Gunt, who had operated upon himself and removed his own head, enabling him to simply slip the collar off. Tragically, while he was leaving the castle with his head safely tucked under his arm, he misjudged the distances, and fell down a flight of stairs.

Sanaa considered this. "So…if this guy really isn't your boyfriend, then that makes him fair game, right?"

Othar stopped, shocked. Then he whipped round and thundered at her. "For any young lady of extremely questionable morals and taste *who is not my sister*—I suppose it does!" he roared. "But you will stay far away from him or I will send you back home to Mother aboard a livestock transport scow!" He paused. "Actually, I really ought to do that anyway. Mother will be worrying, and that always makes her break things."

"Oh, no you don't! Just because you're a Spark doesn't mean you get to push me around!" Othar shrank before Sanaa's fury. She continued. "You already left me behind once, and I ended up here! You owe me! I want in on this!"

Othar threw his hands up in surrender. "Very well! Just this once." He scowled and shook a finger at her, "But no romantic ideas. Remember—he is a nefarious fiend who must ultimately die."

Sanaa squeezed her eyes shut and danced in place. "Whee! I finally get to rescue a Prince!" she sang.

Othar gave up.

In the Great Movement Chamber, Gil was back on his slab, with Agatha, von Zinzer, and Sleipnir reattaching him to the newly repaired array. Tarvek stood by, keeping an eye on Gil. Agatha was describing to von Zinzer what she was planning to do next, and Gil was awake, listening in woozily.

"I guess you could say it's sort of like galvanizing," she was saying.

"What?" Von Zinzer asked. "You're going to dip him in molten zinc?"

Agatha laughed. "Only metaphorically!" she assured him.

"Huh," Tarvek said. "It'll probably feel similar."

"It'll probably be a step up, actually," Gil added.

"Yeah," Tarvek told him, "but then you'll be completely stable and we can…" Tarvek's voice trailed off and his eyes lost focus.

Violetta appeared and looked at him critically. "Tarvek? Are you all right?" she asked.

Tarvek swooned slightly and abruptly sat down. "Sorry," he muttered. "I still don't feel all that good."

Gil rolled an eye toward him and frowned. "Why's he still acting sick?" he muttered. "The secondary core annealing process should have fixed all that."

Agatha looked at the wrecked machinery, the shattered Muse, the busy scientists and their assistants. She bit her lip. "Um…We didn't get to do any secondary process."

Gil's face cleared and he sank back with a relaxed sigh. "Ah, that would explain it." He then snapped upright and began to shout. "Sturmvarous! You never finished the procedure? Idiot! What would your father say to a labman who did something like that?"

Tarvek considered this. "I think he'd say, 'Help me, help me, I'm trapped in this sarcophagus.'"

This checked Gil long enough that Tarvek was able to slam him back onto his slab and tighten a hose that had almost come loose. "We have been kind of *busy* here," he snarled.

Agatha came up next to him. "Yeah. You're the one who still needs processing. We feel great. Well, I do, anyway…" A wave of dizziness gave the lie to this statement. It passed swiftly, but Gil missed nothing.

"You idiots are still feeling the effects of the Post Revivification Rush. Look at how flushed your faces are! You're burning through energy at an unsustainable rate! It we don't cap it, you two will slip into a neurological cascade and we'll *all* die!"

Both Agatha and Tarvek looked about at the damaged equipment. "Would reestablishing the *Si Vales Valeo* do the trick?"

Gil paused. "To stabilize the runaway loss? Maybe…that's a good start…are the machines intact?"

Tarvek waved this aside. "Enough of them that we can rework them. It'll be a lot simpler this time, since we'll just be artificially equalizing—"

Agatha placed a finger on Tarvek's lips. "I could listen to that kind of stuff all night," she said. "But don't *explain* it—do it!"

Tarvek took a deep breath and hurried off. Gil tried to grin at Agatha and whispered, "I could explain it better than *he* could."

Agatha snorted. "Well, let's hope you get a chance to prove it." Red-faced, she turned to Professor Mezzasalma, who had found an enthusiastic student in Theo. The two of them had been attacking the aging electrical system.

"Can you two get us a stable power flow?" she asked them.

"It's tricky, but I think its possible…" Mezzasalma answered.

"Good." She walked to Tarvek, who was busily scribbling calculations onto ragged sheets of paper.

"There!" he told her, "I've calculated the galvanic essence levels we'll need for each of us."

Agatha peered at his work. "Oh, very elegant!" she told him. "Now work out the most efficient shunt layout."

After making sure everyone was busy, Agatha slumped onto a stool and closed her eyes. A while later, von Zinzer prodded her with a sheet of paper. "Here's the power figures from Mezzasalma, plus the latest readings from the three of you."

Agatha took the paper and scanned. Von Zinzer saw her face freeze. "Hey—what?" he asked her. "What's wrong?"

"It's too late," she whispered. "Between the three of us, we don't have enough Galvanic Essence left."

Von Zinzer stared at her. Impatiently she pointed to a column of numbers. "Look at these readings. This is the three of us, from twenty, fifteen, and ten minutes ago, right?"

"Yeah…" Von Zinzer frowned. "Oooh. They're dropping fast," he admitted. "If this progression continues…"

"Yes. You see it, too." Agatha said. "All of our energy levels are decaying. Tarvek just felt it first. We don't have enough energy between the three of us to finish the process."

"Can't you just get more?"

Agatha rolled her eyes. "This is…is *Élan Vital*. Galvanic Essence. Not regular electricity. You get it from living things, or… or…"

Von Zinzer interrupted. "Well, then, why not just add someone new to the circuit?" He paused. "Who isn't me?"

Agatha shook her head. "Because adding someone new, who hasn't undergone the first part, would destroy our current level of synchronization."

Von Zinzer looked at her blankly.

"We'd all just fry," she clarified.

"Ah." Von Zinzer nodded. "Okay, well, let's go. We've got, what, five Sparks here? The pack of you should be able to come up with something, right?"

"No!" Agatha grabbed his arm. "That's exactly what we *aren't* going to do. There's too many Sparks. Everyone will have their own ideas and we'll waste far too much time arguing about which path to take and by the time all the shouting dies down it'll be too late to do anything!"

Agatha snatched up some more paper and began scribbling furiously. "No. We'll do it my way and skip the debate." She began passing papers to von Zinzer. "Give that one to Tarvek. This one to Theo and Professor Mezzasalma. The third to Sleipnir. Don't let any of them see anyone else's."

Von Zinzer nodded. "What about Wulfenbach?"

Agatha glanced over to see Gil talking Violetta through a bit of rewiring. "Don't let Gil see anything."

Von Zinzer glanced through the papers and frowned. "Wait a minute…Now you've got all the energy coming from you."

Agatha blinked. "How do you know that?"

Von Zinzer glared at her. "Hey. I *am* trained as an electrical machinist, among other things, and if you don't learn something about how this kind of crap works in here, you'll find yourself hooked up to power someone's coffeepot." He slapped the papers. "They'll be fine, but you'll die. I mean, for real die."

Agatha looked at him, impressed. "No I won't. I've got some ideas. Anyway, even if I do, I'm betting that if anyone could bring me back, it'll be Gil and Tarvek."

Von Zinzer stared at her. "I don't know if that's fatalistic, optimistic, or just crazy."

Agatha gave a small smile. "That's my life. Go hand those out."

Von Zinzer patted her shoulder sympathetically and hurried off. Agatha sighed and slumped to one side. A hand holding a field cup full of water materialized before her face.

Startled, she looked up into the sanguine face of a Wulfenbach airshipman.

"Thank you," she said as she took the cup. "Who are you?" The question seemed to catch the man by surprise. He pulled himself to attention. "Higgs, Ma'am. Airman Third Class." He gave her a casual salute. "I'm currently assigned to...help young Master Wulfenbach." He glanced over at the man in question. "Is he gonna die?"

"Not today. Help him do what?"

Higgs scratched his head. "Well, hold his hat, mostly." Agatha stared at him. "But he's here to help you." He looked at her with frank curiosity. "Are you really the new Heterodyne?"

Agatha sipped the water. "Yes. I could cackle maniacally for you, if it would help."

Higgs considered this. "It might."

"I beg your pardon?"

"Oh—not for me." The airman reached back and hauled up the remains of the mechanical angel. It had been reduced to a shattered, one-armed torso and a head with a cracked cheek. Even in its ruined state, the eyes tracked her every movement. "This contraption claims to be Castle Heterodyne."

The angel's eyes flared. "You-you-you can-are-not be Heterody-dyne. You-you are-were-are a vessel for Lu-Lucrezia."

Agatha folded her arms and drew herself up. "I am Agatha Heterodyne. Daughter of Bill and Lucrezia Heterodyne. Mother just...visits."

The clank clacked its jaw at her. "You will prove this! Or you will die."

Agatha rubbed her jaw. "You certainly sound like the Castle," she muttered. "But I shut the Castle down. Why are you still active?"

"I-I-I ha-have been...contained." The clank explained. "You-you have shut-shut me do-down?"

"I did. The Castle had shattered into warring segments of itself. They went mad. So mad that they would not obey me."

The clank looked impressed. It stared at her and evidently made a decision. "The La-Lady Lucrez-zia prided herself on her-her abilit-ties in Consciousness Transferal.[98] When sh-she had mastered organics, she sought to-to-go-go even further, to transfer artificial consciousness."

Agatha nodded wearily. "If we had the time, I'd find this fascinating, I assure you. Doctor Beetle, my old teacher, taught that automata consciousness simulates animal consciousness through the expression of scripted responses to pre-delineated stimuli. But...he wasn't sure that organic minds were all that different. He sometimes hinted at the hypothetical possibility of isolation and transfer of organics and mechanics." She took a deep breath.

The clank nodded. "Tar-Tarsus Beetle. Transylvania Poly-polygnostic University. Ye-es, and Beetle was-was her te-eacher, was he not? Lucrezia wa-was never much interested in untested hypothesis."

"It was her-her great triumph: Co-coherent transfer of intellect ac-ac-across systems mech-anical and biological."

Agatha sat down. "This explains so much," she muttered. "If she had ever managed to perfect artificial to organic transfer..."

The clank clacked its jaw in evident amusement. "Oh, that was-was an-an easy one." It jerked its head towards the hole from which it had crawled. "And-and the result wai-waits-waits for you down below—at the-the bottom of tha-that pit."

Agatha's mind raced. The clank made a dry chuckling sound. "Curious? But you ma-may never see-see it. Even if you-you *are* the Heterodyne, you are st-still merely a-an unprotected hatch-hatchling.

___
98   Yes, yes, the whole "brain swap without surgery" thing. In a rare display of solidarity, Sparks have universally discouraged this particular field of research for two reasons. The first, that science is regarded with enough suspicion as it is, without allowing plausible justification for the whole 'Is my ruler/boss/lover who I *think* they are? Or has their mind been replaced by an agent of a secret cabal that is out to get me?' thing. The second, that it's really hard to do, and those who manage to successfully pull it off are bloody insufferable about it.

"By shut-ting down my-my maddened systems, you-you have removed your best defense.

"Your fortress is now-now merely a slowly-crumbling heap of stones. The-the enemies of the Heterodynes will mo-ove to crush us with-without pity.

"They will not wait-wait for you to become strong. But I-I can help you gain strength quickly, if-if you are truly what you claim,

"And then-then you may save us-us all."

Agatha was staring at the bottom of the cup the airman had given her, and grinning madly. She could feel the tingling in her mouth and throat.

"Ah. You're saying that you've had your lackey here give me water from the Dyne."

The clank nodded. "He-he is not *my* lackey." It said. "But ye-yes. The wat-ters of the Dyne have-have always contained an ex-excess of what you-you may call *élan vital*. You said-said you were ter-minally deficient—yes-yes, my audio receptors are quite ex-excellent, even in this damage-ed carapace.

"I have-have tak-en it upon my-myself to maximize your chances of sur-survival."

Agatha felt a growing tingling sensation spreading through her chest. She focused on Higgs, her eyes growing wilder by the minute. "Excellent!" she said. Her voice was thick with the tones of the Spark.

Higgs took his pipe out of his mouth. "So you're not mad-er-*upset*, then?" he asked.

"Don't be ridiculous!" Agatha laughed. "All you did was save me time! I'll admit, I was planning to use it a little later in the process, but this is so perfect!"

"Yessss…" the clank said, "but let's ju-just add the next step, sha-all we?" It reached out and placed its remaining hand on Agatha's bare arm.

Agatha ignored it. Her voice was rising to a mad, delighted shout, and she was staring into the distance before her. "So many things become clear! I can—"

Her rant was cut off as a blue bolt of electricity flashed through her.

Tarvek was sitting with his back to an electrical panel, examining the sheet in front of him and frowning. Theo stood next to him, double-checking the modifications he'd made to the electrical system. After a while, Theo realized that Tarvek was no longer listening to the running explanation of the brilliant work he'd been doing. "What is it?" he asked.

Tarvek looked up. "I'm not sure…but there's something about these modifications…"

"GET HIM!" The voice was Fraulein Snaug's.

"What?" Tarvek jumped.

Sleipnir snatched the paper from his hands and shouted "Come on! Hurry!"

"Just grab him!" Snaug yelled again, and then she, Sleipnir and Violetta had lifted Tarvek off the ground and were rushing him back toward the array.

"Okay! We got him! Get ready!" Sleipnir shouted.

"What are you doing?" Tarvek wailed.

"What do you think, fool? We're manhandling your royal personage," Violetta said.

"It's okay, your Highness," Fraulein Snaug said worriedly, "It's on the Lady's orders."

"How does that make it better?" he asked.

They slammed him onto one of the slabs. "Hook him in!"

"Set the clamps," Professor Mezzasalma ordered.

"Just ignore the pain, sir," Snaug advised him.

"Wait a minute!" Tarvek tried to break free. "We still have to test it!" He thrashed uselessly, but the women held him down.

"Agatha, tell them!"

"*Nonsense!*"

Tarvek froze. Agatha's voice was…different. The tonal qualities a Spark's voice acquired when the speaker was in the grip of madness usually raised the hackles of normal people. This voice had Tarvek and every other Spark in the room, desperately looking for an exit.

"'*Testing' is for when you're still guessing.*"

The clamps had been set, and his captors stepped back. Tarvek could see Agatha now. It didn't make things better.

Agatha was floating, and her eyes stared out at him from infinity. "And now," she said in her strange new voice, "I have no need to guess. About *anything.*"

CHAPTER 11

We then did as the Master commanded us, and when we were finished, lights, like fireflies, began to gleam in the darkness. P'raps it be but fancy, but I did feel as if a Great Presence, invisible and malevolent, was being slowly roused from a deep slumber, and was looking about like a man roused from a wine-induced sleep.

A most terrible noyse did fill the chamber, and Master Faustus did laugh in glee. "The power of speech is not learned instantly! Try thou again," he demanded.

There followed a most unpleasant span of tyme, but shortly enough, the howls and squeals did slowly transmute themselves unto the very semblance of speech. Horrid and blasphemous though 'twas, I could now understand its words.

"Who...am I?" The horrible voice asked.

This simple question did please the Master right well, more than anything I have ever witnessed in all my time under his hand.

"Didst thou hear that, von Mekkhan? No mere mechanism of rote calculation this! It asks a question! It hath a thirst for knowledge! I proclaim it a thing alive!"

Master Faustus then spun about and spake proudly, "Thou art...Castle Heterodyne."

—From the Private Journals of the von Mekkhan Family

gatha was hovering in mid-air. Her hair was billowing straight up, as if caught in some terribly powerful slow gale.

Around her floated a galaxy of small devices and bits of machinery that were assembling themselves into a cohesive ring. Connectors snapped together and cables coiled lazily towards a belt of sockets that encircled Agatha's waist. Whenever one slid into place, a new segment of the ring glowed to life. All of this was happening without Agatha moving a muscle. A look of knowing bliss filled her face, and her skin glowed with radiant energy.

Because he was shackled to a lab table, Tarvek was unable to do the sensible thing—the thing that his brain was screaming for him to do—which was drop to his knees and await the thunderbolt. He fought to regain self-control.

"Agatha," he ventured. "Are…are you all right?"

To the side, the angel clank stared upwards. "You know-ow-ow, I don't-can't remember that any of her ancestors ever did-id this…"

Higgs shifted his pipe from one side of his mouth to the other. "Sure they did. Remember old Igneous? Just before he exploded?"

The clank nodded. "Ah, yes. My, h-h-ow time does fly."

Agatha turned her glowing eyes to Tarvek and regarded him for a long minute. Then she threw her head back and laughed. Tarvek made remarkable strides towards tearing his straps free from the metal table.

"Oh, yessss! I am far more than all right!" Agatha said, "I am perfect!" She glided toward Tarvek, radiating heat that he could feel from almost a meter away.

"I feel…suspended in an eternal moment of supreme clarity. I can do anything!"

Wires and cables on the devices circling Agatha began to click into place—attaching them to the machines hooked up to Gil and Tarvek. Now Agatha herself was part of the array.

Sleipnir had been watching all of this with awe, but when Agatha connected to the main array, readouts began to glow red all over the board of monitors she crouched behind. Sleipnir gasped. She had worked in enough laboratories that she was able to, with effort, tear her attention from Agatha and shut out everything but the job in front of her.

"*I have so many ideas,*" Agatha continued dreamily, "*So much I want to try! It's all so exciting!*" She stared into space, pure mad delight on her features. Then her expression changed. "*And yet, it really isn't perfect, is it? Not yet.*" She stared back down at Gil and Tarvek.

Gil's eyelids fluttered, and he seemed to notice Agatha for the first time.

His eyes went wide as she continued, "*There are still these distractions that shatter the perfect euphoria.*" A bleak tone had crept into Agatha's voice. A coldness evocative of vast spaces between the stars. "*All this concern because of the imbalances within these chaotic, biological organisms. It would be so much simpler to just snuff them out.*"

Tarvek stared breathlessly up at her. She was beautiful. Shining. He wondered if he would feel his own death.

Agatha hung before them and a thousand years seemed to pass before her head lowered, and the golden light in her eyes seemed to dim slightly. "*But if I let you die,*" she said to them, her voice dropping to a whisper, "*If you die...then all the rest...the rest is pointless.*"

She looked up again and the golden light in her eyes flared. "*So that will not happen!*" As she spoke, a pair of cables unwound from the nest encircling her. They looped once and snapped solidly into the devices strapped to Gil and Tarvek's chests. The last connection was complete, and an explosion of blue light filled the room, knocking everyone to the ground.

Several minutes passed and Violetta's eyes flickered open. "Nrg," she grunted.

"Yeah," Sleipnir muttered from beside her. "Tell me about it."

"Wha' happn'?"

"I dunno, but if she starts calling us pitiful insects, run."

Violetta considered this. "That'll help?"

"No, not really." Sleipnir was getting to her knees. Ruined machinery was sparking around them and smoke was everywhere.

Violetta shakily raised herself up on one arm. "Oh..." she whimpered. "If we feel like this, then Lady Heterodyne—"

Sleipnir rolled onto her back. "And Gil! And Prince Sturmvoraus! They were right there next to her!"

A tear trickled from Violetta's eye. "They must be—"

"*Perfectly splendid*," Tarvek sang from behind her. He turned and called behind him. "Agatha! Gil! I've found the last of them! They're fine!"

Violetta stared. "Tarvek! Aren't you dead?"

Tarvek laughed. "Ha! Of course not!" He practically radiated good heath and animal vigor. He picked both Sleipnir and Violetta off the floor, tucked them under his arms, and bounded back to the wreckage of the array, leaping over piles of half-melted machinery with the grace of a gazelle. "Agatha has fixed everything! I feel amazing! My mind has never been more clear!"

The clank angel was propped up against a shattered wall. It stared at Agatha as she stripped off the last remnants of carbonized machinery, brushed herself off, and began to dress.

"Inge-ge-genious." The clank conceded, "to distribute the ex-ex-extra energy between the three of you."

"Yes, and a good thing I did, too! Another forty-five point three seconds and I believe I would have exploded or something!" Agatha's voice was still resonant with the Spark, but she was no longer floating, or even glowing. Her eyes had returned to normal, only shining with pride and excitement.

"...Or something." The clank continued to stare at her. "Under the cir-cir-circumstances, I am forced to admit that you are most-most likely one-one-one of the family."

Agatha stooped to examine a melted bit of circuitry and giggled. "I have *got* to try that again."

"Yesss. Most likely in-in-indeed."

Zeetha was lounging on one of the slabs watching Gil and Tarvek as they dressed. She was amusing herself by wondering when they would notice her close observation. Both were clearly so thrilled at the success of the procedure that they were happily missing every innuendo in her constant stream of suggestions, comparisons, and helpful advice. Finally, she gave up and asked a cogent question. "So you're all cured now?"

"Oh, yes!" Gil said, lighting up at the question. "Cured, stabilized, and feeling quite fine!" He bounced up and down on the balls of his feet, grinning. "I imagine this must be what a post-revivification rush feels like."

"Well, speaking from personal experience, it is quite similar." Tarvek beamed at the coat that Violetta had flung at him, a long, canvas worker's coat that reeked of mildew. It had obviously been abandoned for quite some time. "But more sustainable, I think."

Gil meticulously straightened his waistcoat and turned to face Tarvek. "Ah, Sturmvarous," he said grandly. "I see that you've recovered! How refreshing to hear you doing something other than whining or raving. A bit of a first, now that I think about it."

Tarvek absentmindedly flicked a bit of burnt metal off his coat and squarely onto Gil's shirt. "Ah, Wulfenbach. I must apologize," he said in his most courtly manner. "I imagine when you discovered that your magnificent selfless gesture would actually inconvenience you for more then fifteen minutes—well, it must have been quite vexing. So sorry for the trouble."

The two men stood eye-to-eye for several heartbeats, smiling beatifically.

Then, simultaneously, they lunged for each other's throats, snarling.

Zeetha blinked, then looked around. "Agatha! You're missing the show!"

Agatha strode over, still operating a screwdriver within a half-finished device. Zeetha saw that it was another one of Agatha's little clanks. "Don't we have enough of those? …By which I mean too many?"

Agatha sighed. "It's just an idea I had. What's the problem?"

Zeetha indicated the two men rolling about on the ground, shouting. Each was clearly determined to beat the other into submission.

Agatha nodded. "Oh, dear. Understandable, though."

Zeetha grinned and raised her thumb approvingly. "This girl's ego? Back up to speed!"

Agatha rolled her eyes and blew a lock of hair from her face. "What I mean is that all three of us are still suffering from a huge build-up of raw energy. *I* can feel it, too. It's pressing against the inside of my head, filling my entire body with this urge to *do* something! We need to burn it off, preferably with short sustained bursts of physical or mental activity." She hefted the small clank. "I myself was getting through it by assembling a new device. But since I'm apparently not allowed to work in peace… I'll just have to join in." She tossed the device to Zeetha and leapt toward Gil and Tarvek feet first. "You two ought to be ashamed of yourselves!" she thundered. "You fight like ducks!"

Tarvek and Gil looked up in shock, but it was too late. Agatha landed several well-aimed blows that had Zeetha alternatively nodding in approval and wincing sympathetically. In self-defense, the two turned from each other and tackled Agatha, trying to dodge her blows and catch her at the same time. All three were alternately laughing madly and yelping in pain.

Agatha tackled Gil and brought him down hard on Tarvek. She fell on top of them and struggled for purchase, wrapping one arm around Gil's neck and grabbing the short knot of hair at the back of Tarvek's head.

She was trying to shove her knee in Gil's back when a sudden wave of water drenched all three. The combatants froze in place, blinking.

"Wow. That worked. I feel better now!" Agatha gasped.

Gil rubbed water out of his eyes. "Yeah, me too."

"Same here." Tarvek agreed.

Von Zinzer lowered his bucket.

"Um…good job," Zeetha said.

Von Zinzer sniffed disapprovingly. "If that hadn't worked, I'd have started hitting them with the bucket."

Wet and dripping, Agatha, Gil and Tarvek stared at each other.

"But…it actually worked," Agatha said. "We really did it. Wow."

They threw their arms around each other and shouted with triumph.

"Yes! Amazing! A successful triple *Si Vales Valeo* shutdown!" Tarvek gave Gil a squeeze around the shoulders. "That was brilliant!"

"Yeah!" Agatha said. "And no one's a ravening monster or anything!"

"Ooh! Ooh!" Gil said. "You know what we should try next? Let's hook *everyone* up to a *larger* array, and—"

Another bucket of water hit them. Von Zinzer glared at them. "Well?"

Agatha held up a sodden hand. "I said we're better!" she protested.

Violetta stared in naked admiration at von Zinzer. Then she glanced sideways to see her expression mirrored on Snaug's face. The woman looked ridiculous. Violetta shook herself and scowled.

Von Zinzer noticed none of this. "Think they'll stay focused now?" he asked Zeetha.

"…Get another bucket," she told him.

Agatha was back in control. "Okay, okay, that was great!" she grinned. "But work now, fun later. I've still got the Castle to sort out, and the town to defend."

She hurried to the angel clank, which tipped its head to one side. "You-you-you—ah—" it muttered. A grinding noise began to rise, and a gout of steam blasted from one side of its head. The clank continued slowly tipping until it crashed to one side.

Agatha gave a shout of fear and fell to her knees at its side. "My Castle!" She tried to raise it in her arms, but it was too heavy.

"I-I-I malfun-fun-function…I-I—" the clank stammered.

"No, no, no, no! No malfunctioning!" Agatha cried. "I have plans for you!"

Gil looked interested. "Nice clank. How'd it get so messed up?"

"How indeed?" Zeetha eyed Higgs curiously.

Higgs looked unperturbed. "Hmmm. Sprocket weevils?"

Snaug nudged the clank with her foot. "What's the big deal?" she asked.

Tarvek was angry. "Well, aside from the fact that the body is a Van Rijn, and therefore priceless, it's apparently being run by the last operational part of Castle Heterodyne."

Snaug squealed and leapt back like she'd seen a snake. Then she thought a moment. "Wait, didn't she want the Castle dead?"

"Only temporarily," Agatha said. "There were so many fractured personalities working at cross-purposes, that I had already considered shutting it all down, if only to sort them all out. That's why I saved all the parts for the Lion." She stood up. "But I didn't get a chance to test the idea before I had to do it."

Gil looked serious. "So, you're thinking we can still get the Castle running in time?" he asked Agatha.

She paced furiously. "Yes! We've got to! It's the only way I can protect the town!"

She strode over to the hole in the floor and looked down. "Having this fragment could speed things up enough to save us, but not if it shuts down, too. She waved a hand at the depths. "Fortunately, I have a pretty good idea that there's something down there I can use."

Gil and Tarvek looked at her quizzically, but didn't argue.

"Well, let's go have a look, then," said Gil.

Soon, a small party had crowded onto the platform and was descending farther down the shaft. Von Zinzer manned the controls, glancing up nervously. "I hope these cables hold," he fretted.

Gil shone a lantern down into the darkness. "From the way the Castle was talking, I didn't think there was anything below the Great Movement Chamber."

Agatha nodded slowly. "I…I don't think it knew."

Von Zinzer looked astonished. "What? How could it not know? That thing knows everything!"

"Well," Agatha said, "I'm not yet sure, but I suspect this is my mother's secret laboratory."

The angel clank flicked to life in Airman Higg's arms. "That is-is cor-re-rect. It was hidden. A-a-a secret place beneath my-my very heart. The audacity…"

At that moment, the platform descended into a large cavern.

Von Zinzer kept his eyes on the cables, but asked. "But how did you know this was here?"

Agatha looked thoughtful, and checked the clasp on her locket. "I didn't. Not exactly, but it just…made sense…"

In apparent reaction to the movement of the platform, lights began flickering on. They revealed a large natural cavern that had been extensively shaped. Banks of machinery lined the walls and collected in islands. Some were covered in dust cloths, others simply left exposed. Furniture lay scattered, tables were stacked with books. Tattered chairs, abandoned machinery, and mildew-covered rugs had been tossed about by some unknown agency long ago. Something violent had happened here. There was evidence of a fire that had burned and melted a huge collection of chemical apparatus. Machinery was tipped and shattered, and debris from a seismic-level event had left dust and shards from the ceiling scattered everywhere.

The more she saw, the more upset Agatha became until, with a gasp, she realized that the emotions she felt were not entirely her own. She took a sharp breath and tried to analyze the source of the distress, but even as she tried, the feelings began to recede.

Von Zinzer gasped and stopped the platform with a sudden jerk a half a meter above the ground. Everyone grabbed tight to the frame and glared at him. He pointed downward. "That looks weird."

They looked down. A trail of what looked suspiciously like dried blood led away from the floor where the platform would settle. At the other end of the red smear was a crumpled form. Gil, Zeetha,

Tarvek, and Violetta leapt from the platform and ran to examine it. Agatha and the rest followed.

As he reached its side, Gil reared back in shock. "It's Madame Von Pinn!"

The fearsome construct stirred. Her eyes fluttered open. Her tongue licked delicately at her lips as she tried to speak. Gil and Tarvek knelt to look into her face. Tarvek fumbled in a bag and offered her a flask of water, from which she took a delicate sip.

"Madame Von Pinn," Gil said firmly. "Don't move!"

Von Pinn's one good eye rolled towards him and she grimaced. "Master Wulfenbach," she whispered in a voice like a wire brush dragged against stone. "What are you doing here?" She closed her eyes wearily, "Such a troublesome child."

Tarvek grimaced as he completed his examination. "Gil, this looks really bad."

Von Pinn stirred and glanced his way. "Ah. And Prince Sturmvarous. Of course…naughty children…always getting into trouble when you are together…getting into places you do not belong…"

Tarvek leaned in. "Just…Just hold on," he said fiercely, "You are severely injured."

Von Pinn's lips twitched in a ghost of a smile. "Tsk. No, child, I am dying." She closed her eye and sighed. "It feels very peculiar, and I do not like it." Her voice grew faint. Her attention was wandering. "But then, I have not enjoyed any of this. I would just as soon be done with it. Still…to have failed…"

Airman Higgs joined them. He still carried the angel clank in his arms. At its command, he placed it near the dying construct's head. "You-you-you will not cease!" it said fiercely. "The-the-these children will he-elp-help."

Von Pinn groggily turned her head toward the clank. "Ah. You! You have returned." Her eyes focused and she took in the full extent of the angel's condition. Her eyes widened and she bared her sharp teeth. "But what have you done to my body?" she growled.

Gil and Tarvek had been holding an intense, whispered conversation. Finally, with the help of Higgs and Mezzasalma, they were able to gently lift the wounded construct and begin moving her toward a heavy table. Violetta darted ahead and began to sweep books and papers away to make room.

"What do you think you are doing?" Von Pinn hissed. "Foolish children." She struggled weakly as she was laid down.

"Violetta!" Tarvek ordered, "Find the medical supplies! This place must have *something!*"

Violetta briefly considered arguing that he no longer got to boss her around, then thought better of it and ran to look.

Agatha merely stood by, watching in horror.

Von Zinzer also stood by, wondering at the activity. He turned to Krosp, who was fastidiously washing his paws in a small laboratory sink. "Uh…aren't you supposed to lick yourself clean?"

Krosp rolled his eyes. "We've been walking across old, deserted lab floors in Castle Heterodyne. *You* wanna lick that?"

Von Zinzer scratched his beard. "You are a smart cat." He glanced back at the bustling scientists. "Do you understand what's going on?"

Krosp looked around and then dried his paws on von Zinzer's shirt. "Yes. I think I do. It sounds like Lucrezia was big on swapping minds. The clank says it's Castle Heterodyne. Fine. So Lucrezia stuffed some of the Castle into the angel clank body. Von Pinn's outburst makes me think that *she* is probably the muse Otilia, stuffed into an organic construct body."

Von Zinzer frowned. "But Castle Heterodyne *had* a mind." He thought about this. "…Of sorts."

"It had a patchwork collection of sub-minds. Why not one more piece, stuck in a smaller frame?"

"Why would Lucrezia do that?"

Krosp just looked at him with half-lidded green eyes.

Von Zinzer shrugged in embarrassment. "Yeah, okay. She was a Spark. I get that. But… She was living here. It was one of the things protecting her and her kid."

Krosp considered this. "True, but remember who we're talking about. I'll bet being under the eye of an all-powerful intelligence she couldn't control was driving her even more crazy than usual. I can see her deciding to see if she could catch a bit of the Castle and put it in a doll she controlled. She'd feel like she had some power over it."

Von Zinzer nodded sagely. "That never works, you know."

Krosp paused, looked around at the ruined laboratory. Then he glanced up towards the ceiling, and the rest of the Castle beyond it. "Yeah…and I'm beginning to wonder just how *badly* it didn't work."

With Gil and Tarvek ordering the others around, a surprisingly serviceable medical setup was soon built around the supine construct. Professor Mezzasalma finished carefully threading some tubes. Gil plucked them from his hands and spun them into place. Agatha and Violetta were slicing away Von Pinn's thick leather outfit, while Tarvek followed closely behind, inserting catheters and assessing the damage revealed.

The professor stepped back and took a deep breath. He studied the two men for a moment. "You two seem… unusually agitated. You are familiar with this creature?"

Gil glared at him. The Spark rang in his voice. "This 'creature', as you call her, is the closest thing to a mother I have ever known."

Tarvek nodded. "She's the only caretaker I ever had who showed me love or kindness."

"She never cared about our backgrounds."

"She never played favorites."

"Yes, she was strict…"

"She was terrifying."

"But she knew the life we'd lead."

"She made us strong."

Gil gently placed a hand on her shoulder. "And now she is reduced to this!"

Tarvek placed his hand on her other shoulder. "Who could have done this?"

They met each other's eyes. "Whoever they are, they will pay!" Gil growled.

"Yes!" Tarvek agreed fiercely. "Slowly and painfully!"

Agatha cleared her throat nervously. "For what it's worth, she did kill my parents."

An awkward silence filled the room. The two young men glanced at each other. Agatha continued. "I...can never forgive her for that, but...

"But if you can manage to hold off on the slow, painful vengeance, I will do what I can to help."

Tarvek tentatively raised a finger. "Erm, are you sure it was her?"

This was too much for Agatha. "I watched her rip them to bits right in front of my eyes!" she screamed.

Tarvek turned to Gil, worried. "Okay, that's all I've got. You got anything?"

Gil rubbed the back of his neck. "Hm...Maybe..."

"Go for it. *Please.*"

Gil took a deep breath. "Actually, I wanted to tell you at, I don't know, a better time, but Punch and Judy? They're still alive."

Agatha was shocked. Then she glowered, and looked like she was going to punch him. "Impossible! Why would you say—"

"Not impossible," Gil interrupted. "Just very, very difficult! After you escaped from Castle Wulfenbach, I had them in my lab within the hour, hooked up to oxygenated nutrients, and being prepped. I stitched them back together and the reanimation process was underway within a week."

Agatha's face was now filled with a look of wonder. Gil continued. "As far as I can determine, there's almost no memory loss. They're still recuperating, but—" All at once Gil found his arms full of Agatha. She was hugging him with almost bone-cracking force.

"Gil! You're wonderful!" She kissed him and thanked him over and over again, still holding him tight.

Gil tried to enjoy the moment, but he could almost *feel* Tarvek glowering at him.

"Seriously? The old 'bring her family back from the grave' gambit?" Tarvek's lip curled. "Have you no shame?" He turned away from Gil and Agatha, picked up a syringe, and got back to work, muttering bitterly to himself. "I mean, jeez, it's such a cliché! The last time I saw it was in Feydeau's *'The Clockwork Pantalettes'*! And the reviews for that were terrible!"[99]

Violetta kicked him in the shins. "Are you listening to yourself?"

Gil tried to ignore Tarvek's jealous rambling. "They're stable now, but they're back on Castle Wulfenbach. I've left orders for them to be transferred to the Great Hospital as soon as it's possible."

Agatha let go of Gil sat down abruptly. "I just…it's amazing." she said in a daze. "She tore them to shreds."

"The thing we should be asking," Zeetha said grimly, "Is what will she do to you if she gets a chance?"

Agatha considered this. "She didn't kill me," she said slowly. "And she had the chance." She looked at Gil and Tarvek. "She's important to these two. I'll help them now, and, well, try to talk to her later."

"You may not get the chance." Tarvek said. "She really is dying, and we don't have a lot of options down here."

The angel clank hissed in distress. "This-is-is must-must-must-must not-not-not-not happen!" Its eyes flared. "You can-can-can-can-could-will-will-will—must do this for us-us-us!"

Agatha knelt down beside the stricken device. "Shh. Take it slow." she said in a soothing voice. "Now…do what? What can I do?"

Lights flashed again within the clank's eyes. "The M-mu-muse Otilia was pried-torn from this vessel. She-it-she must be-be restored to it, and I—returned to my proper function-instrumentality."

Agatha straightened up. "You want to return her to this mechanical body? How will that help? It's dying, too."

"No-no-no. Not dying. Not alive. I am Castle Heterodyne. I am—was—am vast. This engine constrains me. I-I am too much

---

[99]　Georges Feydeau was a French playwright who specialized in comedic farce. His plays are known for their witty and complex plots, usually involving misunderstandings and bizarre coincidences. While not a Spark himself, he found much material in portraying their lives, which tended to be full of complexity, misunderstandings, and coincidences. Aptly, he was killed by an enraged lover, who mistook him for the clank duplicate that an appreciative Spark fan had constructed of him. The duplicate functioned for another two decades, and due to the increasingly erratic nature of its writings (caused by a lack of maintenance), became a key forerunner of Absurdist Theatre. His best known work remains *A Flea in Her Gear*.

for it. But re-re-restore its muse, and this clank can be salvaged. Re-repaired."

It jerked its chin towards the mechanisms that littered the room. "This is where it was done. These are the machines. You-she can do this, and you must do it now!"

Agatha stared at the clank. Her jaw firmed and she nodded once. Then she stood and clapped her hands. "Let's get to work!"

A while later, von Zinzer was peering closely at the inner workings of the control panel on the lift cage. He pushed aside a wire with the tip of his screwdriver and a fierce grin twisted his face. "Oh yeah," he breathed. "There's the problem."

"Herr von Zinzer?"

Von Zinzer turned. "Ah, Fraulein Snaug."

She smiled at him. Without Lucrezia actually giving her orders, she was able to operate as normally as she ever did.

However, Zeetha had hit her hard in the fight, and she now sported a prominent black eye. She held up a sausage and a pot of beer. "I brought you something to eat." She indicated the crowd of Sparks at the other end of the room. "They'll want to get going soon."

Von Zinzer gratefully accepted the sausage and took a bite, which made him realize just how hungry he was. "Thanks," he said sincerely. He then tapped the control panel. "Oh...I was just thinking about you."

Snaug was surprised. "Oh! Really?"

"Sure. That trouble you had operating the lift?" He tapped the panel again. "Not your fault, see? Loose worm gear."

Snaug blushed and giggled. "Thank goodness! I'd hate for you to think me clumsy."

Von Zinzer waved a hand. "Oh, not at all. Clumsy people don't last around here." He looked at her again and frowned. "Hey. Let me look at that eye."

The girl felt an unaccustomed wave of embarrassment sweep over her. "Oh! Don't look..."

Von Zinzer gently took her jaw in his hand and tilted her head to examine her. She was struck by the change that had taken place in him. Snaug had been in the Castle for close to six months. She had seen von Zinzer arrive and had been unimpressed. As far as anyone could tell, he really shouldn't even have been here at all. Everyone thought of the little mechanic as a hopeless screw-up who was still alive only because no new prisoners had lasted long enough to force him out of the kitchen. But now... now there was a calm surety to him that was almost unknown in this place. He nodded.

"Nice mouse," he said with a smile. "But it doesn't really suit you." He turned and began to dig through a rucksack. He pulled out a small ceramic pot, opened it, and taking a finger full of the white paste inside, gently dabbed it on Snaug's eyelid.

"I found this earlier. Up in what the Castle calls 'the red playroom.' Just dab that on every hour or so, and it'll fix it right up." He resealed the jar and handed it to her.

She took the jar and smiled. "You're too kind. And, so...grounded."

Von Zinzer looked at her blankly. "Grounded?"

Snaug waved a hand at Agatha and the others. "Able to work so well with Sparks without getting...you know...It's a rare talent."

Von Zinzer gave a snort. "No way. I've always been terrified around them."

Snaug's good eye was wide. "What? But the way you're dealing with them is amazing. You stand up to them. You contradict them, and you're still mammalian and everything."

"Huh." Von Zinzer considered this and scratched his beard. "You know? It has seemed...easier lately." He found himself staring at Agatha. "Ever since she showed up and started dragging me around..."

Hexalena's face cleared and she looked at von Zinzer with a new respect. "Oh, of course! Dr. Mittlemind says that some people are natural minions, and that their lives are...are all confused until they find their proper Master. And now you have."

Across the room, even the Sparks flinched as von Zinzer's scream reached them. They all swung around to see what had happened. From beside the huddled form, Fraulein Snaug waved at them cheerfully. "Just a small existential crisis," she assured them.

Agatha frowned. "What in the world is Snaug doing to Von Zinzer?" she wondered.

Violetta slammed a tool onto the ground and then picked it back up and seeing that it was undamaged, slammed it down again even harder. "Like I care!" She frowned. Why *did* she care?

Meanwhile, Gil was talking to Professor Mezzasalma and Zeetha. "What we're hoping to do is transfer the Castle mind out of the Muse body and into one of the Castle's own subsystems. That will buy us the time we need to transport it to an area where we can restore its control of the main structure. Our best shot is to use that big watchdog clank at the top of the shaft."

Mezzasalma frowned "Those clanks are enormous. We *might* be able to transport it down on the lift, but it would be much easier to take the Muse up."

Gil shook his head with regret. "Don't I know it. But all the machinery we need is down here, and there's definitely too much of it to move." He looked back to the damaged Muse. "Anyway, we don't need the whole watchdog clank, which is good. Doctor Merlot shot it up pretty badly, if I remember. No, it's all right if we can't get it all down here. All we really need are the cognitive engines and a viable power source to run them."

Mezzasalma nodded wearily. "The head is still large, and decoupling it will be tricky." He straightened up and took a deep breath. "I'll want all my tools then."

Gil smiled. "Good man. It'll still be quicker than building something from scratch." He gazed upwards at the hole in the ceiling. "Now I don't know what's waiting up there, so we'll take—"

Tarvek had come up beside Gil, and now he interrupted. "We'll send Princess Zeetha, Mezzasalma, Snaug, Von Zinzer, and your man Higgs."

Gil's eyes narrowed. "Don't be stupid. At least you or I should go."

Tarvek shook his head. "No, we need you down here." He then leaned in and whispered, "Besides, there's something we need to discuss. In private."

Gil leaned back and examined Tarvek's face. He nodded slowly. "But it could be dangerous up there."

Tarvek nodded. "That's equally true everywhere in here. But that's why I want to send—" He suddenly became aware of Airman Higgs standing silently, right behind his shoulder. "Princess Zeetha," he said smoothly.

Zeetha grinned. "Ha! He *is* a smart guy!"

Higgs took a gentle pull on his pipe. "Sure is," he agreed.

In a few minutes, most of the party once again stood on the platform. Just as it was about to rise, Agatha pulled a small metal ball out her apron pocket and tossed it up to Zeetha, who easily snapped it out of the air. It was the device Agatha had been working on earlier. "What's this?"

"When you get to that fun-size clank up there—if you need any help, just wind that up and tell it what you need!"

The platform started upward. Zeetha looked at the ball dubiously and tucked it into a pocket.

Violetta looked at Agatha curiously. "What was that?"

Agatha shrugged. "Just a little something that'll help them." She considered this. "Probably." She thought a little more. "Yeah…" She looked at Violetta and bit her lip. "Well, it won't hurt them, anyway."

The two women stared upwards. "Oh, gods. They're doomed, aren't they?" Violetta asked conversationally.

Agatha turned away. "Nonsense. They're probably not 'doomed' *per se*…"

As Agatha and Violetta went back to work, Tarvek and Gil lagged behind, watching as the lift disappeared into the shadows above them. Finally, Gil cocked an eyebrow. "All right…So what are we discussing?"

Tarvek took a deep breath. "I'm the Storm King."

Gil went still. "You're *what?*"

Tarvek spoke quietly, urgently. "Agatha and Violetta already know. You need to know, too. Zola is too dangerous—"

Gil interrupted. "Hang on!" He was furious now. "This whole thing with Zola—this is *your plan?*"

Tarvek waved his hands and addressed the ceiling. "This! Was! Not! My! Plan!" he shouted, exasperated. "*My* plan was a gem-like thing of *perfect beauty!*"

"What are you shouting at?" Agatha asked, as she and Violetta joined them.

She never got an answer. A glass sphere suddenly smashed at their feet. A dense cloud of yellow smoke arose, and, with a sigh, she, Violetta, Gil, and Tarvek all collapsed to the ground.

Zola, a gasmask pulled up over her features, stepped out from the shadows. She pulled a small device from a pocket and wound it up. As it ticked, she examined the people lying before her. "Oh, Gil," she said affectionately, "what am I going to do with you? I do hope you don't go all stubborn and force me to kill you. I have such lovely plans for you. More now than ever!"

She then turned and shook her head. "Ha. And Prince Tarvek Sturmvarous. You're still a sentimental fool. Well, we can soon fix that. You'll be a model Storm King when I'm through with you."

Another turn and a smile flitted across her face. "Oh dear, and here's little Violetta. Always the best...at losing. Some things just never change."

Finally she turned to Agatha. The look on her face was now serious. She shook her head. "And Agatha Heterodyne. Unbelievable. Just by existing you almost spoiled everything." She nudged Agatha with her boot. "Still...you may be of use to me yet." The ticking device in her hand chimed and Zola began to remove her gas mask, and pivoted smoothly in time to avoid Violetta's rush from behind. She gave a delighted laugh.

"Oh! You shook that off quickly. Very good! Very *textbook!*" She continued to move and her boot caught the seat of Violetta's pants, sending her crashing to the floor. "And here I was convinced you only passed your examinations because of your family connections!" A graceful flip put her into position to smack her boot brutally into Violetta's ribs. "But you really should have put more effort into your combat training." Another kick. "You know, like *I* did!"

She wound up standing over Agatha, who was still out cold. Violetta raised a hand feebly. "Don't kill her," she wheezed. "She's my…"

Zola looked shocked. "Ooh, you horrid little traitor! She has ruined everything the Order—" she glanced at Tarvek, "and your family has worked so hard for all these years." She swept in and studied Violetta's face as the girl struggled to rise. "And yet you're defending her. Fascinating." She straightened up. "It's well known that Sparks can ensure the loyalty of the feeble-minded." Violetta tensed and Zola punched her in the throat, sending her back to the ground, gasping.

"But don't you worry, I won't kill her just yet. I was chosen for this role because I am very good at improvising when things go wrong!" She looked around and sighed dramatically. "So really, I'm in my element right now, wouldn't you say?" She shrugged philosophically. "There have always been aspects of this operation that were less than ideal in my family's opinion." She tapped her jaw thoughtfully. "But I'm beginning to think that I can fix that…"

Violetta roused herself. "*Your* family? Who—"

With a graceful pirouette, Zola slammed her boot into the side of Violetta's head, knocking her unconscious. "Ho *ho*," she chided. "Wouldn't you like to know?"

After making sure that the girl was in fact out, Zola turned towards Agatha. She giggled. "I don't know why I bother talking to that girl. But it's true, I can turn the very worst situations to my advantage, and this one does have *such potential*." She pulled a small ampoule from a pouch. She snapped the vial and waved it under Agatha's nose. "Wakey, wakey, *cheri*," she sang cheerfully.

Agatha started and her eyes fluttered open. "Mwa?" She saw Zola and gasped as Zola deftly plucked the trilobite amulet from around her throat.

"NO!" Agatha screamed. "DON'T!" She clutched at her head.

With a cry of triumph, Lucrezia roared forth. Then she looked around her, and blinked in surprise. She stared at Zola. "Oh! My goodness. Who—?"

Zola looked down at her and smiled. "Hello, Auntie Lucrezia, I'm here to help you."

TO BE CONTINUED IN VOLUME 4:
Agatha H and the Siege of Mechanicsburg

A NOTE FROM YOUR HUMBLE EDITOR

Here at Pontexeter Publications, we strive to provide the most complete, well-researched and up-to-date listings for our readers. Yet, as any seasoned traveler will tell you, conditions in foreign lands can change overnight for any number of incomprehensible foreign reasons, which is why you should always remember the famous dictate of our founder, Ulysses Pontexeter, "Pack half the luggage you want, twice the money you think you'll need, and keep ready a fast horse."

There is no better exemplar of this than the famous town of Mechanicsburg. In the twenty years since the 9th Edition was published, things have changed so much that we have had to completely rewrite the listing. We apologize in advance for any discrepancies the traveler may encounter. Just remember; this is still Mechanicsburg.

MECHANICSBURG. ROMANIA

When you first glimpse one of the most storied towns in Europa, you will probably be disappointed at its modest size.

For close to a thousand years, Mechanicsburg has been the home of the infamous Heterodynes: that dynasty of merciless Sparks who once roamed the continent at will, plundering and subjugating all before them. Mechanicsburg was and is their capital, but the traveler will discover that it is unlike any other capital city on Earth.

For one thing, it is constrained in size by the very geological features that defend it. Girt by some of the most vertiginous mountains of the Transylvanian Alps and sheer chasms carved by the Dyne—that fierce and unpredictable river which rises within the town itself—Mechanicsburg could only get so big.

This geological unevenness is found within the town's walls as well, and as a result, it is a superb example of extreme land-use management. Indeed, several of the ingenious techniques developed by the masters of Mechanicsburg have subsequently been adopted by the rest of Europa.

Secondly, although Heterodynes easily conquered vast stretches of the land, they were never very interested in holding it afterwards. An area would be conquered and the inhabitants forced to pay tribute, and then, more often than not, would hear nothing more from their conquerors for a generation. For the Heterodynes, as a rule, the thrill was in the conquering.

Thus, the town never received a sustained influx of treasure in the form of taxes or, perhaps more importantly, the swarms of ambitious courtiers and bureaucrats that would follow same. While Mechanicsburg never forbade visitors, it was a rare traveler that went there willingly, and thus any new ideas from the outside world were usually dragged in at the end of a chain.

This resulted in a business class composed almost entirely of subjugated merchants, minions, tradesmen, monsters, and artisans who were directly answerable to an unstable higher authority. Today, this has evolved into a level of service that the visitor may find surprising, if not downright unnerving.

Less than thirty years ago, Mechanicsburg was still a place to be avoided—spoken of only in whispers—a dark stain upon the map.

All of that changed when the last of the Heterodynes assumed the mantle. William (Bill) Heterodyne, and his brother Barry Heterodyne, seemed determined to redeem the family name, and to a large extent, have managed to do so through their exploits and good works.

They opened Mechanicsburg to the outside world when they established The Great Hospital, which quickly became one of the most advanced centers of medical learning in Europa. Patients came, slowly, at first, and the wondrous cures they reported soon ensured a steady stream of visitors.

Once back on their feet, these visitors discovered a town like no other. The Heterodynes of old spent their time and money in their own backyard, as it were, and as a result, bequeathed the town an assortment of truly wondrous spoils—many of which can be viewed in a wide variety of museums and semi-private collections.

Mechanicsburg also contains stunning examples of architecture and civil engineering. Everywhere, you will find evidence of the ingenious and unexpected mechanisms that run the town. These will prove a source of perpetual delight to the mechanically-minded tourist.

After the disappearance of the Heterodyne Boys, Mechanicsburg was quickly absorbed into the Empire of Baron Klaus Wulfenbach, and today is a loyal and law-abiding member of the *Pax Transylvania*, sharing in the Empire's currency, postal, and transportation systems.

The historical adventures of the early Heterodyne family, while unsavory, have left a colorful legacy. Echoes of those tumultuous days can be detected in the traditions still practiced at the numerous festivals and fairs, many unique to the region, that are generously spread throughout the town's calendar year. With an exciting nightlife, vibrant market places, a plethora of inns, and an award-winning restaurant scene taking full advantage of the famous Mechanicsburg snail, it is safe to say that the town has embraced its new identity as a tourist destination and is quickly becoming one of the expected stops on the traditional Grand Tour.

The town is informally divided into five neighborhoods. These are roughly wedge-shaped areas that all meet at Castle Heterodyne, which looms on a pinnacle of rock in the center of town.

The Hospital District is the area most familiar to visitors. It is dominated by the Great Hospital itself, and it is here that you will find most of the related businesses and industries, such as pharmacies, medical supply shops, and some of the more exotic specialists. There are also inns and hostels for outpatients and their guests, as well as a number of shops and eateries to cater to their needs. It is the quietest neighborhood, and revelry is curtailed, especially after dark. It is the result of massive rebuilding and redesign by the Heterodyne Boys themselves, and on old maps, you will find it labeled as *The Flesh Yards*. Usually in red.

Going clockwise, we come to **The Greens**. The old Heterodynes maintained this open greensward within the town and over the centuries, it has been used for everything from grazing, to jousts, to biological experiments, to the hunting of prisoners for sport. These days it has been extensively landscaped and contains assorted water features, gazebos, and botanical curiosities, the more dangerous of which are clearly marked. In older maps, one will find reference to a Petting Zoo. Avoid this area at all costs.

Next is **The Field of Weights**. Here you will find most of the businesses, especially those that cater to visitors, as well as the Government Offices, and most of the towns' restaurants and entertainments. Do explore the famous Poisoner's Market, as well as the many other specialty bazaars and shopping districts, which are clearly marked on any city map.

Next, we come to **The Tumbles**. It is here that the people of Mechanicsburg tend to live. It is a quiet district, with little of interest to outsiders, aside from the occasional restaurant. For those so inclined, it is where you will find some of the town's more interesting architecture, and as always, the residents will cheerfully provide directions and suggestions on how to go somewhere else.

Last, but not least, there is **The Court of Gears**. Here you will find The Factory, as well as Mechanicsburg's freelance inventors, artisans, and builders. Almost any machine or component thereof can be found here, as well as the famous Scrap Swap Yards. For the casual visitor, we recommend *The Dawn Clank Inspection and Activation*, which takes place every morning at six a.m.

—*Pontexeter's Guide to Transylvania, Moldavia, Wallachia, & Croatia. 10th Edition*

ABOUT THE AUTHORS

Kaja Foglio attended the Fine Arts Department of the University of Washington, where she learned how to see past the façade of cultural stereotypes surrounding an object, be able to discern the artistic principles that said object was attempting to express and then elucidate these principles with an awareness of the artist's purpose while acknowledging (without necessarily condoning) said artist's own cultural biases and place in history, and not be embarrassed to ask people for money for doing so. Her first professional art job was for a small, independent, Seattle game start-up called Wizards of the Coast, for whom she produced several iconic Magic: The Gathering cards. The company she set up to sell art prints, Studio Foglio, later morphed into a publisher of books and comics, for which, thanks to the rigors of her university training, she is not at all embarrassed to ask for money.

Phil Foglio has toiled in the fields of science fiction, comics and gaming since the 1970s. He won a pair of Fan Artist Hugo Awards in '77 and '78. He produced *What's New With Phil & Dixie* for Dragon Magazine, adapted Robert Asprin's *Mythadventures* for WARP Graphics, and independently published his own comic series *Buck Godot-Zap Gun For Hire* and *XXXenophile*, as well as doing work for DC, Marvel, Dark Horse, and a depressingly long list of no longer existing companies. He has done work for numerous game companies, including Wizards of the Coast (Magic: The Gathering and Roborally), Steve Jackson Games (S.P.A.N.K. and GURPS IOU), Cheapass Games (Deadwood Studios and BRAWL), and Spiderweb Software (Avernum). He co-wrote the frankly silly science-fiction novel *Illegal Aliens* with Nick Pollotta. In his spare time, he did some medieval dancing and improv sketch comedy.

Phil & Kaja met thanks to a diligent comics shop owner. They have been working on the Girl Genius series since 1993, which puts it in the running for "Worst Get Rich Quick Scheme Ever." They were the first ever creators to take an established comics property and begin putting it up for free online, which to everyone's surprise (including their own) immediately tripled their sales. As a webcomic (http://www.girlgeniusonline.com), Girl Genius won the first three Hugo Awards for Best Graphic Story. They enjoy traveling, the opera, gardening, and various video games.